A bribe, threats, a dead employee, a high-level investigation and a sinister hog farmer: Lowcountry Ag Department manager Carolina Slade is a bean-counting civil servant in hot water.

She better dig up the truth before it kills her.

Jesse drew me to the truck bed, my face barely a foot from the nearest pig carcass. "There's ten thousand dollars in it for you," he whispered, draping his arm around my shoulders. "If you find a way to get me the Williams' farm. We can iron out the details later . . . in private." He winked and clicked his tongue. "If you know what I mean."

Panic coursed through me at the altered state. Like hearing that your church-going mother likes her bourbon straight and sex on top.

He'd offered me a bribe.

"Don't be silly, Jesse," I said. "What's gotten into you?"

The Natural Resources Manager, Sid Patten, stepped out from the group and headed toward us.

"Just think about it," Jesse said, his eyes on Sid. "We can chat another time. I got to get to the feed store before they close." He eased his arm away and regained his six-foot-two height, sneering as if he'd won the state lottery.

A plastic smile held my composure intact.

His voice relaxed and amplified, the regular Jesse returned. "I only got a little over a thousand dollars for my sales this week, ma'am. As you can see, I lost eight more hogs. Need to know you'll help me on this, Ms. Slade."

D1296056

Lowcountry Bribe

Book One: The Carolina Slade Mystery Series

C. Hope Clark

Bell Bridge Books

Carol —
Enjoyed the book club!
Bless you for reading about
Carolina Slade.
Hope Clark

Bell Bridge Books
PO BOX 300921
Memphis, TN 38130
Print ISBN: 978-1-61194-090-9

Bell Bridge Books is an Imprint of BelleBooks, Inc.

Printed and bound in the United States of America.

We at BelleBooks enjoy hearing from readers.
Visit our websites – www.BelleBooks.com and www.BellBridgeBooks.com.

10 9 8 7 6 5 4 3 2 1

Cover design: Debra Dixon
Interior design: Hank Smith
Photo credits:
Field (manipulated) © Mikeashbee | Dreamstime.com
Barn (manipulated) © Pictureguy66 | Dreamstime.com

:Lclb:01:

DEDICATION

First and foremost, I dedicate this book to my own personal "Wayne", who sat many an evening on the back porch with cigar and bourbon in hand, listening to every chapter.

Secondly, thanks to my two sons, Matthew and Stephen, who thoroughly understand what it means for their mother to write.

Next, a bow to my writing mentors and pals. Barrie, Sharon, Jake and Sid in particular. I owe you my soul.

Finally, a sincere appreciation goes out to the farmers in South Carolina, my catalyst to begin this series and mold stories that represent this beautiful state.

CHAPTER 1

O-positive primer wasn't quite the color I had in mind for the small office, but Lucas Sherwood hadn't given the decor a second thought when he blew out the left side of his head with a .45.

As the county manager, I identified Lucas' body for the cops, and gave the poor man a quick moment of silence with thoughts to a higher power that he be let through the pearly gates. He died in a place he didn't like, doing work he wasn't very good at, having no place else to go. No mother gives birth thinking her child will end up like this. The unexpected note scrawled across his desk pad gripped me. "Sorry, Slade." Apologizing for what, I didn't know.

Damn it, Lucas. What were you thinking?

He was a fifty-year-old divorced alcoholic, an agricultural technician five years short of a dreaded retirement. I was the closest thing to family for him, but couldn't dial his phone number without looking it up. What forgiveness did he think I owed him?

Three days later, I stood poised at the door of Lucas' office, hand on the knob. Yellow crime tape blocked the doorway to a room resembling a Tarantino movie set. A cleanup crew waited in the lobby. I'd received the official nod from local authorities to enter his office and have it cleaned. Finally, I broke the spell and opened up the room. Painful or not, we ran a business that couldn't stop long for tragedy. People depended on us . . . on me.

My signature line read Carolina Slade Bridges, County Manager, United States Department of Agriculture. I made government loans on behalf of the American taxpayer to the rural residents of Charleston County, South Carolina. Problem was, I spent more time trying to get the money *back*. Poverty made repayment difficult. My job made for stories the average urban dweller would never comprehend.

Charleston County contains the stylish historic city, which everyone associates with culture, Southern charm, and plantation blue bloods living in antebellum splendor overlooking The Battery. No one envisions small-time farmers scrambling to make a living on Rhett Butler's stomping ground, but the string of islands along the coastline offered them a reasonable subsistence with the support of federal monies. I admired their pride and tried to ignore their plight, so I could sleep at night.

On the Friday after the suicide, the three remaining members of my staff expected directives from me. A pile of work awaited us, and I assigned tasks attempting to create a semblance of normalcy. Normal lasted about five minutes.

"How can we just sit here like nothing happened?" said Ann Marie. My middle-aged, wide-eyed clerk always wore a look of surprise on her face, as if she'd just witnessed a miracle. For some reason she adored me, and her ritual Monday morning sugar cookies were a thank-you for taking the time to explain instructions to her. Her perpetual smile dimmed on rare occasions, and talking about Lucas was one of them.

Jean Sparks, my office manager, sat with a ramrod spine and a steno pad. "Honey, life goes on." She tossed her coifed head of ink black hair locked with sprayed lacquer.

"He seemed so lonely," Ann Marie said, her soft pout bordering on tears.

"He didn't do sh—"

I cut Jean short with my stock, green-eyed "don't start with me" glare.

"He's gone," I said. "Let's honor him with our prayers, but remember the work's stacking up." I turned to Miss Mouth. "Jean, how far behind are you with *your* deadlines?"

My return to discussion about workloads settled them down. We covered the basics, and with a residual mourning of a minute and a half, we adjourned minus the usual chatter about kids, mall sales and local politics. Felt funny without a man in the room.

Lucas Sherwood was death number two. A year ago, almost to the day, my easygoing boss Mickey Wilder drove to one of the islands and never returned. I'd immediately stepped into Mickey's job, but sensed he continued to peer over my shoulder, my perpetual mentor. His leadership spirit still hovered in the office. Based on a string of personal factors I wasn't privy to, the cops had labeled his disappearance a probable suicide. Then they'd moved on. We remained behind, our respect for Mickey shaken, thanks to the whispers and innuendo. At least in Lucas' case, the staff had found closure.

I didn't. Mickey made no sense. I still expected to see either man walk into my office, Mickey telling me to get out of his chair.

By ten, phones rang and clients trickled through the door. I remained in my office dissecting complex applications. Slim chance upper management would replace Lucas, considering the minor contribution he made in the grand scheme of things. He inspected property held as collateral for the millions of dollars in loan portfolios. I would assume his duties, which meant counting heads of livestock, inspecting equipment and monitoring crops. Mud-on-my-shoes work. Duties in the outdoors I'd genuinely come to miss since becoming the boss.

Ann Marie poked her head around the door. "Slade, the Rawlings are out here to see you."

Slade was my maiden name going back to my great grandmother from Mississippi. Only my Mom and Daddy called me Carolina, and nobody who knew me used my married name, Bridges. I loved my heritage, but I didn't love my husband. Slade was the best title for all concerned.

"Did they say why?" I hated drop-ins. I liked order. Especially since I'd seen so little of it lately. I slid the oversized paper clip out of my hair. I'd been too busy to schedule a trim, and the thick dark strands didn't take well to a curling iron once they overlapped my collar.

"Jesse said he has a check to give you, but he's short on his payment." Ann Marie preferred to make nice with the public and direct problems to me, since I possessed a reputation for squeezing money out of rocks.

I stood and smoothed out the wrinkles in my khaki slacks and tugged my sweater straight. We worked with rural folk, and suits screamed authority. My closet held an assortment of JC Penney separates, simple to match and easy to throw on, using the same pieces of jewelry, a watch, my wedding ring, gold posts and an hourglass necklace the kids gave me for Mother's Day one year.

I walked to the front counter with the undainty gait my mother hated. Plowing the lower forty, she called it. The eight-foot wooden barricade stood as a buffer to the disgruntled. We aided many people in the rural community and loved doing good deeds, but money issues brought out the worst in some. Thus the counter.

"What can I do for you, Jesse? Ren?"

The brothers always arrived together, Jesse doing the talking. Ren was the eldest but the simplest, incapable of completing eighth grade. Dark hair draped thin and limp on his shoulders. He often repeated his brother, as close to a shadow as a being could get. His denim jacket hung long and loose, and his ball cap sat cockeyed. He was tall but chose not to appear so, his stoop making him shorter than Jesse. Rumor was he'd been conceived via some form of incest. I fought to hide my pity.

Jesse, however, was another tale to tell. The broad shouldered hog farmer grinned with a hint of the romantic, flashing white teeth and peppermint breath from candies he carried in his pocket. Here stood a comedy of errors in fashion. He usually traipsed into the office in fresh denim overalls, a John Deere cap and a tan and black hounds tooth sport coat he'd inherited from his daddy. Wearing the coat was respectful of my position even though he towered over my average height. I reciprocated that respect.

About my age, Jesse had finished high school and held a universal, good-ole-boy quality that commanded a smile and a handshake. Not the cliquish redneck sort, but the down-to-earth kind one slapped on the back. A man to discuss the weather and commodity prices with, and admire for taking care of his brother.

I felt Jesse held a mild affection for me since I'd exercised some mighty creative financing to keep their farm afloat. They'd lost money three of the last five years, and I'd found a means to stave off liquidation each time.

Jesse chuckled and gestured for me to lean closer. I obliged, straightening my V neck to block his view of my garden-variety 34Bs, not knowing whether to expect a joke or a plea for a payment extension. Either way, we'd laugh, discuss it and tell each other to have a great day.

"You know how I ain't been making my payments, right?"

I nodded.

"Well, I've got a great idea on how to fix that."

Oh boy, here we go. Some of my clients concocted schemes of borrowing more to make more. In the agricultural world, more debt meant a quicker demise. I waved my arm toward my office, but he shook his head and curled his finger, drawing me in like an anxious kid with a secret to tell. Ren glanced at me and smiled. I returned it, and he tucked his head, embarrassed.

Since Jesse was prone to bouts of silliness, I whispered back, "I'll give you some advice. Just bring in the money when you sell your hogs instead of telling me they keep dying. We both know you've sold some on the side."

"Listen," he said, with a face like stone. "I ain't jokin'."

I kept smiling at the round-faced country bubba, wondering if he played a different tactic to skate paying. Maybe he'd listened to too many boys at the bar. "I'm not joking, either, Jesse. I'd hate to see you lose your place because you don't pay your bill. What would Ren do?"

A calloused hand, fingernails caked with God-knows-what, grasped my arm. A strong whiff of porcine manure filled my nose as Ren drew close. I'd forgotten. He got frantic at the concept of living anywhere but on that small farm with his hogs. I patted his hand.

Jesse loosened Ren's grip on me with a tender tug and handed him a peppermint. "It's okay, buddy." Ren exchanged a grip on me for the candy.

Jesse turned back and spoke flat and cool. "Sorry, Ms. Slade. Come on outside. Got somethin' to show you."

"Somethin' to show you," echoed Ren.

"We can talk here," I said.

"Please, ma'am. Need you to see my truck. Might help you

understand."

Ren reached up again and yanked me toward the counter door. To keep from stumbling, I obliged him, and once on the other side, I pulled away. "I'm coming, Ren," I said loud enough for others to hear. Ann Marie glanced up from her desk, analyzing the threat level. I shook my head and waved, assuring her things were fine.

The brothers led me outside, into the clear autumn day. Ren peered back repeatedly, snickering and gesturing for me to come. My flats crunched on the crusher-run gravel.

Thirty feet away from their truck, I stutter-stepped as I caught the sight of dead flesh. Ten feet closer, rot smells accosted me. Jesse leaned over the tailgate. Ren mimed him. I held a yardstick length back.

"Dead," Jesse said. "Not sold. Not stolen. Dead."

Eight, market-sized feeders lay crammed in the truck bed, making hundreds of flies orgasmically happy. Some pigs appeared dead for a couple weeks. Others just a day. A sow lay eyes wide and bloated while a young shoat had lost much of its hide, dark, rotting muscle exposed. "What'd the vet say?" I asked, trying not to inhale.

"Ain't showed him. He'd charge, and I can't afford him."

And so the cycle went. We'd never be sure what killed the animals, but we could count on the next payment being short.

Back at the building, my staff stood at the door along with a half dozen employees from other offices in the county agriculture complex. Carcasses tended to draw a crowd.

Jesse drew me by my stretched sleeve to the truck bed, my face barely a foot from the nearest body. "There's ten thousand dollars in it for you," he whispered, draping his arm around my shoulders. "If you find a way to get me the Williams' farm. We can iron out the details later . . . in private." He winked and clicked his tongue. "If you know what I mean."

Panic coursed through me at the altered state. Like hearing that your churchgoing mother liked bourbon straight and sex on top.

He'd offered me a bribe.

"Don't be silly, Jesse," I said. "What's gotten into you?"

The Natural Resources Manager, Sid Patten, stepped out from the group and headed toward us.

"Just think about it," Jesse said, his eyes on Sid. "We can chat another time. I got to get to the feed store before they close." He eased his arm away and regained his six foot two height, sneering as if he'd won the state lottery.

A plastic smile held my composure intact.

His voice relaxed and amplified, the regular Jesse returned. "I only got a little over a thousand dollars for my sales this week, ma'am. As you can see, I lost eight more hogs. Need to know you'll help me on this, Ms.

Slade."

Ren handed me a piece of paper from his overalls, the check smeared with various hues of brown. I gingerly took it, fingering the cleanest spot on one end.

"Jesse, if you've got more money, just pay up."

Reaching over, he rubbed his finger over the back of my hand. "I can't pay if I ain't got it, Ms. Slade."

I yanked my hand away.

Sid reached my side and made a hesitant last step at the sight before slapping Jesse's arm. "Hey, man. How's it going?"

"Just great, Mr. Patten. Needed to show Ms. Slade what happened to my pigs."

"I see that," Sid commented.

The farmer lifted his hat and ran a hand over thick locks of black hair. He slid the faded, broken-in John Deere cap on from front to back, and adjusted it in place—a move saying, "I got to go" in country talk. Then he buttoned the sport coat like he'd just stood from a pew in church.

"Y'all have a nice day now. I'll be in touch about our payment arrangement, Ms. Slade." He bowed, touching the brim of his hat. He stopped and turned at the truck door. "Shame you losing Mr. Sherwood. Kinda sad when someone kills himself. I'm just glad it wasn't murder, or a crime or somethin'."

Ren bowed and opened his door. "Kinda sad."

The men entered the truck cab, slamming squeaky doors. The truck moved away, creaking with its load, grunting as it hit the dip at the road.

"What the hell was that about?" Sid asked, a hand rubbing his chin, the elbow resting on his other crossed arm.

"Another excuse why he couldn't pay. I made the mistake of saying I didn't believe him." I took his arm. "Come on. The excitement's over. Time to get back to the grindstone."

The crowd returned to work, happy for the afternoon distraction. Back inside, I wrote a receipt for Jesse's check with a slight tremble in my hand, tossed the payment in the safe for the next Treasury deposit.

No mistaking his offer: money in exchange for abusing my position. If I didn't report it, I was as culpable as if I'd taken the bribe.

The loan manager in me wanted to scold him and return to dealing with the funny, lackadaisical farmer I knew. The hairs bristling on my arms, however, told me to tread carefully. Government officials like me easily wound up on the front page of national papers over simple matters. Stupid misunderstandings got feds fired, sometimes imprisoned. A manager in Calhoun County lost his job over something bribery related, and last I heard he worked at a feedlot in St. Matthews making half his former pay.

I hurried back to my office and sat down to think. Whether anyone found out about this bribe offer was up to me. Would it be so bad if I didn't report it? This was so out of character for Jesse. How he'd find ten grand was beyond me.

Instincts told me to forget the conversation. Federal law told me I didn't have that option. A stupid, pissant dilemma.

On the other hand, my redheaded assistant manager loved problems, especially when they fell on my plate. I felt Hillary's eyes on me before I saw her tall lanky frame leaning against the door. So stinking predictable.

"What went on out there?" she asked, a hand twisting one of her diamond ear studs. She wore them with every outfit. A gift from a boyfriend whom we all knew well.

"You know Jesse. All mouth and excuses. I'll have to go out to his place and count hogs. They crawl up and drop dead in his truck now. No telling how many are missing."

She threw me a sly smile. "So what did he whisper in your ear?"

"He said I looked damn good. That's what all the farmers say in my ear." I moved toward her and she stepped back. I smiled and shut my door.

Hillary hated having a female boss, especially one ten years her junior. It wasn't my design to be younger, higher ranking and more affluent, but she acted as if I were the architect of the stumbling blocks to her life. We'd endured several heart-to-heart talks about her attitude, but even so, she stood next in command in this little kingdom of ours. Some days I bit my tongue, remembering her rough upbringing as a foster child, with a husband who beat her when his tractor trailer rig hit town. But if she heard one word of my conversation with Jesse, she'd use it to her benefit. An opportunist all the way.

I paced my office, a ground level room measuring twelve by twenty with three floor-to-ceiling windows on one side. My desk sat at one end. A long table, perpendicular to the desk, hosted meetings with loan committees, applicants and my staff. A cheap prefab table next to my chair supported my computer, manuals, and management books on how to be perfect at my job.

The room's length made for good pacing, and a hard look showed the rut in the carpet. Walking beat the hell out of sitting still and rocking my leg like someone needing to pee. A quiet way to vent my frustrations without exposing my doubts to my staff.

A half-joke, half-serious insinuation about a measly ten thousand dollar bribe seemed minor in comparison to what happened to Lucas, but I had to consider the consequences of not reporting it. Why did Jesse have to turn wild boar now, of all times?

My record was as close to pristine as you could get, and a black mark on it concerned me more than a hog farmer. Recalling the touch of his rough finger on my skin sent a shudder somersaulting through me.

I didn't need this right now. Too many threads unraveled in this office already, more than I could control, especially with an upcoming audit by the bean counters in Washington. No time for weakness, either. I'd instinctively learned to hide mine, thanks to a husband who relished sticking a verbal knife in anyone's soft spot. Just like Jesse'd tried to stun me with pig death. My hide stretched thick over my emotions.

Decision made. Somebody somewhere would consider me an absolute idiot for calling in the authorities, but my career and well-earned reputation were more important than anyone's half-assed opinion. Rules were absolute; that's the way I was raised. If I followed the rules, I'd be just fine. That's how life worked.

CHAPTER 2

I sat in my office chair, picking at the half-inch rip in the seat. I lifted the receiver, then hung up. What if someone overheard our conversation? What if Jesse pursued me again and a bystander learned I kept the first offer quiet? Found under a pile of pens in my desk drawer, the Inspector General's business card flipped in my fingers, the number printed in black next to an ominous gold-foil badge.

Management gave us the cards at a conference last year, but I knew no one in the Office of the IG other than the agent who investigated Lucas' death a week ago. Mr. G-man in his dark green suit acted distant and formal, searching for a mystery where none existed. He didn't know Lucas like I did. I would've thought a suicide warranted sensitivity, but the US Department of Agriculture didn't dabble in death, at least not of the human variety.

I decided it safer to ring State Director Pete Edmond, my second level boss and a professional who respected my work. A clammy hand punched speed dial. My District Director Henry McRae would be pissed I went over his head. McRae called himself my immediate supervisor, but I wasn't asking a man inept at his job for a judgment call. The man couldn't pour pee out of a boot with the directions on the heel.

Edmond's secretary Angela answered. "I'm sorry, the Director is away today."

"This is Slade in Charleston. Would you give me his home number? He asked me to call." I gave her my neediest whine. "It would be my head if I waited until Monday."

She snickered. "Oh, sure. Like he'd have *your* head."

She was right. He'd favored me since my stats kept him looking good in D.C. eyes.

I got the number and dialed. "Mr. Edmond, I hate calling you at home, but—"

"Hey, Slade. Excuse the noise. I'm on the patio setting up the grill. What's up?"

"A farmer just offered me a bribe. Not a large one, so I wasn't sure—"

The fatherly tone turned to pure boss. "Talk to me."

Short of the dead hogs, I covered the details, hoping he'd tell me not to worry since I didn't take the farmer up on his bribe. Wasn't sure what to think about Ren overhearing the offer. I waited for Edmond to tell me the buck stopped on his desk instead of mine so I could go home.

"Stay there," he said, "until someone calls you back."

"Um, okay. I—"

"Damn, girl, I gave you better credit than this."

"Sir?"

"I'll call the IG. That's what you should've done. Don't phone me again about this. Bad protocol, girl. You of all people should understand the regs."

I hung up and flopped back in my chair. Damn it all. I should've shrugged off the brothers.

My heart sank from the scolding. Pissing off the boss was not on my to-do list. A loan file needed attention in my "In" basket, so I diverted my disappointment to something more productive. All I did was flip papers.

Keys soon jingled in the outer office, and I glanced at the wall clock. My staff prepared to head home. I sat and waited . . . for whatever it was I was supposed to wait for.

"Slade, you coming?" shouted Ann Marie.

I hollered back, "I want to finish this loan file. Go on ahead. Lock the door, please."

"You can't work all the time," she said. "You've got another life, you know."

I grimaced. Not much of one. My husband suckled the government teat as an accountant at the Air Force base. We'd enjoyed a few early years of blind and giddy love when lust made you think you're perfectly matched, but we couldn't stand each other now.

No sooner had the door lock clicked when the phone rang.

The voice projected businesslike, professional, almost curt. "Mrs. Bridges? This is Mark Ledbetter. I'm Assistant Regional Inspector General in Atlanta. I understand you've been offered a bribe?" The Boston accent rubbed me like sandpaper.

"Yes, *sir*, and it's Slade, please, not Bridges."

"Are you certain he meant it as a bribe?"

"Yes, sir. No doubt in my mind."

"Could you have misunderstood?"

I raised my voice. "No, sir."

"I'm just trying to ascertain the details. I have to make sure you have your thoughts straight."

Did I sound stupid or what? "Let's see. He asked me to get him the farm and promised to pay me ten thousand dollars to do it. What would you call it?"

Mr. I-Am-Important-And-I-Want-You-To-Know-It sharpened his

tone. "First of all, you should *not* have contacted Edmonds. You should have called us directly. You're a manager and should know better."

Three "shoulds" thrown at me in one breath.

He paused. "You worked with that employee who committed suicide, didn't you?"

Would my answer earn me brownie points or make things worse? "I was his supervisor."

"What is your home address?"

"Why?"

"We have to send an agent to your house. We take attempted bribery of a federal employee seriously, as I'd hope you would."

Talk about overreaction. He hadn't seen the ragtag team that offered the bribe.

"I take it seriously or I wouldn't have called. Wait a minute . . . I've got plans with my children this weekend."

"We all have to make sacrifices. I'm assigning an agent," he said. "Don't go home until he calls."

"That's it?"

"We appreciate what you're doing. Good-bye."

A cue card response. He probably took a shower with his gun sitting on the toilet in readiness for an Amber alert for rustled Herefords. Geez, this was the U.S. Department of Agriculture, not the CIA.

I wasn't used to orders.

Nandina bushes danced outside my window in the October evening breeze, the leaves half red from the cool season. What would an agent do? Surely he could just get Jesse to confess. Alan would be full of sarcasm about this once he . . . "Aw, hell."

The clock read six, and daycare closed at half past. God, I hated asking Alan to do anything. I picked up the kids most evenings because their little faces were sweet enough to eat. I threw my gnawed pen on the desk.

Speed dial got my husband on the second ring. "I won't make the daycare in time."

"What's this, twice in one week?" he said.

I sighed and stared up at the ceiling. "Do I need to call Mom?"

"Mom to the rescue." His laugh rang hollow. "You and your fucking mother. Peas in a pod."

My second line rang, caller ID indicating a Georgia area code.

"Alan, just get the kids. I have to answer the other line."

"Yes, *ma'am*. Whatever you—" I cut him off.

"This is Wayne Largo, Senior Special Agent from the IG Office in Atlanta. Understand you've got your hands full over there?"

Another twenty-five dollar title. I tried my best to play nicer this time. No point in an agent catching grief because his boss was a twit. "Yes, sir. Someone bribed me."

"Hopefully, you mean attempted bribe, Ms. Slade. If you've been bribed already, I'm after the wrong person."

Was that dry humor or a jab? At least he used the right name. "Of course it's an attempt, Mr. Largo. Think I'd call if he'd handed me the money?"

"I'm not sure. Don't know you well enough yet. It happens."

I twisted my wedding ring, ruing my remark.

"I know what you mean," he said, filling the silence. "Listen, it's your weekend. Mine, too. But I need to make arrangements with you so we're prepared for Monday."

"What's Monday?"

"Not on the phone. How does Sunday at one sound?"

Not on the phone? Since when did hog farmers bug government lines? "Fine," I sighed. "How will I know you?"

"A white Impala in your driveway and my photo credentials." He hung up. He was nicer than the other guy, but still . . .

Walking to the parking lot, I felt icky and devious like a kid planning to hit a convenience store. The Jesse I knew wasn't bad enough to warrant this trouble. I mean, he was trouble, but not the kind that got arrested. Wasn't like he was a drug dealer or pedophile. What if he learned I'd turned him in? A prickly sensation shot down my back.

Once in the vehicle, I hit the electric locks and drove slowly from the crushed gravel parking lot to the asphalt pavement. My shoulders relaxed as if I'd touched home base. Stress melted into the seat as I belted beach-shagging lyrics with General Johnson and The Chairman of the Board on the oldies station. With thirty miles to go, I sang and tapped the steering wheel, my unwinding ritual. This drive kept me sane, readied me for the destination. Once home, I'd face my blessings and my curse and pretend I lived a homespun life.

I eased my Taurus into the snaky trail of commuters leaving Charleston via I-26, riding the bumper of the car in front of me like a dog in heat. This downtime allowed me to reflect and try to make sense of personal obstacles. My car was my Zen Zone.

Alan Bridges, my husband, ate up a lot of my Zen.

He and I had once danced to shag tunes. We'd attended Clemson University in the South Carolina foothills, where tiger paws adorned every bumper, tee shirt and lamppost during football season. My hot-bodied, hip-hugging days.

As my betrothed, he'd pitched college baseball and briefly courted a professional contract, but at twenty-two, fate ripped opportunity away with a fastball and a shoulder injury. A degree in accounting replaced the

Atlanta Braves. We married two weeks after graduation and slid downhill from there – his high points courtesy of painkillers he thought he'd hid.

Two kids and innumerable slings and arrows later, we lived alone together. We'd even argued about who would cave and start the papers first. I considered myself mostly misunderstood, especially when it came to males . . . especially those of the idiot persuasion.

Home at last and inside the door, I sighed deeply, then smiled as my kids rushed to greet me. I squeezed them to pieces, showering kisses on warm cheeks and foreheads. They didn't need a performance from me. We were real.

"Momma, Zack said something nasty today." Ivy was my dark-haired, bossy but adorable, eleven-year-old daughter.

"She's making it all up." Zack, my tow-headed inquisitive six-year-old, addressed life head-on, demanding explanations while hiding his. They were my weakness and my strength.

"Let me change my clothes, okay? Then I'll cook dinner." I walked past them, shedding my earrings. "Any ideas what you guys want? And don't say pizza."

Ivy said, "I don't care."

"Whatever," echoed Zack. Then in an afterthought he shouted, "Nothing green!"

In my bedroom, I kicked off my flats and put on my threadbare tee shirt and fleece gym shorts. Barefooted, I grabbed the laundry basket and pulled the closet door closed with my toes. Still time to start a load before dinner.

As I separated darks from lights, Jesse's words played in my head. *"Ten thousand dollars, Slade . . ."* Dang, I needed a sounding board, someone to bounce off my doubts and analyze whether I'd overreacted calling in the feds. Maybe it wasn't too late to call them off.

I shouted from the laundry room so Alan could hear in the den. "Some pretty heavy stuff went down at work today." I snapped a towel to fold it, pleased with my civility.

"You drive another employee to suicide?"

Screw him. Screw the laundry. I should have known better. I threw the towel back in the dryer and slammed the door. I stomped to the kitchen. Leaning on the pantry door, I scanned the shelf for something quick for dinner while inhaling deep cleansing breaths. No fangs. No bloodletting. Not tonight.

Blood reminded me of spaghetti. Oregano, basil and sage fell unmeasured into the tomatoes as meat sizzled. Onions and garlic sautéed in a puddle of olive oil. My stomach rumbled like distant thunder as the aromas saturated the air, so I snatched a piece of sausage from the skillet.

Zack plowed into my leg. "Momma, look what I did today."

I laid my knife on the counter and scooped him up. "Ooh, show me."

He clamped a pudgy hand over his nose. "Ewww. Don't put any onions in my sketti." He then gripped his picture in both hands. "This is my short story, and this is my picture to go with it. It's called an ill-us-cra-tion."

I asked for my daughter's daily report as she sat at the kitchen table with her nose buried in a Judy Blume novel. She gobbled books like butterscotch.

"Nothing happened today," she said without eye contact. "Let me read the rest of this chapter, Momma."

Ivy flaunted a prissy air that masked her shyness. The thought of her reaching puberty scared me silly, especially if she tried any of my teenage stunts, even as goody-goody as I'd been. My dates consisted of the dean's list; then I married Alan. Go figure.

Dinner concluded uneventful. Kitchen cleaned, Madge the cat and Smokey the dog fed, laundry put away and kids tucked in bed, I poured a cup of coffee. More tired than usual, I chalked up my fatigue to stress and a certain stupid farmer. I felt sorry again for Ren.

I lounged on the sofa, hot mug in hand, and tucked my feet between the cushions to chase a chill. Coffee never kept me awake, so I often closed my day with a cup. My blood pumped about thirty percent caffeine anyway, putting eight ounces of java on the nutritional level of a multivitamin. I eyed the top of Alan's head over his newspaper and decided to give the husband a last chance.

"One of my farmers tried to bribe me today."

Alan dropped the paper in his lap. "How so?" Eye-to-eye contact from him was rare, and his reaction startled me.

"If I fix a land deal in his name, he pays me ten grand."

"You take him up on it?"

My mind stumbled. "What?"

He snickered once at scoring a point against me. "Never mind. Who was the farmer?"

"Jesse Rawlings. I've mentioned him before. He weirded me out. The IG is sending an agent here on Sunday."

Alan sat up. "You contacted the IG's office?"

"It's standard procedure."

"You should've told the guy to take a leap." He snatched the television remote. "You and your feminist career."

"Why? You work under the same government umbrella I do. No one bribes a federal official."

He flipped through channels. "And who would know if you blew him off – nobody. Just another way for you to make a name for yourself, sweetheart." He dropped the remote on the end table, stood and walked to the kitchen. "And what if this farmer tries to find you at home?"

My mouth fell open at the thought.

"Stupid, Slade. Not a brilliant move – not by a long shot." He grabbed a box of crackers and a beer and flopped back in his recliner. "But then, you aren't noted for having much common sense."

I counted to ten while my hand trembled, resisting an intense urge to throw my cup. Twelve years of this slice and dice treatment had calloused me from most of his crap, but each time I thought I'd reached invincibility, he broadsided me with a new demeaning angle.

A lump formed in my chest. "I'm not trying to prove anything or impress anybody. It's the legal thing to do. I'm not exactly excited about it."

He snatched another handful of crackers out of the box, one falling in his lap. "So why do it?"

"If I didn't report it, I'd be in a world of crap if someone found out. I don't see much choice."

"Whatever."

"Go to hell, Alan. You're never there for me." Not exactly lethal, but it felt good.

He smiled, unaffected. "You gotta learn to stand on your own two feet. One day I *won't* be there."

Oh, God, let it be soon. I drained my coffee, rinsed out my cup in the sink and went to the bedroom, fingernails scrunching into my hands. I prayed he wouldn't follow anytime soon.

The kids deserved better that these daily marital aftershocks. I'd stayed with this relationship for them—time to dissolve it for the same reason. Monday I'd call and jack up my attorney to prepare the papers . . . again. This time for real. A tear welled, and I willed it away. Alan pounced on any sign of weakness.

As I lay in bed, my thoughts shifted to Lucas. I'd Googled a web site at lunch and studied the warning signs of suicide. No obvious indicators, as far as I could tell. I didn't expect him to blow his head off, but I wasn't all that surprised. Was I that insensitive?

My mind now firing on all pistons, my focus shifted to the agent. Would he show up with a welcome smile or a snap of his wrist as he shoved a badge in my face? I pictured a firearm on his belt and a badge on . . . what? Surely an agriculture agent didn't sport a shield on his shirt.

The television clicked off, and my husband's footsteps headed toward the bedroom. Damn. I rubbed my head on my pillow to wipe away another errant tear. Why couldn't he watch some late night talk show, read the paper . . . sleep in the guestroom?

He sat on the bed. Time stopped. With a sigh he reclined and drew the covers over him. His breaths soon came easy, and I quit holding mine.

God, I hated weekends. No telling what mood tomorrow would find him in. Weekdays engrossed me in work. Weekends ate at me like three-alarm heartburn as I fought to focus on kids, avoid Alan, and count the minutes until Monday morning work.

But this weekend wasn't about our joke of a marriage. The kids and I would spend Saturday at the park after a neighbor's birthday party. Sunday would make me the object of a federal agent's interest. Alan and I could afford to miss one day of spit-fighting. I had an appointment to rat on Jesse.

CHAPTER 3

The morning sunlight's wash magnified the yellow curtains on my bedroom windows, the warmth slowly arousing me from a cozy sleep. I'd once entertained a rare Martha Stewart moment, as evidenced by the tiny yellow flowered wallpaper and matching sheers.

Alan threw open the curtains, blinding me, knowing full well I liked to wake up slowly.

I bolted upright. "Chicken spit, it's Sunday!" Not exactly the best way to greet the Sabbath, but I forgot a federal agent was about to drop by.

I tossed on sweats and ran to the kitchen. To the delight of my children, I whipped up French toast sprinkled with powdered sugar. Cooking magic to them. Bundled in jeans and layered shirts for the unpredictable autumn weather, they leaped at the chance to visit my parents, three miles away. After kisses and little arm hugs, I dropped them off at Grandma's.

When I arrived home, Alan slammed doors and drawers, cursing, in search of his wallet. "Your wallet's on the kitchen counter next to the coffeepot," I said. "Found it in the clothes basket." Without a thank-you, he stormed out back to talk to our neighbor Mike.

Dishwasher loaded in record time, I jumped in the shower. I presumed agents were observant by nature, so I shaved my legs. Once my hair dried, I combed the white streak I inherited from my grandmother to the right, my lone chic attribute.

The next daunting task lay with the wardrobe. At the office, I'd wear a suit as an equalizer – charcoal, navy or black with a bright colored blouse that sizzled, and a teeny drop of Chanel to show them a woman stepped to the plate. Ironed, creased, corduroy shorts and a long-sleeve rust-colored polo won the toss after trying on jeans, pants and even a jogging suit.

Nerves. I hated nerves. A waste of time and energy. The guy was probably insolent anyway, disgruntled at missing his Sunday football. Most Southern boys held football sacrosanct, and the man had sported a drawl. The Department of Agriculture couldn't have much in terms of James Bond personalities, either. After all, we're talking livestock and beans, for God's sake.

I reached for my lipstick, feeling naked without it, wondering if I ought to use the deeper bronze color I kept in my purse.

Alan stormed into the bedroom. "Where the hell are my gym shorts?"

"You leaving?" I asked, passion peach on one lip.

He shouted from the bathroom. "Mike and I are shooting baskets with a few other guys." The snap of a medicine bottle told me he'd downed another Percocet.

No time to fight about his habit now. "That agent is coming by. Thought you'd hang around."

He walked into the bedroom and propped a foot on the bed. "He's not coming to see me," he said, jerking his shoelaces tight.

His short temper forever festered below the surface, keeping me primed for the next argument, my defenses piqued. "That's not the point, and you know it," I said. "He's coming to your home, to see your wife. At a minimum, he's a guest."

"And I won't be here. I'm going to enjoy my weekend in spite of this ridiculous *investigation* you've conjured." He jerked his blond head toward the backyard. "Even Mike thinks you're insane."

The crease in my brow reflected in the bathroom mirror. "You discussed this with Mike?" He'd tell Sharon, then the whole neighborhood would know.

He shrugged, a smirk glued to his face.

"God, you're pathetic." I fought the quiver in my voice. "Why the hell are we still married?"

He snatched up his gym bag. "File the papers, sweetheart."

I threw the lipstick in the drawer. "What about the kids?"

"What about them?" His lip curled to the right, like it did whenever he told a ripe joke to his buddies. He brushed past me into the hallway, his sneakers squeaking on the kitchen floor as he left the house, leaving my question unanswered.

He didn't think me gutsy enough to leave. Closing my eyes, I decided Alan wasn't going to rattle me. Not today. Not now. Not ever. I'd file the damn papers.

I finished my makeup and walked out on the front porch, stopping tears with the back of my finger, salvaging the mascara.

Sitting in one of my wooden rockers Mom had dragged back from Gatlinburg, the toe of my sneaker started a rhythmic back and forth, but my nerves weren't so easily soothed. I jumped up, grabbed a broom and swept leaves off the porch. The mild autumn air roused goose bumps on my bare legs.

Mockingbirds cackled noisily overhead as though they knew something I didn't. Madge the cat sprawled on the railing, hypnotized by one of the fat birds perched in the crape myrtle four feet away. Our Lab,

Smokey, stretched out on the lawn without a care in the world. I envied him.

Dusty brown leaves and dying pine needles fell into the flowerbeds as my arms pumped the broom. I focused to keep it together, on getting my answers right for the agent. No surprises. Like the way I preferred my mornings.

A garage door opened across the street. Looking up, movement caught my eye to the left as an unmarked white Impala turned into the neighborhood a block down. The car drove slow, the driver probably checking addresses. The vehicle stopped alongside my curb. This was it. I reset the grip on my broom. Smokey released a good-natured woof and rose to greet company.

The driver stepped out and put on his black leather jacket. He rose to six feet, wearing stonewashed jeans, cowboy boots, and an open neck dress shirt. A revolver latched onto his left side in a cross-draw fashion I'd never seen before. The dark hair, stout shoulders and trim waist caught my eye. I guessed his age to be around forty, but the close cut beard made it hard to tell. Could be older. He tousled the fur on Smokey's head and walked toward me with a laid-back air and an expressionless face. More a Texas Ranger than a James Bond, more sour mash whiskey than a dry martini. The government's eclectic taste in agents surpassed my expectation.

He stopped at the bottom step. "Ms. Slade?"

I leaned on the broom, unsure how to smile. "That's me."

He flipped opened his wallet credentials, and sunlight glinted off the badge. "I'm Senior Special Agent Wayne Largo."

We did the power-grip thing, a moment of measurement, his hand firm but gentle. I kept eying the gun. "Nice to meet you. Have any trouble getting here?"

"GPS makes it easy," he said. He nudged the badge in my direction again and I changed my focus to the gold in his hand. "You need to check this, since I'm required to identify myself before we get started."

His Georgia drawl eased off his tongue natural, comfortable. I gave the credentials a cursory glance and drew back. He put the black leather bifold back in his pocket with his left hand – no wedding band. I tried to imagine mine ringless.

"Come right on in," I offered. "Did you arrive last night or this morning?" My words sounded like a bad accent from a *Gone with the Wind* sequel. Like a cheap flirt, I'd stepped into bimbo mode. I was more used to being in charge.

"Arrived this morning. I like getting up early."

My radar went off. I didn't trust the smile. Too pleasant. Federal workers knew agents reputedly flipped scrutiny onto employees.

However, Mr. Largo would find no skeletons in my closet, regardless of how large the smile. Dust bunnies, maybe, but no dirt.

He climbed the stairs and held the door open for me to enter. Conscious of his gaze and flattered by the chivalry, I wondered if my shorts showed too much thigh. I should've worn the slacks.

Alan had come back in. He walked briskly toward the garage, gym bag in hand. "I'm gone."

I wished. "Alan, wait. This is the agent I told you about."

He waved us off. "Gotta go. Mike's waiting outside. Don't know when I'll be back. Y'all have a dandy time." The door shut behind him.

My blood boiled, and I felt the heat in my cheeks. "Um . . . sorry about that."

Largo didn't bat an eye. He gestured to the floral loveseat. "Should I sit here?"

"Yes. Would you like iced tea?"

"That would be great. Sweet?"

"No other way." I walked around the bar that divided the kitchen from our breakfast table and great room, grabbed two glasses and opened the refrigerator, putting the huge door between the agent and me. I inhaled the crisp cold blast of the freezer. An ice cube tumbled out of my fingers, bounced on the tile floor and splintered into a dozen pieces. After elbowing the door shut, I smoothly kicked the ice chips under the counter. I'd wipe up the puddles later, or better yet, just let them evaporate, like my marriage.

The agent took his glass with a nod of thanks, and I parked myself in the opposite armchair. He rested his glass precisely in the middle of a white napkin on the coffee table between us and opened his briefcase. My fingers encircled my drink and rested the glass on my knee.

Largo glanced around the great room, taking in the family pictures on the fireplace mantel. We'd designed the room for family living and dodged formal plans, choosing beige paint and Berber carpet to accommodate kids, pets and an active lifestyle. Teal green and coral-colored touches gave it color. I still loved it.

"Nice home," he said.

"My mother helped me decorate. She lives nearby." I sipped my tea like a proper lady, but my mouth stuck dryer than burnt toast.

He opened his notepad. "Now, what name do you want me to use?"

"Slade. I don't use Carolina, and I certainly don't use Bridges. But that's another story. Let's just say Slade fits the mold." He grinned. I was glad to see he sported a sense of humor. Relieved to know mine hadn't tucked tail and run.

"So tell me, how did you become head of the Charleston office?"

He listened to my brief one-year history with apparent intent. "What does your husband do?"

"As little as possible." The words fell out too quick to stop. "Sorry." I set my glass on the table. "He's an accountant at the Air Base in Charleston." Largo checked off items instead of writing what I said. I sucked in air, then tried to release it without being heard.

"Henry McRae. Is he a good boss?"

"He does his job." I almost spoke again without thinking. This guy didn't need to know I despised Henry, and I didn't want the agent to think I hated all men. I just hated ones who stifled me, kept me from feeling comfortable in my skin, or made marital promises they never intended to keep.

Thirty minutes passed as he asked his questions. Common sense dictated he had to know me to work with me. Still, I felt like I was sitting for a high-powered job interview, with all the wrong qualifications. The ice melted in my glass.

Speed was not his virtue, nor his plan. He studied his notes. "Tell me about . . ."

"You want another drink?"

Largo set down his pen and notebook. "That would be nice."

I couldn't read him. This whole affair was gravitating into "much ado about nothing" from where I sat. Alan would grin like a fat possum when the IG told me to forget about Jesse and do my job.

I went to the kitchen for another refrigerator reprieve. When I returned, Largo set the glass down again in the center of the napkin without taking a drink. "Tell me what Jesse said."

Finally we were cutting meat. "He said he'd give me ten thousand dollars if I found a way to get him the Williams farm."

"Did you feel threatened?"

Should I have? If I didn't, was I blowing the offer out of proportion? I rubbed a hand on my chair cushion. "No, not really. I see Jesse all the time. Everybody likes him. Why should I feel threatened?"

"Did he say he had the ten thousand?"

"He offered it to me, so I assumed he has it."

"So you don't know."

Hell, I hadn't given it a thought. Was I supposed to ask for a copy of his bank statement? "Um . . . no."

"Did he ask you in those exact words?"

"He didn't say that precisely, but that's what he meant."

"Then let's start over and you tell me exactly what he said, not what you think he meant." His pen hand moved furiously across the pad, spreading too much blue ink.

Why did he copy what I said if it wasn't what he wanted to hear? I inched to the edge of the armchair and banged the glass down on the table, tired of repeating myself. "If he meant nothing, I wouldn't have called you." I pointed at him, a bit theatric, but we'd sat too prim and proper for too damn long. "Don't toss innuendos at me. You ought to be glad I'm honest and called the authorities, not dirty enough to take Jesse up on his offer."

He lowered his pen. "We can take a break, if you wish."

I waved a dismissive hand. "No. I'm nervous. Just remember who called who first."

"And I'm here . . . asking questions." He moved slow, returning his attention to his pad. No emotion, no counter-attack, no soothing tone telling me it's all right. Disarming. Intentional.

"Does Jesse have that kind of cash?" he asked.

"I don't think so. I'd break his neck if he hid that much money and didn't pay his loan."

"So why would he offer it?"

Good point. I crossed then uncrossed my legs as I pondered it. "Maybe because he thought he'd get my attention. Maybe he deals drugs. Maybe he has a rich aunt. Who knows?"

Largo's eyes lit up. "Tell me about the drugs."

I rolled my eyes. "I don't know anything about any drugs. There's rumor in the county that his momma moved here from Washington to get away from some bad sorts." This wasn't about drugs, damn it.

"How long ago was that?"

"Ten or more years. That's why it's a rumor."

He stared, forcing me to stare back. "Have you ever seen him with drugs or dealing drugs?"

Terrific. Why did I mention drugs? His steel blue eyes held me fast, though, making me want to answer. He was damn good at this job, making me feel like a fool at mine. "No. I suspect he's been selling off a few hogs and not using the money to pay his loan, but I don't have any proof of that either."

He leaned back and rolled the pen between his fingers. "Why does he farm if he doesn't make any money at it?"

Ah, the million-dollar question. Bet he thought it was original, too. "Have no idea."

"Why do you let him keep farming then?"

That's it. Largo touched a nerve usually delegated to the reporters who whored themselves for an anti-government story.

My eyes narrowed. "I don't dictate those half-baked procedures Congress pulls out of its—out of the air. I just follow the rules. Farming is damn hard work with ridiculously small rewards. The press eats my agency alive every time there's a drought, a flood, a freeze or some freak heat wave. We don't help the farmer enough, or we pour too much money into losing enterprises."

More writing. More silence. He laid his pad on the table, pen on top. "Listen, Slade. Just bear with me and we'll get through this. Cooperation would be nice."

Properly chastised, I hushed and stared at a large flower on the sofa next to Largo, the spot where Alan's buddy had puked after a Super Bowl party last year. "I make agricultural loans for a living, and I'm good at it. I don't get in people's minds as to why they like stepping in hog dung. I dole out government funds to keep farmers feeding everyone's belly, and I follow all the rules to do it." For a brief moment, I caught a raised eyebrow. I didn't know how to read that. "Okay?" I asked.

He smiled. "Yes, ma'am."

He shoved the notepad in his briefcase and stood. Dang, I should've mouthed off earlier.

"Tomorrow morning I'll be at your office around ten with a colleague. Tell your staff we're auditors. After all the agents who snooped around here last year on Mickey Wilder's disappearance, and Lucas Sherwood last week, a few auditors should mean nothing to them. The less they know the better."

He was right. After Lucas' suicide, we were sick of cops.

He reached out a hand and I shook it. "Thanks for the afternoon." There was that smile again. I glanced at the wall clock. We'd been at this for three hours.

I saw him to the door. He reversed the car in the driveway and drove off. Overall, I suspected I'd done pretty well chatting with someone who put people in jail for a living, but I didn't know for sure. And he'd left me with no clue what to expect for tomorrow. Amazing how a farmer's whims of bribery garnered such quick attention from the IG. I never figured them to be that efficient.

I stared down the empty street. Surely the agent recognized me as a patriot. One question got lost in the shuffle between us, though. What would happen when Jesse figured out I'd turned him in?

I went back in the house and changed into my softest jeans. When I called Alan's cell, it went to voice mail, and I left word I'd be at my parents'. Like he cared. Like he'd even be here when I got back. Like I cared if he ever came home again.

CHAPTER 4

I arrived ten minutes late for work, as usual, and brought my Taurus to a stop right outside the door of my two-story office building. Because of our rural customers, the department planted its branch offices on the edges of towns, making parking a non-issue. I bolted inside, scanned the office and released a sigh of relief that Largo hadn't arrived.

Hillary leaned over the counter, explaining an application to a farmer in flannel, denim and dusty work boots. I said good morning as I stepped past them, desperately needing my coffee injection. Wayne Largo's instructions weighed heavy on my mind. I wasn't sure how to play-act and lie to my staff, so I bee-lined to my office.

To keep from dwelling on the pending visitors, I studied Friday's unfinished file and considered a new appraisal. After signing the document, I threw it in my out-basket, lifted another loan application off the stack and sipped my coffee. Before I could double-check the balance sheet, Agent Largo walked in the front door with another man. I shut the file and listened, waiting for my cue.

"We're here to see Ms. Slade." Luckily he hadn't used that deep tone yesterday, or I'd have wet my pants.

My pulse jump-started as the ploy began.

Ann Marie rapped twice at my door. "I'm sorry to interrupt you, Slade, but a Mr. Largo and a Mr. Childress are here to see you. They don't have an appointment."

I looked up from my pretend reading. "It's okay, Ann. Tell them to come in."

No doubt heads turned as the two agents strolled through the lobby. The staff knew every soul in the county who fattened livestock, planted seed, sold supplies or scratched his butt with a pitchfork. Loud enough for everyone to hear, Largo introduced himself and his colleague as auditors, then closed my door. I exhaled.

Eddie Childress stood six inches taller than Largo and ten feet wider across the shoulders, appearing fresh out of college. His deep brown skin and large, box-like head cast an ominous presence. The Western boots and black leather jacket finished the quintessential bounty hunter look. Largo's smile was slow to surface, but Eddie's flashed the moment he made eye contact. The tiny diamond stud in his ear seemed an effeminate touch to the macho package. Both agents were eye-candy in so many ways.

Largo set his briefcase on the floor and draped his jacket over the back of a chair. He wore a tie and no gun. His beard had been neatly trimmed since the day before. He made a fine auditor.

I handed a file to Largo. "Here's Jesse's information." I acted upbeat and congenial, in spite of my urge to get this over with. The sooner they concluded this mess, the better.

Largo set the file on the table and leaned an elbow on it. "Slade, you're going to help us catch this guy."

The heck I was. I fell back down in my chair and held up my hands. "Hey, no need for that team-player stuff. You can carry the ball. I'll cheer." I knew the drill. They wanted my buy-in, basic Management 101. "Go arrest the creep. I'm not expecting any reward."

Eddie laughed deep, and I jumped. "Man, I see what you mean. She's a piece of work."

Largo grinned. "Told you."

"Told him what?" Male humor escaped me on most days, but especially on this one, when I had no time for jokes.

"Let me explain. You're the cooperating individual, Slade," Largo said. "The offer came to you. Jesse won't repeat it to us. You're an intelligent lady, so don't think for one moment you can't pull this off." He crossed his legs, one foot on the other knee – the first relaxed sign I'd seen from him. Guess he was in his element.

I twisted my wedding ring, remembering I forgot to call the lawyer. "Pull what off?"

Eddie's voice commanded attention. "Wayne says you're sharp." I pictured him pinning a crook with one hand and placing a phone call for pepperoni pizza with the other. "I'll be learning from him, too, if that makes you feel any better. Folks in Atlanta say he knows his stuff."

My gasp wasn't intended. "A teaching case?" I turned to Largo. "Guess bribery doesn't rank as high as I thought."

"You'll make a good CI," Largo said.

"And what does that mean?" I knew full well what it meant, but this was my office, and no one made a fool of me.

"Cooperating individual. You are cooperating, aren't you?"

"This is what you do for a living, not me." Nervousness exposed my nasty side. I leaned forward and picked up a paper clip, tumbling it over and over on my desk. "I'm not trying to be contrary, Mr. Largo, but chasing criminals is neither on my agenda nor in my job description."

"The name is Wayne, and we'll put the cuffs on him. You just pave the way."

After that, the agents set up shop in Lucas' old office. I figured they could break the death feel of the place. I went back to my desk and opened the same abandoned file.

Largo appeared in my doorway. "Slade."

"I'm kind of busy, Mr. Largo. Work doesn't go away just because you decide to visit." Thanks to one too many years with Alan, sarcasm rolled off my tongue easier than my mother would like.

He shut the door behind him. "Call Jesse."

I swallowed. "You're kidding, right?"

He dragged up a chair. "Make an appointment with him for tomorrow. Tell him you want to talk about his farming plans."

Wayne played hell with my need to remain in control. "Won't he get suspicious?"

"You'll pique his interest. My bet is he'll offer the bribe again." Largo laid his briefcase on the table and drew out a small device.

"What's that?" God, I sounded like a hapless female.

"A recorder." He grinned. "Haven't you ever seen one before?"

"I'm not stupid."

He hooked a lead into the phone, making adjustments here and there. I simply stared, feeling a need to say something . . . intelligent. "Don't we need a warrant?"

"I do this for a living, remember? Call him." He leaned in to the table, pen in hand.

I searched for Jesse's file. Where was the damn file with the number?

Largo slid it to me. "Need this?"

I bit my bottom lip.

"Wait a minute." Largo tapped the table with his pen. "Let's practice a bit first." The twitches in my eye eased as he ran through scenarios and suggested replies.

Finally, I dialed Jesse's number. Thank God his mother answered, a woman I'd spoken to a few times in dealing with the farm operation. She said he wasn't in, didn't know when he'd be in, then gave me a dial tone.

Despite the woman hanging up on me, being proactive began to sooth my nerves.

"No problem," Largo said. "We'll try later."

"You mean I'll try later, don't you?"

Not a frown, grin or cutting glance out of the guy.

"You can give me that file now," he said. "I'd appreciate it if you'd download his account history. I'll be next door . . . doing my *audits*."

After printing Jesse's full account, I sat with Eddie and Largo in their temporary space. Eddie wedged in Lucas' chair, pecking at a laptop. Wayne's chair sat beside the desk, almost resting against the wall to allow room for his crossed leg supporting the file. I felt like an applicant, victim, anything but a manager, seated across the desk from them answering questions. The room warmed up with the door closed, and I caught a strong whiff of Eddie's cologne and somebody's deodorant. My suit jacket came off, and I wished I'd not worn panty hose.

We covered every angle of Jesse's less-than-stellar history with the Department of Agriculture. He held the keen ability to lose hogs to one disaster or another and sell beans at a lower price than all his neighbors. He tolerated his mother, and vice versa. She slept around, and he ran the household, including the care of his brother. Half the county sympathized with the guy for having such a slut for a mom.

Financially borderline, the farmer never reached a level bad enough to foreclose. Short of the ill words beside his truck on Friday, he was the textbook bubba.

Largo flipped pages, stopping to read about hogs, payments and crop sales. I already knew the file, so I chewed the end of my pen.

"How well did Lucas Sherwood know Jesse?" Wayne asked.

The name flashed an instant recall of brain bits sliding down the walls and the middle-aged Lucas slumped over the desk where Eddie sat.

Largo waved his hand in front of me. "Slade! Did Jesse know Sherwood very well?"

At the mention of Lucas, my thoughts wouldn't gel. My brow creased as I tried to collect myself and answer like a professional.

Largo leaned back in his chair. "Maybe we should have talked about Sherwood before now. I'm sorry about what happened. My condolences . . . really."

Guess adding "really" to the end of his sentence meant something in his world.

"He died in that chair," I said, nodding toward Eddie.

Eddie eyed his seat on one side, then the other, and returned to typing.

I snorted softly at the nonchalance. I could like Eddie. "I miss having Lucas around, even if he wasn't much good at his job. He didn't have to die like that." A sigh escaped at the memory. "But, to my knowledge, there wasn't anything abnormal about his dealings with Jesse."

"Wasn't Jesse behind on payments?" Largo had read the correspondence side of the file, so he already knew the answer.

"Lucas never mentioned him other than as a routine borrower." I'd never thought about Lucas and Jesse involved in extracurricular activity, but then I never expected Jesse's bribe, either.

"What about Mickey Wilder?" Largo asked, eyes still reading paper.

A mild cramp caught in my neck as the tension in my upper body made sitting awkward. "Mickey? A straight arrow and downright anal about regulations." I knew Mickey as more than a supervisor. A twenty-year tenured manager, he'd molded the rest of us.

"When he vanished that Friday, it stunned everybody," I said. "We traipse up and down dirt roads and wander through backwoods to serve these farmers. His disappearance made us feel vulnerable, you know? *We* trusted him." I waved one arm toward the files stacked on a table. "The farmers trusted him."

Back when Mickey disappeared, I'd hated the questions about his ethics and motives. When investigators discovered antidepressants, a serious second mortgage and his wife's medical bills, we'd felt his pain but never questioned his sanity or his judgment. Mickey could handle anything served him. He wasn't a suicide-type of guy. It'd been a year now and still no body.

Largo glanced at Eddie, exchanging unspoken thoughts. How rude.

"I think you're mistaken if you sense a connection," I said. "Neither Mickey nor Lucas . . ." I broke eye contact. Suddenly, bells clanged in my head and something didn't ring true. Within forty-eight hours after my bribery call, I'd hosted Atlanta's finest, at least per their view, on my doorstep. Atlanta handled too many cases across the Southeastern United States to warrant this level of attention. This was about something more than good ol' Jesse. I felt dumber than blonde.

"What is it?" Largo asked.

"Huh? Oh, nothing. Thought I left the coffee pot on at home," I lied. We returned to our reading.

So who *were* they after? And why? I ran down a list of people connected with this office, and nobody jumped out in my mind. On Sunday, Largo had thrown ambiguous questions at me about Alan and my boss. Alan wasn't affiliated with agriculture, so he was out. McRae schemed about little more than on which bed to bang my assistant.

They must be here about Mickey. Victim or culprit? And why a year later?

A lone shiver rippled through me. Lucas' suicide might have been an end to something else. I'd been his final thought per the note on his blood polka-dotted desk. The message made no sense to me, but it may have to these 007 hayseeds.

What shoe was fixin' to fall on me?

Largo caught me watching him and raised his brow, as if asking me what I wanted. I smiled and shook my head once, redirecting my eyes to the paper in my lap.

The rules to this game had changed.

I could play cooperating individual for Largo. Just call me Little Miss Collaborator. I'd faked it with Alan for years. Acting for these two agents couldn't be any harder, as long as they didn't reclassify me from CI to target. And if they solved Mickey's disappearance, all the better.

I felt like I worked in a gingerbread house with the devil stirring crap in the basement. Soon it'd come up the stairs and through the vents, poisoning the air, maybe coating my pristine career with filth. No way. I'd have to stay keen, keep my eyeballs peeled on Eddie's and Largo's actions, words and subtle nuances.

But there was no reason we couldn't take out two trophies with one shot–Jesse and whoever else Largo pursued. The sooner the better. Then I could send these law-boys packing back to the Peach State and concentrate on my divorce. Maybe get some credit for helping nail a criminal element in the process.

Eddie stood and stretched, his knuckles touching the paneled ceiling. "Let's eat lunch before my stomach gnaws through my backbone."

"I agree with Eddie," I said, stepping into my role with newfound swagger. "Never investigate on an empty stomach. Isn't that a secret agent motto or something?" I reached for my suit jacket. "Melvin's lays out a great spread." I offered this place to most of my male visitors. I took my female guests to refined eateries without foam plates and packets of finger wipes. Personally, I preferred the barbeque.

"You like pickin' a pig, Mr. Largo?"

"Matter of fact, I do. And for the last time, it's Wayne."

In the serving line at Melvin's, the two large agents squished me between them, making me feel protected. The meager contents of my plate paled in comparison to their mounds of chopped pork, coleslaw and onion rings. No one spoke while forks shoveled food. Eddie licked his fingers incessantly then wiped them on the napkin draped across his chest. I resisted reaching over to wipe the sauce off his cheek. Largo ate each item at a time, his napkin in his lap.

Plates cleaned of all but sauce dribbles, we sipped our tea. Performing as the perfect CI, I waited for them to spill more than sauce. A tiny bit of info about their clandestine reasons for being here would be nice, and in this laid-back air I waited for something to slip.

Eddie bragged about his all-too-brief professional football days and shrugged off his ankle injury, the cause of his career shift. I began to tell them about Alan's parallel baseball story and cut it short. Every word I said was one less I heard from them.

The men spun stories about office politics, arrests and rural criminals, but dropped no clues as to their purpose. As I chewed on my straw, my loan manager job seemed a dry profession.

Eddie tapped me on the arm. "Ready?"

"Yeah, let's get back to it." I dropped the straw on the table, grabbed my purse and slid out of the red vinyl booth. I paid my tab at the protest of both men. I wasn't ready to feel obligated to them just yet.

Back at the Ag building, Wayne followed me to my office while Eddie disappeared into the one next door. I laced my fingers and rested my chin, awaiting instructions.

Wayne laid out index cards with handwritten notes. "These are the items to cover when you meet with Jesse. Memorize them until they become second nature. Keep him from straying. You don't have a problem with meeting him, do you?"

I slumped back. Sure I had a problem with it. The harmless farmer who lived with his mom and brother flaunted a new, slick personality that creeped me out.

I picked up the first card. The words sounded natural, and my heart slowed. I could do natural. If this was it, I could do natural with my eyes shut. I reminded myself this was part of the game, and two bona fide agents had my back.

"Get Jesse to repeat what he said Friday," he said. "We need corroboration for the grand jury."

Grand jury sounded awesome—suspenseful and exciting. Would I testify? I'd buy a new suit. Charcoal or navy blue. Block heels, nothing high.

"Got it?" Wayne said.

I smiled at him like a kid who'd aced extra credit on the exam. "I'm all over this."

"Good. A little role-play then. I'll be Jesse."

By the time we finished practicing, the leading questions and tactical phrases were seared into my head like the chorus of an old Baptist hymn. A tap at the door broke the rehearsal as Ann Marie peeked in. "Jesse Rawlings is on the phone."

"Remember, business as usual," Wayne said to me, then turned to Ann. "Thanks. That's one of our files. Your timing's perfect, sweetheart."

Ann giggled as he nudged the door closed, her shyness melted with that one little flirty word. Slick.

The hold light continued to blink. "What do I do with the recorder?"

"I'll handle the machine." He sat to the left of my desk and donned a headset. "Just be yourself." He pointed at me. "*Go.*"

I pushed the button. "Ms. Slade, may I help you?"

"Momma said you called," Jesse drawled.

I studied the plaque on the wall to my right, afraid watching Wayne would throw me off track. "Can we talk?"

Jesse hesitated. "Hey, I called you back, didn't I?" Another silence. "Wait. What's going on?"

I'm setting you up, you idiot. Oh God. My brain forgot what to say.

CHAPTER 5

Wayne must have read the panic on my face. I sat frozen behind my desk, phone in hand, Jesse on the other end of the line.

"Ask him to come in," Wayne whispered, writing it on a pad at the same time.

I nodded. "When can you come in, Jesse? We should talk."

Wayne winked.

As my heart raced, I scanned the index cards for reminders, but the words ran into one another. Two cards flipped onto the floor when I tried to spread them out. "The hogs. We need to talk about those missing hogs. Bring in your sales tickets. Anything from the vet, too." I found *that* card and turned it over with sweaty fingers.

Jesse's voice turned lively. "Oh, yeah, and I meant what I said. I'll take care of you."

"We can discuss that, too."

"I'll try to talk Ren into staying behind. How's Wednesday?"

"Let me check my appointment book." I paused for effect. This investigation stuff wasn't so bad. Now I was making up my own cards. "How's tomorrow?"

"You that anxious to talk about pigs, or you wanna see me?"

"Wednesday's booked," I said, ignoring the come-on. "It's got to be tomorrow."

He agreed to show up at ten in the morning and chuckled a good-bye. I wondered if he'd show up – almost hoped he wouldn't. Then I remembered to breathe.

Wayne switched off the recorder. "You did fine."

"He didn't say it like he did before." I collected cards from the floor and added them to the stack, tapping all four sides on the desk to make them even. Then I tapped them again.

"You're not face-to-face. Makes a big difference," he said, crow's feet wrinkling with a grin. "He said enough, plus he's coming in for you to have another go at him."

He secured the recorder back in the briefcase. "I'll give you a break, CI, and let you get some work done." He stood and left.

Finally alone. But after bitching about no time to work, now I couldn't, not with adrenaline pumping through my system. Instead, I strolled into the main office for a cup of coffee, hoping a pot of decaf lay waiting for me. Ann chatted with a customer at the counter. Hillary's door was shut, and Jean studied a stack of folders. Alone in the middle of all these people with no one to confide in. *Hell, Slade. Who do you ever confide in?*

Harboring an intense desire to pace, I retreated to the ladies' room, then upstairs, then down the hall. I'd opened this dam and couldn't hold back the current now. Jesse expected something of me. I almost ran into a technician from another office, grabbing her shoulder to keep from steamrolling over her. I apologized and paced on.

Sooner or later Jesse'd be pissed; I would be if I were him. I needed to ask Wayne when they intended to throw cuffs on him so I didn't worry about the weirdo tailing me home, or waiting for me in the parking lot. Jesse's clandestine nature could blow any time, if he got a wild hair or a beer in him and talked. I shouldn't have told Alan. Damn. He'd tell people just to spite me. Already had. Maybe I needed to hold off on the divorce until this case cooled a bit.

My hike brought me back to the office where my staff gathered their coats to head home. The urge to spill my guts no longer gnawing on me, I said goodnight, and then knocked on Lucas' door. "Everyone's gone, guys."

Wayne let me in. They were packed, ready to go to their motel.

"What time can you get here in the morning?" Wayne asked as we left, him holding the outside door for me.

"Whenever you need me, I guess." I started to ask him how long this mess would take, but heck, he wouldn't know. Not yet anyway.

"How's six? I need to set up before your staff comes in."

Alan was going to love this. "Sure, I'll be here."

"Good. Get in your car and lock up. We'll wait for you to leave."

Largo exuded calm, but Eddie stretched and scratched his washboard belly, like he'd had a long day. They didn't disturb me as much anymore, but they weren't drinking buddies either. I could do this for a few days.

I got into my Taurus and locked the doors. Eddie gave me a thumbs-up, and I had to smile. Easing out of the parking lot, it hit me. Gentlemanly qualities hadn't brushed my life in a long while.

ALAN CONFRONTED ME before my keys hit the kitchen counter. "So how did the meeting go with Columbo?"

"I have to go in early tomorrow."

"Quite the heroine these days, eh, Wonder Woman?"

"Cut it out, Alan."

He shook a blond lock off his forehead, like a movie star seeking attention. His hand reached in his pocket and jingled change, once, twice, pause, then three times. Did he have to flaunt all his stupid habits at once? Snatching off my gold loops, I pinched an earlobe and whispered a curse.

He leaned against the dining room entrance, sneering like a middle school bully. "When you lock up this big bad crook, you gonna write a book?"

I strutted past. "Don't be a pain."

The kids rummaged through the refrigerator, leaving jackets, book bags and shoes in their wake. They'd no doubt heard us and hadn't thought twice about the banter. A blessing *and* a sad state of affairs.

"You able to take the kids in the morning?" I asked quieter. "I promised the agents I'd be there around six."

His mouth slid to the right, flashing annoyance. "For what?"

"Whatever they need. We're trying to catch Jesse making the bribe." The kids ran between us into the den.

He shook his head. "Silly shit."

I snatched a dishtowel from the drawer, mad at his games. He leaned toward me, whispering, "I've been invited to the White House to be briefed about a secret mission. I might have to fly to London after that. Not sure I can make it home before daycare closes."

Throwing the dishtowel down, I turned on the water to rinse a glass. "Yes or no?"

"Like I have a choice." He walked away.

I went to the bedroom and changed into leotards and a sweatshirt. At dinner, everyone ate in silence except Zack who hummed the Spiderman theme song.

With the dishes done, I herded the kids through their baths and told them their father would take them to school in the morning. After exclamations of cool and wow and discussion about what their dad would let them get away with for breakfast, I tucked them in bed, warning them I'd tie them with yo-yo string if they got up. Sleepy giggles told me they were done for the day. The night-lights shined soothingly in the dark, and I slipped back downstairs, fighting the urge to slide in bed with Ivy.

Wine in one hand and a bag of spicy hot potato chips in the other, I curled up in my bentwood rocker in the bedroom, seeking a cozy spot to practice my Jesse phrases. Even in the embrace of a rocking chair under Mom's handmade quilt, I didn't feel good in my own house. My husband was the enemy – my home the battleground. My parents surely wondered why I had married this nitwit.

I reached for the phone on the bedside table and discreetly dialed my lawyer. My hesitation to follow through with divorce last year would probably make my attorney dawdle this time. I'd worried about robbing the kids of their dad and back-pedaled. All this could have been over by now.

Emboldened by voice mail, I left a message to proceed with the same legal papers we'd completed the last time, reminding him I still had him on retainer. I hung up. That felt good.

Being proactive made me think of Savannah — not the city, but my best friend. I dialed, and her answering machine clicked on.

"This is Slade. Call me at work tomorrow."

"Wait a minute! I'm here," my friend shouted, gasping over the recording. "What's up?"

Savannah Conroy was my counterpart in Beaufort County, home of Hilton Head Island. Her clients rarely enjoyed the celebrated restaurants and secluded beaches known to tourists. Beaufort harbored rural poverty and agriculture just like Charleston. When I'd signed on with the agency, she'd taken me under her wing. Right after that, I'd nicknamed her Savvy.

"Don't let the gender remarks get under your skin," she'd lectured her new protégé at an after work social. "Farmers are a tough bunch. They don't like it much when the banker wears a bra." Savvy's good-natured disposition, lubricated by tequila, had broken the ice and forged our friendship that night. She carried a heart as big as her flamboyance.

Tonight I needed to hear that friendship. I whispered. "All hell's breaking loose, that's what."

"You know my opinion about that bad boy. Surely, you recall our last talk."

We'd attended a manager's conference in August and, as usual, reconnoitered at the motel bar before dinner. A strong-willed, beautiful woman with close-cropped hair and high Cherokee cheekbones, Savvy'd scolded me over the top of the hors d'oeuvres. "You do well. Alan hates it. You hold yourself back for his sake and shortchange yourself. You can't win."

Now she recognized my quasi-whisper over the phone. "He hasn't hit you or anything, has he?"

"No, no, nothing like that. It's just that work's turned my life upside down, too."

"Girl, you don't have work problems. You're the budding young executive according to Edmonds. I'm honored to rub elbows with someone so impressive."

"A farmer tried to bribe me, Savvy."

"No shit! You call the IG?"

"Yeah, and you aren't supposed to know, understand?"

"What if they tapped your phone?"

I hesitated. "Oh jeez."

"I was joking, Hon. Chill. So what did they do?"

A thread poked out from the corner of the blanket. I spun it around my finger. "They're here – in Charleston. They sent a pair of agents, and they actually tape conversations and stuff."

"Sounds kinda cool. So what's the big deal?"

"Alan's riding my case saying I should've swept the bribe under the rug. And the farmer gives me the willies. The agents say we have to make him repeat his offer or come up with money to catch him. Alan flat-out deserted the day I met the agent here at the house." I yanked the blanket thread loose and dropped it on the floor.

"Forget about that bum. Are you safe?"

"Yeah. The farmer doesn't know anything." I paused again to get the next words right. "I told my attorney to proceed with the divorce papers."

Nothing stunned Savvy, and she didn't miss a beat. "Divorce is hard, Slade. Even when it's necessary. He doesn't deserve you, though, but you've heard that before. You did the right thing."

Savvy had divorced a drunken, cocaine-sniffing insurance agent who envisioned himself a rock band mogul. She could talk the talk. We didn't discuss those details, but they existed unsaid as a lesson well-learned.

Her next words clarified my decision. "Look at it like this, when the kids are grown and gone, Slade my dear, do you want that asshole to be all you see across the dinner table?"

While Alan didn't fall into the same husband category as Savvy's, the fact was I didn't love him anymore. I didn't even like him. Question answered.

After thanking Savvy for her support, I said goodnight, folded my lap blanket and climbed into bed. With the heavy comforter gathered under my chin, my consciousness descended into what I hoped would be a dreamless night, however short.

The television switched off. Alan's feet plodded across the floor.

Crap.

He entered the bedroom. He undressed noisily, and his weight on the bed jostled me. He shifted closer, blowing hot air in my ear. No chance he'd get a piece of me. I controlled an urge to flinch and feigned sleep. Two minutes later, he sang his signature throaty snore. My shoulders relaxed.

It'd been a long time since we'd entertained sex, something Alan considered set apart and far removed from a loving relationship. He played nice in order to get his two pathetic minutes of grunts. The last time he pulled that trick was four months ago. I intended it to be just that . . . the last time.

THE ALARM BUZZED AT 4:15. I dozed to 4:30 then reset the alarm for Alan, tempted to not set it at all if it weren't for the kids and school. I dragged my numb body to the shower and all but dozed under the water. My brain didn't stir until my skin shone rosy pink from the steam.

After donning charcoal slacks and a sweater, I nudged Alan. "I'm leaving. Don't forget about the kids." Wow, those words had a premonition feel to them.

"Whatever," he mumbled.

I threw earrings and lipstick in my pocket, snatched the car keys off the wall hook, and glanced at my watch. Time enough to pick up a black coffee and a honey bun from the convenience store.

Headlights reflected in my rearview mirror when I turned onto Interstate 26 eastbound. I'd expected minimal traffic this time of the morning. I tilted the mirror to avoid the glare and slowed to let a vehicle pass. The driver hung close.

"You've got three lanes to drive in. Pick another one, you idiot!" As if hearing me, the person drifted back a few car lengths. I pulled my foam cup from its cradle and opened the plastic top. The lid snapped loose and a few drops sprayed me in the face.

Bam! The car lurched forward, hit from behind. Spilt coffee burned my hand. My car veered across the road, straight toward the concrete median. I swung the wheel to the right and scraped my bumper against the median before regaining control. I plopped the cup in the console holder, slinging liquid across the floor.

Every muscle tensed as I eased my foot off the accelerator. Slowing down, I expected the moron to follow suit so that we could both pull over and exchange insurance information, but as I looked in the rear view mirror, I saw the vehicle accelerate. I clutched the wheel in a death grip and punched the gas too late.

Bam! We bumped again.

Son of a bitch! I held the car stable this time. Gritting my teeth, I braked hard and peered into the blackness to identify the culprit, almost driving over the centerline again. Headlights backed away, coasted for a moment, then accelerated. Instinctively, I faced forward, hoping to remain on the road and not careen into the pines and live oaks to my right. My butt, legs and forearms tightened.

The lights approached, filling up my mirror, blinding me. The car shot past—the plates too hard to read before the taillights disappeared into thick predawn darkness.

My pulse hammered. I strained to see.

Instinct told me to call the cops, until I realized I held no inkling who'd rammed me. The strong coffee called my name, and I took a moment to admire my hold-it-togetherness. I reached for the Styrofoam cup. My hand shook, sending ripples across the liquid. So much for poise.

The Arthur Ravenel Bridge spanned the Cooper River in all its steel and cabled glory against the orange-pink sky as the sun broke over the horizon. The car's digital clock read ten to six. Miraculously, I would get to the office on time.

As I reached the parking lot, Eddie and Wayne stepped out of the white Impala, their boots crunching gravel as they approached, briefcases in hand. Wayne wore the same blue suit, different shirt, a boring blue tie.

"Great morning," Eddie boomed, his breath a white cloud in the chilly dawn air. The sun was already changing grays to color.

I slammed my car door. He was one of those energized early risers you needed like a root canal. "I'm not a morning person, Eddie." Especially not *this* morning.

He watched me walk around the car, pressed a big finger over his lips and whispered, "I'll remember that."

He made me grin.

I studied the bumper, the damage way less than I imagined for two strong taps. "Some idiot rear-ended me for no damn reason this morning."

"Are you okay?" Wayne asked, walking over, rubbing his hand across the dent.

"I'm here, aren't I?" A mixture of embarrassment and impatience washed over me. "The moron hit me twice. It's a miracle I didn't wind up kissing an oak tree."

Wayne frowned and reached for a notepad in his pocket. "See his face? Get the tag?"

"Nope, and that's why I didn't call the cops."

Both men stared incredulously.

I blew a frustrated sigh, my arms rising out to the side in a "why me" pose. "It was dark. I was alone. The car isn't demolished. The driver disappeared, and there's nothing I can do about it."

Wayne stared at me like I'd changed color. "You're dismissing attempted murder?"

"Murder? We shared paint." I pointed to the dent. "I can't prove anything, and the damage isn't worth raising my rates. Cut the dramatics."

Dramatics or not, Jesse came to mind. I buried the thought. I'd known Jesse too long to envision him going that far. Not for a piece of dirt.

Wayne thrust the notepad back in his pocket, tight-jawed. "If it happens again, you call me immediately. Whatever time it is."

Like that remark didn't warrant suspicion about their presence on my turf.

I stepped up to the building and tried to insert the key into the front door. The key trembled. Wayne grasped my hand to steady it, his grip warm and firm. We worked the key, and the lock clicked open.

"Thanks," I said. "I'm good. I'm fine." So why had I said it twice?

He let me enter first, his morning shower fresh in my nose. I hit the light switch, and the fluorescent tubes hummed, then flickered on, one at a time. While I made coffee, the men wired my office. Wayne turned just as I yawned. "You could have slept in if you'd given us a key."

Waving a hand in front of my mouth, I shook my head. "I'm responsible for this place. My head would roll if something happened."

"Your call," he said. "I could get a set anyway, you know."

Oh my, a taste of sarcasm from the lawman. "Not if you want to keep me happy," I replied. "By the way, how long do you think we'll be doing this cloak-and-dagger thing?"

Wayne shrugged. "Don't know. Depends on the farmer."

Non-committal. Exactly what I'd expected.

"So why didn't *you* call the cops about my bumper car incident?" I asked. "I'd have thought one cop would want to call another."

Wayne spoke over his shoulder, his hands busy with a wire under my desk. "We can call right now."

"Forget it."

He stood and admired his work. "There. The recorder and wires are well hidden. The mike is in your vertical files there. Sit in your chair and give me a test."

We played "testing-testing-1-2-3" like kids on walkie-talkies until he felt comfortable with the reception.

Eddie poked his head in the door. "The picture's good."

I stared at the young agent as if he'd grown antlers. "What picture?"

Eddie strutted into the room. "See Wayne's briefcase parked in the corner?" The case sat on my two-drawer file cabinet, across the room from my table and desk. "There's a pin-hole camera in there. It sends a live feed to me in the next office. I'll be watching you on a tiny monitor, so smile pretty when the camera rolls."

"I'm impressed," I said, lying. I wasn't rocking and rolling with all this.

Wayne laughed. "Don't be. We borrowed the equipment from the FBI. Two-bit guys like us don't have tech departments." He rubbed his hands together. "We're 10-8 here. Wanna grab a bite, Big Man? Slade?"

Eddie snapped to his feet. "You know it."

"I ate a sticky bun from the convenience store," I said. "Thanks anyway."

I watched them through the front window as they left and wandered over to my car. Eddie rubbed his finger across the bumper again. Wayne waved him toward the Impala.

The guys were growing on me. While they choreographed most of the behavior to seek my alliance, I liked to think they respected me. No man had liked me in a long time.

But there was still that other agenda.

CHAPTER 6

Around ten, with the two men in the next room, I paced my office, waiting for the phone to ring. The last time my stomach climbed Mount Everest like this, I'd given a speech to a deputy secretary and a couple of congressmen on behalf of my boss Edmonds, and performed brilliantly. Surely I could ace a one-on-one chat with a hog farmer only high school educated.

At ten thirty, I buzzed Wayne. He said to give Jesse another half hour.

At eleven, I marched into Wayne's office. "Now what?"

"Calm down and call him."

We repeated the phone exercise from yesterday, and left a message on Jesse's answering machine.

We killed an hour, only this time together in my office. Wayne took the sting out of my anxiety by making me laugh at tales about bootleggers, illegals, even abandoned cattle they'd rescued. Then he tried to crack a joke and the punch line fell flat.

We were about to give up for the morning when I decided to check my voice messages. Without thinking, I listened to them on speaker as usual, while the two agents chatted.

"Slade, this is Craig McCurry. The separation papers will be delivered to Alan around four this afternoon. Call me if you change your mind—"

I cut the message short. My lawyer's finger-snap response to my kick-ass message last night surprised me. My cheeks turned cold and pasty. Wayne glanced in my direction. I was jumpy to leave, go home, tell the kids . . . get out of the house for a day or two. Oh wow.

Then Jesse called.

My phone's hold button flashed, ordering me to switch back to work mode, but I couldn't. How many days' clothes should I pack? Daddy would back me up, but what would Mom say when she heard I no longer needed a husband?

Wayne switched on the tape and mouthed silently that I should stay calm.

"No, wait a minute," I said, home too prominent in my head.

Wayne clicked off the tape and rewound it. "Breathe deep. You can do this," he said, composed and assuring, implying he understood.

After the second inhale, I took the call. "What's the problem, Jesse?"

"Truck broke down," Jesse drawled. "I'll get there tomorrow morning about ten." He hung up without a cordial goodbye or his usual corny one-liner. I held the receiver out, stared at it, then replaced it in the cradle as Wayne shut off the recorder.

Eddie shrugged and rocked his chair back on two legs. "Not unusual," he said. "Guy's not gonna be all that reliable in any of this. Won't surprise me if this thing falls through altogether."

Wayne turned quickly. "Can it, Eddie."

"This plan isn't working, is it?" I asked. Jesse loved being impromptu, dropping in one time and forgetting an appointment another. I saw him when I saw him, just like the day he dropped in with the bribe offer. Problem was, this was a new Jesse Rawlings, even more unpredictable. Our roles were reversed with him calling the shots. Knowing Jesse and his lack of resources, I halfway expected this event to flop. How the hell would I deal with him then?

"It's working fine so far." Wayne retrieved his jacket from the back of the chair, making Eddie stand in kind. "Are you all right?" Wayne asked, settling the jacket on his shoulders.

"Yeah, I'm freakin' great."

They reached the doorway and looked back. I glanced at my watch. Did my attorney say four? Four thirty? I got up and walked to the window where I could watch the shrubs and not feel like the focus of attention.

"I'm sure everything will turn out fine," Wayne said. "In both cases." He closed the door gently behind him.

Jesse was a tomorrow issue. Home consumed me now. My fights with Alan were finally coming to an end, in a big crescendo overlap with Jesse's crap.

I needed to skedaddle to drop the bomb on my mother that the kids and I were coming to visit until Alan got his belongings out of the house. She knew we were having trouble, but divorce wasn't a casual word to her. I felt like the bruised banana in the bunch – still edible but not as pretty as the rest. I dreaded facing Mom more than Alan. Guess in a way, that had something to do with respect.

I phoned my boss McRae in Aiken to take the afternoon off. As my first line supervisor, he'd been promoted only after I'd foolishly declined the position so Alan could stay in Charleston and keep his job. Ironic or what?

His clerk took the message. The man would love an emotional chink in my armor. He had no heart, no brains or balls, either—and very little hair.

I sighed, rubbed my temples to stop thinking about the office. First things first.

I powered down my computer, grabbed my bag and stepped into the agents' room. "I promise to practice my lines and be ready in the morning, but I've got to take off the rest of the day." Wayne brushed my arm. I held up the palm of my hand, turned and left.

Walking to my car, my guts tightened, ready to implode. This was one of those one-way-no-return things, and my conscience whispered I might be leaving calm water for the rapids.

"Slade . . . hold up."

Wayne jogged down the building's brick steps, and my instincts told me to run. "I gotta go, Wayne. It can wait." I opened my car door, wishing he'd leave me alone. This wasn't any of his business.

He caught up and held the door for me. "Hey. Let me follow you home."

I fumbled with my keys, touched by the offer. "You still have to unwire the place."

"Eddie'll do it. You have a lot on your mind, some of it thanks to us. I want to see you get home in one piece and make sure no surprises await you on the other end."

"He won't hurt me." My hand grasped the door handle, angry at myself for defending Alan on any level, but my husband had never raised a hand to me. "He's not that way, Wayne."

"Then humor me. It can't hurt."

With no time to argue, I nodded, and he shut the door for me.

I drove out of the parking lot and froze at the stop sign. Half of me feared another rear-end collision and the other dreaded walking in my front door. A driver honked from behind Wayne's Impala, and I jerked into traffic with him tailing me two car lengths behind. I cranked up the radio but couldn't recall any words to the songs. His white car hung behind mine all the way to Ridgeville, maintaining the same distance back.

This was like putting a dog to sleep. Alan and I were miserable, in pain, unable to heal and get well, and somebody needed to end it. I turned on the heater to stop my arms and legs from shivering. It was sixty degrees outside. Gritting my teeth, I called Mom on my cell.

Forty-five minutes later, the kids flashed happy, surprised faces when I met them in the principal's office, saving them a bus ride. I procrastinated telling them why I'd picked them up and drove straight to my parents' house. Mom took Ivy and Zack inside for snacks, and I went home to pack for the three of us. Wayne waited at the curb.

I flew through the place, collecting this and that. Bags full, I almost tripped over Madge, then took a moment to write a note to Alan about feeding the animals. I returned to the garage and threw the baggage in the backseat of the Taurus. Smokey could stay in the garage overnight with food and water. Suddenly, the dog started barking, scratching to get outside. I hit the automatic button, and the garage door opened to arguing voices. My blood froze.

"I'm just making sure Slade is okay, Mr. Bridges." Wayne's tone held firm.

"And why wouldn't she be?" Alan fired back. "She doesn't need a damn escort to our house. Get off my property."

God only knew what the neighbors thought. "Alan!" Both men turned toward me. "A lot happened today, and Wayne was just making sure I was fine."

Alan stepped toward me. "Oh, it's Wayne now? What happened to Special-fuckin-Agent Largo?" He stared wild-eyed at the agent. They stood at the same height, but Wayne loomed so much bigger thanks to the shoulders and leather jacket. Alan used to be that big.

"Calm down," I told Alan. "If you want to talk later, we will, but I'm not discussing anything with you like this."

Alan stood in the middle of the driveway, breathing heavy, his cheeks hot and strawberry-tinged in contrast to his blondeness. He tossed back hair with a shake of his head, then raked fingers through it when a piece fell over his eyes. He clenched his fists and moved forward.

I stepped back. Wayne stiffened.

"The kids and I will be at my parents." I stepped toward my car. "Call first, because I can't account for Daddy's attitude if you just drop in."

Seeing Wayne's arms crossed, hand prudently close to the Smith and Wesson revolver beneath his coat, prodded me to keep my mouth shut and get in my car, before serious shit went down in my yard.

Wayne drove behind me for the short three miles. He flashed his headlights after I'd parked behind Daddy's Jeep, and then drove off.

An hour later, Alan called and asked to come over and discuss our plans. Worried about an emotional explosion inside my parents' home, I agreed to a chat on their front porch.

He drove up, parked and stepped hesitantly to the steps.

"You showed more guts than I thought," he said, sitting in a rocker three feet from mine. "You won. You filed first."

"Nobody wins," I said.

"Well, give me a few days to move out. Visiting the kids won't be a problem, will it?"

"Of course not."

He stood and reached over to kiss me, and I pulled back. He dropped his eyes and grinned sadly. "I'm really going to miss that cat." Then he left.

I went inside before he backed out the driveway.

Daddy greeted me from behind his front door, shoving his .45 firmly away in his belt. "Think he understands? He isn't giving you any trouble, is he?"

I smiled at my security system. "I think it's okay, Daddy. He's actually kind of pitiful."

"For the kids' sake, I hope you're right, baby girl."

Pointing to the pistol, I asked, "Would you have used that thing?"

He smiled. "With a choice of him or you, he'd be fertilizer on my grass."

Good old Daddy. He was a knight in shining armor to me as a kid. In high school, he required boys to come to the door and ask for me. In spite of the wrinkles in his neck and the blue veins on his hands, he remained my hero. To this day I drank bourbon, thanks to him. The occasional taste for wine came from Mom. My mood dictated which I preferred, which often meant a can of beer just to be me.

For dinner Mom heaped chicken and dumplings in our bowls. The aroma of homemade cobbler drifted from the oven. After dinner, the kids helped wash dishes while I took a bath, relaxed in my temporary bedroom, and studied my Jesse script under a quilt. A box of tissues mysteriously appeared on my nightstand from Mom. A lowball glass of Jack from Daddy.

I drifted off to sleep mumbling lines off my index cards while I thought of my children becoming adults, praying they wouldn't hold the split against me. Three times I awoke from ugly dreams.

I wadded up tissues and left them on the bed for Mom's sake. Daddy would know better.

AS DAWN BROKE OUTSIDE my office, the agents performed their electronic duties, while fresh percolating coffee gurgled in the background, scenting the air.

I leaned back in my chair, my eyelids drooping like lead weights. A voice whispered to me. "Here's your coffee, sleepy head."

I awakened expecting to feel Mom's butterfly quilt tucked under my chin. Seeing Wayne brought me to an embarrassing realization. "Oh, my goodness. I'm so sorry."

"You really *aren't* a morning person, are you?" He handed me the coffee, stepped back, and leaned on the corner of my desk.

I smiled through my haze. "Last night wasn't very restful."

"We all go through crap. Drink your coffee."

A soft order, as if saying he knew what I needed at the moment. I focused on my cup. He was an easy man to be around. So accommodating – so easy to call him Wayne instead of Mr. Largo.

A few sips of caffeine and my brain fired up. Before Wayne asked me about the night before, I explained about the separation and pending divorce. He leaned over and studied me, taking me in as I covered more ground than I planned to.

"I sensed something wrong between you two on Sunday," he said. "Would love to reschedule this case to a better time, Slade, but you know I can't." He cocked his head. "Are you okay handling all this?"

At least he cared to ask. "Sure. I'm fine. The bad part is over."

"Hopefully so. I need you sharp when you meet with Jesse."

Then he shifted personalities again, and in a softer tone added, "Just take care of yourself." His knuckle rapped the table for emphasis as he left. I noticed he liked rapping on things.

"I'm fine," I said, then as he turned his back, I mumbled, "Don't have to lose any sleep over me."

I wasn't as tender as he thought, but his concern was duly noted – get Jesse, or whatever else he was there for. I swiveled back to my desk and knocked two files on the floor.

Leaning over, I cared little about the order in which I retrieved the papers and stuck them in the files. Tossing the heap on my desk, I stretched back in my chair. Who was I kidding? Even if he showed up today, Jesse would spot me lying a lot sooner than I could nail him.

An excruciating three hours later, miracle of miracles, Jesse showed up. He fidgeted at the counter, twenty minutes early for his appointment, decked out in his hounds tooth jacket. The tractor cap sat askew on his head, and he'd parted his hair and combed it to the side instead of slicking it back. In my office I tried not to look up from my phone.

Wayne schooled me over the intercom line, a last minute prep talk. "Speak to him like you rehearsed," he reminded me. "Don't leave him alone. We only have a consensual monitoring authorization, meaning you have to keep him in view of the camera, close to the mike and always in your presence. Otherwise, we can't use this in court." He hung up.

After a few deep breaths, I buzzed Ann Marie. She sent Jesse back at my request. He shut the door behind him and broke into a wide grin. "Just you and me now, lady. Cozy, huh? Puts a whole new perspective on customer service."

I stood and waved my hand at the chair facing my desk. "Have a seat."

"I've heard more from you in the last week than the last six months," he said. "Am I a gleam in your eye?" He reached out to shake my hand.

I begrudgingly obliged and grasped the bulky broad palm. He then slumped into a seat, draping himself over the back.

I glanced at the center of my blotter where I'd practiced my lines off index cards no longer there. "We need to talk." A pen rolled between my fingers for a pacifier. I furrowed my brow, acting intent on our dealings.

"What about?"

"You know what about. And keep your voice down."

He wiggled a pointed finger, like he forgot where he was and gave me credit for reminding him. Then he got still. "I need that land, Ms. Slade—or can I just say Slade, since we're partners now?" He took off his hat, laid it on the table, and stretched his legs out.

"Let's keep this professional. We don't need anyone to get wise." Did people still say "get wise"? I crossed my arms and tightened my jaw for show. "Now what's the deal?"

"You heard me the other day. Nothin's changed. I need the pond on that place for my crops and hogs. Used to piss me off during a bad summer to see those watering machines running on a rich man's place, while my crops and livestock baked."

"Regulations make this deal . . . difficult," I said, acting hard to convince.

"Yeah, you're good at rules. When I lose hogs, you tell me about the rules. When I can't pay, you spout more rules." He tilted his head toward my bookcase. "Well, this time we're talking about an understanding that ain't in no book."

The pungent mix of his Walmart aftershave and my sweat stole the air. "And that understanding is . . . ?"

"Well, ma'am," he puffed up and lowered his voice. "Slade . . . sweetheart."

Sweetheart? My skin prickled.

"We need some mutual cooperation."

Versus what – individual cooperation? *Idiot.* I nodded to keep him talking, then remembered I was on audio. "Um, yes we do."

His voice deepened. "I don't deal well with dishonest partners. You've been good to me. I respect that. Now, that Wilder fella? He wasn't so likeable."

"You mean Lucas?"

"Nah, Wilder."

Jesse leaned back, rocking the chair. A sly grin split his three-day growth of beard.

For an eternity we watched each other, then he scooted his chair closer. I pinched my thigh to get a grip.

Then I got pissed at my timidity. This office was my domain, damn it. "If you have money, why don't you get the land the right way? Buy it." If he wanted to spar, we would.

"Hey, my cash flow is tied up in ventures, you know? Plus, I got you."

"You don't have me, and obviously you *don't* have the money." I stared him down. His face tightened. I pointed at him. "You intend to pay me a measly ten thousand dollars for putting my neck on the chopping block, but your money is supposedly tied up. I'm not stupid. You're broke."

He didn't back up like I'd hoped he would. "I'll pay part up front, and part when the deal's done. I've been slipping a hog to the market here and there and storing the cash." He winked. "And I got partners."

"Sure you do. When you have the green in your hand, let me know." I crossed my arms.

"Come on now, Slade. I'm a nice guy. Trust me." The snake tried to measure me. His dark eyes locked on mine. I looked away, over his shoulder, but still could feel that stare. "You're smart. You're pretty, living good, got a handsome son and a sweet girl you pick up from daycare most evenings when us farmers don't keep you late."

My eyes darted back at the mention of my children. *Where the hell was he going with this?*

"Pets, too," he said. "I just got a yard dog, myself. Momma don't let dogs in the house. Can't get many women in there, either." He winked.

I shoved back from my desk. "That's it."

"You've got to give me time to meet your demands, Ms. Slade."

I froze. "*My* demands?"

"You are some business woman, gotta hand you that," he said, nodding as if honoring my expertise . . . and acting for an audience.

"You're out of your damn mind. You came in here last Friday and made an offer to *me*." I fought to control my rising pitch. My rapid breaths grew louder and shallower. The only noise in the room.

After hearing my family mentioned and seeing the ease at which the farmer could spin a tale, I realized I'd been played like a bingo card . . . by both the agents and Jesse.

"Nothing happens without the money that *you* offered," I said. "We're done here." The G-men had gotten all they were getting from me. And Jesse could walk off a pier. This case could fall flat on its ass and make me hysterically happy.

"Give me a few days to get your money together." He stood and reached to shake hands. "Listen, it's been good talkin' to ya, Slade. I like your spunk. Kinda spicy!"

I refused his hand and waved to the door. "I said we're through. Get the hell out."

Jesse touched the brim of his hat. "I'll be back."

"I don't care if you ever come back . . . or if you ever pay the money, Jesse."

I trembled and knew he could tell. The filthy asshole had spoken about my children in menacing undertones. A sharp urgency to reach Zack and Ivy clouded my senses as the man left my office, then the front door.

I sat down hard, my head dropping into my hands. I should've known better than to get involved. I'd finally found the guts to file the papers to get out of bed with Alan. Now I was in bed with a new son-of-a-bitch.

This lunacy was ending . . . now. I started to get up. Wayne appeared in the doorway.

"What was that about?" I demanded. "You didn't tell me—"

"Hang on." Wayne shut the door and moved toward the recorder to shut it off. "Pretty good job for an amateur."

"We didn't rehearse threats to my children." Wayne put a finger to his lips. Remembering the staff, I lowered the decibels, my teeth clenched. "You know a hell of a lot more than you're telling me. You're using me to get information. Fine. But nobody uses my children!"

He sat in Jesse's still-warm chair. I wasn't sure who I hated more.

"You called me a smart lady. Well, this 'smart lady' knows that Atlanta doesn't deliver two agents to nab a small-time hog farmer. I didn't make manager by sitting on my ass or lying on my back." I inhaled again, refueling. "Why are you really here? A step up the ladder to Super-Agent in Charge of North America?"

"Hold on," he said, restraint evident. "Let me get a word in."

"No." I wanted to retain the momentum. "I don't—"

"Listen to me," he said. "Discussing anything other than the bribery deal would've rattled you," he said. "You wouldn't have been natural. We took a chance you'd have enough guts—"

"*You* took a chance?" I smacked a stack of folders with my hand. "I didn't see you in here getting drooled over. He even accused me of putting the bribe idea in his head."

"Standard ploy," he said, waving his hand. "Doesn't mean anything."

"It's on the tape."

"Look, you did well—better than many agents." He leaned forward, his hand on his chest. "I didn't expect him to mention your kids, and for that, I'm sorry." His eyes softened. "Investigation isn't an exact science, Slade, but we now know more about who we're dealing with. It was a glowing success."

The apologies, the smiles, the overt attention to my needs had snared me for the last time. "There is no more *we*. *This ends right now*." I turned to stomp out of the room, then stopped. Hell, this was my turf. Understanding registered in his eyes, and he stood and left.

Out of the office, down the hall and past the bathroom, I marched my anger out the back door to where the smokers congregated. A soil technician ground out a butt and held the door open. My disposition apparent, he left without a spoken word.

I'd never smell hog again without thinking of this day. I sat on the curb, leaned back on my hands and closed my eyes, letting the midday sun rest on my cheeks. All my life I'd made the best of any circumstance. The strong willed firstborn, the obedient daughter, and the disciplined working mother. A trouble-shooter who put everything back to right. I rocked . . . until today.

Jesse was a predator. No man had ever frightened me like he had, not even Alan in his worst fit of temper. In the last twenty-four hours, I'd unraveled my home life, scurried home to Mom, and sparred with a pork farmer who'd tucked me into his pocket, confident he owned me.

I assured myself I'd done all the rights things. Then I assured myself again.

"Screw you, Alan," I yelled. I threw a stone across the lot into a clump of honeysuckle entangled in the chain-link fence. He'd be laughing at me now if he knew.

"Damn fine arm," said a voice behind me.

CHAPTER 7

Sid Patten stepped outside where I sat on the sidewalk, restructuring my sanity. The soil conservationist stooped over my shoulder. "You all right?"

"Bad day, Sid. Real bad day."

He sat beside me. "You mind?" he asked, holding up a cigarette.

I was in the designated smoking area anyway. "Go ahead."

He lit up and blew out a long stream of smoke. "Haven't seen you since Jesse Rawlings brought you all that dead barbecue in the back of his truck. Where you been?"

I snorted. "Up to my butt in catastrophes. How about you?"

"The same."

Yeah, right. Like surveying ponds was a crisis. Soil conservationists had no clue what controversy was unless someone's pond leaked.

He flicked ash against the curb. "Received three requests about confirming wetlands this week. One from our buddy Jesse."

I turned. "He doesn't have wetlands on his farm."

He shook his head. "He asked about the Williams place. I told him to talk to you, since that's one of y'all's foreclosed properties. That boy isn't trying to buy more land, is he?" He laughed and took another drag. "He can't handle what he's got now."

"Nope."

"He's a good boy, you know that? Look at what he deals with every day—that trashy mother of his and a brother who's just damn pitiful. You've done a good job keeping him farming, Slade."

I stood and dusted off the seat of my pants. Conversation about Jesse's attributes was more than I could stand. "Got to get back, Sid. Thanks for the chat." I'd remind him of this conversation when they led my hog farmer off in cuffs.

Back in my office, I closed the door. As soon as I sat, I realized my seclusion would sprout curiosity from staff, so I returned to the door and opened it a wedge.

Hillary's sassy alto was unmistakable. "I don't think Henry knows what's going on here."

"They're just auditors," said Jean.

Hillary scoffed. "I don't think so."

"You're paranoid."

"I've been through audits. They sure aren't pulling many files."

"Maybe they already know what they're looking for." Jean lowered her voice. "Ooh, maybe we have a client wanted for something."

Hillary dragged out her words. "Maybe. I just think Henry ought to know."

My boss and Hillary's Economy Motel buddy, Henry McRae, would drop in on me now. He didn't miss a chance to visit his floozy *and* torment me.

I opened my door, letting it bang against the wall. Jean jumped, but Hillary turned her back, composure intact.

Both possessed brains and efficiency when they kept their noses clean, but their gossip irritated the crap out of me. Biddies, my grandmother called such people. Chicken biddies poking their silly little heads into everyone's business.

The noise alerted the agents. By the time I returned to my chair, Wayne stood in my doorway. His tarnished image placed him not much higher on the food chain than Jesse. At least the farmer identified what he wanted from me.

"Hillary and Jean are suspicious," I said, motioning him closer. "McRae'll drop in unannounced to see what's going on." My eyes met his, and I forgot what I was saying, confused as to how far to trust him. "Play your damn part and at least look like an auditor. I've sure as hell been playing mine."

Wayne stuck a pencil behind his ear. "What do you think? I might find a pocket protector somewhere."

I rubbed my forehead. "I don't have time for your shenanigans."

"So it seems," he said.

No sympathy from him, no pity. Made me dislike him even more. Of all the people in my life, this one owed me. I'd reported a bribe offer. Employees didn't do that anymore, just because of situations like this. You couldn't trust badges.

I rammed the head of my pen into my blotter, ink oozing. "No more tricks. Otherwise your 'cooperating individual' becomes uncooperative, and I don't give a damn who you turn me in to."

He tilted his head, waiting for more. I searched for signs of patronizing. Finding none, I wondered how well he hid his feelings. He'd been trained; I was shotgun scattered all over the place.

"Appears I've gotten myself in a situation with Jesse that can't be reversed. Right?"

"Affirmative," he replied.

"Then let's get this over with. I want this guy locked up. I want you gone."

He raised his chin, still listening.

"And one more thing. If you're here for something besides Jesse, keep me out of it."

His jaw muscles worked just under the skin. Finally, a sign I could read.

"Are you hearing me, lawman?"

His mouth tightened, then released. "I hear you."

"Either you think I'm not trustworthy, or I'm not worth your trouble. Don't underestimate me." I opened my desk drawer and took out my purse. "I think I'll go home and hug my kids before something happens to them that you helped cause. I'll be here the same time Monday, whether you are or not. I don't care."

Then I left him sitting there.

I checked my office voice mail from my cell, driving ten miles over the speed limit up Interstate 26. Five messages. Two ranchers wanted to start a partnership. Mom called to say she'd pick up the kids; Savvy checked to see if I was sane; and Alan said he needed one more day to relocate. In spite of the craziness, life marched on. I allowed myself to take meager comfort in my screwed up personal life, because my career now swayed on a precipitous ledge owned by Wayne Largo, for reasons I was clueless about.

THE FALL WEEKEND DAWNED bright and beautiful. Zack didn't complain once about missing Saturday morning cartoons when we left for the ocean. Sullivan's Island, with a more native appeal than the Isle of Palms, was my choice of beach. The abundant pools of trapped water at low tide captured attention with teeny silvery fish. Terns sprinted in spastic spurts, chasing leftover foam from the waves. I often found myself wandering the water's edge when life threw darts at me. The majesty of the place dispelled whatever moments of gloom clouded my mind. The location and the kids' laughter would hold me together.

I needed a break from my parents, and though they wouldn't admit it, they needed a break from the kids. We held slightly different views on discipline.

The gusts made us slip on gloves and coats. We walked a mile, searching for sea inhabitants that may have strayed out of the water. The briny aroma on the damp air cleared my sinuses, forcing me to pull a tissue from my pocket.

After a while, we turned back to find a picnic place in the dunes. Ivy collected more shells, and Zack hunted for crabs before we sat, sipped hot chocolate, ate Oreos and talked about divorce. They asked questions, and I struggled with answers.

The discussion about their daddy moving out ended up rattling me far more than them. Ivy put her arm around me, choking me up to a point where I pretended sand lodged in my eye. Zack made a couple of mouthy comments about his father, a protective exhibition for me, and I corrected him for not honoring both his parents. They returned to the beach fifteen minutes later, the wildlife commanding more of their attention. I wasn't sure how to read that.

Minimal traffic ventured to the beach in cool weather, so a white truck parking alongside my vehicle in the small visitor lot caught my eye. Jesse drove a white truck.

"Ivy, Zack! Get over here," I yelled, an urgency climbing up my throat.

A young man hopped out of the truck and moved around the vehicle to open his date's door. They hugged and headed to the sand for a romantic stroll. I relaxed, angry that Jesse could have such an impact on my life.

LATER THAT AFTERNOON, when we reached my folk's place, the kids and I smelled chocolate as soon as we opened the door. Daddy eased me aside as the kids ran to see what Mom had cooked up in the kitchen.

"He's out of the house," Daddy whispered, handing me a bourbon. "He called and left a message."

"Why'd he call you?" I asked, happy for the glass, reaching in my pocket for my cell. Two messages. "Guess that explains it. You didn't say anything . . . ?"

He shook his head. "We didn't talk. Anyway, you want me to go with you to make sure everything's fine?"

"No, Daddy. Might make the kids uneasy. I'll call when we get there."

An hour later, we entered our home as if seeing it for the first time. The animals appeared fed recently, Madge's wet food remnants still moist around the bowl's edge. We found Smokey running loose outside. Zack walked straight to my bedroom and peered in. Ivy went to her room after ordering Zack not to leave his back pack on the floor.

I walked from room to room, scouting for change. The bedroom closet still contained a few suits and shoes Alan rarely wore. Otherwise, it was all mine. I shrugged out of my coat, hung it up and pulled out a dresser drawer for sweats. A pair of Alan's underwear fell out when I unfolded a deep green sweatshirt, my favorite piece of loungewear. The briefs weren't fresh. I wrote off the mix-up as laundry confusion.

That evening, I crawled in my bed once the kids crashed in theirs. My huge bed, where my single body could spread out, ball up or sleep crossways and use all four pillows. *Wuthering Heights* still sat on my nightstand, three months since I'd read chapter twelve. The title seemed appropriate. I understood Catherine's marriage to someone she didn't love, but damned if I'd die over a poor choice of spouse.

When the words blurred together, I reached for the bookmark parked in the back cover. It fell out along with a grocery ticket. On the back, Alan had written, "Dream about me tonight."

I crumpled the paper and hurled it across the room. The underwear was no mistake.

SCREAMS FROM THE FRONT PORCH pierced my Sunday morning reverie in the kitchen. The breakfast dish slipped from my sudsy grip and shattered in the bottom of the sink.

I bolted outside. Zack stood at the top of the front porch bawling. Ivy coiled in the rocking chair. She pitched back and forth, her face buried in folded knees, sobbing.

Smokey lay dead on the lawn. Madge mewed and meandered around the corpse. I quieted Zack and eased the story out of him.

A white truck had jumped the curb, careened across the yard and over the dog. Some sorry hit-and-run driver had taken a beloved pet . . . and come too close to killing my kids.

I ushered them into the house, placing one on each end of the sofa, a blanket thrown over their shivering bodies. Something warm and soothing was in order. Water splashed out of the sink from the still-running faucet when I entered the kitchen.

A couple of minutes later, towels on the kitchen floor, the children held hot cocoa mugs with floating marshmallows. The police were en route. I sat on the sofa between my children, aching to snatch the memory away, rubbing their arms and legs.

I only knew one person who drove a white truck, but surely he wasn't capable of this. "Madge is awful sad and is going to need extra loving from you guys, you know."

They stopped crying. Zack stood, ready to rescue his kitty. "I'll get her, Momma."

"No, I will. You stay here and keep the sofa warm for her."

Madge curled up next to the front door, eyes wide and frightened. After burying my face in her fur once for a kiss, I deposited her in the midst of the kids' blankets. I rummaged through the DVDs, intentionally selecting *Mary Poppins* to ease everyone's frayed nerves, then returned outside to watch for the police.

Joyce, the mother of twins from across the street, stood in amazement about six feet away from Smokey, her neck craned to see, fearful to come any closer. "Oh, Slade, I'm so sorry. I can't believe this happened in our neighborhood."

Alan's basketball friend, Mike, walked up and covered the body with a tarp.

My hand eased back the tarp and brushed over the furry Christmas present we'd received five years ago, straightening his ears and feeling the warmth fast leaving his body. "Did either of you see anything?"

"No," Mike said. "We came out when we heard the kids scream. Whoever hit the dog drove off like a bullet. I heard him take the corner hard down the block."

Crisis management ranked as one of my strengths, but usually the crisis involved other people, not me. Playing the victim felt unnatural, and one patronizing deputy didn't help. He wrote up a report in minutes, saying they'd be in touch if they uncovered anything. My mom didn't raise an idiot. I knew they'd never get a lead, assuming they even looked.

But then the other young deputy, last name James on his name tag, paused over my pet almost as if saying a prayer. "I'm terribly sorry, ma'am," he said, his overly lanky frame hunched in respect. "There's no cause for this. My condolences for your family's loss."

His sincerity drove the pain into my heart. "His name was Smokey," I said with a hoarse voice.

He smiled at me. "I'll make sure that goes on his report then."

Fighting tears, I replied, "Thank you."

MONDAY DAWNED as miserable as I felt. Grey clouds hung so dense they seemed stuck on the tips of the long-leaf pines, appropriate with Smokey's death leaving a hole in our routine. The last place I wanted to go was work.

Ann Marie tackled me with a hug when I stepped through the door. "I'm so sorry," she said softly. "How are the children?"

"They're sad, Ann—real sad. How'd you find out?"

"Jean told us," she said, eyes moist. "She got a phone call from Alan, I think."

I tried to hide my surprise. My insensitive ex hadn't even bothered to console me or the kids after I'd left a message on his cell.

Jean didn't glance up until I stood close enough to smell her hair spray. "Morning, Slade. That's awful about the kids and your dog. Just awful."

"Thanks. I understand Alan told you."

She spoke into her lap. "He said he wanted everyone here to know, in case you didn't come in. He sounded worried."

I didn't bother deciphering Alan's intentions. My desk chair groaned as I fell into it.

Wayne and Eddie were still absent. No messages on my voice mail. Good. By my second cup of coffee, I'd immersed myself in loan files, no longer preoccupied with investigations.

"We're back."

I jumped. Eddie filled my doorway wearing a leather vest and a big-toothed grin. "Bet you missed us, huh?"

I forced a smile for Eddie. Wayne walked up after a moment at Anne's desk, and I dropped it.

"Be quiet, Eddie," he said. "Sorry to hear about your dog, Slade. He seemed like a good fella. Kids okay?"

"Not really."

They came in and sat down opposite my desk.

"Did you see who did it?" Wayne asked.

I started to recant what happened, then stopped in mid-sentence. Why did he even care? Just like he'd asked about my divorce before, his only interest was my presence of mind regarding the damn case. "The police said it was probably a drunk. They don't hold any hope of finding the guy."

"Hopefully it's just another random incident. I'll speak to the authorities. Did you get the deputies names?"

"One of them has the last name James." But this accident wasn't random. "I'm not slow, Mr. Largo. First, someone tries to drive me off the road and then my dog is killed. What I want to know is what you're going to do about Jesse? Take at least one problem off my back." I snapped my fingers. "I got it . . . how about you being honest?"

Eddie lost his humorous grin as my ire sent sparks through the air.

"I'll check with the officer who handled the call," Wayne said in a monotone. "See what I can learn about this white truck. Meanwhile, Eddie or I'll tail you. Okay?"

"Whatever you think."

Our conversation ended on that cool note. Wayne rigged up the recorder while Eddie returned to his office. Not ten seconds after Wayne finished, the phone rang.

"Slade?" Ann Marie said. "Jesse Rawlings is on line two."

Wayne pointed to the phone and nodded. Terrific. Here we went again.

"May I help you?" I asked, not nearly as nervous.

"I've been collecting money," Jesse said.

"So?" I replied, staring at my calendar and all the work not getting done.

"So, when you bring papers for me to sign, you'll get the first part of your share," he said. "Told you, I'm a man of my word."

Was there such a thing? "It'll take a day or two, Jesse."

"Oh. I ain't meeting you in your office again. Does hundreds suit ya'?"

The change of place startled me. "Depends." I stalled, glancing at Wayne, my hand on the mouthpiece. He nodded and scribbled on his pad, and then twisted it toward me. "How much money?" and "Where?"

Removing my hand, I said, "Exactly how much you got?"

"Four thousand."

My loan manager instincts kicked in on top of the pissy attitude of having to go through these motions. "Where'd you get that kind of money?" Jesse never sold enough hogs to pay a bill this size. "That's not even half of the ten thousand, either. Thought you were a man of your word?"

"I am. This is all I could get. If I can get the rest by the time we meet, I will. How about meeting me at the farm?"

"Not sure I can."

Wayne gestured in agreement.

I sighed. "Okay," I said, not too keen on meeting Jesse on his turf. "When?"

"Thursday at ten. That gives you two days. I might surprise you with the whole ten grand by then."

I rolled my eyes. "I won't hold my breath."

"Oh, I will, Slade. I'll hold my breath until I see you. *Alone.*" His guffaw echoed loud.

Jesus.

Wayne wrote hurriedly.

"By the way, Jesse," I said, reading Wayne's notes, "do you really want this land in your name? Everyone knows the place is coming up for sale, and your financial reputation isn't all that keen."

"I was getting to that. The papers will show Palmetto Enterprises."

I turned a new page on my notepad. "What is this, a partnership or a corporation?" The questions rolled off my tongue like for any kosher loan closing. I ignored the fact I collaborated with the devil.

He rattled off an address and pertinent information, then made veiled threats about involving anyone else before abruptly hanging up. I turned to Wayne. "What do we do now, Sherlock?"

Wayne clapped once. "We're going to a meet. Well done." A corner of his mouth rose. "Oh, and Sam Spade's more my style."

He left the room, his steps light with purpose. My butt sat like lead in my chair.

Last week, I'd naively labeled investigation work entertaining, but the novelty of the game had withered, even as it came to a climax. Who was being set up—Jesse or me?

Wayne joined Eddie in the next office. I picked up a file and shuffled through the papers, like they made sense. My office had deteriorated into a mess. McRae would have a certified reason to chew my backside if I didn't find a way to make these loans happen.

I took a real business call and felt odd not acting a role.

"Mike Hatchwood, Ms. Slade. Tell me about any property you have coming available in your island areas. I can pay cash."

I recited my spiel, relieved at the mundane conversation. I pitched him two tracts, including the Williams' place since I still needed to unload it once Jesse was out of the picture.

"Can you fax me the survey? That might be exactly what I need. I'm from Brunswick, Georgia, but I'm in Charleston a lot on business." He paused. "Any wetlands on the farm?"

The unusual question caught me off guard. "Just a few acres on the back corner. Why?"

"Just knew someone who got stuck with swamp land."

"Feel free to walk the acreage, Mr. Hatchwood. You'll see there's not enough to hinder any kind of development."

"Okay . . . that's good." He didn't sound all that happy about it. He'd probably read just enough environmental propaganda to be a worrywart about facts he didn't understand.

I faxed him all the information and returned to my number crunching, making a note on my calendar to call him back in two weeks.

The phone rang. I picked it up, glad to be too busy to think.

"Hey, Slade," Jesse drawled. "I forgot something."

My blood turned to ice water. The recorder wasn't on. Wayne wasn't feeding me instructions. I grabbed a pen and wrote down the date, the time, and his name like I'd heard Wayne do when starting a new tape on the recorder.

"Sorry about your dog."

I couldn't remember how to write.

"I know I told you 'bout my yard dog." His voice oozed calm and smooth as the black water eddies of the Ashley River, and just as treacherous. "Well, the bitch gets knocked up every time I turn around, but the puppies turn out cute. She's due anytime now. They won't be shaggy like yours, but kids don't care what a pup looks like. Puppies are puppies."

Wayne walked in, saw me on the phone and started to back out. I threw my pen at him. He turned back. I pointed to the phone and silently mouthed, "Jesse."

He rushed over to read my pad. Seeing it blank, he motioned for me to write as he grabbed the headset and turned on the recorder. I opened my drawer for another pen.

"You got another customer or something?" Jesse asked.

"Tell me how the hell you knew about my dog."

"News travels fast. Bet those kids are just tore up."

"Don't ever mention my kids again, or I'll shut this whole thing down. You got it?"

A laugh echoed through the line. "Maybe after all this, we can celebrate—at your place. That empty bed ought to be mighty cold by now."

CHAPTER 8

I shivered at Jesse's telephone offer to share my bed, but his veiled references about Smokey's death and my kids curdled my blood. "That filthy piece of hog shit. The murderous, repugnant, revolting son-of-a-bitch." I inhaled for another string of superlatives, staring at Wayne like he raised hogs, too.

"Whoa." Wayne reared back. "Chill."

"It's obvious he killed my dog."

Wayne swung the headset in his hand. "I caught most of it, but it's not concrete evidence."

I rocked my chair forward. "He admitted to everything . . . the bribe, the threats . . ."

His mouth flatlined. "Thin threats at best. When the money passes hands, and he clearly states what it's for, then we arrest him."

I shoved a notepad away from in front of me and picked up the phone. "I'm calling my parents." The phone number jumbled in my head and I dialed it wrong. I disconnected, then dialed again. I'd grown up with that number, written it on my school records since the fourth grade.

"Aren't you overreacting a bit?" Wayne asked.

"Not when it comes to my children."

Wayne reached over and laid his hand on my phone. "You'll scare your family to death. Slow down."

I didn't want to slow down. I needed to react, take preemptive measures, move to stay a step ahead of Jesse. Sitting still felt like standing in traffic, hoping the cars would swerve and never hit me.

He laid down the headphones and his pen. "You're tough, you know that?"

"Don't patronize me."

"I'm not. You're spinning off into space here. I'm just reminding you of what you're made of."

A juvenile spunk coursed through me, and I didn't care. "Exactly how does my behavior make you feel? Does it make it harder to take me down—pin this junk on me?" I bounced a fist off my chest. "I called you. I worried what was the right thing to do, not the easy thing, not the admirable thing . . . the right thing. Instead, you get a hard-on trying to take me down with the guy who started this mess. I've endured your testosterone up to here!" I held a stiff, flat hand over my head.

The hand shook as I lowered it into my lap. I was going to make sure Jesse made it behind bars. I was finishing what I started if for no other reason than to make my life one less headache.

"Why the silence?" he asked, eyebrows raised. "You were on a roll."

I picked up the phone again. "Daddy? Would you mind picking up the kids from school when it lets out? I'll explain later. Thanks. Love you, too."

That one proactive move settled my nerves to subatomic level. That's why I usually paced. I needed an energy release from somewhere other than my mouth. "What next?"

"You know the drill," he said. "Prepare fake papers—deed, note and mortgage."

The man sat perfectly still, whereas I couldn't talk without swatting imaginary mosquitoes. "Fine. Let me do it, then. Get out."

He winked, pointed at me and started to rise from his chair. "Gotcha. That's what I like to hear."

"Don't do that," I said, teeth gnashed together. His words smacked me by surprise no different than if he'd bitch-slapped me upside the head.

He stiffened, his face washed with an ambushed awe. "Do what?"

"The wink and the finger-thing. Jesse does that. Can't you even try not to piss me off?"

My scathing temper did nothing to him. Instead, he counterpunched with an apology. "Sorry. Do your paperwork," he said quietly. "I need to devise Plans A, B and C for Monday with Eddie." He strode to the adjoining office, leaving me to deal with my unraveled self.

My hands twitched, adjusting my blotter, straightening papers. I opened my desk drawer, then, not sure why I did, closed it. We'd do this sting with Jesse, and I'd be there as they pinched his wrists and drew blood with cuffs. Maybe they'd bang his head on the door when they threw him in the backseat of the cop car. I'd testify, wearing the best damn navy suit I could afford, convincing jurors what a worthless schmuck Jesse was. Even applauding when the foreman pronounced him guilty and the judge sentenced him to twenty years.

My hands no longer shook. Working myself into a hissy fit proved the same effect as talking to Jesse. I arched my back, stretching to release tension, then stretched my fingers, popping knuckles. Sliding my notepad back in front of me, I listed what I needed to prepare for this meeting.

Creating "funny" paper was a no-brainer. I finished a legitimate-looking thirty-page docket for Jesse in just under an hour. I then turned to real applications, recommending approval for one tractor and supplies for four hundred acres of soybeans. Uninterrupted, I slung government paperwork like the pro I was supposed to be . . . like I was.

Wayne rang me on the internal line. "McRae's on his way."

That's all I needed. "How do you know?"

"Eddie has taps on all the incoming lines. Your boss called Hillary. Hide all the paperwork about Jesse."

I didn't have much spread out, but I collected it in a stack. "Nosy jerk."

"Well, we're not hanging around. Get your coat and act normal. Eddie's already in the parking lot." He hung up.

Outside I squinted and raised my hand over my eyes when we stepped into a clear autumn day. Eddie sat in the Impala, but Wayne directed me by the elbow to the other side of the parking lot. "Let's take your car. Eddie'll follow."

I took the driver's seat, and Wayne rode shotgun. "Do I drive around in circles or do you have a destination?" I asked. "Why are we running away?"

"Ann Marie told me about this place off Rutledge. The Hominy Grill?" he said, waving toward the road for me to move on. "And we're not running away. We're choosing our own time to meet the man, and it's not now."

King Street in Charleston conjured images of big-ticket expenses, but the Hominy Grill was a little neighborhood restaurant tucked away in what used to be a run-down section of town, eight blocks over. The place collected wall-to-wall patrons for breakfast and lunch. The chef was famous for country style pork ribs with red rice, pinto beans and a blackstrap molasses barbecue sauce—a plate-full of ecstasy. Yankees retired south for the chef's buttermilk pie.

We lucked out and found a table near the back. Wayne practically barked our order at the waitress so we could get down to business. I wasn't all that crazy about sitting in the midst of such a crowd. I needed another trip to the beach in the worst way.

"Listen," I said. "McRae and I may not be bosom buddies, but I'd have handled him. Did we really have to come out like this?"

"Hillary knows McRae well, I assume."

"Oh, intimately . . . Makes work a challenge when my boss is screwing my assistant silly."

Eddie laughed. "Moving up the old-fashioned way, huh?"

"So she thinks." I put my napkin in my lap then looked back at Wayne. "I'll handle McRae." My green tomatoes arrived, and I prepared to dive in. McRae was stale news; Hillary even more so.

Wayne reared back. "Guess I underestimated you, CI. With all that's going on in your world, I was worried this might tip you over the edge."

"Again, don't patronize me. You're more of a problem than he is. I told you he'd come snooping." I swallowed. "I've had my belly full of men lately. You included. File a discrimination charge. I don't care." My fork stabbed another piece of tomato.

"I swear nothing's going to happen to you," Wayne said, "on the heads of my children."

I rested my fork on my plate. "You have children?"

The back of Eddie's hand popped my arm. "Hell no, he doesn't have kids," he snorted. "Mini-Largos . . . ha . . . that's a scary thought." He busted out laughing again, turning heads at the next table. A chuckle bubbled up from my gut as I envisioned mini-Waynes . . . with beards.

"Seriously, you're handling this thing well," Wayne said once we'd sobered.

"It's all about the case to you, lawman. Get over yourself."

He hushed and retrieved a biscuit. I was happy for the silence. It didn't last long.

Eddie stuffed his face with a sandwich and spoke through the bread. "What we doing about McRae?"

"We won't go back this afternoon," Wayne said. "I'd prefer he not be able to identify us."

I pushed a bite of tomato through a puddle of gravy. "You could have just left for the afternoon."

He tipped his glass in mock toast. "Maybe I needed an excuse to try a new place to eat."

Running out of the office like we did was still way over the top. Eddie was too busy shoveling food for me to get a read on him. Obviously, their desire to dodge my boss carried a lot of weight in the grand scheme of this caper. Or they really did think I couldn't handle McRae's surprise visit.

Time I exercised a bit more control. I laid a ten on the table and stood.

"We got you covered," Wayne said, sliding the bill back toward me.

"I pay my own way, thanks." I weaved through the tight tables and headed back to deal with my boss.

AS I GRABBED A COFFEE, McRae sauntered into the office. He perched on Jean's desk, his shoulder cocked forward and body language implying he owned the three women hovering around him, like some government pimp. I covered my contempt with a smile as plastic as my spoon and walked back to my office.

While he was six-feet tall, lean and in fair physical shape, the genes that blessed him in stature refused to grace him in countenance. His lips held a perpetual pucker and a sickly, blue pallor. When he smiled, his eyes remained dull, almost lifeless. His hair combed left, the part too close to his ear.

How this man reached the level of Regional Director was beyond all sensible reason. He couldn't balance a spreadsheet or greet people without pissing them off. Yet, he fancied himself a charmer. In my estimation, he contained as much charisma as an alligator gar.

My lipstick freshened, I pulled out a tiny brush from my purse and addressed my hair. I relished the fact I intimidated him. Each time we completed our quarterly checkups, he'd leave with my reports immaculately accurate and his temper aflame. I knew my job. Hell, I knew *his* job, however, his macho annoyances grated my nerves.

He waltzed into my office as I tucked my purse in my desk. Without a doubt, he pursued a newfound mission, hoping to catch me off my game.

"Mr. McRae. What a surprise," I said, closing the drawer. His long narrow nose appeared to bend left when he grinned.

"Just thought I'd see how things were going."

"Hectic, Henry. We'll match last year's lending."

"Really?"

"Meaning?"

"The loans aren't moving fast enough," he said. "But that's the problem when auditors are underfoot."

"They're a nuisance, but nothing I can't handle."

We jousted as usual. An investigation now bottlenecked my loans enough for him to harass me. He claimed auditors were no excuse for being behind, then asked where they were. I told him they were in the field.

"Yeah, shame. If you weren't so behind, you could've gone along." He studied his hands, with white nails far too long for a man. "What about the Williams' place?" he asked. "Unloaded it yet?"

"None of the neighbors seem to want it, but a man named Mike Hatchwood sounds promising."

"Don't let him get away." He paused. "You talked to the highway department about any issues?"

"With the Williams farm? What for?"

"What about the highway expansion?"

I struggled to guess his motive. My mind usually stayed light-years ahead of his, but he stumped me with this. "That's old rumor. Even so, beach development is ten miles away."

"Lower the Williams' appraisal," he said.

"Why do that if you think the highway's expanding? Doesn't that make it worth more?" What a weird line of conversation. "Besides, I don't have that authority, Henry."

"I'll get it for you. Better to sell it cheap than to let the government own it."

We didn't alter six-month-old appraisals. "We can't justify that."

He squinted at me. "You'll do what you're told or be considered insubordinate. You walk that line enough already."

We often tested each other, but he'd never outright ordered me. And no way was I doing something that could land my butt in trouble. "I'm the best manager you've got."

He leaned forward, the scent of fried chicken and spearmint gum preceding him. "Don't test me. I'll win."

I needed a job, so I bit my cheek and checked my combative tone.

He eased back into his chair with a haughty smile. "I approved your time off the other day. Anything I need to know about?"

"I'm getting divorced." Gossip delivered right from the horse's mouth. The illustrious Carolina Slade stood tainted and flawed, as if he didn't already know, thanks to Hillary. Now he could say I was distracted from work due to personal problems, too. God I hated handing him ammunition.

His mouth twitched. "I'm sorry."

A hundred smart-ass retorts tempted me: comments about him screwing Hillary, his professional ineptitude, his pitiful relationship with his wife. I buried my quips in favor of common sense. "These things happen."

On that note he stood and nodded toward the adjoining office. "The auditors working in there?"

"Yes."

"Any idea what files they're checking?"

"Not really. They've asked me directions and minor questions about Hodges, Hancock and Frampton." I tried to hold eye contact through the lie.

"I'm sure they won't mind if I take a glance." He disappeared into Lucas' old office and my heart leaped. The only papers in there would be Jesse's. I stood, pondering whether to interrupt my boss and arouse his suspicions, or let the agents deal with their own undoing later.

McRae came back out before I could meet him. "Guess they carried the files to the field." He turned his back and picked up his briefcase. "We'll talk again soon."

I commended myself for maintaining a sense of calm under fire as he strode to the front door.

Once he'd left the building, I threw myself back into my work, shedding the new threat best I could. For someone known for problem solving, I had ample opportunity to hone the skill. I saw every man in my life with an ulterior motive. Everyone but my son, and he just wasn't old enough to try yet.

Ann put a direct call straight through. McRae must want another stab at me from the safety of his car.

"Hey, loan lady." Wayne's voice eased the knots in my shoulders before I thought to be defensive. "How did the meeting with the boss man go?"

"Fine. How were your *inspections?*"

"We might give you an A-plus when we finish this *audit.*" I removed a paperclip from my hair, readjusted a lock and clipped it back again. Tape and staples anchored hems. Paperclips kept hair out of my eyes.

"How about taking us to the farm tomorrow?" he asked. "I want to see what's so attractive to Jesse about that piece of dirt." He told Eddie to hush in the background. "Eddie's pumped full of conspiracy theories. I told him maybe Jesse wanted that farm for all the normal reasons a farmer wants a place."

My appointment calendar showed no guests. "Sure. Another daybreak appointment or can I sleep in?"

Wayne relayed a muffled comment to Eddie. A duet of guffaws echoed in the background. "Sleeping beauty can drag herself in late if she likes. Will that be around noon?"

"I can manage eight-thirty."

We hung up, and I glanced at the clock. Time to polish off one loan approval before five. I opened the application and scanned the cover page. More goddamn hogs. Before this ordeal was over, I'd be a friggin' vegetarian.

CHAPTER 9

The next day, an overcast sky locked the temperature in the moderate fifties, raising goose bumps on my arms. In boots and khaki pants I'd dressed casual enough to run up on a slobbery cow or rust-eaten tractor, but neat enough to greet a client. When you mixed with farmers, business casual had its own meaning.

I drove my no-frills, government-issue, white Ford Fusion to the motel at a quarter to nine. Wayne took the passenger seat. Eddie was nowhere around, the Impala gone.

Wayne knew about my kids, my divorce, even the way I decorated my house, but all I knew about him was he liked barbecue and cowboy boots. I'd witnessed traces of a keen sense of humor behind the stern veneer but somehow knew he meant to be received that way. This man pushed buttons I didn't know I owned and read my mind more than I cared to admit, which stirred a desire in me to know him equally as well. For balance.

"Why aren't we just riding with Eddie?" I asked.

"He had something to do," Wayne said.

"I never know how to take you," I said.

"That's good," he replied, his face impassive. "You could learn from that. I've been trained by the finest agriculture investigators in the world. Hard-core agents, one and all."

"Oh yeah," I said. "Hard core cases about renegade Brahmas and rabid roosters, I'm sure."

His laughter carried a reassuring quality. "You're a pretty decent CI, in spite of yourself."

There was that reference again. Why should I call him Wayne with only letters in return? Maybe I shouldn't. I wanted to remain formal, but my fate rested more than I preferred in those big hands of his. Plus, my name wasn't that hard to remember. "I'll take that as a compliment, since I don't have any idea what kind of competition I'm up against."

"Your peers aren't the sharpest tacks in the box, but there are a few with some sense. You have more than your share," he joked.

"Like it takes more than a thimble of brains to put people in jail who aren't smart enough to rustle a cow," she said.

I'd reached the highway. Conditioned hay lay swept in neat lines across fields. We passed crisp clean rows of dark green turnip, mustard and collard greens. I waved at an elderly gentleman driving a truck heavy with sweet potatoes. Out here we raised a hand on the steering wheel in casual acknowledgement whether we knew the other party or not. A subtle sign of roots. Otherwise you were from the city or up North.

I turned onto Highway 162 and headed to Hollywood, a far cry from its sister-city in California. The only neon in this Hollywood flashed on the portable sign outside one of two sit-down restaurants. Burger was spelled with two e's.

"You worked for Agriculture long?" I asked.

"For a few years. I've put people behind bars, even busted stills."

"Really?" I hadn't heard anyone mention stills in a coon's age. "A farmer I once worked with made moonshine. His wife stayed shnockered, rocking all day on her front porch with a Mason jar of corn liquor. During the drought two years ago, he told me he could bury a grasshopper in the ground head down and make it rain. I told him if that was so, he ought to make it rain and save everybody's crops."

Wayne chuckled. "I can guess."

"He didn't want to cause a flood." Smug at having told a good story, I noticed my mouth flapped more than his. I was supposed to be extracting information, not filling in the void.

I braked at a four-way and let a tractor with a lifted Bush Hog cross in front of us. Then I continued south toward the Toogoodoo community and the Williams' farm.

"I assume you're a married man. Already know you don't have kids."

His tongue worked against his cheek—a dead giveaway he was withholding history.

"Why do you do that?" I asked.

His brow furrowed. "Do what?"

"Wait before you speak. Makes me feel like you're judging whether or not I'm worthy of an honest answer."

He studied the distance. "It's not you. All my life I've divulged information on a need-to-know basis. My dad taught me that as a kid. He was a beat cop in Augusta." He glanced toward me. "Nothing personal. Just habit."

"How many brothers and sisters have you got?" I asked, keeping the momentum going.

"That's enough of the Q&A about me."

I'd pushed a button. I mentally jotted a tick mark in my win column and gripped the wheel tighter. He focused on the scenery.

"If you want to build trust, Mr. Largo, you gotta give as well as take. I *know* they taught you that in interrogation school. Spill it. What's your life like? I have one sister. How about you?"

"One sister, and she's not up for discussion."

"Married?"

"No."

"That wasn't so hard, was it?" He had a leathery smell, and a hint of cologne I could barely make out over the coffee aroma.

"Not really," he added. "My divorce is final any day now." The car cruised on, tires humming on the pavement.

How did I respond to that? "Sorry."

"It's okay," he said. "We aren't angry or anything."

He'd opened a door to his life. Curiosity carried me across the threshold. "What's her name?"

"Pamela. She's an agent, too."

The husband-wife combo sounded like a slice of the silver screen. I wondered how fit she was and what weapon she carried. I didn't possess secret agent hormones that made me want to jump off roofs and crash cars, so I didn't understand that sort of dynamic, especially in a marriage. Maybe Wayne wasn't as macho as the other agents, and she preferred someone who ripped off her clothes and placed her in strangleholds, cutting off her oxygen, cuffing her to the bed.

Man, I was losing it, wandering down speculative lanes I had no business traveling. "That must have made for interesting supper conversation."

"Not really."

The speedometer read ten miles per hour slower than the road sign allowed. I gunned it back to the limit. "Again, I'm sorry."

"I served the papers, so don't be."

I paused. Oh wow. As a soon-to-be divorcee, guess I was just as curdled in someone else's eyes.

"I hope it goes smoothly." What else do you say to someone getting unmarried? I'd have to remember my own awkwardness now when people walked on the other side of the hall from me at the kids' school functions.

Then again, I wondered if he was playing me. He had a dark, sad side to him, with no real reason to display it out in the open. As he'd said yesterday, like Sam Spade. His attention to me furthered his goal to solve my case, now his case. Wayne owed me nothing, and I was foolish to think he gave a damn about me or my situation.

He pointed to a dirt road about eighty yards ahead on the right. "Is that the drive?"

I slowed the car. "Thought I was showing *you* the place?" I eased the car off the highway and crept over gravel that popped and crunched under the tires.

"Over by the barn," he said.

The farm wasn't anything special, and I'd seen it a dozen times. Apparently, Wayne had seen it, too. The irrigation equipment lay stacked in the thirty-year-old barn, pipes and wheels rusted red and thin. There wasn't even a house on the place, just two kudzu-covered outbuildings where old man Williams once stored seed and fertilizer. The homestead had stood on another tract sold a year ago.

The fields and structures lay abandoned for two years, and while I'd checked out the buildings during cursory windshield inspections, I'd not taken the time to walk every acre or climb into the loft. Lucas had drawn those duties.

Eddie parked behind us. I hadn't seen him follow. He got out and walked past us, disappearing in the weeds to reconnoiter Mother Nature, I guess. I opened my door and stood, stretching.

Wayne strode around the front of the vehicle. "Tell me about Hillary."

"Thought I already did?" I leaned on the car, sliding away when he came close. "Why can't you shoot straight with me? You've already been out here." My fingers did a rapid-fire tap on the hood. "You're probably married to a schoolteacher and have six kids."

"I'm not, and I don't. I haven't lied to you, Slade."

"Oh wow, you actually said my name this time." Give the man a gold star.

I marched toward the barn, angry over my passing flash of pity for him in the car. As for Hillary, she might be a jerk, but she wouldn't jump into something dirty. Her world was filled with the minutiae of hair color, shoe styles and the size of McRae's appendage. All this gossip wasted more of my already limited time.

Wayne caught up to me in three strides. "Well?"

"There's nothing to know about Hillary," I said. "She's worked with me for three years. She was a superb clerk, and management recognized her skills. Mickey offered to take her on as an assistant. She's a pain in the ass, but good enough at her job for me to overlook her faults." I flashed an annoyed stare. "That's it."

He snatched a long dry grass blade and stuck it in his teeth. It looked comfortable there.

With hands on my hips, I stopped and stared at the fallow field. "Those two have been bonkin' each other for two years. They're both married but don't like their spouses. Her spouse is abusive; his is a country club whiner with a heart condition. Hillary could do better."

"Did she—"

I turned away and marched closer to the barn. A wren swooped over the tall grass to our left. This line of questioning bordered on soap opera.

"So far you haven't told me anything," he said catching up.

"Maybe you ought to ask the right questions."

"What's your honest opinion about McRae?"

"He's an ass. Arrogant, unprofessional, condescending, and he seeks every opportunity to blemish my record. I'm forever running to stay ahead of him, and he's forever trying to find fault with me. A perpetual pissing contest."

Wayne caught up easily and walked in stride. "How did he get along with Lucas Sherwood and Mickey Wilder?"

"Lucas was a deadbeat, but McRae gave him the benefit of the doubt since he was a *man.*" Wayne studied my animation and the cocked hip. I'd learned he noted every movement, every word of everybody he crossed. "He never would let me discipline Lucas," I said. "They knew each other in college, and McRae covered for him."

Wayne nodded. "How did McRae respond to Mickey's disappearance?"

"Now you're asking a decent question. I thought he'd behaved too calmly when Mickey never returned." I sensed McRae's aloofness now as more than a simple lack of etiquette. If that asshole proved responsible for Mickey disappearing, I would do back flips and work twenty-hour days to put him away. My pulse quickened at the thought of that chance. "He thought Mickey was dead from the beginning," I said. "Should I wonder about that?"

"And how did he feel about Lucas' death?"

I'd asked a question, one friggin' question, and Wayne couldn't answer it. That's how we'd communicated from day one. I held up a finger and wagged it back and forth. "That's it. Enough of your game."

He shifted his weight. "This isn't a—"

"Nope." My palm stopped his sentence. "My turn to ask the questions."

He hushed. His easier stance relayed a compromise.

"What's with the interest in my boss? Tell me the real reason you're here . . . and don't say the bribe. I don't buy it."

"You don't?" He crossed his arms in our verbal game of chicken.

I shifted weight. "No, I don't."

Grasshoppers jumped out of his way as he turned and stepped through the dry, thigh-high yellow grass. The breeze wielded a crispness, tempered by the mid-morning sun. Autumn farms held a musty scent of loam, fertilizer and livestock. The metallic and earthy aroma of this farm hovered faintly over the dust and weeds.

A few crates lay stacked against the east side of the barn. After testing them with his boot, Wayne sat down on one and motioned for me to do the same. Glancing behind the crates for a creepy crawly, I jumped when a lizard scurried up the wall to disappear among the eaves. I shook my crate to scatter any hidden kin, and then sat down. The seat warm, I leaned back against the weathered planks, tucking my hands in my pockets. For a change, I shut my mouth and listened. His turn to talk anyway, and I wanted to hear every word.

CHAPTER 10

Wayne leaned with his back against the weathered boards of the barn and glanced over at me. Either he was preparing to reveal some serious back story about his visit here, or I was about to be led by the nose again.

"McRae's involved in fraudulent real estate deals."

"Sweet!" I exclaimed. "I didn't think the man was ballsy enough to crap in his own backyard, though." I stretched my arms in front of me like a cat in the sun. I'd be rid of both McRae and Jesse, and Hillary might as well be spayed. *McRae screwed up* sang singsong in my head.

Wayne failed to see the humor. "You can wipe that smile off your smug little face. I need you to keep quiet about this." My eyes rolled for effect, and he frowned. "We needed to know you weren't involved before telling you."

The myth that agents checked out the employees before the thugs wasn't fiction after all. I didn't care, having nothing to check.

"When you called about the bribe, the real estate involvement caught my attention," he said as he reached in his shirt pocket and extracted a cinnamon toothpick in a candy striped wrapper. "Since I knew about the Wilder case, I asked to come. A bribe on top of two deaths in the same county is one coincidence too many."

A cool breeze prompted me to button my coat. "Are you even concerned about my dog murderer anymore?"

The toothpick hung precariously on his lip, but he talked around it with ease. "We're not sure of Rawling's involvement in all this. He could be working solo with the bribe."

Wayne stopped moving the toothpick. "Watch yourself around your boss."

"I know him better than you do."

He leaned over and grasped my arm. "Listen, Slade. This isn't a TV show. People do nasty things when they're going down. He's an unknown quantity in this equation. Don't trust him."

I shook free, rubbing his presence off my arm. "Chill out."

He returned to his pose on the crate. "He searched your office last night."

"What?" I pivoted on my seat. "How do *you* know he was in my office?"

"We wired it for visual. Last night, Eddie and I waited in the car across the street and watched your favorite boss while eating our take-out."

"You're filming my office?" I scanned my memory for a straightened bra strap or underwear twisted wrong, moments preserved for Atlanta headquarters to snicker at over doughnuts and coffee. "You'd better cite me some law that gives you that right."

"I have the right. It's not on all the time." He leaned back and stared off at the tall grass twenty yards away. "Trust me."

"Yeah, right. Like you've earned that." I fanned an annoying gnat away.

"McRae ruffled through files in the outer office then entered yours," he said, in the same monotone he'd used with me Sunday a week ago, that now seemed like a year. "He picked a file, sat in your chair and read every single page. Eddie and I *thoroughly* enjoyed that show."

"Then what?"

"He put the papers back and walked out."

I slapped my hands on my thighs. "Jesse's file. McRae pilfered your office yesterday when he dropped in. I thought your cover was blown."

"Give me some credit," he said, removing the wood sliver from his mouth. I rose, not happy sitting below his eye level. He could look up at me for a change. "He also walked into Hillary's office," he said. "He left empty-handed, even raising the blinds back the way they were when he arrived. Does he usually show up after hours?"

"Not that I know of." But then I wouldn't have known about last night without cameras stuck in my ceiling. Bet Hillary snooped through my stuff on McRae's behalf, though. Wouldn't put it past Jean, either.

I tucked hair behind my ear, craving a paperclip, my thoughts abuzz about everything I did *not* know. I wondered if I'd tipped off McRae somehow yesterday, or did he rummage through my office on a regular basis. In my instant replay, McRae's comment about prematurely lowering the price of the farm triggered a concern. "Hey, that reminds me—"

I jumped as the bushes rustled to our right. A mockingbird burst from his cover and flapped madly toward the sky.

Eddie stepped from around the back of the barn, brushing weeds from his shirt and picking brambles off his trouser legs. His country boy getup of jeans and denim shirt hugged his muscles in all the right places.

"You're sporting a piece of broom sedge in your hair, big guy," I said. "How far'd you get?"

"Ten or twelve acres." He slapped his pants and brushed the top of his head. "Whew! I'd hate to come out here in the summer. Bet there'd be copperheads all over the damn place."

Wayne stepped over to him and they whispered.

"See anything?" I asked, not expecting much of a reply.

"It's obvious you haven't inspected it lately," he answered.

I stiffened "Why? What'd you find?" Someone's dead livestock or marijuana patch would label me a suspect all over again. I should've known Lucas shirked his inspection duties.

Eddie laughed with gusto. "Nothing's out there. Just a lot of weeds and a creek that tried to suck off one of my boots. Damn, gotta get 'em buffed now." He lifted one mud-covered foot. "I love these boots."

I laid a melodramatic hand on my chest. "You about made my heart stop. What were you doing?"

"Wayne wanted me to lay out how we're meeting Jesse. But I routinely check for pot and bodies."

"Bodies?"

They laughed and heat rose across my face. I couldn't separate their fact from fiction and tired of being a butt for their entertainment.

"So what's the plan, big man?" Wayne asked.

Eddie pointed to the northwest. "See that thicket over there?"

Wayne raised a hand over his eyes to shield the sun. "You think that'll keep you within decent range?"

"Sure. From the look of the road, nobody's been there in ages, and the transmission ought to be fine. It's only about a hundred yards." Eddie turned around and stared at the barn and the tall grass and kudzu around it. "Now you can stand—"

"Uhn-uh," Wayne interrupted and glanced at me. Eddie followed his look.

"What?" I asked.

"You don't need to know where I'll be. You'll be standing somewhere in that vicinity," he said circling his hand toward a bare area near where I'd parked. "Don't let him take you into the barn, and try not to get in his truck. He can even sit in the vehicle and you hand things back and forth through the window."

"Why can't I know where you are?" I scowled. "What if I need help? Eddie'll be too far."

"If you know where I am, you'll glance in my direction, cluing Jesse." He spit out the spent toothpick. "You won't need any help. You'll be a natural in your element of papers and red tape."

Enter here. Exit there. The agents told me where to lure the farmer and play my role. But it wasn't like Jesse could be trusted to follow the script, and I didn't feel too cozy about the arrangements.

"Suit you?" Wayne asked.

"I guess." My gaze traced the plan, roaming from the parking place to the barn then up to where Eddie would be. "This is a lot to ask."

"You having cold feet? *Now?*"

"I've never done this type of thing before." I waved my arms over the stage. "Jesse could shoot me dead in nothing flat with this setup."

"Nobody's getting shot, CI. It's a bribe. Money for paper. Remember, he needs you."

Sure. More like if I refuse, I'm subject to penalty and administrative discipline. "Yeah," I said. "I think I can do this."

"I'll be close enough to hear, and in case I can't catch it all, we want to ask a favor," Wayne said.

"I knew it." My fanciful thought from the day we met at my house took form. It's what all agents were supposed to do.

"A wire bother you?" Wayne's passive aggressive manner reeked "double-dog dare."

"Not at all. So who gets the honor of wiring me, or is this a *ménage a trois*? Strip me and wire me any way you like." A sports bra and jeans would cover all my prime parts anyway. I'd take evidence on Jesse any way I could get it and end this case any way I could.

"I'd love the honor, but you make the call, CI," he said. "We want you to be comfortable." He rubbed a hand across his face and left two fingers over his mouth, hiding a smile.

Damn it, I wished he'd quit playing me.

Eddie's big hand patted me on the back as he snorted then laughed. I stumbled. If he'd been any louder, Jesse would have heard us at his place. "What now?" I asked. "You coming back to the office with me?"

"No, ma'am," Wayne said, his voice back to business. "We're going to check out the area a little more."

"You turn over all the rocks you want. I've got work to do. McRae blames you for keeping me from making his quota." I threw hands on my hips, mocking them for a change. "Watch out for the wrath of McRae."

Wayne shook his head. "Don't mock the guy. He has the most to lose here. After two deaths in your office, you can't afford to consider him a joke."

Wayne sure stored a short supply of humor. "I'm too worried or I'm not worried enough. I'm Slade, then I'm CI. What is it with you? Do you want to do this?" I said, refusing to be rebuked. "I'm *sure* you can handle it *much* better than me." I spun on the heel of my brogans and walked to my car.

"We just want you alert, Slade," he said. "We want you prepared," he spoke louder as I reached my car.

"I am," I yelled back. "Give *me* some credit." I slammed the door, and my tires kicked dirt as they carried me away from the theatrics. Wayne invariably rubbed me wrong. Almost like he did it on purpose.

I FINISHED WORK, confident Uncle Sam extracted more than his fair share of money out of my hide. I even helped Hillary complete a nasty loan reamortization.

The day returned to the strange comfort of the old bureaucratic routine. Downright peaceful. Like any family, we juggled our black sheep, spats and spectacles, but we could make things happen for the constituents of Charleston County.

Having a reason to go home and no excuse to delay, I shut down my computer and headed north to collect the kids. Alan now lived across town in an apartment with a pool.

"How about a breakfast supper?" I asked my dynamic duo as we left the daycare lot.

"Can we do pancakes?" Ivy asked. "We still have some blueberry syrup."

"I want waffles," Zack demanded.

"You could at least ask, Zack, instead of shouting orders."

He glowered at me through the rearview mirror. "I'm the man of the house now."

I stared back. "I'm still your mother, and that means respect, little man. Is that clear?"

"Yes, ma'am," he mumbled into his shirt. "But Grandma named me the man now since Daddy left. Doesn't that mean I'm in charge? Daddy used to be in charge."

My decision to split from Alan made even more sense.

"No. That means you should act more mature. I'm in charge at work, and I'm a woman."

"But you have a man for a boss."

Not for long, I thought. "A man or a woman can be in charge, sweetie. It's the job you do, not whether you're a boy or a girl. Okay?"

"Okay. But can I still have waffles?" he asked, the lesson ancient history.

While the kids took baths, I cooked supper. The family room television displayed a game show. I guessed the right answer as my phone rang. "No. Where do you get off thinking it's Thailand?" I scolded the contestant who hung his head to groans from the audience. The emcee turned over another question. I answered the phone. "Hello?"

The party hung up. I scrolled back through the numbers in the memory and read "unknown caller." Probably a telemarketer. Who else called and hung up this time of evening?

Hot fat popped my forearm as I turned the last piece of bacon. The contestant lost the round, and I called him a moron instead of shithead in case the kids wandered within earshot.

Smelling of bubble bath, they scrambled into the kitchen. "Um, bacon!" Zack said, zipping past fast enough to snatch a piece.

"I get an extra piece to make it even," Ivy said. She scrubbed her chair across the floor and found her place at the table. Zack jumped into his seat. They soon ate like ravenous squirrels. Bellies full, they showed signs of crashing a half-hour before bedtime.

I placed the last glasses in the dishwasher. "You guys brush your teeth. I'll be there in a minute." The phone rang.

Again no reply.

"I don't have time for this." I hung up. Someone loved pranks, apparently.

Would Jesse call and not speak? Or Alan. Wouldn't put it past him, either. Vulnerability nudged me, and I started humming. I glanced out the window facing the back porch. Nothing glared back. I drew the shade.

Collecting the videos, books and mini-racecars in my path, I lowered each window shade as I made my way to the kids' bedrooms. Book askew on her chest, Ivy's eyelids drooped. I took the book and tucked the covers under her neck. Zack snored. I kissed his peaceful face and fought the urge to wake him, then rock him back to sleep. He was my cuddler.

With my life slowed for the moment, I poured a glass of wine and settled on the sofa.

The phone rang. I almost dropped my glass reaching for it before the ring woke the kids. The deep breathing on the other end erupted my temper. "Who the hell is this?"

The exhales amplified. A man cleared his throat. I hit the disconnect button.

My heart pounded against my ribs so hard I could count my pulse in my ears. I slipped around the house double-checking locks and latches. One minute I was sure Alan toyed with me, then by the time I walked to the next window, I convinced myself it was Jesse. In front of the bay window, I imagined the caller as a perverted stranger, maybe someone I'd rejected for a loan.

The sheers over my dining room windows made me feel like a sniper target, so I wrote on a sticky note to buy drapes and stuck it to the refrigerator. All secured, I decided I didn't know who the hell it was and ended the debate.

I rummaged through my nightstand and pulled out the .38 and laid it on the coffee table.

Then I wadded myself into a protective ball amidst cushions and a blanket on the sofa. Local television reporters infused crisis into everyday events, bordering on the comical. Hell, my life held more drama than this. Warm and relaxed, I dozed with the lights on, my muscles melting into the couch. Going to bed seemed too much trouble, so I eased down flat and raised the blanket over my shoulders.

The phone rang two feet from my head. I grabbed it, enraged at being jolted awake. "Hello!"

"No need to shout," Alan said.

"What the hell are you doing calling this late?"

He laughed. "It's not that late. I need to pick up a few things. Can I come by?"

"Hell no, you can't come by. It's . . . what time is it?"

"It's ten. You're usually up this late. Wonder Woman tired from her investigation?"

"Have you been calling me and hanging up? Is that all you have time to do?"

"This is the first time I called. I've been playing basketball."

Oh yeah. League night. But he could've called from the gym. Or his cell.

"Slade, do I need to be worried about the kids? First the dog, now this?"

Now I understood his plan. "Not over a couple of hang-ups. Quit blowing things out of proportion and quit calling. Come by tomorrow night before the kids go to bed. Say around seven." A female voice said something unintelligible in the background.

"Who's that?" I asked.

"Who's what? I'm watching the news. I'll see you tomorrow night." He hung up.

The woman's faint voice rang a bell in my head, but I couldn't place it. Frankly, I'd appreciate someone screwing his brains out tonight. I'd forgive his prank calls if someone else wanted him.

With sleep totally out of the question, I turned off the phone, cranked up the coffeepot and turned on a late night talk show. I'd rather stay up than have some idiot wake me from a sound snooze and shake my senses again. Tomorrow would be a grumpy, drag-ass day. So be it.

As the hardwood floor finish flickered with the reflection of the television, I sank into my sofa, reminding myself I was strong. Prank calls were just that, silly pranks. The refrigerator hummed and dropped cubes in the dark kitchen behind me. A crape myrtle ran its fingernails across the dining room screen as a midnight breeze stirred. Hugging a pillow, I flipped the remote through channels and stroked the unconscious cat next to me to make her purr.

This was ludicrous. I was becoming my own worst enemy. I bounced up and switched on more light, pretending not to snatch a peek behind the furniture. I picked up the phone. One person in my life would understand the frayed edges to my sanity.

I dialed and nestled deeper into my blanket. "Savvy, you up?" I asked when the answering machine clicked on. "Come on. It's Slade."

A sluggish Savannah Conroy picked up. "I'm here in body, honey, but not sure about the spirit. What time is it?"

"A couple minutes before midnight."

"You okay? The kids okay?"

"We're all fine. I'm curled up on my couch hiding from spooks, falling apart."

She muffled a half-yawn. "You're the last person I'd expect to come unglued, but go ahead and spill."

After all these years, this woman knew my calls held purpose. We didn't do the shopping, giggling girlfriend chitchat much.

"This case is kicking my ass. I chewed Alan to pieces just because he woke me up. And I keep waiting for someone to jiggle my front doorknob. I feel like such a . . . *girl.*"

She laughed. "Give me a sec." The phone clunked as she set it down. I heard footsteps, then ice dropping in a glass. "Okay," she said when she returned, slurping something. "Needed a glass of ginger ale to play counselor. This might take a while."

I loved the woman. She slung me doses of her philosophy as I relayed my concerns and fears. "First," she said, "tell that secret agent of yours to do his job and catch this idiot. That's what your tax dollars pay him for. He works for you."

The image of giving Wayne an order made me break a smile, and I sure appreciated Savvy not seeing it. "Girl, you know I tried," I said. "But seriously, I think he's trying as hard as he can. These cases don't get solved in an hour. TV it ain't." Wayne's own words. I sipped my coffee. "Once the sun comes up, it'll be less spooky, and I'll be able to talk to Wayne without sounding like a wimp."

"Wayne? We're on a first name basis with the guy? Wish I had an agent to keep my ass out of trouble. Wait . . . what's he look like? Maybe I don't want him after all."

"Give me a break. We're working a case." I played with my cuticles, the phone wedged between my neck and shoulder, the cup now on the end table. She'd calmed me already.

"Is he ugly with a pocked face, no eyebrows and the charm of an artichoke? Kinda what I picture in an agriculture agent. I'd think all the hunks work for the FBI."

"Oh, no. He's not bad at all. Nothing like you'd expect. Broad shoulders, nice eyes and a gentle nature. So unexpected. Damn if he can't scold and respect me in the same sentence."

She whistled. "Honeydew, I declare! The budding executive has gone sweet on a new man."

"No, the hell I haven't." God forbid. "It's not like that. He makes me feel like I have a brain, at least part of the time. Wayne . . . Largo admires what I can do, not what I can dish out, if that makes any sense."

I could sense her smirk long distance.

"This investigation is wearing me thinner than cheap toilet paper," I said. "McRae's leaning on me, the farmer's turned nasty, and I don't trust Alan. Don't necessarily trust this agent, either, so don't start."

She snorted. "Like Alan is something new? You're just tossing that one in for effect, honey. Remember who you're talking to."

"Well, he rolled over and played dead when I served him his papers. I can't put my finger on why that doesn't feel right."

Ice cubes clinked in her glass. "Does sound non-Alan-ish, doesn't it?"

"I can't dump the case. They'll discipline me if I don't see this through. Even if I refused, this farmer'd still be on the warpath. These calls tonight are probably from him. I'm sure he killed Smokey. He says he knows where my kids go to daycare, and McRae . . ."

She waited. "McRae what?"

Wayne said keep quiet about McRae. "Um . . . let me pass on that before I get myself in trouble. Just don't ask."

"You'll tell me sooner or later anyway." She clucked her tongue. "Poor baby. I've never heard you this uncool."

Sitting here in the dead of night, I craved a grownup in the room. "I'm scared, damn it." There, I'd said it.

"I can tell. Change your locks," she ordered. "And get an alarm system. Go proactive. Always makes me feel better."

Alan would be mightily pissed at new locks. "I'll consider it, but I hate locking a guy out of his own home."

"It's not *his* home anymore. At least get the alarm system," she said. "I know Alan, and I'm sure locking him out isn't a bad idea. Men get weird in a power struggle. Been there, honey."

"You're probably right."

"I'll send you my bill. Two margaritas ought to do it. My ginger ale's gone, I have a loan closing in the morning, and I need my beauty sleep. You better now?" she asked.

"Some." I curled my feet under me and rearranged the blanket. "Looks like moving forward's the only choice I have."

"I don't see that as a problem for you," she said, then switched to a more somber tone. "Just be careful, Slade. Listen to those agents and watch your back. Call me. I'll keep you sane. God knows you've done it enough times for me."

I hung up. She was right. Using the remote to find an easy listening country channel, I lowered the volume, wadded the blanket over me and closed my eyes. Willie Nelson crooned me into a dreamless slumber, giving me a temporary reprieve from being a heroine.

CHAPTER 11

I woke at 5:30 a.m. tangled in my blanket, a sofa cushion on the floor and a crick in my neck. A slow, hot shower relaxed some of the knots. Wrapped in my chenille robe with the tattered belt and ink stains from a felt marker used to label the kids' school stuff, I considered sitting on the porch with my fresh-dripped coffee. I could watch the sun rise. Seeing my breath hang in the cold morning air changed my mind. Curled up in my blanket, I finished my coffee on the sofa watching predawn exercise shows on television, despising their abs, then woke the kids for school.

I parked my Taurus at the office forty-five minutes early. After opening the blinds and starting the java, I leaned back in Jean's chair. She owned the most comfortable seat in the place, with lower lumbar support to die for thanks to her doctor's note to HR. She probably lied about the back, but if it made her generate more work, I couldn't care less.

A big whomph meant the heat had kicked on. Coffee gurgled and dripped painfully slow into the glass carafe. Hearty Colombian brewed instead of Hillary's sickening vanilla hazelnut. I kicked off shoes and propped my feet on Jean's footstool and waited, expecting agents to walk in any second. I closed my eyes for what I thought would be a few seconds.

I recoiled as a hand touched my shoulder. I smiled, realizing I'd fallen asleep again in front of Wayne.

"Slade?"

I opened my eyes. Jesse Rawlings grinned in my face.

I jumped to my feet and lost my balance, ramming my bare toes into the desk corner. "Shit!"

Jesse's rough hands steadied me, a wide, goofy grin covering his face. "Jumping into my arms now?" he asked.

"Jumping, jumping," repeated Ren from three feet behind him.

I wriggled, trying to tactfully ease away from his fingers. But his hands moved up my back then forward under my arms. His fingers brushed across my breasts. I instinctively yanked an arm across my chest and swung the other at Jesse's face. "Keep your hands off me."

He blocked the fist with open palms. I felt a sick fear that this whole bribery charade could have been for no other reason than to get me alone.

Jesse snickered. "Slade, you gotta be more careful around here . . .

alone. Any pervert could walk in off the street and hurt you." He pointed to the desk. "You all right? That was a powerful wham on the toe." He stepped back and peered at my foot. Ren stooped in unison.

I fought to control my alarm, but I was a fool not to think my face broadcast terror. He was right. A pervert *had* walked in off the street.

"You scared the hell out of me." My finger quivered on the end of a tight fist. "Don't you ever . . . and I mean ever . . . touch me again. You got that?"

Jesse's lip curled. Ren tilted his head, analyzed his brother's expression and aped it.

I straightened my sweater where it'd bunched up above my waist, giving them a peek at my middle. "What are you doing here?"

"I came by to see about our deal, thought now was a good time, before your people came in to work. Watcha done so far?" He reached toward my shoulders as if to hug me. "I'm excited about all this."

I smacked his hands away. He put them in his pockets, but his body leaned toward me, bent at the waist, a dark, playful smirk across his face.

No recorder, no video, and, worse, no Wayne or Eddie. "I've been making sure the title to the property was straight," I said. "I didn't want to deed you something you couldn't legally own."

He leaned on the desk. "You know better than me how these things work, so I'm trusting you to make 'em right. We still on for tomorrow?"

"Sure." I glanced at the front door. "Someone's going to be here any minute, Jesse. It might make people wonder what we're up to if they see you."

"Okay. Just one more thing. Put the papers in my name."

Didn't matter to me whose John Hancock went on the fake deed, but Jesse sure put himself on a limb recording a fraudulent deal in his own name. I didn't ask why, because I didn't care. His request would tie him to the crime even better, so I just nodded.

"Good. I'm outta here." He buttoned his worn out sport coat, turned and ambled toward the door. Ren left light tracks of dirt or something worse on the carpet. Guess hogs ate early. Jesse spoke over his shoulder. "Found another dog for your kids yet? My offer still holds. I can get you that pup." He'd reached the door and did his signature wink just as Hillary sidestepped the pair in the entrance, puzzlement on her face.

"Don't forget your receipts next time, and call before you come. I might not be here," I said for Hillary's sake.

Jesse cocked his head, winked again and left, Ren in his wake.

"What's *he* doing here?" Hillary said, unbuttoning her coat. "Come to think of it, what are *you* doing here so early?"

Leaning against the counter, I gingerly rolled my foot trying to decide if my toes were broken. "I couldn't sleep."

She grimaced as if she'd stuck her nose in a garbage can. "Oh, yuck. Don't tell me you fixed that strong coffee."

"Dump it. I'm gone." I limped to my office, picked up my briefcase and grabbed my coat. "Call McRae and let him know I'm on sick leave. I'm sure you intended to call him anyway." As I passed her, she stood with her coat still on one arm, amazement spread across her face.

The drive home was a delight, traveling in the opposite direction of rush hour mayhem. Once inside the house, I donned jeans, a cable knit sweater, windbreaker, and thick socks, coziness personified. With my bruised foot slipped into an untied sneaker, I headed east—to the beach.

My shoe eased off the gas when I realized Wayne wouldn't know where I was, then I returned to the posted speed limit. Mr. Special Agent could call and leave a message. That reminded me . . . I placed my phone on vibrate.

Due to the light traffic, I reached the beach in record time. Seated in front of a favorite dune, I dipped swollen bare toes in a saltwater pool left behind at low tide. Seagulls chattered overhead, as if they laughed at me. The sun rose higher, warming the surrounding air in spite of the breeze, but I stayed snuggled in my layers, the water on my feet refreshing. I needed the chill, needed to chill. I'd come close to real trouble and handled it like an oaf. But whether I finessed or clumsied my way through this mess, my choices were simple.

I could resign or see the case through.

Giving up my job would jeopardize my custody of Zack and Ivy. Keeping it risked . . . what? Jesse probably killed Smokey. Would he cross the line to hurt or murder a human being? If his veins pumped that kind of poison, what difference did it make if I quit or not? He'd remain a concern.

A seagull waddled ten feet away, no doubt checking out the interloper on his sand, and I wished I'd brought bread to feed him. I could usually coax them within three feet of me. Sitting still, I waited to see how close he'd come. He hopped twice, jumped, spread his wings and then flew off with a serious squawk.

A hand tapped my shoulder.

I started, scrambling to stand and run, but slid in the sand. My butt hit the wet ground, and saltwater from the tidal pool splashed my jeans.

Wayne held me still by the shoulder. "Whoa, didn't you see me coming?"

"No, damn it . . ." I swung my arms, shoving him away. "Don't ever creep up on me like that."

He stepped back. "I came to check on you."

The drumbeat in my chest almost hurt.

"I was worried," he said.

I cast him a hard stare, then scooted crab-like away from the wet sand and up on the dune, stretching out my damp legs to dry in the sun. He sat uncomfortably close to me, his broad shoulder skimming mine as he patted my knee. What the hell was this?

I elbowed his hand away. "How'd you find me?"

"I followed you. It was my turn. Eddie's shift is tonight."

Of course he followed me. Why not? Everybody else was controlling my life except me. A little silver fish flashed and darted away in the pool, disappearing like I wanted to do. "Jesse surprised me at work this morning. I came out here to consider my options."

"I know." He reached under his leather coat and brandished two small bottles of water. He opened both and handed me one. "I was going to come in, but you got rid of him pretty well on your own. Saved my cover."

I took the bottle and swilled half the contents, buying time to weigh how I liked being watched.

"What did he want?" Wayne asked.

"Nothing. Just to scare me, I think." Slow gray waves rolled in on top of one another. "I didn't see you when I left."

"You wouldn't have seen *anyone* the way you stormed out." He took a sip of his water. "I saw Jesse's pickup in the parking lot and waited for him to leave. You came out right on his heels."

"You could have helped."

"I'm undercover, remember?" he said. "I watched him on camera, like I did McRae the other night. Bet you're glad I rigged those cameras now."

I crammed the half-full bottle into the sand. "Glad to know I'm an actor for your entertainment pleasure." I stood and brushed the sand off my bottom. Hobbling like a peg-leg pirate, I marched down the beach.

My reputation of confidence had evolved from a talent to maintain control. Now I served as a marionette for a half-dozen people. Throbbing pain soon overcame my pride. Feeling foolish for venturing so far away, I leaned to take the weight off for a half a minute, then turned around. Wayne jogged over.

"Why don't you just arrest this asshole?" I said, tottering. "I don't know why I ever called you people."

"Because you're a good person, Slade. A genuinely decent person."

"Like you give a damn."

"But I do." He moved closer, his arms out, palms spread wide in a gesture of peace.

I wondered what his catch was. What investigative maneuver he needed me for next.

"I'm sorry I scared you. I'm sorry Jesse scared you. I'm sorry life isn't giving you a fair shake these days." One arm reached out further, tentatively looping through mine to support me. "I'd fix it all if I could."

His expression of support sounded real, something I sorely needed to hear. My legs weakened, caving at the chance of an ally. He'd been less than forthcoming, but intent on finding answers to some serious wrongs. I was so confused. So flustered. "Will you cover for me when I shoot the bastard?"

He laughed. "If the opportunity presents itself."

Loved his answer. "This wasn't supposed to work out this way, you know. I just thought—"

"I know."

"No, you don't. You don't have kids." I reached up to push a strand of hair away from my mouth, but he did it for me. I tensed.

"We'll get him," he said.

That's when I realized his gray eyes matched the water. "I'll hold you to that."

"Fair enough."

I was so tired of fighting enemies. So tired. He helped me back to my tidal pool. Animosity drifted away as warm, strong muscles enfolded me.

"How's your foot?" he asked.

I sat and moved my toes in the water, slowly flexing. Water rippled and rebounded against the sand. "Hurts like hell. If you don't shoot him next time he does that, then I will. I mean it."

"I'm so sorry he touched you, Slade."

My frustration melted and ran into the saltwater at his use of my name. A warm sensation surged up through my core. His touch was something I wanted, and I blushed at my emotional naiveté. I'd been badly married for way too long.

"Am I forgiven?" he pleaded with a mock downcast gaze.

"Just kick his ass next time."

"Will do."

"Tell me about Pamela." The move was bold and probably ill-timed, but the moment had turned on a dime from work to personal. Time he coughed up some his own reality as a symbol of trust. I'd sure spilled a heap of mine.

He delayed, looking down and thinking before he spoke again.

He shifted a little away from me. "I met her in Chula Vista, California, while with the Border Patrol," he said, squinting at the horizon. "Got sick of seeing those poor illegal saps die in the desert and couldn't see spending my career recycling people. So when a transfer to USDA opened here in the southeast, I grabbed it. She came with me."

I listened, afraid to interrupt this new taste of honesty.

He gave a mild shake of his head. "She worked for the BP as well.

Even though she's hardly a hundred pounds soaking wet, she's nailed her share of bad guys."

A petite female dynamo. Every man's dream. She was probably a natural blonde with a backside as firm as a watermelon and a waist as big as my thigh. "She sounds, um, ominous."

My remark drew a half-smile from him. "Oh, she was. She is. She volunteers for every task force, case and committee that comes along. She went to work for the DEA in Atlanta. They love her." He sighed and tightened his lips. "But I'm done with her."

Pamela had to have flaws. Not that I wanted to hear something horrible, maybe just a closure with a teeny hint of bitterness. Enough to let me know he'd shut and locked the door on her. I started to say something about Alan, but he spoke up again.

"She worked a lot of overtime with her pumped-up DEA guys. I loved her enthusiasm and she loved my maturity. I turned into her father." He took a long swig from his bottle. "Hence, the divorce."

Finally, a glimpse behind the badge. His arm dropped from my shoulder. "I hear she's dating one of the DEA trainers now," he said.

Okay, that sounded like a period. I wanted to ask if it hurt to talk about her. My selfish side wanted him to say no. The adult in me understood that leaving a spouse, however incompatible, still chipped off a piece of your heart. I decided to let well enough alone since I sensed the wound was still a bit raw. He'd finally become human to me.

"So what happened between you and Alan?" he asked.

That history didn't take long, and I didn't have secrets. He already knew most of it anyway. "The relationship began eroding before Alan and I ever married. Kids and routine carried us from our wedding vows to divorce in a continual mudslide." I brushed my palms back and forth across each other. "And that's that."

He curled up one corner of his mouth. "Aren't we a pair?"

"No point crying in our beer."

His arm slid around me, again. "That's why I know you'll handle this case."

Again the case. Still, I let him pull me into him, my body stiff at first, unsure how to react. Was he seeking my trust or . . . caring?

"Still not sure I'd call you guys if I could do it all over again," I warned.

He closed the space with a tight hug. "Oh yeah you would."

I fought to mask the pep rally taking place behind my ribs. "Can I ask you a question?"

"Sure, loan lady."

"Don't you ever lighten up? Let your hair grow an inch longer?" Scrunched in his grasp, I couldn't see his smile, but I knew it was there.

"I'm fun at the right time. Otherwise, it has to be all business to maintain professional confidence. Get too casual and everybody lowers their guard." He eased me back and gazed into my eyes. "Do you trust me now?"

A hormone hurricane whirled inside me.

With his free arm, he reached over and put a finger under my chin, a touch that set me afire and tossed all reason out the door. "If you have to think about that answer, maybe I led you wrong," he said.

I shivered and realized I was being every bit the *girl* I'd whined about to Savvy. "Are you leading me now?"

Logic told me to resist him. His divorce was barely final and the ink on my papers wasn't dry. What were the chances this was an honest attraction and not a rebound—for either of us? I felt adulterous, yet excited about the allure.

As my thoughts scattered, an ache grew inside me, and I shut my eyes as if doing so would keep me safe and gather my wits. But other senses seized control. I relished the scent of his aftershave, the firmness of his shoulder, the depth of his breathing.

He brushed my cheek with his finger and my lips with his own—just a whisper of a kiss, leaving me starved for one of greater substance. His combination of tenderness and confidence was intoxicating and sucked me in.

I leaned back, the abrupt halt dizzying.

"What's wrong?" he asked.

My heart still thumped fast, fighting my logic. "Does this feel right to you?"

He stared at me. He fixated again on the water. "God, Slade, no. That wasn't supposed to happen."

Weren't our lives frustrating enough? I leaned close. "I wish we *could* make something nice out of all this."

His fingers combed through his hair. "Damn conflict of interest, sweetheart. They'll yank me off this case in an instant if they suspect a relationship." He gently took my hand off his leg and laid it back on mine. "It would be a disaster if they removed me from Charleston and you got stuck with another agent. An agent who was told you almost sabotaged the case with your feminine wiles." That million-dollar grin flashed, then left as quickly as his kiss.

I swear I felt an attraction. I'd sure reacted like I had. Or was this another control feature of his profession?

"Stop and think. Jesse is not the loveable fella you once thought," he said. "McRae isn't any better. You have an ex I'm not too sure about, either. I'd be an idiot to leave you alone in the midst of all this. The risk is too great."

"I'm not made of tissue paper. Plus, I've known these people for years."

"Maybe it takes a fresh eye to see them for what they are."

Now my heart beat harder for a different reason. "Maybe you don't know them as well as you think."

I couldn't help feeling he saw me as vulnerable, needing protection. Like I had no power of my own. To think I'd almost asked if I would see him once he returned to Atlanta.

He tempted me, threatening to overwhelm my doubts about his intentions. I knew better, but, Jesus, I couldn't remember wanting Alan like this.

Savvy was right. I'd gone sweet on Wayne. Problem was he hadn't gone sweet enough on me. His attention remained anchored on the investigation.

Dammit, he'd reeled me in before I knew it. Whether he did it to catch Jesse, catch McRae or catch me was yet to be seen. I just couldn't read him.

But I still craved that kiss.

CHAPTER 12

Wayne followed me from the beach back to Ridgeville, then veered off with a quick honk of his horn. After collecting the kids, I ordered pizza, planted myself on my sofa and tried to balance my emotions. When the doorbell rang and I identified the deliveryman at the door, I let Ivy take the pepperoni pizza while I returned to my pillow, the ice pack on my foot.

Ivy assumed command, placing slices on plates and pouring glasses of diet root beer. She sat Zack at the coffee table in front of the television, then handed me my dinner. She assumed an overseeing position at the other end of the sofa. I so adored her at that moment—at her ability to take charge.

I felt old *and* depressed.

At a quarter after seven, the doorbell rang. Alan let himself in.

Zack yelled, "Daddy!" and ran to him, wrapping his father's waist in a hug. Their hair matched perfectly, the genes obvious. Ivy stayed on the sofa.

For the sake of the kids, I hid my annoyance that he'd waltzed in uninvited. "What are you doing here?"

"This is still my house."

Savvy had been right again: time to change the locks. "Well, let me answer the door for you next time."

He gestured to my ice pack. "You don't look like you could answer a door."

Ivy came to my defense. "She kicked the desk at work when she fell out of her chair. I'm taking care of her."

"I see that." He smiled at her. "Wanna hug your daddy?"

She jumped up and headed to the kitchen with the dishes. "My hands are full."

"Just like her mother." His sarcasm missed Ivy but struck me, as intended.

"What do you need?" I asked. Thoughts of the day at Sullivan's Island unsettled me, like Alan could read that I'd embraced a man so soon after I'd filed divorce papers.

He held a pad of paper in one hand and a large gym bag in the other. "I need clothes, some junk out of the medicine cabinet, CDs. I'll make arrangements for the big stuff, but no rush. Brad has just about everything covered at his apartment."

I pointed to the bedroom. "Help yourself."

"I believe I can find my way."

I bit my tongue. My attorney had told me to be careful. Nothing exposed raw emotion more than a divorce. Alan would be on a seesaw until he adjusted to being single—the Mars and Venus kind of thing. I didn't have to understand it, just be wary of setting him off.

I stayed where I was, and Ivy brought me a cup of tea, bless her heart.

From the sounds of his movements, Alan rummaged around in the bedroom then moved to the bath. Moments later he strutted into the kitchen, then moved to the dining room followed by the garage. Forty-five minutes later he announced his departure.

Zack walked him to the door. Ivy didn't.

I'd have to deal with that. Apparently her emotions weren't as settled about her father as I thought, though I appreciated the allegiance.

Once Alan left, Zack walked by his sister and popped her on top of the head. She slapped at him and missed. He sat down with his handheld game player, and I flipped to the news.

Alan walked back in.

"Don't do that!" I said, the mask gone from my irritation.

"I forgot something." I suspected he'd left a basketball jersey or a baseball glove. He entered the bedroom and returned with a .22 in his hand, half pointed at me. "My gun."

My blood turned arctic. "Glad you're taking it. I forgot that thing was in the closet," I said, turning toward the television, struggling to hide the panic, wondering what the kids would think.

Zack searched the TV for kiddy channels. Ivy watched her father, wary.

"Where's your pistol?" he asked me.

"At Daddy's for him to clean it," I lied. My revolver hid under the corner of my mattress at night or in my glove box by day. "Now go."

He left with that twisted grin of his. I'd have the locks changed first thing tomorrow.

Ivy moved closer to me. "Momma?"

"It's okay, baby. Come keep me warm."

She scooted under my arm and we watched Zack's cartoon.

Damn that man.

THURSDAY DAWNED uncommonly bright for an October day, a good omen for my meet with Jesse at the Williams' farm. Just to be safe, I opted for my Reeboks so I could book it out of there should things turn ugly.

Ann understood I planned to work field inspections when I collected my silver Ford Fusion government car from the office. The white Impala followed me to Wayne's hotel at a discreet distance, Eddie at the wheel.

I arrived at the mid-rate, two-decade old Ramada Inn, a large colonial brick building with ground floor rooms facing out. I put the car in park and realized I bit the inside of my cheek.

Wayne opened the door to room 115.

"Here I am," I said, arms out, then slapped back to my side. I hadn't seen him since our personal moment, and awkwardness took me back to the first day we met.

"Come on in. You ready?" he asked.

"No, but I'm not sure that matters."

The lawman's concentration hid any sign of a smile. Eddie jogged over, stepped in behind me and shut the door.

My hand brushed my face before I recognized the flirtatious gesture. Not even a peck on the cheek from Wayne. God, when he said hold back for the sake of the case, he meant it. All morning I'd tried to not think about that sand dune kiss. Best to forget it. Wayne obviously had.

His toiletries lay in order on the bathroom counter, the toothpaste squeezed from the bottom, cap on. A half liter of Wild Turkey sat more empty than full. He'd made his bed from the looks of the sheet corner sticking out from under the spread, and left the do-not-disturb sign on the door to deter housekeeping staff. Moisture remained in the air from his shower.

The butt of the Glock peeked from its shoulder holster on the dresser, along with brass knuckles and a black-handled, five-inch Spyderco knife. The Smith and Wesson .357 sat apart from the arsenal, as if exclusive and preferred.

I pointed to the ample supply of testosterone substitutes on display. "Expecting trouble?"

"Hate surprises," Wayne said, his jesting half-hearted. He nodded toward my briefcase. "Got the papers?"

I handed him the briefcase. Nervous, I moved clumsily, almost dropping the thing. But soon my life would be smoother sailing as a single parent with a routine job and no men. Hard days would mean soccer and PTA in the same evening.

Wayne produced a body wire and demonstrated how it worked, but I paid little attention to the words. I'd have to unbutton my shirt. I'd worn my imagination thin on how to play this, conjuring ideas to diffuse any erotic imaginings, but shedding my top now raised the heat of embarrassment.

But he seemed all business, almost too anxious to get this done. He finished his explanation of how a wire worked, and stood in the middle of the room holding it, brows raised. Eddie started to excuse himself.

When neither of us made a move, Wayne said, "I need your help if we're going to use this thing."

"Fine," I said with a haughty air. The shades already drawn, I slowly slid my shirt out of my pants. Then I undid the buttons one at a time, eyes locked on him.

He tried to stare me down. I wasn't about to glance away. He wasn't besting me this time, not like on the beach.

Finally, I stood exposed in my best fitting khakis and a new sports bra, my shirt held back off my shoulders.

"Pink?"

"You got a problem with it?" I sucked in my gut.

He forced back a grin I could've done without and carefully installed the wire, each brush of his hand sending a tiny sensual wave through me. I ordered my reflexes alert, my eyes still fixed on him, standing my ground.

Wayne repeated how the wire worked and awkwardly tried to help me back into my shirt. I let him. Then I buttoned back up, lingering on each piece.

Eddie stood against the wall, as if keeping a distance, amazement in his eyes. "What the hell is going on here?" he muttered.

"You say something?" Wayne asked harsh.

Eddie pushed himself off and sat on the edge of the bed. "No, man, not a thing."

Then Wayne eased out one of the cheap wooden veneer chairs for me. "Sit down, Slade."

I sat, crossed my legs, relieved the act was over, ecstatic I'd gotten him back.

Lipstick, wallet, hand lotion—Wayne emptied the contents of the briefcase onto the bed. Then he opened my wallet, checking each compartment.

"What are you doing?" I asked, remembering the living room interview when he questioned my motives. "All you need are the papers. They're right there," I pointed, fighting back indignation.

"Just hold on," he said calmly. "Standard procedure. Prior to meeting a target with a payoff, I have to search the vehicle, purse, briefcase, pockets, so I can testify that the CI carried no money going into the meet. From this point on, I can't let you out of my sight." He winked, and my heart tripped. "Not that I'd want to, of course." He tucked my money in his shirt. "I'll give this back to you later."

Eddie waved his hand like a first grader. "Can we save the sexual overtures for later? This is my first time on the wire, thank you very much."

"There are no sexual overtones, dude," I said.

"Whatever," he mumbled.

Wayne patted me on the arm. "Did you eat breakfast?"

"A pastry. Why?"

"I don't want to have to pick you up when you faint in the middle of this. Need something on the way?"

"Are you serious?" I said. "I've never fainted in my life."

His cell phone rang. Glancing at the caller ID, his face made a terse change. "I've got to take this," he said, heading outside.

Eddie shrugged at me, and I peered around the curtain at Wayne pacing the sidewalk. A frown turned his face to stone. Ten minutes later, he still argued with the caller.

Eddie turned on the television and kicked back on the bed. I glanced from the program to the door a dozen times, occasionally scratching at the wire. "What's he doing?" I asked.

"Have no clue," he said. "I don't ask when he gets those calls."

What calls? The boss? Another CI in play? The ex?

Thirty minutes later, Wayne strode in and shut the door, locking it behind him. His eyes stared cold at the closed cell, his teeth grinding from the movement in his jaw. "The meeting is off. Call Jesse."

Eddie clicked the television to dark and rolled off the bed to his feet. I stood, feeling the color drain from my face. "What do you mean it's off? We've—"

"I've got a family emergency back in Atlanta. Eddie, pack the car."

Eddie rushed back to his motel room. Wayne threw toiletries and clothes in a suitcase. He checked the cap on the bourbon and gave it a brief glance before packing it. I stood in the middle of the room, stepping out of his way twice.

He pointed to a case on the dresser. "You can take off the wire and lay it over there. Be careful with it."

I unbuttoned again, as if undressing before my sister. He didn't notice. As I laid the wire down and covered back up, he opened the door. "Sorry about this, but it can't be helped."

"Someone sick? Anything I can do?"

"Nothing I really care to discuss, if you don't mind." He stepped through the door, a bag in hand.

"Um . . . okay. But what do I tell Jesse?" I suppressed a sprouting sense of panic and followed him outside. "What if I can't get him and he waits out there and we don't show up?" Not only could Jesse get riled, but I'd be alone at home again, waiting for prank calls and white trucks. "How long will you be gone?"

He gripped my shoulders. Seeing me wince, he eased his fingers. "I'm hoping no more than three days. I'll be back as soon as I can. Tell Jesse whatever you want. Just buy us at least three days."

He went back inside the motel room and reappeared with hands filled with two duffle bags. "Eddie?" he hollered. "Let's move it."

I stepped toward my car and opened the door. "I hope all goes well for you," I said over the hood.

"That would be too much to ask, believe me," he said.

Eddie tossed his suitcase in the trunk and Wayne shut the lid. Both slid into the vehicle, and Eddie threw a brief wave as they drove off.

I stood wondering what the hell existed in his world with the power to shut him down so fast. The man apparently toted baggage, something seriously dark and ominous worth dumping a federal case over. Wayne's stern emphasis to keep us at arm's length from each other now made more sense, just not for the reasons he claimed at the beach.

And he'd kept my money.

NO FARMER had ever dropped the F bomb on me before, but Jesse threw it at me three times. "What the fuck kind of trick is this?" he yelled in my ear after I'd called him from my office. The boyishly smiling face and charm he spread over the agricultural community didn't match the words pouring over the phone. I told him my boss had called, demanding to meet with me, causing me to cancel.

"We don't want him curious, Jesse. We can't afford that."

"If you did your fucking job right, he wouldn't be coming over." His voice grunting and gravelly, he sounded like a mobster. "Stinking fucking bitch."

A shiver ran through me, as if air-conditioning caught me in the face after a sweaty run. I'd led this man through one farm crisis after another, all but holding his hand and hugging Ren with support. I'd spent mornings checking hogs and hot noon days riding through fields with the guy. Everybody I knew saw Jesse as a congenial, good-old-boy. This rabid badger streak of his freaked me out, and it was becoming routine. His next words frightened me more.

"Ren, Ms. Slade isn't helping us very much." Jesse spoke to his brother in the background. "We might lose our farm."

A wail rose and fell, icy pricks dancing down my spine. "I didn't say that," I said.

"She hates us, Ren. She's gonna take your hogs away."

The wail howled louder, an animal sensation that cut through me. "I didn't say anything like that." I swallowed down the lump of shock in my throat. "Put Ren on the phone. Tell him he can keep his pigs."

"No, no, no," Ren continued. The no's went on and on with Jesse egging him on with warnings about losing everything.

"Stop it," I yelled. "That's cruel. I said we'd still meet. We just can't until next Tuesday. Tell him that's only four days away. Four stinkin' days."

Ann appeared in my doorway, Hillary behind her. I waved them away, silently mouthing that everything was fine. They didn't believe me, of course. I covered the mouthpiece and asked them to close the door.

"Tuesday," Jesse said low. "And don't screw with me again."

"I'm doing my best," I said. "I'm not used to this kind of thing." The howling reduced to whimpers. "Please tell Ren everything will be fine."

"Not until we meet, Slade. Not until you do what you said you'd do. Just remember you were the one to upset him, and I'll remind him of that every morning and evening until you keep your end of the bargain." He hung up.

Oh, Jesus. I rested elbows on the desk and covered my face, massaging my cheeks. Fright crawled into my head. My pulse hammered behind my eyes. I covered my face again, sighing deep, wishing the world would slow down a minute.

"Slade?"

I leaped out of my chair at the voice two feet from my face.

"I'm sorry," said Hillary, backing away. "Ann Marie was frantic. What's wrong?"

Of course she was. Ann had a heart. But no guts, since she sent the second-in-command to check on the first. Hillary was the last person I wanted to see in a moment of weakness.

"The divorce," I said, reaching for a tissue in a box on my desk, struggling to produce a tear. "Dumb attorney, stupid husband. That call caught me off balance, I guess." I stopped myself before I wove a story too hard to untangle. That, and I was afraid I might actually *talk* to Hillary, an act that would haunt me in the worst way at some future date.

THANK GOD FOR FRIDAY. Didn't know why I should, but it was better than cursing Him for it. My day hung in this limbo, purgatory dimension, as would my Saturday, Sunday and possibly Monday. I didn't think "what else could happen," because fate would prove how bad things really could get. I still waited to hear from Wayne.

Alan carried the kids to the movies on Saturday. I watched my own pay-per-view at home, new locks on my doors, shades and blinds drawn. He returned my children stuffed with junk food and wired with a sucrose overdose, so I grabbed a yogurt, then a Snickers bar chased by a Chardonnay to run at their speed. Once the sugar crash hit, cat naps carried me through a long night while my babies slept like . . . babies.

Not up to church, the next morning I authorized hooky from all routine. In our pajamas, we made pancakes in the shapes of stars, pirate hooks, ballerinas and daisies. Chocolate chips and blueberries accented our art. I laughed so hard my ribs ached.

Around three, we watched animal bloopers on The Discovery Channel as Ivy braided my hair with beads and barrettes. Zack painted my toenails once I promised to keep his manicuring talents a secret from the world.

The phone rang, and I let it.

"Answer it, Momma," Zack said. "Might be something important."

Yes it might, I thought. But I didn't want to know what. "That's okay," I said. "They'll call back if it's really important."

"We're not doing what's normal today, Zack. Like Momma said." Ivy poked a barrette in my ear. "Sorry, Momma." I forgave her with a smile.

The rings began again. "They called back," Zack warned. I held out my hand and wiggled my fingers, body staying still not to disturb Ivy's handiwork. Zack handed me the phone, laughter on the television catching his attention. He moved to the recliner and draped on his belly over the arm to watch a cat stuck in a cookie jar.

"Hello?" I asked with hesitation.

"It's me." Wayne said, back on my planet.

"Are you okay?"

"Yeah." He did sound better. "Family deal. Not fixable, but it's as under control as crap can be."

"Is she okay?"

"Didn't say it was a she, but yes, I think so."

I read that message without needing an antenna. Might be the sister he wouldn't talk about, but the ex-wife felt more right. "You coming in tomorrow? I scheduled Jesse for Tuesday at the same time."

"Tomorrow afternoon. I want to brief the boss while I'm in town, hit a lick at a couple of other files, then we'll hoof it back down there. Nothing's happened, I hope."

He'd interrupted work for his family. Now I interrupted it for mine.

"Nothing at all," I said. "Let me go. I'm in the middle of something."

I handed the hung up phone back to Zack.

"You're not doing anything, Momma," he said, eavesdropping.

"I'm getting my nails and hair done. What could be more important than that?"

We were the epitome of normal, and I might as well enjoy it while I could. Tomorrow, Wayne would strut back in calling the shots, tugging me away from anything that hinted of normal. All he wanted was a case. I'd about decided the beach was a hormonal blip for him, and I'd foolishly

Lowcountry Bribe

fallen for it. Guess that's why they called it a rebound.

CHAPTER 13

Monday, the agents arrived around two in the afternoon, waving at me, and feigning interest in the staff before docking in the spare office. Eddie stayed in Wayne's shadow, as if knowing better than to speak. Ten minutes after they arrived, they came into my office, pulled out chairs and sat.

"You remember what to say?" Wayne asked, his eyes cool. Eddie sat across the table, fingers interlaced on hands resting respectfully on my table.

How could I forget the drill we'd practiced so many times? "Engraved in my head, lawman."

The senior agent flaunted professional detachment. After an abbreviated overview of the rescheduled meeting for tomorrow, Wayne headed for the men's room and I cornered his rookie partner.

"What the hell's wrong with him? He's a different person."

Eddie rolled his eyes. "Somebody in his family pissed him off. He about sliced my jugular on the way home Friday, so I knew better than to ask questions this morning."

I went ahead and asked. "Is this girl his sister or his ex?"

"I didn't ask. He didn't volunteer."

Anne Marie held up the phone and waved it. "Mr. McRae on the line."

Eddie left for his office and I took the call, wondering what business the crooked-nosed devil wanted with me now. Once a month suited us ordinarily. Now I was his pet project. "What's up, Henry?"

"I'm coming by tomorrow. How's lunch time sound? Thought I'd try to catch up with your auditors while I was there."

"Um, might be a problem." There was a problem all right. "The day's booked tight. They're running out of time and want to start closing their audit."

"Why don't I come by early, then? We can have a working lunch—my treat."

He knew better than to buy lunch for an auditor. "We're leaving early and eating wherever we wind up. Can't this wait?" I asked.

He cleared his throat. "How about letting them speak for themselves."

"Hold on then." I ran into the guys' office. Wayne was back and looked up with nonchalance. "McRae is demanding to meet with you guys tomorrow," I said. "Preferably around lunch. *His treat.*"

"Which line?" Wayne asked, clipping his words.

"Two."

He hit the button and answered. "Largo here." His eyes slanted as he listened to McRae's attempt to squeeze himself in. "Tell you what. I'll call my boss and see if he can grant me another couple of days. I'll call you back if I can." Wayne hung up. "There."

"There what?" I asked.

"I don't call back. In the off chance he decides to drop in anyway, don't bother coming by here in the morning. Leave the government car at the motel tonight." He returned to his laptop.

I stood in the doorway, ignored. "Something wrong with your sister? Or Pamela?"

"We don't have time for this," he said, still studying the screen.

The brutality of his demeanor took me aback. "Time for what?"

"Anything other than the business at hand." He looked up. "Got any questions about Jesse? Those I'll answer."

"Hey, don't put yourself out. I've got plenty to do without you, too."

I turned and went back to my office, nails raking across my palms. I decided not to give a damn about him anymore either.

THE NEXT MORNING, we replayed the wire routine without the electricity between us. Without Eddie, too. He went ahead to the farm. The air was flat, Wayne's attitude miserable and introspective, his behavior barely reaching acceptable manners.

"What's wrong?" I asked.

"Nothing you need worry about," he replied gruffly, refusing to make eye contact.

"You sure? I'm sort of going out on a limb doing this meeting with Jesse. Can I trust you?"

With that, he straightened in his seat and glared. "And why wouldn't you?"

"You tell me."

"We're ready," he said, then tried to grin. "And I'm good. Let's go."

Wayne's wall remained guarded en route. He stared out the window, flashing a brief strained smile when he felt my glances on him. After this meeting, we'd have the goods on our man. Wayne, Eddie and I would go our separate ways. Like the last day of summer camp, we were tired of being here.

His cell rang. "Largo." After listening without comment, he covered the phone and annoyingly pointed to a gravel road. "Turn in here."

"This isn't the right road," I said, slowing.

"Please. Just do it."

I eased in, placing the car in park.

His attention returned to his caller. "What's the emergency, Pamela? I'm in the midst of something here. You've got sixty seconds."

Confirmation. The ex was still an itch.

"She doesn't want to be involved," he said. "You sure this isn't about us?" He listened and I pretended not to, staring at the cracks in the road's asphalt.

"So arrest her." He hung up and whispered, "Bitch."

I sat, awaiting orders, wanting to know the whole story as bad as I'd ever wanted sex or chocolate in my life. He faced out the passenger window, tension thick in the air.

"Wayne?"

Still glaring at the weeds, he waved toward the windshield, and I drove back onto the road.

"You okay?" I asked, picking up speed.

"Let's just do this, Slade."

At least he used my name again, but Jesse had culminated into an errand. "Well, I've tried nice, and you didn't bite, so now I'm going straight to the point. How about assuring me your mind's on my case and not some mess in Atlanta."

"I'm good," he said.

"So you said. Convince me, because I'm nervous about whether you've got your act together."

"I won't let anything happen that shouldn't."

"Didn't stop you from abandoning me last time." My attention roamed from the road to him, trying to understand his mental state. We passed the farm entrance next door to the Williams' place.

"This isn't exactly the time or place, but I'm sorry," he said. "I'm wrong to take anything out on you. You've been a trooper."

I didn't buy his game face.

"Don't worry," he continued. "This'll be over before you know it."

We arrived thirty minutes early, from the direction Jesse would expect. Wayne slid low in his seat as I turned in. The worn drive took us through the yellow, weedy fields straight to the barn. I focused my energies toward what to say and how to say it.

"Eddie is right over there." Wayne pointed at the top of the hill near a familiar thicket. I couldn't see the Impala. "He'll man the receiver. I'll listen in."

He called Eddie on his cell phone and told him to be ready when Jesse appeared. Then he patted my arm and eased out of the car, losing himself in the barn's shadows before I could say "focus."

I left the engine running and the radio volume on low, feeding my need for music and an easy escape.

Kudzu vines snaked up the back of the barn and halfway over the tin roof, offering cover where they entangled in the limbs of a few pin oaks. I craved knowing where to look for Wayne in the cover. That kudzu covered a lot of ground. The patch was forty or fifty feet away—might as well be a mile if Jesse decided to get weird. A wariness filled me in spite of my attempt to will it away. What if Jesse didn't have the money? What if this meeting was for other reasons?

Daddy would kick my butt if he knew I was doing this. Suddenly I wanted to call the whole thing off. Wayne's head wasn't on straight, and I felt exposed as hell.

A katydid hopped on my windshield and crawled down to the wiper blade, then jumped off into the grass. A C-17 aircraft crawled into the clouds from the local Air Force base, and I remembered when my master sergeant daddy let me go inside one when I was in grade school.

Movement in my peripheral vision shifted my attention to a dust cloud just off the highway. I straightened my shirt and spoke into the microphone. "Someone's coming." Speaking into my boobs made me feel oddly protected.

Sure enough, Jesse's white pickup bounced up the gravel drive, shocks older than my graduation gown. Window down, elbow hanging out and a cigarette butt in his lips, he cruised up to my car, stopped and threw the truck into park with a clunk. The heap coughed and shut off.

Ren peered over from the passenger seat, across his brother.

It took a concerted effort to begin my performance and go against the grain of everything I'd ever learned. Nothing felt natural, making it doubly hard to act the lie.

Grabbing the envelope with the papers, I stepped out, leaving the car door wide open, a trick I'd learned from collecting delinquent payments from drunk and irate borrowers. I walked to where I thought Wayne had told me to stand, but I couldn't find the rock I'd seen when we walked through rehearsal last week. Damn. Was I in the wrong spot? Could Wayne see me? God, how I wanted to look over my shoulder and see him nod and tell me I was doing this right. No wonder he didn't want me to know his location.

Jesse remained in the truck, wearing his business-only hounds-tooth coat. "Ms. Slade," he drawled. "Welcome to my office." He made Ren open the passenger door. "Come on in and have a seat. I brought you a coke."

"Brought you a coke," said Ren.

The envelope crinkled in my sweaty grip. "I'd prefer to stand."

Jesse turned the side view mirror toward him and stretched his face, scratching his nose. His cap sat on the dash. "You got the papers?"

"You got the money?" I spoke as if throwing my voice to the kudzu.

"Show her, Ren."

The brother held up an envelope. He drew out a handful of bills, waving them with a smile. "See?" he said. Some of the bills dropped from his grasp, and he leaned over, out of sight.

"I need to see some papers now," Jesse said, watching his brother.

I slipped my hand inside the manila envelope. "Let me explain these documents to you." I moved toward the truck so he could see.

Jesse nodded to Ren who dropped off the seat to the ground, like a ten-year-old. The simple brother held the door like a denim-and-plaid-clad chauffeur, peering up at me, through the truck cab, grinning as if he'd practiced for a recital. Jesse threw him a peppermint.

Ignoring Ren, I extracted the deed from the envelope and leaned toward Jesse's window. "Now this document—"

"Get in or we don't deal."

The F word sat on the tip of my tongue, but I remembered the wire. "Then we don't deal," I replied, hoping I played the right move as a partner in crime. But then I regretted my words. If he drove off, this case was done. Much ado about nothing, leaving me alone to manage a pissed off farmer.

"I have the money right here," he said. "And it's better to sign papers out of the wind. What's up with you?"

"Nothing," I said.

"You sure?"

With every ounce of me screaming "don't do it," I walked around the front of the truck and stepped on the running board to slide in and bring this meeting to a fast conclusion. Then I stopped, Wayne's warning to stay outside the truck pinging in my head. So I strode to the truck's hood and laid out my papers, leaning on them for effect . . . and to keep them from blowing away.

I patted the hood once. "Come on, Jesse. Quit messing around, and let's do this."

He frowned and opened his door. Soon he stood to my right. Ren rubbed up against my other side. Moving away from him put me closer to Jesse, so I chose to remain nearer the lesser brother. Ren's stare remained glued on me, somewhat glazed, his smile stuck in one position.

Jesse's lust-filled leer, however, snaked over me. A shiver caught me by surprise as I smelled the splash of cheap cologne on him, telling me he wanted more than paper.

He reached over, grabbed my lapel and jerked me toward him. Ren leaned in more, his left arm resting on the hood.

I shoved Jesse away. "I told you before, keep your damned hands off me."

He frowned. "I was just closing up your jacket so's you wouldn't catch your death."

"Bullshit. Pay attention to business. The title is straight now. Sign here and here. You'll have a loan on the books. I altered the appraisal so you're getting it for eighty percent less than market value."

His head reared back. "I gotta pay for this place? Why can't you just give it to me?"

Ren tapped my arm. I turned and he said, "Gotta pay?" His eyebrow raised like his brother's, only his was sprinkled heavy with dandruff.

"Um," I turned back toward Jesse. "Because I have to show a loan for the place or a cash sale. Obviously you don't have the money. If you can't pay the loan, I'll restructure it. You understand how that works." Jesse paid on some emergency loans still on the books from drought years long past. Our rules allowed us latitude in reworking payments for those with unfortunate circumstances. Some farmers took more advantage of the government's loopholes than others.

He cocked his head, as if proud of a new idea. "You've got a good job. How much you got in the bank?"

"What's that got to do with anything?"

"I bet you it's all in your husband's name. That's why you're willing to do this." He laughed mockingly. Then he wrinkled his nose and brow. "Or you might be a greedy bitch."

Finish this, Slade. "Anyway, downstream when you can't pay, I can write off part of the debt. That's the best I can do."

He studied my face for an uncomfortably long moment. "I guess that's fair. So here's something for you, ma'am." He reached for the brown envelope in Ren's hand. "You know you could just put that money on my debt and make me look downright legitimate."

"Thought you said you were paying me for the paper." Inside lay a stack of hundred dollar bills. "This doesn't look like five thousand."

He shrugged one shoulder. "That's because it ain't."

I didn't want to touch the bills. Didn't want my fingerprints on the paper. "How much is it?"

"Three."

I held the envelope to my chest and tapped it on my jacket pretending to contemplate a plan. Then I yanked it away, remembering not to inhibit the transmission from my wire.

Jesse treated this deal like he did his loans, promises half kept, thinking he had enough charisma to carry him the rest of the way. Out here, however, I could afford to get pissed about it. "Papers shred easily, and no one knows about 'em but you and me." I almost sounded like

Jesse. I could envision Wayne shaking his head to my ad-lib.

But Jesse didn't think twice. "The last one that backed out on me, well, let's just say he regretted it. But I see you're a lady who likes to play. I wish I'd dealt with you before, but you wasn't in charge then. Patience pays off, huh?"

My brashness melted as I caught the reference to Mickey.

Jesse's features lightened. "In case you get a prick of conscience, just remember your kids. You got no man at your house."

"Uhn-uh. No man," echoed Ren.

I closed my eyes for a moment to collect myself.

"I see you understand," Jesse said.

Anger whipped through me. "I'll kill you if you even think about touching them."

Jesse waved his hand. "Been tried before." Then he leaned toward me like he wanted to make sure his words recorded crisp and clear on tape. "You'll get more money when you're through doing what you're supposed to. If you don't, I'll say you pressured me for those bucks instead."

"My word against yours, Jesse, and mine carries more weight." Then as an afterthought. "You came to me first, remember."

"We'll see who McRae believes," he said.

He knew my boss, and now Wayne heard him say so. "You don't get the finished papers without the money," I said.

"Sure I will, but I'll give you some money anyway. Just call me honest." He chuckled. "Let me know, and I'll come in like a good little farmer and pretend we did this by the book. Shake hands and be buddies for all the world to see. Everybody loves me."

"Are we through here?" I waved my hand for Ren to step away. He stumbled back. I moved away from the truck toward my car. Slowly. My means to escape getting closer. Breath held, I counted my steps.

"Wait a minute, Slade. Let's shake on it," Jesse shouted.

I stopped five feet from my vehicle, my getaway so close. "No."

He strode over and blocked my path. I backed away, bumping into Ren, of course. Cigarette butt twisted into the dirt with a boot, Jesse wiped his hand on his coat and reached to shake to the deal. So mannerly, so commonplace, such an easygoing country boy image. I'd once thought of him as the embodiment of small-time agriculture, the type of person I loved to help stay on the family farm.

I held my palm out in stop-sign fashion. He grasped it firmly with a calloused hand. With a snap of his arm, he yanked me against his chest, my arm pinned behind me.

He planted lips on mine, his tongue capitalizing on the short moment he had to taste me. Tobacco-flavored saliva oozed into my mouth.

He drew back. "Let's consummate this deal." He rubbed my breast not an inch from the wire. His two dollar cologne clashed on a ridiculous scale with the mustiness of the old coat and the manure on his boots.

I twisted away from him. "Not if you want this farm."

"I'll get it one way or another."

Without thinking, my knee jerked up into his crotch like Daddy taught me to do. A move I never thought I'd use.

"You bitch!" he yelled, doubling over, almost toppling.

"The only consummation you'll see is the title recorded in the courthouse," I said, gritting my teeth. "And don't ever threaten my children again."

Adrenaline kicked in harder. Seeing him handicapped empowered me, and I wondered how to kick the man without him grabbing my foot, or Ren jumping in to help.

Then Jesse laughed.

A hint of fear crept in as I sensed the unexpected.

"Didn't see that coming," he said, and laughed again, raising back up to his full height. "No sirree, didn't think you had it in you, Ms. Slade. Cold shower for me tonight." His chuckles continued through his grimace as he recovered.

What had I done? This wasn't some stranger in an alley. Jesse knew where I worked and where I lived. He wasn't going away anytime soon.

He bolted up and shoved me against my car. "Okay, lady. We're good, but I'll take a rain check on that tight little body until the papers are filed." He clicked his tongue, winked and pointed at me. The move that gave me chills. Then he turned back to his truck.

Ren baby-stepped toward me, his mouth puckered for a kiss of his own, emulating his brother.

"No, Ren," I said, allowing him a judgment error, but unwilling to let him touch me. He kept coming, this time reaching. One hand latched onto my sleeve. "Let go," I said, holding out a straight arm to his chest. "I don't want to hurt you, too."

"Ren? What're you doing?" Jesse hit his door with a fist, the bang echoing on the old metal, like seeking an animal's attention. "Get in the truck. Ms. Slade ain't in the mood today."

Ren smiled, but when I didn't return the gesture, a scowl clouded his face.

Jesse started the engine. "I'm leaving you, man, if you don't get in." His door creaked with a pop as the hinge succumbed to closing. His brother shuffled to the passenger side and crawled in, the pout still stuck on his mouth.

Jesse leaned out and spat on the ground. "Lookin' forward to a phone call—say in three days? Maybe next time we'll do dinner. My treat."

He shoved his truck into gear. "Leave that knee at home."

The hundred-yard road went on forever, the billowing dust adding another layer to a tailgate already primed with dirt. He reached the highway and turned right, the direction toward his farm.

I flopped into my car seat. The envelope fell to the floor when a wave of stomach cramps hit me. I raked my tongue across the sleeve of my coat to get the taste of Jesse out of my mouth.

Wayne entered the car. He put the cash-filled envelope in an evidence bag, sealed it and stuffed it in his coat pocket. "Come closer. I need the mike."

He formally signed off the taped conversation. I swished a mouthful of bottled water and spat it out the window.

"I'm through," I said. "Completely done with this crap."

"Oh, we're not completely through," he said, humor tinged with demand. "Now we get him indicted, pick him up and—"

With complete command, I leaned in his face. "Get out of my car."

His head rocked back a few inches, brow raised.

"You can take your personal problems, your badge and your authoritarian attitude, stuff them in your Glock and shoot your brains out." I twisted the cap back on the empty water bottle and held it by the neck, wishing it were his. "Pack your arsenal up and high-tail it back to Atlanta, lawman. Today."

He dialed his phone, pointed it at me then raised it to his ear. "Settle down. You're in this for the long haul."

I was sick of these oral competitions. "No, I'm not."

Wayne hung up and dialed again. "That's odd. Eddie's not answering his phone."

I squeezed the bottle. "Maybe he's fed up with you, too."

"Get off your high horse for one damn moment, would you? I'm serious," he said. "I can't get Eddie."

CHAPTER 14

I started the car, shuddering with thoughts of Jesse's hands and mouth on me. Wayne repeatedly tried raising Eddie on his cell. The junior agent's hiding place sat near a stand of white oaks on the ridge facing the barn. Took us minutes to reach the spot.

"Eddie," Wayne shouted, as we got out of the car. "Let's wrap it up, man."

He walked slowly, so I slowed behind him. Since he was searching the area carefully, I did, too.

Wayne eased out his Glock.

My gut flipped against my rib cage. "What's wrong?"

He held up his hand for me to wait. I hushed and darted to the right behind a large oak. If this was Eddie's idea of a joke, I'd slap him out of his size thirteen boots. I already itched to belt Wayne.

The woods remained oddly silent, without a bird twitter. Wayne crept silently over pine needles and yellow oak leaves toward the Impala. He scanned around the car. The driver's side faced us, the door slightly ajar. He bolted to the opening.

"Slade, get over here!"

Eddie slumped sideways on the seat, blood splatters on his white shirt. A rivulet of crimson trickled from his left ear. Wayne felt for a pulse, reached into his pocket and tossed me his cell. He shifted Eddie's bulky frame to the passenger side of the car. I juggled the phone, almost dropping it while dialing 911.

"Tell them we're carrying a twenty-four year-old black male with head trauma—unconscious," he said. "What's the nearest hospital?"

"St. Francis."

"Tell them I'm driving him in."

I crawled into the backseat. Before I could inform the operator, Wayne spun the car around and headed up the dirt road. With a phone in one hand, I held onto the door handle with the other. The speedometer bounced around a hundred. Wayne yelled at Eddie, telling him nonstop that he'd be okay.

"Wayne," I yelled over his barking to Eddie. "Did we get the tape?"

"The whole damn recorder's gone, Slade. There is no tape."

Jesse was on to us. I flipped open the phone and hit automatic dial three but some woman answered, "U.S. Attorney's Office."

"Shit," I said disconnecting. My cell remained in my car, with my purse.

The car turned onto Highway 17, and I rebalanced myself. Then I dialed again.

"What are you doing?" Wayne asked in a tight, controlled tone, both hands white-knuckling the wheel.

"I've got to call the school, damn it. To check on my kids."

"Now?" he yelled, his voice angry. He turned to Eddie as if enlightening me what was important. "Stay with me, buddy."

The school secretary answered. I commanded her to scramble to both classrooms, confirm by sight the kids were safe and prepare them to be picked up by my parents. Then I called home, shouting for my father to retrieve them.

Jesse rambled pompous and devious all over the county now, happy we'd been duped. I wasn't going to wait for the menace to show up again on my doorstep.

We covered twenty-five miles in fifteen long minutes. The car screeched to a halt under the hospital canopy. Eddie mumbled from the gurney as they rolled him away. I stood staring at the swinging doors, adrenaline coursing through my system.

"Come on. Let's go inside," I said, trying to will myself calm.

Wayne didn't move. He dragged his hands down his face. "I'm responsible for him."

His world had collapsed, but the obvious needed to be said. "Jesse's obviously not working alone."

Wayne's painful stare took me aback. "I should have made contingencies."

"You can't foresee everything," I said, resting a hand on a bicep.

"That's my damn job," he yelled.

I hushed, telling myself not to get upset. I held it together for him for a change.

"It should've been so simple," he said.

Yes, it should have been. We'd underestimated Jesse. "Do I understand this right? We're back to my word against his?"

"No, it's *our* word against his."

An ambulance drove up, and we stepped aside.

"Listen," he said, his face drawn. "I've got to call Atlanta. Would you please find us some coffee? Come get me if they come out with news about Eddie." Like I needed caffeine to jolt a system barely bridled to sanity.

Returning with two cups, I found Wayne seated in a corner, speaking on his cell. I stepped away and leaned against the wall across the room, watching cable news television. Surely the powers-that-be would understand. Things go wrong.

When I glanced over, Wayne's body language was stiff and awkward. Someone was serving him a serious ration of shit.

EDDIE REMAINED in St. Francis hospital, the doctors uncertain about the extent of his injuries. He had no short-term memory or balance. At minimum, a concussion.

OIG headquarters in Atlanta ordered Wayne to return immediately. After we retrieved my car from the farm and searched the area for the slim chance of finding the recorder, we met at the motel. Street lights blinked on here and there. The day aged into night, almost over. Our troubles weren't.

Wayne tossed his clothes into a suitcase.

"How long do they put a case on hold in situations like this?" I asked, trying to control the fear that had been threatening to rise up and beg him to stay.

He grunted. "Have no clue."

He was abandoning me again. "That's fine for you."

"What does that mean?" he said, pausing with a shirt in hand.

"Jesse's coming after *me*, not you."

He laid the shirt on top and closed the suitcase. "I have orders. I'll straighten things out with Atlanta and get back as soon as I can. On the way out of town, I'll stop at the sheriff's office and file a report about the stolen recorder, and talk to them about protecting you and the kids."

He rattled off his plans like they were ingredients in a recipe for cinnamon buns. His promise didn't assure me. "I live in the next county, lawman. Different sheriff, different police department in Ridgeville." Alarm rang loud and clear in my voice. I was vulnerable. We both knew it, and I could no longer pretend it wasn't true. How dare he leave now?

Wayne reached out and gripped my shoulders. "Listen. It'll be okay."

"How can you say that?" I pulled away from his hands. "Jessie just attacked a federal agent. What's to keep him from coming after me or my kids next?"

"We don't know it was Jessie."

I just looked at him, not believing he'd even voiced that.

"Okay," he said. "You're right. I'm sure Jessie had something to do with it. But all eyes are on him now. Coming after you would be a really stupid move. He's going to lay low for a while."

"You don't know that."

"If I didn't believe we had some time here, Slade, I wouldn't leave. But we have to regroup, and if I don't report, I have no badge. Then I'll be unable to help you."

A fat lump stuck in my throat. "This is all wrong. All of you have dumped on me." God, I sounded like such a victim, not my way at all.

He studied me. "I'm also going to call that deputy."

"What deputy?"

"James, Donald James. The guy who handled your dog."

The guy's Barney Fife appearance didn't instill confidence in me. Nice, yes. A dynamic mass of brawn against Jesse? Not in my craziest imagination. I tried to swallow the emotion still building in my throat. "What can he do?"

Wayne rested his hand on my hair, then let it slide down to my shoulder. "He can be aware. I'll give him your number and ask him to drive by your house a few times a day. I spoke to him about the dog incident when it happened, and warned him about Jessie. That will give you a direct number to someone nearby who understands your danger." He hesitated a moment, then picked up his suitcase and headed out to his car.

I followed, thinking maybe he was right. Maybe things would be okay for a few days. "So I just wait?"

"I'll call you as soon as I know what's going on." He loaded his suitcase into the trunk, then turned to me again. "I'm not forgetting you. Surely you know better."

"No, I don't." Again, I fought down the panic.

"Listen. Go stay with someone. Your parents." He shut his trunk and opened the driver's door to leave, then paused and moved toward me . . .

Instinctively I stepped back, trust, loyalty, desire . . . all of it gone.

He closed the distance between us and hugged me anyway. "Please be careful."

My arms started to respond in kind, but I held back.

"Goddamn it," he whispered as he walked away. "I'll get back as soon as I can." He got in his car, his face older than the one I'd met barely two weeks ago, and drove out of the parking lot, not looking back.

Alone in a crisis, inadvertently of my own making, I drove toward home. No Wayne, no Eddie, no Alan and no protection from Jesse. The local police held nothing to use against Jesse, and I wasn't stupid enough to expect them to watch me around the clock because of a botched federal operation.

Five miles from home, my cell rang. I didn't recognize the number other than it was local. I tentatively answered. "Hello?"

"Ms. Slade, this is Deputy Donald James. Just wanted you to have my number in case you need me. Senior Special Agent Wayne Largo asked me to check up on you periodically."

His forced bravado and use of Wayne's mile-long official title would be cute under other circumstances, like a kid cleaning the board for his favorite student teacher. "I appreciate that Mr. James."

"Call me Donald, ma'am. Don't be afraid to contact me. Better I handle any trouble than you."

"Um, thanks, Donald."

The deputy was eager, but his fervent assurances didn't remedy my stabbing fears. Driving to my parents', I couldn't contain the negative thoughts. The agents would say this wasn't my fault; Alan would say it was; and Jesse would enjoy the show and wait for an opening to get his due. No telling what my parents would think.

Did Jesse know we'd set him up all along? Of course he did. Jesse or his accomplice didn't just walk up on Eddie.

That night, my sister, parents and I established a schedule of carrying the kids to and from school and ballgames. We threatened the school within an inch of the principal's life not to deviate from the plan. Ivy cancelled a sleepover, and Zack attended ball practice accompanied by at least two relatives.

For the next couple of days, I altered my route to work and arrived whenever I felt like it.

On Friday, Wayne called me at the house. "How are you holding up?" he asked.

His voice mule-kicked me as I stood in the middle of the kitchen preparing the kids for school. I shooed them to get their shoes and bags. "What's happening?" I whispered.

"I've only got a minute," he said. "Meet me at the Waffle House in West Columbia tomorrow. The one off of I-20. Can you get a sitter?"

The argumentative side of me withered. Only logic made sense at this point, minus any emotion. My old sense of preservation returned, chastising my interim bout of impotence. "I'll be there."

"Good."

"Are you okay?"

"I'll live. We've got to talk." He hung up.

DADDY HAD RECEIVED the abridged edition of the investigation's events the day of Eddie's attack, but when I asked him to babysit so I could meet Wayne, he demanded more. His annoyance wasn't directed at me, but it was unpleasant nonetheless. When I recognized his dilemma over whether to accompany me to Columbia or protect the kids, I removed the burden. I told him Mom didn't need to be left alone with his grandchildren while he was a hundred miles away in Columbia. Daddy loaned me his Jeep to avoid detection.

The drive passed quickly with so many worries to choose from.

Three days had passed since the farm incident. I couldn't sleep. Whether he knew it or not, Jesse held me under his thumb.

While I doubted anyone would recognize me at a Waffle House, I still wore shades and pinned up my hair.

As I walked in, grease, maple syrup and coffee odors hung in the air amidst silverware clinking and the sizzling of a griddle. The diner's early morning crowd gone, the lunch mob hadn't found its way in yet.

A heavyset man perched at the counter, his butt overflowing the stool. His ball cap sat atop stringy hair peppered with white. I guessed he was the owner of the semi-rig outside. He gave me a nose to toe scan and winked.

Wayne sat in a booth in the rear, his coffee steaming in a thick white ceramic mug.

He stood as I slid in the booth and tucked my glasses in my bag. His million-dollar smile was missing, a buck-fifty model in its place. "How you doing, loan lady?"

I adopted an upbeat expression. "I'm holding it together. How's Eddie?"

"He's fine. Another week or two and he'll be back. The bastard who cold-cocked him didn't crack that thick skull of his. He can recall bits now, but he didn't see who clobbered him."

"You think it was McRae?"

"I'd like to confirm where he was when Eddie got attacked."

"Coffee?" asked a middle-aged waitress as she turned over the empty cup. She snatched her order pad from a taut, white apron and extracted a pencil from behind her ear.

"Thanks," I said. "Black."

"Sure thing, sweetie. Anything else?"

"Just toast, please." Pencil back behind her ear, the waitress marched off yelling my order in code to the fry cook.

"You look thinner," Wayne said.

"Fear does that. So what's up with Atlanta?"

"They're removing me from the case."

He paused, and my stomach tightened, awaiting the second half of his message.

"They're going to investigate you," he said.

Surely I'd heard him wrong.

He dropped his chin, searching. "Did you hear me? The IG is going to investigate your involvement with Jesse."

I was still waiting to hear a but . . . an explanation as to why I didn't need to worry. "Guess I shouldn't have trusted you after all."

His facial muscles drew tight. He sat back in his seat. "They've placed me on leave until they complete their internal investigation, pending disciplinary action."

The weight on his shoulders now mirrored mine. I regretted my sassy retort but wondered where the heck this predicament left me. "Idiots like Jesse have to upset the best of plans sometimes," I said. "Surely you don't solve every case?"

He sighed heavy, fingering the corner of his napkin. "You took money from a farmer. I screwed up. That's all they see."

This outfit cannibalized their own as well as crucified my kind. The myths about badges were truer than I'd imagined.

"My boss has never liked me or my methods," he said after downing the last of his coffee. "He doesn't have a clue how to handle detective work, since he came from an audit background. A pencil geek. He's come after me twice." He stopped for a few seconds and set down his cup. "They reckon I exposed Eddie and jeopardized the case."

"I don't get it. What could you have done differently?"

"In my best judgment, we acted appropriately. But the whole field meeting concept didn't set well with headquarters."

But a crime remained unsolved. "There're two bad guys and an attempted bribe of a Federal official still on the table."

"Listen," he said. His deep inhale told me to get a grip. "Someone called and complained about us. About a relationship."

The cup in my hand tipped coffee onto the table before I righted it. "What?"

"Both Atlanta and the US Attorney's office are discrediting me as a witness. I'm sorry, Slade. I take all the blame. Both you and Eddie behaved as I directed, which compromised you both."

Had someone followed us to the beach? Had our energies been too obvious? Maybe McRae muddied the waters from the start.

"Can they do that? I mean, can they kill a legitimate investigation like that because of some gossip?"

He shrugged. "Absolutely. You and I'd be the key witnesses for the prosecution. A fling could plant enough doubt in a jury to land an acquittal. The US Attorney's office doesn't take anything they can't win. They're backlogged."

"So, who called them?" Being around a snitch I couldn't identify was like being a hen in a snake-infested coop. Eventually, one of them was going to strike . . . again.

"Don't know." He plucked napkins from the dispenser and wiped up my spill. "My biggest concern is you."

As it should be. I'd called the IG. They'd swooped in, screwed things up and were now leaving without so much as a tip of their hats.

I licked dry lips. "I won't lie to you. I'm petrified. I don't know why Jesse hasn't come after me yet. Or the kids."

"I know."

Did he? Really? His issues resided in Atlanta now. I might never even see him again. Jesse might barge in and have his way with me at any time. I thought about baiting him, blowing him away and claiming self-defense, but from what I'd learned about the law lately, they'd just as likely arrest me for killing a poor defenseless hog farmer who worried about the cost of feed.

My job would fall next. I didn't even care what people thought anymore. How would I feed my children? Crap, *keep* my children?

"So what do I do, Wayne? What the hell do I do?"

"I'm not sure."

He'd led me into this, and now he didn't know? He was the damn cop. I stiffened and then whispered, spitting the words. "Your 'cooperating individual' has jumped through hoops for you and been dumped on the side of the road like some unwanted cur dog. You aren't allowed not to have answers."

His eyes narrowed. "You aren't the only one who's sacrificed, Slade."

I threw myself back against the seat. "Don't talk to me about sacrifice." My throat constricted, breaths turned difficult.

Wayne reached over and put his hand on mine. "I understand you're scared . . . and I wish I could make it all go away."

I laughed once. "Like at the beach? When you promised you'd take care of me for being such a good, noble individual?"

His tongue worked inside his cheek as he held words in check.

"So when are they sending me another agent?" I asked. "They'll probably send a greenhorn, or someone they dump the trashy cases on." I sipped coffee to avoid crying and tried not to look in those gray eyes. I couldn't think straight.

"They've closed Jesse's case."

I nearly choked. "What?"

"They believe there *isn't* a case. Didn't you hear me? They believe too much has been compromised to make it stick in court, regardless of the agent."

"What about McRae? You came to Charleston more for him than Jesse."

"It was my idea to study McRae in addition to Jesse. Since I'm out of the picture, they aren't interested."

"And the money?" I asked. "You took three thousand dollars with you. Where did they think that came from?"

"They look at that as one of his payments. Where would Jesse say the money came from if he were asked? His own hogs. They're going to tell you to put the money on his loan."

I shook my head. "Jesse won't be able to prove his sales." Jesse's and my most common argument was livestock count and maintaining books.

"They aren't going to question a farmer who wants to pay on his debt, Slade. They're more likely to question why you tried to hide hog sales *from* the record. They'll wonder even more why you met with him, collected money and didn't assume it was a payment."

"But he executed documents," I said a bit too loud. "We have his signatures!"

"Slade. Think. He'll say you made him sign them. How could he refuse when you offered him such fantastic terms? They're building a case against us."

The same doubt that hovered the day Jesse offered the bribe, resurfaced with new vigor. What if someone didn't believe me? Now they didn't. Of course they didn't.

"I know, I know," Wayne said. "Let me deal with Atlanta, then I'll be back as soon as I can. Two days, three tops."

"You're leaving me again. That's marvelous."

"I shouldn't be here now, Slade." He clenched his fist then opened it, two fingers pinched together. "I'm this close to being terminated. We're both screwed if I have no badge. Do you get it now?"

I hitched a breath. He was right. "You could really lose your job?"

"I could lose my sister, too," he said, head hung low.

He said the word sister so painfully. I didn't know how to ask who, what, or why. I drank my coffee with both hands, because one would shake the cup.

His head didn't move for the longest time.

"Wayne? Is your sister the reason we rescheduled the meeting with Jesse?"

"Yes," he said almost indiscernibly to the table.

"And?"

He remained still. "And she's a coke addict. Or used to be. And she's involved in a deal with DEA that just might get her killed. And my goddamn ex-wife had a hand in it. My agency knows all about it, which doesn't make my predicament any better."

"Oh, Jesus."

"Yeah." His gaze held no warmth.

I was on my own, a selfish but realistic conclusion. Wayne couldn't cover all the people in his life, including himself. He'd tried up to now and failed. I couldn't be at work and at home at the same time to protect everybody no more than Wayne could be in Atlanta and Charleston.

The waitress put the toast in front of me and asked if I needed anything, but I couldn't get past the finality of Wayne's message. No matter how I looked at the situation, I was screwed.

"Sweetie, you okay?" she asked.

"Bring her some orange juice," Wayne said.

The woman waddled quickly behind the counter and returned with a tall glass of juice.

"Want me to get Josh to whip up an omelet for her? Maybe some pancakes?"

Wayne smiled. "No thanks. Appreciate the offer. We're good now." She left and moved down two more tables, glancing back to make sure I didn't faint or fall on the floor.

Wayne rubbed the arm of my sweater. "We're going to get through this, Slade. I'll drive down later this week. I'm not leaving you hanging. I'm trying to do damage control so we can contain this disaster, maybe even nail Jesse. You understand?" He held my hands.

All I heard was "trying" and "maybe." But I couldn't afford to believe in him now. Someone assumed Slade was now cornered, beaten and scared. Hell yes, I was frightened, but seated in a Waffle House on Sunset Boulevard I declared no one would make me suddenly disappear in some creek or blow my brains out.

Numb with visions of imminent catastrophe, I left Wayne seated at the small diner and drove toward Ridgeville. McRae was an unknown quantity now. Jesse would be angry I'd betrayed him. If I lost my job, Alan would campaign to take custody of Zack and Ivy. I wasn't sure Wayne could save his own hide, much less mine. And while I was sorry for his sister, right now I couldn't afford to give her a place in my world of worry without losing grip of something precious of my own.

CHAPTER 15

On Monday, I arrived at the office on time for a change. Tardiness would have fueled more criticism from McRae. A snitch resided right here under my nose, and she didn't need another reason to rat on me. During the staff meeting, I doled out duties. Ann Marie wrote furiously, nervous and scatterbrained. Jean glared at me from the corner of her eye, and Hillary concentrated her pissy stare in the middle of my forehead like it would laser a hole through my brain.

"It's been ugly around here lately," I began, calm words masking anxiety. "If I snap, I don't mean to. I have a lot on my mind." I took a long pull of hot coffee, craving one of Daddy's bourbons, even at eight in the morning. "Hope you understand I need you guys." I needed them to watch my back, not stab it. My eyes met each individual, one by one. Only Ann Marie held the look.

A customer walked in the front door, interrupting the awkwardness. I adjourned the meeting, and the vacated chairs reminded me of how alone I really was.

I wasn't sure how long this charade could last. The lack of mutual trust within these walls would erode us. We'd clash again and again until someone folded. When that happened, I'd be transferred, disciplined, or worse.

A clean day on the appointment calendar gave me ample time to work quietly and alone, escape for a while. I told Ann Marie to keep my schedule clear, but a minute later, she buzzed a call through.

"Mr. Largo on the line, Slade."

I grabbed the phone, missing his guidance, craving somebody on my side. "Wayne?"

"It's me, baby." Jesse laughed on the other end.

A sharpness pierced my chest hard enough for me to grab my shirt. He'd disguised himself as Wayne, evidence my henhouse snake still thrived.

"How's the deal coming along, sugar?"

My thoughts short-circuited, and words dissolved. Jesse knew everything.

"Hey. I know you ain't got nobody there now, so why aren't you talking?" He laughed again.

"Who else would be here, Jesse?"

"You do think I'm a hayseed, don't you?"

My voice came out raspier than I wanted. "What do you want?"

"I paid you. The deal's still on. Just making sure you understand." The line went dead.

I punched Wayne's number in my cell. He'd supervised so many of Jesse's calls that I instinctively sought his assurance. But what could he do?

I hung up. If I didn't come through for Jesse, my family would pay the price. Yet fulfilling the deal confirmed to the feds that I was Jesse's willing partner. Either way, I was done.

"What a surprise." Hillary's voice amplified in the outer office, happy to see someone come in. The swinging door at the counter creaked. "What brings you to town?" Her tittering could only mean one thing.

McRae's loud and scripted reply made my skin prickle. "Need to chat with Slade. How's it going around here?"

I remained seated and quiet, listening. It would be too much to ask of fate for this to be a loan visit. My fists clenched and relaxed, twice. I slowly counted to ten.

"Slade's busy with the auditors all the time, so it's hard to get much done," Hillary said, then she lowered her voice. "Then there are her *personal* issues."

My mechanical pencil filled in the holes of all the eights on my desk calendar, waiting for McRae to make his way to my office. He took pleasure in the delay, knowing I could hear him.

"Jean?" he asked. "How're you doing?"

"Working hard, sir. Too many disruptions." Strike two.

His attention turned to Ann Marie as he neared my door. "You don't look so chipper this morning."

"Just busy." Thank goodness for one loyal fan.

McRae stepped across my threshold and closed the door. *Good.* My ass chewing didn't need an audience and neither did my retorts.

His intimidation meter seemed charged to capacity from the animated strut in his step. He walked to the table in front of my desk, laid down his briefcase, pulled out a chair and sat. His long manicured fingers unfastened the one jacket button, then he crossed his legs. I turned to my computer, hands on the keyboard, trying to ignore his bravado.

"Give me a sec," I said, "and I'll have your figures for you." No way I'd sit like a deer in his crosshairs.

"Forget the reports. Let's talk." He extracted a pen from his coat pocket. "I have a few things to cover, manager to manager."

IQ and intelligence mean nothing when the boss thinks he has something on you.

His smoothness indicated he thought me overcome, ready to rope and tie. I prepared to parlay, trusting my instincts still held an edge after the past week's adventures. During normal times, I outmaneuvered him slicker than a weasel on a mud bank. But these weren't normal times.

"Director Edmonds called me last night," he said.

The federal government did not communicate after hours unless there was a hurricane, flash flood or act of war. For the big boss to call the little boss ranked pretty high on the crapper scale. "Is there a problem?" I asked, knowing he meant his remark to shock me.

"Atlanta's removed the *auditors* from Charleston. You are to have nothing more to do with either of those *agents*."

So he knew. And Edmonds knew. Great. That meant Hillary knew, which was as good as talk radio. By the end of the week, word would be out that I'd screwed both the agents and the farmers, probably asking payment from all four.

But somewhere in that pea-sized brain, McRae surely knew how close he'd come to being discovered in his real estate scheme. Federal agents slipping in on his home turf when he was up to his neck in illegal activity had to set off an alarm. Maybe he wondered what I knew. I doubted the IG called him, anyway. Why call a potential criminal target when they could intimidate the State Director?

"If they've been removed, then there shouldn't be a problem," I said.

He rested an elbow on my table, the other hand tapping his Bic on the surface. "It's best you do what I tell you. They're still considering action against you."

"Thank God you're not me, huh?"

What did "taking action" mean? My fingernails raked the arm rests on my chair, digging in until I felt pain in the quicks. I could be stubborn, too.

He sat erect and stared down his long, bent nose. "You've wasted everyone's time, compromised an investigation and endangered the life of an *agent*." The bastard knew nothing of what went down, but he milked his advantage for all it was worth.

I rested both elbows on the desk. "I compromised no one. Mr. Largo compromised no one."

"Speaking of Mr. Largo," he said, slurring out the name. "I understand there's a *thing* going on with you two."

"We've been completely professional. In no way did we endanger the case."

"Really?" He slid the word out in a teasing manner.

"Really," I mimicked. "Just like you and Hillary don't mingle work and . . . um, pleasure."

His grin slid off his face, like spit off a mirror.

Mine spread wider. "I followed the book in calling the IG, and you know it, Henry."

He sneered at my use of his first name. "You overreacted. I would've advised you differently and avoided this predicament. Face it, woman. You're behind on work, your staff has lost respect, and a poor sucker lies in a hospital thanks to you. And that doesn't count anything illegal you've done."

I tossed my hair. Feminine, but the gesture was as defiant as I could think of without running a letter opener through his sternum. "First, federal regulations do not let me call you when there's a bribery attempt. A righteous decision. Second, my staff is okay. Third, the agent is recuperating fine."

He tsked three times. "The impropriety of your actions may cost you. We'll know more in a couple of weeks."

"Impropriety? A word you know as well as the condom instructions on the side of the box in Hillary's nightstand."

His pen slammed on the paper. "Say it, Slade."

"Two things. One, you're the last person to talk down to me about impropriety in light of your affair with my assistant."

He didn't falter this time. "And the second?"

I'd run my mouth too fast. I was totally unfamiliar with the details on the McRae property scam. Using one of Wayne's pregnant pauses, I searched for words. "Fishing." The pinch hit remark was worth it from the stunned ignorance smeared across his face.

His eyes squinted. "What?"

"I know someone who saw you go fishing on government time." The man did have a penchant for striped bass, so I took a stab at the fact he'd abused his position to wet a line.

McRae snickered, even more confident than before.

Common sense told me to cut my losses. "So do I go home until something is decided, or do you need me to make your loans and help you keep your job?"

His lanky frame stood and hovered over my desk. "You'll fucking well stay here until you're told otherwise."

I acted properly rebuffed. "Stay here. Make loans. Got it."

He buttoned his coat with the exaggerated swagger of a guilty man. "Ms. Slade?"

"Mr. McRae?"

He rested a hip on the corner of my desk, after sliding files aside to make room for his long skinny hands. "Are we playing dirty now? "

I stood up, and he straightened. "No, we're playing fair—only the facts."

"We'll see. I'll be checking in more often . . . without notice." He shoved the chair back under the table and left without acknowledging Hillary's wooing smile. I gave him two minutes to clear the parking lot.

"Hillary? In my office, please." God, it was more fun ordering than being ordered.

She strutted in. "Yes?"

"Close the door. Don't bother sitting down," I said, taking my seat. "This won't take long."

She stood at attention in her black polyester slacks, then tried not to. She was tall enough to pull off a pants suit but could never accessorize. The necklace fell to her navel, over ruffles. Ick.

"I've had a belly-full of your pillow talk with McRae," I said. "You keep undermining me and you'll regret it faster than you can say, 'Do me again, Henry.'"

"You're in too much trouble to bother me, Slade."

"Don't be so sure. If I go down, I'll take you with me somehow."

Her face blanched.

"You know your job, Hillary, but your choice of men sucks. Think about what you're doing before selling yourself to McRae." I was a fool advising her, but I did it more to piss off Henry than anything else.

"Kiss my—"

"Watch it." I pointed my finger at her. "You don't want to be insubordinate to your boss."

Her face twisted, searching for words to hit me with without doing herself in.

"I'm on to you, Hillary. Now get out."

"Henry won't like this."

"What part of 'get out' didn't you understand?"

The woman left with her nose in the air.

I dropped my head, stretching the steel-knotted muscles in my neck. I had one more call to make.

Surely my position as State Director Edmonds' protégé still carried some weight. He'd been my confidante when Jesse propositioned me that fateful Friday. He promoted me to manager. He once said he wished he employed a dozen more like me.

"This is Slade. I just met with Henry McRae and thought you needed to be brought up to date."

He coughed lightly. "Did you two talk it out? I can't afford for that office to fall apart."

"He didn't want to talk about the office," I said. Tattling would make me look bad, so I launched into damage control. "This situation has totally blown out of proportion. We pursued this farmer for his bribery attempt and now the IG has dismantled the case as the result of some kind of internal office politics. Jesse Rawlings is an unsavory character,

Mr. Edmonds, and we can't let him off the hook."

"Who?" he asked.

"Jesse . . . Jesse Rawlings. The hog farmer who offered me the bribe. Has Atlanta briefed you?" Whether ignorant or apathetic, Edmonds' mental stutter didn't sound good at all. My mentor's formality distanced himself from me and the stink of a scandal. I'd seen him back-pedal and feign ignorance before . . . only with other employees.

"They're reviewing your actions to determine whether you wasted their time. So I'm waiting as instructed." He cleared his throat again. "I'm not too thrilled about aggravating the IG."

Then silence. Big bosses could do that to you. Intimidate you with nothing but dead air.

I drew spirals on my blotter since I couldn't pace. This was October and the thing was already tattooed into December. I wrote S-H-I-T in block letters as I talked, then outlined them over and over, wider and wider until they looked like pop art from a 1960's lunchbox.

"Sir, if they don't deal with this farmer, not only will we have further problems with him, but my life is in danger."

"Haven't you exaggerated enough, Ms. Slade? What bothers me more is they consider you a partner to this Jesse's plans. I heard something about him giving you money."

I dug the pen into the blotter. "Of course he gave me money. That was the whole point—to make him come across with the money in exchange for a deal."

"Stop, Slade. I don't want to know. Let's see what Atlanta does and take it from there. Do your job until decisions are made. Anything else?" He asked the question like I'd asked for an extra day off for Christmas.

"No, sir. But don't you think—"

"We'll call when we hear something. Don't bother me about this again."

My finger ended the call first so I didn't get hung up on. He only cared about office production; he'd made that clear. Just how did I run the show while under investigation? It wouldn't take Hillary long to sabotage me, with Henry's blessing.

A sickening idea crept into my head along with the beginning of a headache. Two ideas, as a matter of fact. If I'd taken Jesse up on his bribe offer, I might have called his bluff and scared him away. Or I could have accepted his offer, taken his money and put it on his account. Both scenarios played out clean. Had I over analyzed this whole mess?

The confrontation with McRae had fused my back and neck muscles stiff. This day was done. More than done. I left the office without a word to a soul. I drove out of the parking lot at straight up five p.m., before my staff reached their cars. In my mirror, I saw them gossiping in a huddle.

Wayne hadn't called once.

The kids and I had developed a routine without Alan, a simpler, more synchronized evening where everything ran in order from dinner to homework. I fought to stay task oriented and dodge the day's instant replay. Efficiency led to everyone ready for bed before the clock struck nine.

"What are we supposed to do now?" Zack asked.

Ivy stood with a hand on her hip and a glare beneath her tiny brows. "This is weird."

I motioned upstairs. "How about going to bed?"

"You've got to be kidding, Momma. It's eight-thirty." My daughter's sarcasm was plain cute. God, their antics kept me sane.

"You can stay up as late as you like then."

Zack's eyes widened like silver dollars. "Wow! On a school night, too."

My daughter knew better. "What's the catch?"

"You have to be in bed to do it. I don't care if you read, listen to music, or take a toy with you. Just stay in the bed with your bedside lamp on."

"I can live with that," she said.

Zack watched his big sister and replied in echo. "Me, too."

"Okay, then, scoot. I'm taking a bath, so nobody get up for anything, especially don't open any outside doors."

"What you scared of, Momma?" Zack asked.

"Nothing." I started to remind them of Smokey's death in the front yard and decided against it. "That's just my rule."

They scrambled upstairs, giggling.

Wayne probably knew more than I did about the IG contacting my agency. So why hadn't he called? He'd likely tell me more than I cared to hear, and I sure didn't want to get in the habit of asking him for direction, but he could at least check up on me. I opted to wait instead of chase him down. I lifted the phone to snag Savvy for a rant session, but the idea of an hour chat depressed me. I needed sleep, pure unconsciousness. and escape from a world of dung.

I eased my tired body into a steaming bath. The water from the brass faucet churned rose-scented bubbles from a bottle someone gave me eons ago for Christmas. My legs braced against the end of the tub in case I dozed off. I did.

In my dream, a faceless man chased me up and down fence rows near the Williams' farm until I fell into Toogoodoo Creek and bumped into Mickey's body, his eye's wide. Tiny fish flitted in and out of his mouth.

I jerked awake, splashing, and pulled the plug. My tension flowed down the drain with the bath water, carrying some of my toxic day with it. I smeared lotion over my legs and tossed on an extra-large tee shirt. A quick check confirmed the kids were asleep in spite of their intentions of staying up. Back in my bedroom, I burrowed into bed with a novel. Words blurred only one page into the chapter. I rolled over and bunched up the covers.

My eyes snapped open after what seemed seconds since I'd cozied up with my pillow. Madge the cat slept two feet away from me. The numbers on my alarm clock glowed three o'clock.

A kitchen cabinet door closed with a muffled whump.

CHAPTER 16

An intruder was in my kitchen. I froze in my bed, listening hard, then closed my eyes to listen harder.

I inched my way across the mattress. Easing the sheets and quilt off, I slid to the floor. The nightstand held my phone. My gun was under the corner of my mattress. I eased open the drawer a quarter inch at a time. The gun came out easier. The two items rested one in each hand now. Papers rustled and a cabinet door thumped again.

What burglar rummaged in kitchen cabinets?

My instincts identified the man, but my common sense told me to verify first. Gun in hand, I stooped down and slipped out of the bedroom, hunched and creeping along the wall and down the stairs until I reached the archway between the dining room and kitchen. I flicked the switch, spilling light into the kitchen. "What do you think you're doing?"

Alan spun around, his getup positively eerie—very un-Alan-ish, as Savvy would say. His dark jeans, black turtleneck, skullcap, hiking boots and gloves contrasted stark and ominous against my white enamel-painted cabinets. He was finishing off a glass of milk. As silly as he looked, I reminded myself he'd still broken into my house.

"I could have shot you," I said.

"The magic words are 'could have'," he said, then drank the last of the milk. "You didn't. You wouldn't want to scare the kids."

"I'd want to protect them, you idiot. Why are you in here?"

"So what are you up to these days?" he said, ignoring my question, leaning against the sink like he still owned the place. Well, maybe he did still *own* the place, but that didn't give him the right to . . . what kind of silly-assed question was that anyway?

"None of your business what I'm up to," I said, hiding the .38 behind me as I remained hugged against the archway wall.

"I need to know what's going on at your office." He wiped his mouth on his sleeve, and for a moment I saw Zack in his expression.

"Since when do you care about my work?" And how did he even know about it?

"Since you're seeing someone. Since you've been making backdoor financial deals with farmers." He pulled off his gloves and stepped into the den, crossing to the desk where he started rummaging through my open briefcase, which had been closed and on the floor when I went to bed.

I set the phone on the credenza to free a hand, reached over and slammed the briefcase shut, barely missing his fingers. "Get out of there. Why do you care if I'm seeing anyone? You dared me to file the papers first, so I did."

He spun toward me, his mouth tight. "Your farmer friend, Jesse. Did he come through? I hear you don't have a leg to stand on."

How the hell did he know about all this? "Who've you been talking to?" I pondered microphones in the wall and cameras in the ceiling. Anything was possible these days.

An intense urge to justify myself came and went; he was the wrong person to blab to. He'd have reason to fight me for the kids, as if his stellar behavior would woo a family court judge. Breaking and entering wasn't high on the Good Samaritan list, and I'd damn sure use it against him.

"How did you get in?" I asked. "You don't have a key, which means you broke in." My thoughts raced, wondering which window was busted, door jimmied, sliding glass door compromised.

He reached into his pocket and held up a ring with a lone key dangling. "Oh, but I do have a key."

Some locksmith was going to pay. "I changed the locks. How did you—"

He stepped closer, and the hairs rose on my arms. My fight or flight trigger clicked, probably later than it should have considering he'd burgled my house camouflaged in black.

"Has he screwed you?" he asked.

"Has who screwed me?" I replied, even as I thought of Wayne. My thumb rubbed the gun. Geez, the kids. "Are you crazy? Lower your voice—"

"You kicked me out of my own house, stole my children, and humiliated me. Now everybody in Ridgeville assumes I did something to you." His brow grew deeper, his eyes darker. "I can't show my face in church."

The absurdity of the conversation almost shoved me back. "Are you kidding me? This is about your reputation?" And church?

He rushed toward me. I dodged under his arm, his fist missing me and hitting the wall. I scurried around the corner of the desk. My heart jolted, throwing me into a fast pant. I almost threw up as it pummeled my insides. Oh my God, who was this guy? "What's your friggin' problem, Alan?" I swallowed to avoid the shake in my voice. "Go home, and I won't call the police."

Not showing fear might compose him. He'd never hurt me before, but then he'd never cat burgled either. His grimace slipped into a sweet placid smile. That familiar expression had flirted with me long ago, wooed me, seduced me in our scrapbook days. The picture on the mantle behind him displayed the exact same pose for the photographer who took our family portrait. Alan then put his gloves back on with slow and easy deliberance.

I gripped the .38 in both hands, pointed the weapon at his chest and swallowed. "You know I can use this." A chill rushed from my shoulders down my arms and into my hands. I wondered how I would scrub blood out of natural hardwood floors and how to keep the kids from seeing it.

Shoulders drooped, he stepped back. He donned the face of a scolded toddler, making me look like the aggressor when I was the damn victim. Barefooted in a nightshirt, I cringed. Seconds dragged, but I wasn't dropping the gun. Not with the man so possessed

He straightened, relaxed, and removed the gloves. "Can I pick up the kids on Wednesday for pizza?"

Oh my God, this man had lost it.

"Um, sure," I said, leery of another emotional switch—wondering how early my attorney woke up.

Alan stepped out into the night and turned back. "I'm sorry about this. The divorce has me kind of strung out, you know?"

This had to have been orchestrated, a pretense, a move to rattle me. No way this was the real Alan. But what scared me worse was that he was capable of such fantasy. And what else did he have in his plan to drive me batty?

I wanted to call him a son-of-a-bitch, or wait until he turned around and shoot him in the back. I wanted him a part of everyone's history, especially mine, but he was Ivy and Zack's father. God how I hated that reality. My hands shook. A weirdness hung in the damp air like the final moments of Halloween night. How was I supposed to deal with him on a regular basis with behavior, no . . .danger, like this?

It took me three tries to clasp the lock on the door after he finally left. I wedged a dining room chair under the knob then carried another chair to the kitchen door and did the same. Then I checked the windows, drew the blinds and stacked pots around the doors. No entrance was broken, so he had used the key.

When I was done, I straightened papers in my briefcase, just to put more to right.

What was Alan really doing here in the middle of the night? I downed a glass of water and eased to the recliner. Lowering myself, I wrapped my arms around me and closed my eyes. I'd never seen this side of Alan. He was the devil I didn't know versus Jesse, the devil I did. What should I do with the kids now? A protective urge exploded in me, and I fast-stepped up the stairs to Ivy's room. Asleep, her face buried in her pillow. I left her door cracked open. Next Zack's bedroom. He lay sprawled on his bare belly, his pajama shirt bunched under his chest. His babyish snores came even through his wide open mouth.

After tucking quilts, I returned downstairs and crawled under my own. Madge slept unaffected in the same position I'd left her. The clock read four. In two hours I'd be awake and expected to act normal.

I said the word aloud, with nasal and pursed lips. "Normal."

Disturbed at my movement, the cat circled once and sank into the goose down, her tail softly settling over her paws. "Normal," I said, kissing her head. Her warmth and steady motor suppressed my fear as I lay in the dark stroking her, wondering what kind of demented, broken-down, crazy woman I'd be a year from now.

"CRAIG MCCURRY, PICK UP!" I shouted on my cell. Two hours' sleep and a blinding sun readjusted my disposition to proactive mode. I'd dropped the kids off at school before phoning my attorney, giving me the freedom to raise a ruckus. My driving matched my mood as I dodged rush-hour traffic like a hummingbird through my abelia bushes.

"What's happened?" Craig asked. "It was a gorgeous morning before you screamed me awake."

Two eighteen-wheelers slowed traffic to the speed limit. I rode almost on top of one's bumper. "Alan broke into my house last night dressed in black, like some ninja."

"I warned you about some guys' reactions to divorce," he said. "He didn't hurt you, did he?"

"No, not that he didn't take a jab at me. If you want proof, I'll show you the knuckle print in the wall."

"Did you call 911?"

"No, I didn't want to wake the kids."

"Did you call your parents?" Craig asked questions like he read from a list.

I passed a Lincoln, then slowed when a Volvo pulled in front of me with no signal. "No, Daddy would've killed him. And I'm not joking."

"Did the kids see it?"

"No, thank goodness."

"Then how do you prove he did anything?"

I eased into the slow lane to think about that. Craig had a point. "Shit."

"I think that about sums it up."

"What about him picking up the kids? Should I allow it?"

"Slade. His anger is with you, and so far he hasn't hit you. Has he ever harmed the kids?"

"No."

"Then there's nothing you can do to stop him from seeing his children. How did he get in?"

"He had a key. I changed the locks and he still had a key . . . or so he said. I couldn't find where he damaged anything to get in, so I guess I have to take his word on that."

"My guess is he told a locksmith he lost his keys and needed new ones cut. Probably while you were at work."

I might as well be living in a tent. What if he'd watched me sleep? Exposed at work and naked at home. I'd say my safest place was on the highway, except someone had already proved that hypothesis wrong by going bumper cars with me two weeks ago.

"So, Counselor," I said, with marked annoyance at his casualness, "what's your expert advice? Get a bodyguard? Go into hiding? Leap off a bridge?"

He chuckled. "I'll file a restraining order."

Traffic backed up, and I braked to slow down for my exit. "I never expected him to be like this. He's a wimp."

"Well, now he's not, and you need to be careful. Next time, call 911. You hear me?"

"But the kids, Craig."

His voice turned edgy. "You want your kids to lose their mother next time?"

I laid my hand over a gurgling stomach. The convenience store coffee wasn't agreeing with me, and the thought of food turned me off. Had to be a peppermint in the glove box somewhere.

"I just thought my bed should be a safe haven, Craig." I rummaged through the box. A loose butter mint from The Magnolia Restaurant popped out from under a cellophane-wrapped fork and spoon.

"It will be, Slade. This ordeal will be over before you know it. I promise."

Promises meant squat to me these days. People had promised me money, an investigation, and safety with none of the assurances coming to pass. Plus, an assurance from a lawyer was like the weatherman predicting clear skies for an outdoor wedding. There was always a disclaimer.

I headed toward the office, watching my mirrors more than the road ahead, my fear of Alan still fresh in my mind. My .38 rested in my lap.

A SOYBEAN FARMER needed operating funds in the first loan file on my stack, and I thought its simplicity would jump start my thought processes. It didn't. I couldn't focus on the paper.

The intercom buzzed, Ann Marie's whiny voice on the speaker. "Andy Burroughs on line two."

I depressed the button. "Hey, Andy."

"Ms. Slade, haven't you gotten my messages?"

Andy was an annual customer with an uneventful operation. Three dozen more like him would make my world spin so much smoother.

The man recited new plans for a cotton-picker and two new implements for his tractor—a six-figure, ten-year loan. When these guys ran ideas by me, I high-fived myself. This kind of lending was fun. I gave him my blessing and asked him to drop off an application. My God, I'd done my job again.

A tall man in a black suit smacked his briefcase on my table, and I jumped. He motioned for me to hang up the phone. I shook my head, waved an arm for him to leave my office and mouthed, *Get out*. Nobody waltzed into my territory unannounced.

He stood rock-steady and crossed his arms.

With a scowl I covered the mouthpiece. "Please wait outside. I have a client on the line. I'll be with you in a minute."

"Hang up."

"Get out."

The stranger strode over, held his finger over the disconnect button and cut off the call. He reached under his coat, lifted out a black billfold and flashed his IG badge in my face. My own personal investigator. He'd sure shown up fast.

But I'd seen badges before. "You realize I'll have to call that farmer back and apologize?"

"Lady, what you'll do is listen." He spoke hard and sharp with the curtness of a general, disguised in a gray pinstriped suit, lavender tie and polished leather shoes. "Senior Special Agent Julian R. Beck, Ms. Bridges. Care to read the credentials?"

The ID seemed authentic, not that I'd spot a forgery. But I'd bet a week's pay no one had ever taken him up on his offer, so I accepted the credentials and studied them, turning them around, doing anything to stall the moment. "How do I know this is real?"

He took them back and ignored my question. "We have a lot of ground to cover, Ms. Bridges. Your undivided attention would be appreciated for this interview."

This agent possessed a strange air about him. Too pretty. I couldn't see him traipsing around kudzu-covered barns or hog pens. His cuticles looked better than mine.

Beck spread his tablet, pen and laptop on my table in neat alignment and sat down, his back stiff. "I'm from OIG's Internal Affairs, here to investigate the relationship between you and Special Agent Wayne Largo.

The quicker you cooperate, the sooner I leave, Ms. Bridges."

"Relationship" rang nasty coming from his robotic government mouth. Mom would have a fit at his deportment and his erosion of my reputation. She'd give him an earful. Then she'd blister me good for getting myself in this situation.

Didn't I have rights?

I angled my desk plate in his direction. "The name is Slade. That's how you spell it, in case you need help."

"Ah, yes. The pending divorce." He clicked his pen and ticked off a box.

What an ass. "Shouldn't I call someone? Get my one phone call or something?"

"Up to you," he said, scribbling on his pad. "You're not the target." When I continued to sit still, he looked up. "Well?"

Who would I call? My attorney only dealt with divorces. Beck would never allow me to contact Wayne. Savvy either. I'd be damned before I called my parents. Guess I winged this on my own.

I tried to nudge away the disappointment that Wayne hadn't called with a warning.

"Forget it," I said. "One thing, though." I tapped my desk with a knuckle like I'd seen Wayne do, flexing what power I could muster. "Please drop the attitude. I get paid the same whether we chat or I keep my mouth shut." I stood and pointed at him. "Now . . . *you* can wait a minute."

He showed mild amusement as I stood.

I stepped outside my office and instructed Ann to hold my calls. Then I returned and shut the door. "There. Now we won't be interrupted."

"I've already ordered your staff not to interrupt our meeting."

"You seem to forget I'm the manager here."

"We'll see about that after today."

CHAPTER 17

Special Agent Beck sat across from my desk with a wicked smile, evidently enjoying the battle of wit. "Do you know Mr. Largo?"

"Of course," I said.

"Raise your hand and repeat after me."

"Why?"

"This is a formal statement, and once we write it out to both our satisfactions, you're going to sign it," he said. He pointed to the row of books behind my desk. "Your job depends on it."

He swore me in, made me sign a statement saying he swore me in, then turned through several pages of his notepad. He read questions already listed, some with blanks in them, others with red question marks in the margins.

"Was this a legitimate case, Ms. Bridges?"

"The name is Slade." We both knew he held the reins, but I wasn't going to let him run roughshod.

His dark eyes seemed to recognize the early impasse. "Let's try this again," he said adjusting his tie. "Was this case legitimate?"

"I didn't go through blue blazes for the fun of it."

"Try to keep this civil."

We hammered out preliminary details as he took slow, methodical notes about my work, my family, my coworkers. Much like Wayne's interrogation in my living room a millennium ago. Then Special Agent Beck dug into the heart of his visit.

"When did you first meet Agent Largo?"

I explained how the case played out and how Atlanta set up my meeting with Wayne and Eddie.

He checked off a question. "Do you feel Mr. Largo stayed fully focused on his duties?"

"Absolutely."

"Do you think he took too long on the case?"

I craved the urge to turn away, but felt he would dissect my body language. In hindsight, the case took longer than I'd expected, but who was I to judge? We'd spent a lot of time waiting for Jesse. Damn it, what was the right answer?

I rested forearms on the table. "He obviously didn't spend long enough. Jesse's still loose."

Another tick mark. "You spent a lot of time together according to his travel records. How many times did you sleep with him?"

We hadn't slept together. So why did I feel we had?

He tapped his pen on the table. "I have to ask these questions. Standard procedure."

"No problem," I said. "I never slept with him."

"How many times did he say he wanted you?"

"The only person he ever said he wanted was Jesse Rawlings."

"Did you wonder why he strung out the case?"

"I have no idea how long a case takes."

"Are you a police groupie, Ms. Slade? Do cops turn you on?"

My mouth dropped open. What gall. I clenched my hands. His lips gave a slick upturn.

I waved a hand in the air, then crossed my arms. "I harbor no love or hate for you guys. Sorry." That was a lie first class. I abhorred badges now.

He seemed delighted at my clumsy response. Embarrassed or not, I realized he wasn't there to find the right or wrong of the case. He was there to make one against Wayne.

His gaze returned to his pad. "Then why did you tell your office you'd be in the field that day when you were in Largo's motel room?" His eyes rose to meet mine, timed as if the next step would fall into place.

"We prepared for the meeting," I said. "I wore a wire. We couldn't exactly do it here in the office."

"Do it?"

How juvenile. "Rig the wire. We didn't even go in the field that day. Something came up."

He wrote, stopped, then wrote another couple of lines. So someone saw my car and assumed the worst. Taking my shirt off for the wire now held serious sexual connotations. If this guy read people, I was as cooked as Mom's Easter ham.

"Eddie was there," I said, in attempt to preempt the man's question.

Beck nodded. "And his memory is spotty, assuming he tells the truth."

I scoffed at his tacky retort. "You're reaching now, Mr. Beck."

"Why didn't you go into the field that day?"

I shifted in my seat. "Mr. Largo cancelled at the last minute."

"Did you two get distracted? Is that what cancelled the meeting? After all, you were in a motel room."

He clung to this tryst accusation like a hound dog with a soup bone. "No-thing hap-pened." I dragged out the words for effect to jam the message through his thick skull.

He eased reading glasses out of his pocket. He flipped back through pages of notes, pages filled with more writing. Preparation for today. He found the page he wanted and took off his glasses, peering at me. "Why did Largo leave that day?"

All I knew was Eddie's comments about family. "I don't know."

"Did he get interrupted often by personal calls?"

"No."

He badgered me with six more questions about Wayne's personal business, testing what insight I could give as to his extracurricular activities. He wanted names, numbers of calls, Wayne's reactions and my take on how the calls interfered with plans. I disappointed him on all counts, but with each question, I pondered what the hell Wayne had done to draw this kind of attention. Someone pursued him hard, and I sensed a vendetta dating much further back than Jesse's bribe.

"Did you expect Rawlings to come through?" he asked, coming back around to what I considered relevant.

"Yes, because he did."

His pen wrote, the scratching the only sound in the room. He looked over my head then back at me. "When Mr. Rawlings gave you money, how do you know it wasn't for his existing loan?"

"Because he told me it was a partial payment to deed him the Williams' farm. Wayne heard him say it. Eddie, too."

He wrote faster. "But you have no proof."

"We have the telephone tapes. We recorded setting up Jessie for the real meeting at the farm." I stuttered and hated myself for doing so. "And we have the signed papers."

He looked at me, grinned and wrote. "When *you* set *him* up?"

God, that didn't come out right. "Wait a minute. Don't you twist my words, and you damn well know what I mean . . . if you're any kind of agent at all."

He didn't take the bait. "But still no proof of the exchange itself?"

"Well, Agent Beck, who the hell hit Eddie and why? The meeting was taped, and someone felt threatened enough to steal that proof."

"After going through the tapes of Mr. Rawlings' visits to your office, on one of them he asserts that *you* offered the farm to him for money."

"He may have said that, but you'll find there's no trace of me asking such a thing. In fact, I recall refuting his words."

The weasel grinned. "If you were having a liaison with Mr. Largo, isn't it possible the tape could have been doctored?"

"I'm not a tape expert."

"Do you know how long I've been an investigator?"

I blew a loud, irritating sigh, reading the arrogant mind of someone who thought he hid his thoughts well. "You've heard them all, huh?"

He frowned. "You make too light of a very serious matter."

Lunch came and went. I almost asked to leave for some water, but didn't want to walk past inquisitive employees with their stares . . . Hillary's smirk. Instead, I dug in my purse until I found a roll of mints. A moment later I dug in again, then peeled paper off a pack of antacids as the agent typed up my statement, asking questions to fill in gaps.

Time dragged like an auto mechanic's waiting room. "I'm going to the bathroom," I said, impatient at the man's dawdling typing skills.

"I'll go with you," he replied, pushing back from the table.

"No, you won't, unless you want to add sexual harassment to that statement. You have your answers. I'll pee while you peck." I stood up.

He sat back down. "Don't take long."

All three of my staff ladies pretended to study anything but me as I left. In the bathroom, I hunched over the sink dying to splash my face, knowing if I returned with wet hair and no makeup, tongues would wag harder than they already were. I should have brought my purse, my cell phone. I could have called Wayne and asked how the hell to handle Beck, assuming Wayne even knew the IG'd sicced someone on me.

Wait. I could stop by Sid Patten's office on the way back. The Natural Resources office situated between the restrooms and Beck. If I skipped the potty break and hurried . . . I jerked open the pneumatic door and bolted for Room 104. I grabbed the handle and ran headlong into Ren.

"Hi," he said, his thick-tongued greeting loud and slurred.

I looked frantically behind Ren, to other doorways leading to various employees. Ren went nowhere without Jesse.

"I'm right here, baby," Jesse whispered into the back of my neck.

"Ahhhh!" My feet ran in place, my arms lashing out.

Sid rushed out of his office. "What's going on out here?"

My pulse thumped in my head, kicking my chest. "I need your phone, Sid. I'm in a hurry."

A puzzled expression wrinkled his face. "But your office isn't thirty feet that way," he said, pointing.

"Not now, Sid. Trust me. I can't explain," I said.

"Well, sure, Slade. I don't mind, it's just—"

Dress shoes echoed on the tile floor. "Excuse me. Has anyone seen Ms. Slade?"

Jesse nodded toward me, and stepped aside. "Right here, sir."

Beck hinted at a grin, telling me the jig was up. "Wondered where you went to. I'm on a deadline and would sure love to finish up our meeting before I catch my plane."

I gripped Jesse's coat sleeve. "This is Jesse Rawlings."

Sid cast a questioning stare at me and my excitement about a farmer we'd known for years. Jesse held out his hand. "Yes sir. I'm Jesse Rawlings. You work with Ms. Slade? My brother and I think the world of her. She's helped me stay on my farm when I thought we'd lost all hope. Y'all hired a good 'un in her."

Sid joined in. "She's one of our favorites. I'm Sid Patten." He reached out to shake. "Natural Resources Director."

Beck gripped his hand, then Jesse's, then Ren's. "Nice to meet you all. I'm just reviewing some files for Ms. Slade's office, one of them Mr. Rawlings'. Good luck with your hogs, sir."

"Thank you much," Jesse said, the good ole boy oozing out of him. "'Scuse me, ma'am." He tipped his John Deere cap at me. Beck touched my elbow, directing me toward my office.

I returned to my desk, imprisoned in my own place of employment.

The agent shifted his suit coat as he sat. "Ms. Slade, we think Mr. Largo has several lady friends in different states. Women like you he's met on cases. Would that simplify this interview for you?"

My heart fell through my stomach, and it must have shown like a beacon on my face. The lines in his forehead disappeared. He'd found the right button to push, and we both knew it.

"Our relationship was purely professional," I finally said.

My legs quivered beneath my desk. I envisioned my parents, Alan, Mr. Edmonds, my staff and peers standing around me shaking their heads as my career flushed down the toilet. *How could she have been so blind?*

My silence told Agent Beck all he needed.

He probed for another half hour, and I answered each question dry-eyed and somber. When I didn't give him answers he liked, he repeated questions until my replies watered down to something closer to what he preferred.

He directed me to sign the five-page statement. I read the document three times, refused to sign and demanded changes. He preferred to word things his way, continually badgering me about the "real" answers, the "best" answers, the "right" answers to send back to Washington, reminding me I wasn't the target of his investigation.

The interview took three hours total. I aged five years.

I wanted out. I didn't know where *out* was, but I wanted it badly.

I couldn't make Beck understand about Jesse's threats and insinuations. He didn't believe my dog's death connected to the case, nor someone calling me in the middle of the night. Jesse had fallen from the IG's spotlight. Wayne had taken his place. I ended the ordeal the best way I knew how—by signing the statement with the agent's pen.

Beck introduced me to the excrement of internal affairs, tapping what he needed at any cost to anyone. I saw few remnants of my career surviving this. Who would believe I'd done an honorable deed? The human factor unraveled procedural guidelines. Naïve used to mean innocent to me. Now it meant nothing more than stupid.

Beck called Atlanta from his cell, giving someone instructions to collect Wayne's gun and badge and place him on administrative leave. I recognized the garish flare and knew they'd already stripped Wayne of his authority. Purely for my benefit, Beck informed Atlanta he'd completed his mission. His haughtiness made me wish a human being dead for the first time in my life. The last thing he told me before he left was not to make contact with Wayne. I wasn't sure I wanted to.

My knees wobbled even as I sat, unable to pace and burn off the anxiety. What did I have left to ponder, to fix, to pace the floor about?

Outside, the office staff sat in silence. No typing, no voices. I knew in my soul that one of them had sabotaged me. Ann Marie buzzed. I told her to hold my calls and hung up.

An hour later, I stood and faced the spotlight.

Ann Marie jumped up from her chair. "What's happening, Slade?"

"That man was an agent checking on a client suspected of a crime, Ann. They wanted a statement from me. Nothing you need worry about." I scanned the room.

Jean hid behind an open file drawer, pretending to search. Hillary stood against her door fighting back a smile. Ann Marie appeared frightened, but she always looked that way.

The clock read three. "I think in light of the disruption today, y'all can go home. I'll close the doors at five. No one worry about that guy. He's not looking at us." The last phrase meant nothing. Of course, no one looked at them. The only potential suspect in this office was me. "Maybe one day we'll be done with cops and agents. I've had my fill."

They disappeared fast.

A few minutes before five, I picked up my bag and walked across the silent lobby, blessed that no customers walked in. I switched off the lights.

"Hey, Slade," came a voice from the dark shadows beside the counter.

I dropped my bag and screamed.

"Whoa. It's me," Wayne said, stepping out of the darkness.

My chest heaved, one hand gripped on a chair back. I shook so hard I crossed my arms, tucking my fingers away from sight. Beck's words about Wayne's infidelities snagged my memory, and I stiffened.

"Let me cut the lights back on," he said.

"No," I said. He didn't need to see the confusion on my face. And God help us if somebody saw us together. I sat in Jean's chair.

Wayne moved into the light coming from the parking lot, squatted in front of me, bringing his grey eyes level with mine. He wore dress slacks and a button-down shirt rolled up at the sleeves, open at the neck, wrinkled from the long-distance drive. He'd run his hands through his hair too many times that day, leaving it tousled and unkempt.

"I've been wondering when you were going to allow yourself to be human," he said, grasping both arms of my chair. "Damn, Slade, I don't know how you've held things together this long. I'm here for you. I'm still on your side."

"What side is that, Wayne?"

He released the chair. "What do you mean?"

"I really don't know you. People are turning on me from all directions, so what makes you any different?"

He rubbed his forehead and stood. "Damn Beck. He worked on you."

I turned away, surprisingly ashamed at the cold fact from Wayne's lips.

"Of course he did," he said, saving me the shame. "That's his job, and he's an expert at it." He sounded tired. "Try not to believe all he said."

The crossroad of accepting or refusing Wayne in my life lay before me. I could lose a lot either way.

He sighed. "Well, I came to check on you and give you a heads up."

I released a lackluster chuckle. "What else you warning me about, lawman? A nuke on my car?" I was cruel . . . but only if he wore the white hat. Right now I could not tell where he stood and couldn't afford the vulnerability.

"I couldn't help you with Beck," he said, a hint of plea in his voice. "They confined me in Atlanta this morning while he grilled you here in Charleston. I drove like a rocket to get here." He blinked, trying to connect with my internal battle. "Slade, it's a known fact that these people twist words to mold answers."

I took the offensive to steer clear of any emotional entrapment. "So what's the *heads up* about?" I was prepared to doubt the Pope.

"Two of your employees have been on the phone chatting about you non-stop since Eddie and I came to town."

"Who?"

"Hillary and Jean."

"No big surprise about Hillary." I released a bitter laugh. "If McRae's screwing both of them, I wouldn't be surprised, but I thought Jean had more sense."

He hid his hands into his pockets. "Jean didn't call McRae."

So she gossiped. What did I care?

"She talks to Alan. She's been in contact with him for over a year. They meet on Sunday afternoons."

"He plays basketball on Sundays."

His eyes fell soft on me as he waited for my thoughts to gel. "Come on, Slade."

So much for my judgment of men. I'd known Alan for fifteen years and Wayne for fifteen days, and I'd bombed on both counts.

"Wonderful," I said, my temples throbbing. Wayne sat on Jean's desk. How many Monday mornings had my clerk Jean sat through staff meetings, reliving the moves she'd put on Alan the day before?

"You've filed the papers," he said. "It's over. Don't let it bother you." He reached out for my hand to draw me from my chair.

I ignored him. "How long have you known? And don't give me any of your hidden agendas."

He reached out again, wiggled his fingers for me to take hold. "Come on, Slade. It's not important. I'll walk you to the car."

"Answer me, damn it!"

He hesitated. "Since the beginning, okay?"

"And you found it imperative to rush over and tell me today? I should've known you'd put work before me."

"Hey, I'm sincerely sorry."

I quit counting the times he'd apologized since this chaos had begun. "Don't feign guilt for my sake. Did you treat me like all the others, or am I the best you've run across . . . up to now?"

His head jerked up. "What?"

"It's the vulnerable ones you go after, isn't it? That how it works? No wonder you sped back here from Atlanta. You figured Beck had made me ripe for the picking."

Wayne froze.

I stood and stepped closer to him, my ire gaining momentum, sickeningly thrilled at having the upper hand after a day of being under an agent's thumb. "Was the story about your ex-wife bullshit, too?" I clenched fists. "God, I'm so stupid!" I nodded toward the door. "Just get out." Hiding Alan's behavior from me went hand in hand with Beck's portrayal of Wayne . . . the lawman kept secrets. We hadn't slept together, and I was probably overreacting, but his behavior led me to believe we could have become something. He walked to the door, but waited and silently held it open for me.

Bastard.

I left the building and drove off fighting back tears.

CHAPTER 18

I drove too fast from the office, down the interstate with an anger difficult to control. Alan having an affair didn't upset me as much as I thought it should. Wayne waiting to tell me, however, ticked me off.

Jean forever fought to claw back her years. Dye left her hair brittle as pine straw. And she packed her ass into a skirt like a butcher stuffed pork in a sausage skin. Whatever possessed her to join at the groin to a man like Alan? A man who despised any woman with the guts to escape the kitchen sink and pursue her dreams?

Wayne remained a dark horse, very dark, and I cursed myself for a lapse of sense in my attraction to him. Maybe he did prefer the vulnerable ones, drawing them into his bed. Thank goodness I hadn't gone that far. Damn Alan. Damn Wayne. Damn the whole Department of Agriculture and its pillar of testosterone. To hell with all of them.

I cut in and out of cars. Taillights flashed ahead of me. I braked hard as the traffic stopped, striking the steering wheel with the palms of my hands.

As I took the freeway exit hard and gunned it through a yellow light, the grocery store caught my eye. A bottle of wine seemed in tall order. No, too civil. I needed beer. A six-pack. I turned late and clipped the curb.

The teenage cashier smirked through thick sparkly lip gloss as she ran my grocery items over the scanner. Beer, two sticker books and a large bag of spicy hot potato chips must've screamed *lonely single mother.* To hell with her, too. I swept up my bags and headed for the car.

I left the store and turned right, winding behind a subdivision instead of sitting in line to get back on the interstate. With five miles left to home, I chose the back way, two-lane roads that kept me away from the rush-hour madhouse and bumper-to-bumper mayhem at the exit ramps. The kids and I often came this way, past the pastures, away from billboards and eighteen-wheelers.

I didn't expect company, but a brown rusted Ford gained fast on me. I would let it pass. Maybe he harbored a piss-awful day as well.

The car began to come around, and then swerved violently into me. Metal crunched metal. I accelerated and grappled to keep the car on the road. The Ford struck again and shoved my vehicle onto the edge. My right front bumper toppled a row of three mailboxes, throwing one up high enough to send spider vein cracks across my windshield. Grunting, I piloted the Taurus back onto the asphalt, raking the passenger door with another mailbox. I glanced to get a look at the madman, but he'd dropped back.

As my hands strangled the steering wheel, my mind raced through options. If I stopped, the asshole would corner me. If I headed home, he'd nail not only me but my family. So I drove as determined and fast as I could, in hopes he'd head off like he'd done on the interstate the week before.

Logic said this was the same guy. No way on God's green earth had I antagonized two people bad enough to swap paint like this.

The current road would take me to Highway 78, on my way to Ridgeville and my street. At Lott's Crossroads, I veered right and headed north with the Ford sticking to my bumper. I flashed my headlights, seeking someone who'd recognize an SOS. Then I left the lights on to see through the shadows of pending night. My clock read almost six thirty.

I stomped the gas for the one-mile length of road, the Highway 78 intersection pictured clear in my head. If I couldn't stop, I could at least lay on my horn and draw attention. In an unexplainable second of error, I slowed to get a better look at his face in my rearview.

The Ford accelerated. I swerved across the road and back again, zigging against his zag, but the impact to the rear came hard, snapping my head back. My elbows locked.

The intersection appeared in my sights. I traveled too fast to make it. I braked hard to make the turn. The car struck me again.

The collision jolted me through the intersection onto Jedburg Road, headed away from Summerville. Two miles stretched before I would reach the Interstate.

Then the air got silent except for a rattle in my fender. The Ford's motor revved higher, the engine timing off from lack of upkeep. It drew alongside. I saw the glint of gunmetal in the side view mirror as we passed under a streetlamp. I cut the wheel as a gunshot rang out.

The car jerked to the left. The steering stiffened.

My vehicle fought me and careened left from a flat tire. In a simultaneous motion, I yanked the wheel right, another mistake. As the Ford pivoted left to avoid me, the driver gunned it, burning oil, and left a cloud of white smoke in his trail. My foot jammed the brakes, slinging the rear end to the left. I yanked my foot from the brake, then hit the accelerator again. The clockwise spin disoriented me to where I couldn't tell which direction to steer. I closed my eyes. The vehicle went airborne toward a stand of pines.

The touchdown lurch broke my seat back, and my door flew off. The whole world convulsed as I hit a thick pine and the airbag blew out.

Dead silence.

Then I smelled gas.

Opening my eyes, I recognized the tan ceiling and dome light. I couldn't see anything else for twisted branches and the airbag. I fought and scrambled upright, unfastened my seatbelt, grabbed my purse strap and lunged for a carpet of pine needles. I tripped on wisteria and kudzu, ran on hands and knees for a few feet then regained my stance, sprinting for all I was worth.

I stopped behind an immense pecan tree, my aching back against the bark while fishing in my purse for my phone. I peered back at the car. That's when I saw him.

He stood atop a hill fifty yards away, right before the road turned sharp, a trailer park spotlight barely backlighting him. Tall, average build, wearing jeans and a dark, probably camouflaged, hunting coat, he observed me. Masked in the sage-colored dusk, his face remained unrecognizable. I crouched, uncertain.

A giant puff of smoke belched for the sky as flames engulfed my Taurus. I dialed 911. When I peeked around the tree again, my assailant was gone.

Sirens ripped the air as a fire truck arrived accompanied by two sheriff patrol cars. When a deputy hurried down the slope, I ventured into the open. I held out my hand to make an introduction and blackness washed over me.

"Ma'am? Ma'am?"

I opened one eye, then the other.

"Yes, can I help you?" I asked, rote memory of my job kicking in first through the haze.

A handsome twenty-something uniform stared down at me. "I think I need to be helping you, ma'am. Don't move, okay?" Sirens screamed in the background, and I wondered why he didn't turn them off when he parked. That's when a pair in black pants and blue shirts ran up, latex gloves on their hands. I tried to sit up and someone held me down.

"Hey," I said. "I'm fine."

"We'll decide that. Do you remember anything?" A light flashed in my eyes. Someone else pumped a blood pressure cuff on my arm.

"Ma'am? Do you remember your name?"

I waved the free hand. "Carolina Slade. I live in Ridgeville. I work for the US Department of Agriculture. I'm perfectly fine."

Finally they let me sit up. After prodding, measuring and gauging, they couldn't find anything wrong. "You want to come with us?" asked the young blonde female EMT.

"No. I'm going home . . . if I can catch a ride from someone."

She shook her head. "Not real smart, ma'am. I imagine a doc would want to keep you overnight for observation."

Oh yeah, sure. The ambulance takes me to the hospital, the madman following on my butt. My parents babysitting, Wayne in Atlanta and Alan not giving a damn. That's exactly what I needed . . . to be alone so someone could finish the job.

"I'm not going with you." I stood, brushing off my slacks, an EMT on each side of me. My teeth chattered though I wasn't cold. My knees wobbled, and I tightened them. That's when I saw I was barefoot. I dropped like a rock, and the EMT's caught me. "Guess I will tag along with you guys."

The deputy stepped forward. "Ms. Slade, right? Can you tell me what happened?"

"Some idiot rammed my car, repeatedly. Then he shot a gun. He chased me for miles."

"A gun?" he asked. "Only one set of skid marks on the road, ma'am. You sure?"

"He stood up there on the hill and watched, for Christ's sake." I sighed and dropped my head back, exasperated. "Anyone ask you to keep a watch on me? Like a federal agent? As if I might be in danger or something?" Then I remembered. "Do you know Donald James? Has he said anything about my being in danger lately?"

"James?" The deputy cracked a slight grin. "Haven't swapped any stories lately with Scarecrow."

"I'm not a story."

"No, ma'am." The deputy shifted toward the EMT, giving me part of his back. "She have a concussion?"

So much for the sheriff's office watching out after me like Wayne promised. And I'm supposed to trust law enforcement after Wayne and Beck?

"Any chance you can read what happened from the car? Like forensics?" I asked.

His doubt read loud and clear via the expression on his face. "I know you're shaken, and I'm not making light of your ordeal here, but . . . take a look at your car. Dorchester County isn't CSI New York. That vehicle's toast."

I sat up, shoving away the EMT's hand when he attempted to stop me. "So, Deputy Sherlock, tell me what really happened."

"Well, hard to say with the car burned and all, but I'd say your tire blew."

"Damn, imagine how I misinterpreted that," I said, my tongue sticking to the top of my mouth. "Anyone have a bottle of water?"

"No point in getting upset, ma'am." His pen still hovered above the clipboard. "Do you want me to write up your story like that? An unknown man chased you, shot at you, and ran you into the trees?"

For a moment we intently focused on each other, me trying to decide which story made the most sense. Him probably wondering if I was coherent enough to even make a statement.

"Write it up like I said."

The deputy shrugged and went to work.

The EMTs helped me into the ambulance. I called Daddy and told him not to get upset that my car was history, and I might need a ride home later. Thank goodness today was my parents' day to pick up the kids.

I laid back on the gurney. So this was how it was going to be. Jesse and me, head-to-head. He wanted his farm, and I had to protect my children. Nobody knew how to nail an ignorant hog-farmer without a high school education. Neither did I, but it was up to me to figure it out now.

Maybe not. I dialed my phone.

"Wayne? There's been an accident."

"Are you hurt?" he asked, without the first reflection on our confrontation at the office.

I paused, figuring how to answer the question. "I have no idea. I'm in an ambulance."

"Which hospital?" he demanded.

"Trident Memorial, I think . . ." I said, shrugging and staring at the EMT who then nodded in confirmation.

"I'll find it." He hung up.

TWO HOURS LATER, a doctor stood before me, checking my scalp one more time. "I don't see anything, Ms. Slade, and I feel pretty comfortable writing this off to adrenaline and shock. Don't be surprised to find a bruise or two tomorrow. Sounds to me like you earned a few in that accident. I'll give you a prescription for a mild pain reliever. Just—"

Wayne snatched the curtain open, then jerked it back in place. "Slade. What do they say?"

"And who are you, sir?" asked the doctor.

"Her husband," he replied. "What's the deal here?"

I opened my mouth to protest and then hushed. No point.

"She'll tell you," the doctor said, smiling. "In summary, she'll be fine. I'll leave you to talk."

Wayne checked behind the curtain as the man left, glanced around for others, then turned to me. "Sorry it took me so long to get here, but I was already past Columbia when you called."

Still stunned to see him, I started to speak but couldn't put words in order. Then I remembered calling Daddy. "Did you see my father in the waiting room?"

"I called him on my way here and convinced him to watch your mother and the children while I came for you. He's probably crazy waiting for your call. Where's your phone?"

I pointed to my bag of belongings. Daddy answered the first ring and went nuclear on me once he learned I was okay. Knowing a federal agent would escort his daughter home calmed him to the level of ballistic. Reluctantly, I hung up, knowing I now faced that agent, not sure how to handle him.

"He's not happy," I said, and sighed. "Someone tried to kill me tonight, Wayne. My car is a pile of scorched metal upside down on Jedburg Road."

He straightened my collar then stopped, as if afraid he'd hurt something. "Damn, Slade. I should've followed you home. What are the police doing about it? Who's the deputy in charge?"

I held up both hands. "They think my tire blew. I think it was shot. I made them write it up my way, but what's the point? I saw no one I could recognize. But whoever it was waited to see my car burn. I saw his silhouette on the road, watching."

He rubbed his beard. "Damn it to hell." Silence. "How do you feel?"

"Numb." Confusion messed with me. We'd argued just hours ago, over his questionable loyalty, yet here he stood, tending to me. "Beck said I'm not supposed to talk to you," I said.

"Screw Beck," he said "Look, I'm about to be suspended. I'm coming back to hunt this guy."

I stared at the lawman. Wayne's life lay in shambles. Without a badge, his capabilities were limited, assuming his motives were genuine. He kept secrets. What if the IG used him now to set me up?

"How do I know you're not like Beck?" I finally asked, no energy behind the words.

He inhaled deep then said nothing.

My surge of fevered emotion broke the lull. "How do I know you're not sacrificing me? Maybe they're offering you your job in exchange for me."

"Damn it, CI, listen to yourself."

The title tugged at me, then at tears behind my eyelids. I tried not to blink to avoid the spill.

"You lived a regular life before all of this," Wayne said, his pity sounding so real. "It's got to take a toll on you, honey. Are you sure you're all right?"

No, I wasn't sure.

Did I risk everything with him or by myself? And if I chose to work with Wayne, would he crucify me or improve my chances?

He leaned in making eye contact. "Please don't shut me out, Slade."

I blinked, sniffling. "Listen to me, and you listen good." I held up three fingers. "First, I hate you for hiding Alan from me. Second, you're getting your ass over here to help. You got me in this shit, so get me out of it."

"Okay. My pleasure." He tried to laugh. "I may be unemployed, but the talent is still there. What's the third thing?"

I was far beyond humor, and cut my hand through the air to shut his off. "Don't bring any of your personal trash over here. Your boss, your ex-wife, any other case. I don't care what it is. My concern is that hog farmer. I want no more rules, no more IG, none of your crap."

He sobered. "I know you're scared."

"I'm a target."

He paced the room once, a hand on his waist. "Like I told you before, let me see what I can find out while I have federal resources at my disposal," he said. "Two days."

I froze. "Two days? You are kidding, right?" My life was being ripped apart and he was asking for days, again. "I'll be stone-cold and buried by then."

"Don't," he ordered. "Don't even joke about that."

"Then do something about it." Exhaustion suddenly weighed me into the gurney. "Soon. Please."

He squinted, as if trying to see a new thought better. "Okay. Screw Atlanta. They're about to can me anyway."

"Why do they need you back anyway?"

"Beck's still interviewing me. Not only about this case, but a dozen others. If they get rid of me, the ripple effect jeopardizes all of them in court. As long as I'm on duty, which won't be long, I'm sure, I'm tethered to them—by orders from all the way up the line. "

"Two days, then," I said.

"I promise," he said. "In the interim, I'm asking someone to watch your house."

I snorted once. "Call Scarecrow."

"Who?"

"Deputy Donald. I had him pegged as Barney Fife, but the uniform this evening told me his moniker was Scarecrow. Didn't sense a lot of admiration there."

Wayne didn't find the nickname humorous. "He's a little gung-ho, but that's good in my book. You have his number in your phone?"

"Yes, sir."

"Come on then," he said, lending his arm for me to get off the bed.

"Get dressed. I'll take you to your parents'."

The ten-mile ride seemed too fast. I still felt the need to talk, but I was tired and he had an eight AM appointment with Beck. Something told me he'd drive straight there from here. If he was lucky, he could stop for coffee along the way.

We parted on the doorstep, with Wayne literally handing me over to my father. After a handshake with Daddy, he was gone.

My son gave me a sluggish hug as I checked on him in his temporary bed. Noticing the shake in my hands, I quickly tucked the quilt and walked to the hallway. Ivy had gotten up to see me. She gathered me in a hug. My stomach did a queasy twist at how close I came to not coming back to her. "It's gonna be all right, Momma," she said.

"Thanks, sweetheart." I sent her off to bed with a tighter squeeze than usual. Since when did an eleven year old get so wise?

Feeling generally worthless, I neglected the facial treatment, brushed my teeth and crawled under the covers.

The nightmares came thick and fast. McRae stood behind a pulpit with a black curtain backdrop, grinning at the blight on my career. Hidden in shadows, he read judgment on me. Alan silently watched from a location I couldn't define, but his laughter was unmistakable as it mingled with Jean's. Someone breathed on my neck like Jesse had at the office. I shot up, awake, my pillow soaked with sweat.

With my throat dry, my breaths were eerily audible, quick and shallow. The clock read two. I'd been in bed less than two hours. The house lay silent, Madge the cat nowhere around.

"Oh damn, Madge." Stuck at home, she'd missed her dinner.

Not eager to return to my dreams, I eased out of bed. Skulking down the stairs was easy, since Mom slept with a television on. Nothing stirred her short of the lack of white noise if the cable went out. Daddy dozed in his recliner, all the lights on, a John Wayne flick on the classic movie channel.

I dragged myself to the back door. The creamy white box sat aglow on the wall, the lights on red. Chicken crap. Daddy set the alarm, and I didn't know the code.

I returned to bed, glad for the excuse not to go out in the dark. "One minute at a time," I said. "A year from now I'll laugh about all this."

A year from now I could be worm food, too.

CHAPTER 19

With the kids at school, I called in sick to the office—legitimately. Every bone and sinew in my body ached. A bruise adorned my cheekbone. When I went to the bathroom, I found one on my hip as well. Standing naked in front of the mirror, I inspected every inch of skin and located half a dozen more. I threw back four aspirin with coffee and a slice of Mom's coffee cake and headed to my house under her protest. Daddy's scowl could blister paint off a car. I compromised by letting them keep the kids for another night, giving them something to protect.

Madge the cat tried to trip me twice as I took care of her needs. While she ate her salmon gunk, I threw laundry in the washer and folded a load of clothes cold from the dryer. I called a different locksmith this time, one who swore he didn't know Alan. He assured me tomorrow morning I was first on his list.

Still in yesterday's work clothes, I changed into a tee and gym shorts. I tried to put away the rest of my freshly folded t-shirts, but the dresser drawer hung up. Each year I swore to rotate my winter and summer wardrobe, and each time I just crammed the off-season pieces to the bottom. I tugged, trying to reach my extra-large tie-dyed tee, one of four I wore around the house. It popped out, bringing others with it.

The force toppled me backward. A small piece of paper fluttered to the floor. I picked it up and unfolded it, the writing unmistakably Alan's.

I know what you look like under this.

I scooted a couple of feet further across the carpet. He could have put a water moccasin in the drawer and raised the same sense of shock. Either he'd been in the house again or the note dated back to the night he'd gathered his things. He had another woman, so what was with the stupid notes?

I crawled over to my nightstand and dialed Alan's number . . . then hung up, furious at my gutless ability to follow through with a harassing phone call. Instead, I stood, stomped into the bathroom and rummaged through the drawers until I found his moustache scissors. From the back of the closet, I jerked his pinstriped suit out of the cleaner's bag and cut a hole up the seam of his pants—appropriate for an asshole. Then another in the crotch. Holes in all the pockets. Then I carefully returned the suit to its hanger in the closet, along with the shreds of his favorite silk tie tucked in the breast pocket.

Much more satisfying than making a phone call.

Madge meowed and brushed my leg. She dangled all fours as I lifted her off the floor and into my arms. We climbed beneath a blanket on the sofa. She purred and I rubbed her soft belly, using her body heat to chase my chill.

The whole damn world had lost its mind. The only people who made sense were in trouble, and the crazies ran the show. I took a nap, swearing off men for at least three lifetimes.

The phone jarred me awake and scared me out of one of those lives.

"Special Agent Mason Ames, Ms. Slade."

Was there a run on agents? Buy one and get two free or something? I rubbed the sleep out of my eyes and blinked at the mantel clock. Quarter to eleven. Madge purred at my feet, apparently too hot to stay under the blanket.

"Hello?" asked the agent.

"I heard you. Is this a customer service courtesy call? The Jesse Rawlings case is closed from what I hear." I yawned, not caring if he heard.

"Any chance we can speak today? Since neither of us wants to waste more time than necessary, may we stop by your house?"

So they'd dropped in my office and missed me. Suited them right for trying to sneak in like Beck. "Don't know why. I swore and signed my name to Beck's contorted statement, just the way you guys wanted it."

"It would go easier on you if you cooperated."

"That's what the last two agents said." I'd already been indoctrinated into the Royal Order of Special Agent Groupies. I knew how they worked. "I was in a car accident yesterday, so I'm not feeling all that well," I said.

"We're sorry to hear that."

Sure he was . . . *we*? But I decided to cut him some slack. Might learn something more about what the IG had up its sleeve. "I'll give you an hour, at my house, at noon."

"We appreciate that, Ms. Slade."

They arrived at five till noon. I started to make them wait on the porch.

"Special Agent Mason Ames." His short arm extended his badge. I had an inch on him in height, enabling me to see the thin spot on the top of his brownish gray-haired head. "And this is Special Agent Ann Reddenbach."

Out flashed another badge. The female agent nodded and strained at a smile that needed more practice in front of a bathroom mirror. She obviously didn't think much of me.

Ames sat in Alan's recliner. I detoured to the kitchen, wetting a dish towel. Returning, I relaxed on the sofa, pulling the blanket around me as if they'd intruded on my sickbed, and held the towel to my temple. Maybe a tad over the top, but my head hurt.

Reddenbach laid her purse on my coffee table and sat in the tufted reading chair. Her nails perfectly manicured and too long to handle a gun, in my opinion, she wore pink lipstick with a blouse too red to match, like a street vamp. "You opened the Rawlings case," she said, "and it obviously didn't pan out. Instead, it raised more concerns." Her Mickey Mouse smile disappeared. "We have questions."

"Good for you."

The agents exchanged looks. Ames poised on the edge of his seat, like sitting back would make him less assertive. To think I'd worried what agents thought about *my* body language.

His colleague, however, seemed eager to flex her young agent muscles. "We aren't the culprits here, and apparently Rawlings wasn't one either."

Who the hell *was* in their opinion? I eyed the prissy woman. "You obviously wouldn't know the bad guys from the good." I didn't care if they reported me, but my muscles ached, and the partial nap had me cranky. "Rush this up. What do you need to know?"

For thirty minutes, they asked me to recap the deal with Jesse. The truth wasn't hard to tell. Every now and then I moved and grimaced for effect, refolded my washcloth.

Ames closed his pad. "We have all we need for now. We'll visit Mr. Rawlings, advise him to ignore the deal, and warn him not to bother you in any way. His only dealings with you will be to pay his debt and keep proper accounts."

I launched from my seat, wincing at the sudden move. "Are you insane? Do you realize where that leaves me?"

Ames spoke up. "Ma'am. We're trying to preserve reputations here. I assure you he won't be bothering you anymore."

I stooped over, closer, angrier. "You don't have a clue how evil this bastard can be, yet you're offering assurances. I'm worried more about my family than a reputation. He calls with threats. He's stalked me, groped me, killed my dog, for God's sake. Doesn't any of that matter?"

Reddenbach raised her eyebrows. "None of which affects the case."

"He offered me a bribe!"

"Money for his loan payment, Ms. Slade," she said.

Muscles knotted across my shoulders. "So, you're tossing me aside, for Jesse Rawlings to do with as he wants."

She sneered. "A little melodramatic, don't you think?"

I rose from my seat. She stood. With the coffee table between us, we dared the other to make a wrong move by our stares alone. Finally, my finger jerked toward the door. "Get out!"

"Thanks for your time," Ames said as he rose. Reddenbach scurried behind him toward the door. Ames turned around on my porch. "We'll drop back by and let you know how it goes."

"My voice mail works fine."

I shut and locked the door before they reached the bottom of my front steps. The government was heading out to give Jesse permission to be his maniacal, demented self. This couldn't be happening. Surely this lunacy limited itself to agriculture agents. If this mentality guarded national secrets, Americans held no chance against foreign terrorists.

The phone rang again, a Georgia area code.

"Your two visitors arrive yet?" Wayne asked.

"They're headed to Jesse's right now. He'll be mad as hell, and those cretins think he'll forgive and forget." My pulse quickened at the thought of them stirring the pot, escalating Jesse into a fury. "I'm assuming you didn't know about this last night."

"Just learned today, Slade. An hour ago."

"You work with a herd of blithering idiots."

"How well I know it," he said. "I'll call when I'm on my way over. One more day of questioning, and I'm out of here. I'm supposed to be in the men's room. Beck's waiting so I don't have but a second. What are you doing this afternoon?"

"Getting a new phone number," I said. "Washing clothes. The locks get changed tomorrow."

"Good." He continued with a laundry list of security issues. Keep my eyes open when driving or walking to and from the car. Lock my doors. Pick up the kids at random times. Check into a motel or stay with Daddy.

"The kids are at my parents' tonight. I'm already doing the other things."

"Damn I wish you had an alarm system. Check on that, too, okay? Lock everything. Avoid being easy prey, but I think he'll lie low for a while."

"I know, I know." The farmer may or may not attack me. What a revelation. "Well, I'll see you when you get here."

I heard a voice in the background.

"Huh? Crap. Slade?"

"I'm here."

"They're calling me back. You be safe, CI. You can do this." He hung up.

Do what? I could do anything I set my mind to including acting the innocent victim if that's what got his butt over here to clean up this mess.

I wasn't his CI this time. He was mine.

Then I had an epiphany. I punched the phone buttons for the Beaufort office. Savannah answered.

"Savvy? The boss isn't supposed to answer the phone."

"She does when the staff's out to lunch celebrating a birthday. Wonderful boss that I am, I offered to catch the calls."

"Well, since you're so nice . . ."

"My girlfriend needs me, huh? Speak."

I rarely asked her for help because she'd hurdle two states to deliver for me. "Would you babysit me?"

She paused. "I love your kids, sweetie, but can't you find a sitter closer than seventy-five miles away?"

"Not the kids, Savvy. Me." I brought her up to speed about Jesse, McRae, Alan, the car accident, then finally Wayne: a twenty-minute conversation.

"Girl, I'm crushed you haven't called me before now. Let me throw a bag together, and I'm yours for the rest of the week. Can you manage 'til I get there?"

"Sure. It's just a precaution . . . and I'd like to see you. I need to vent over a drink."

She laughed. "No problem. I'm dying to hear about that new man, anyway. I want to know more about the charismatic soul who swept Miss Straight and Narrow off her feet."

"Back up. I haven't been swept anywhere. He's just wrapping up this messy situation."

"Sure, honey. The tequila's on me."

Doors and windows locked and blinds drawn, I cleaned up the t-shirts I'd yanked on the bedroom floor. Nerves frazzled, thoughts racing, I wandered the house barefoot, seeking something to dust, vacuum or disinfect . . . checking locks for the second time as I went. When I dusted the table beneath the remote, I wondered what people watched this time of day.

A talk show couldn't hold my interest, so I changed to a home shopping channel. I ran to the kitchen to grab my credit card and order an embroidered jacket when a key clicked in the front door. My parents would've knocked.

Alan walked in like he was coming home for lunch.

"Get out," I said, before he looked up.

He jumped six inches off the rug. Then his astonishment vanished at the sight of me. His face now expressionless, he shut the door and locked it.

I readied myself, shoulders braced. "Where'd you get the key?" I demanded.

He unsnapped his windbreaker, the one Mom had given him for his birthday. He was dressed like he'd left straight from the office, wearing tan slacks and a beige dress shirt with a brown and gold print tie. "I need some things."

My hands went to my hips, appalled that he continued to disrespect my space. "What part of a restraining order don't you understand? I could have you arrested."

He moved in closer, setting his keys on the entry table like the old days. "So what's stopping you?" he asked. "What are you doing home anyway? What happened to your face?"

"My itinerary isn't your business. Leave. Go back to your girlfriend." I moved toward the door.

He stepped in my way. "My personal life isn't any business of yours."

"You stride in here when you aren't supposed to, with plans to pilfer through the house, after cat-burglaring me the other night, and have the gall to say your life isn't any of my business? I don't give a rip if you have a girlfriend. I honestly don't care." I returned to the sofa and folded the blanket. "And don't hide any more of your stupid notes."

He walked toward me and yanked the blanket from my hands.

I stood, pulling it back. "Grow up and get out."

"I'll leave when I'm ready and after I get what I came for."

I pointed toward the bedroom. "Find your stuff and go. You can pay to have the locks changed this time." Savvy and I would have another topic for our evening chat-fest tomorrow. I'd have to ask if her ex had gone half as nuts as mine.

Alan turned toward the bedroom, then stopped and turned back around. He scanned me from eyes to knees. I glanced down, remembering I stood braless in my oversized t-shirt, panty-less in my gym shorts. He'd know that.

Walking toward me, he flashed a sneer similar to Jesse's. My neck hairs prickled, the sensation shooting down my back. His six-foot frame blocked my way to the front door.

Run, Slade. Run until he settles down—like last time. Stay out of his reach and it'll be okay.

I dashed into the bedroom where a sliding glass door led to the small balcony only five feet off the ground. A wooden dowel wedged the slider shut—one of my latest security measures. My fingers fumbled with the pole, but it rolled, evading my grasp. Alan grabbed a handful of shirt. The force carried me back, off my feet, landing me on my behind next to the bed.

I scrambled to my knees. He flat-palmed me upside the head. My body bounced off the mattress and onto the floor.

"Stop it!" I screamed. I poised to defend with my knee or my nails across his face. He lowered his arms, and his vacant look appeared to reconsider his actions. Thank God. As soon as he was out the door, I'd call my attorney. Then the police.

After readjusting my shirt, I rose slowly, and when he didn't approach, I dared to walk past him. His grip on my upper arm didn't register at first, but my back slamming against the wall did as wind whooshed out of me.

Before I could inhale, he covered my mouth with his, pinning me hard with his body, from his lips to his thighs. My muffled scream diffused into his mouth as his kiss suffocated me. His tongue probed my clenched teeth. He pinned me with his body, and I cried out, allowing his tongue to swab my mouth, reaching my throat. His grip on my forearms would add more bruises, but his growing hardness against my groin scared me most.

My struggle impassioned him more. He dragged me to the floor as my bare feet dug into the carpet. With my arms flailing, I tried to knee him, but his slap against my face made the room spin.

"Manager? What a fucking joke. You couldn't manage your way out of a wet paper sack," he laughed. "Hear you got more than a professional interest in Mr. Special Agent, wife."

I wasn't sure what hurt most, my cheekbone or his knee on my chest. I feared he'd break a rib under his weight. He yanked off my gym shorts, then found his way to the femininity I'd denied him for four months. When he shoved his fingers inside, I gasped and renewed my fight only to earn his other hand on my neck.

I tried to wrestle free, the familiarity of marriage telling me he wouldn't choke me. His fingers pressed tighter, proving me wrong. My ears heard a distant white noise that intensified and floated sparkles of light between me and his slanted brown eyes.

I released my grip on his wrist to the hand choking me . . . and used both hands to gouge him in the eyes.

His hands abruptly let go. "Goddamn it!" he screamed, covering his face. "Oh God," he panted. His fingers rubbed his eyelids as he fell off me, stumbling to his knees. "You goddamn bitch!"

I rolled to my side and retreated toward the sliding glass door since he stood between me and the bedroom exit.

My eyes wide and blinking, the room slowly returned to focus.

Alan rose, tears pouring down his face, his cheeks blotched. "You're through."

The dowel that evaded my grasp before found its way into my hands. I wound up like a baseball player. "Get the hell out of my house before I take your friggin' head off."

Alan stood and zipped his fly. Saliva mixed with tears glistened on his chin before he wiped his face with his sleeve. "You're done, Slade."

"Come within a hundred yards of me, and I'm having you arrested," I said. "I'll be armed, too."

Bared and disheveled, I glared at him, wanting him to recognize the damage he'd done. His stare drove a piercing chill through me.

Then he just left.

I locked the door, wedged a chair under the knob, then my legs buckled like a new colt. When breakfast rose in my throat, I struggled to reach the bathroom, only to vomit on the carpet next to my bed. Between heaves, I cursed as coffee cake and caffeine seeped into the wool fibers.

Stomach still cramping, I grabbed paper towels, but I couldn't quite erase the spot. Screw it. I ran a bath of hot water. Actions robotic, my mind hovered in neutral. A half-bottle of bubble bath globbed into the tub. Lavender-scented lather disguised a temperature almost hot enough to blister. The shorts and shirt went in the trash. I sank into the steam, closed my eyes and let the heat burn. I deserved this.

But I drooped my head and burst into tears. They wouldn't stop. I watched them fall over and over and puddle with the perspiration running between my breasts. Crying stopped then started again as I tried to figure out what I'd done to warrant all this.

Yeah, feel sorry for yourself. Let everyone see how a string of men broke Carolina Slade when she bit off more than she could chew. Everyone in Agriculture would label me the fool.

I sniffled in erratic spurts, like Zack.

No way would I cry attempted rape. How would they understand my husband let himself into his own house with a key and attacked me? My word against his. They'd just say I brought this on myself.

CHAPTER 20

When the doorbell rang two hours later, I jumped, sending lukewarm water over the edge of the tub. The bubbles had melted. Realizing the good guys usually rang the doorbell, I climbed out of the bathtub and wrapped my chenille robe around me.

Savvy called out, "The babysitter's here!" as I opened the door. She studied my robe then my swollen eyes and set her goodie bags on the floor. She rubbed her hands up and down my arms, her bracelets clinking against each other. "What happened, sweetie?" Then she held a finger under my chin, turned my head and examined my cheek.

Her cropped, frosted hair and designer makeup made me feel all the more disturbed. I bit my lip to fight tears and twitched at her touch on one spot, raising my hand to the pain on my face. "Alan."

"You mean he . . . ?"

"Attacked me."

"Oh, honey, did he . . ."

I shook my head. "His hands grabbed . . . in my pants . . . but he didn't . . ."

She lifted my chin with two fingers. "Still rape, though, wasn't it?"

She shut the door, locked it and kicked all the bags in the corner. She swung her purse around and rummaged through it, pulled out her phone, and hit three buttons.

"What are you doing?" I asked.

She held up a finger. "Yes, I called 9-1-1. My name is Savannah Conroy. I just arrived at my friend's house to find out her estranged husband raped her about an hour ago." She gave my address, my name.

This wasn't happening. "Oh, Jesus, Savvy." I covered my face with my hands. More cops. More damn cops. And what would Alan think . . . or worse, how would he react when police challenged him? This was Jesse all over again.

She hung up. "Someone will be here any moment. Let's go have a seat. Tell me what happened. Every detail."

I moved as ordered, captive in the chain of events, and too spent to deviate. Admittedly, Savvy used her good common sense reporting what was in essence a crime, but she hadn't been in my shoes these last two weeks. If Alan had tried this under any other circumstances, with no special agents or deranged farmers in my world, I'd have reported him before he left the front porch. But my constitution sat on a shaky foundation as people right and left turned on me, causing my previous trust in a system to erode to dust and disappear.

But Savvy loved me. I could afford to feel safe around her. I answered her questions in monotone syllables, not caring to fall back into a well of emotion right before company arrived.

The doorbell chimed. Savvy answered. I remained on my sofa still in my robe, for effect per Savvy's orders, and dreaded the next moment with a mile-high mound of trepidation.

In walked the same deputy who took the accident report on Smokey.

"Come on it, Deputy . . . James, is it?" Savvy asked. She ushered him into the living room. "Slade, here's . . . what's wrong?"

I glanced up at the deputy, his thin physique accented by the heavy gun-laden leather belt that threatened to tip him over. "We've met. Sorry, Donald. Forgot to call and tell you someone was breaking in so you could rescue me. Seems my timing is off."

My caustic behavior didn't sway him. He remained standing, feet shoulder-width apart, old enough to be ominous in uniform, young enough to lack experience, all business written on his face. "I understand where you're coming from, Ms. Slade." He opened a clipboard. "May I sit?"

I waved toward the recliner.

"Tell me what happened. You were raped by your husband?" he asked.

"Estranged. I filed for divorce. Not exactly, but he attacked me. Hit me. Tried to rape me. He just used his hand . . ." I cleared my throat. "I poked him in the eye and grabbed a pole to scare him off."

He wrote a few words. "So he didn't penetrate? No semen? Anyone around here that can corroborate the fact he was here?"

Eyes closed, I sighed. "I said I stopped him. And I have no idea who may have seen him drive up or drive off."

He wrote more, then looked up. "How did he get in?"

"A key."

"So no forced entry?"

I explained the reason for changed locks, the earlier night when he'd broken in and almost pummeled me, the prank phone calls I suspected were his. Donald asked if I'd injured Alan. I should've hit a home run against his head with my stick.

"I scratched at his eyes, but he seemed okay when he left."

"Ma'am." He paused. "I'll file the report. I'll speak to your husband. But this might wind up being—"

"He said, she said," I whispered.

He nodded. "No witnesses. His house. Just depends on how far you want to fight this. I see your bruises, but he has wounds of his own. He'll claim . . ."

I held up a hand and stopped him. My imagination took it further than Donald even knew. My kids were in danger. My job security rocky. Did I want to air all this in public?

Crap. What was the need for law enforcement when it held victims more accountable than the criminals? I rubbed my forehead, unable to process this absurdity. Systems and processes. They installed structure in an otherwise chaotic environment. Do wrong, and rules existed to right that wrong. So why didn't they work for me?

Donald worked his mouth, pondering. "Do you wish me to file charges? That would mean picking him up for questioning."

Running my teeth over my bottom lip, I studied the man, assimilating his remark. That's when I realized his attitude wasn't against me. It was about what happened to me. Just like he had with Smokey, Donald sympathized and craved to help.

"Slade?" Savvy touched my hand, the one I'd tangled unknowingly in the tie from my robe. "He asked if you—"

"Yes," I said with a jerk of my head. "Pick his ass up."

Donald cocked his head. "Are you sure?"

Alan sure wasn't Jesse, but for now he'd do. And I sensed Donald relished the opportunity. "Absolutely."

I gave him a smile. He returned one in kind with an approving nod.

After collecting a few more questions and my signature on a form, Deputy James left.

Savvy locked the door behind him and turned around, a smirk showing her satisfaction. I shook my head, tucked feet under my robe, and sank into the sofa cushion, resting my forehead on my knees. Savvy left me to myself.

She kicked off her shoes, and her padded footsteps went to the guest room, then the kitchen. I heard a bag rustle, then heavy glass clank. "Where's your blender, girl?"

I lifted my head and pointed to the pantry.

"Get in here," she said with emphasis on the IN, her finger pointing to the floor beside her.

I unfolded and honored her wishes. "What?"

"Stand here," she shifted me to one side of her, "and hand me what I tell you."

She barked orders as she salted glass rims and sliced limes, operating as if she tended a bar at Hooters. When she completed her recipe, she handed me a glass of the light green liquid.

Her manicured fingers tucked a lock of hair behind my ear. "Drink it.

And don't spill any or it'll burn a hole in your floor."

I sipped the tequila and licked some of the salt, wincing as it stung my lips.

"Shit, honey," Savvy said. "Suck it down. You can sip the next one."

I chugged the contents, enjoying the burn. She passed the second one to me, then sipped one of her own. "Now come over here to the sofa. Sit next to me and tell me what's going on. Then I'll decide who needs killing."

An hour later, she could name the agents, describe Jesse and hate Alan as well as I could. She stopped at one margarita while I'd swilled four. I cursed and complained about everything on my chest. Like a best friend, she agreed with it all, with a few reservations about Wayne.

"You got a camera around here?" she asked.

"I got kids. What do you think?" I licked more salt. "Why?"

She touched my face. "I want proof of those."

"Unh uh. Nope."

"Then take a picture with me." She jumped up, hands on her hips. "Later I can show you what you look like drunk. And we can show your insurance company the bruises in case they want proof for your car accident."

"Whatever. Look in the credenza drawer down the hall."

She rose from the sofa.

I hollered, "How come I don't have a picture of you for my wallet?"

She returned. "Well, we'll take care of that, too, won't we?"

We finished posing and hugging for the camera just as the battery died. "I'm still in my robe. Ain't that a crock of shit?" I said, slurring my words as she set the camera back on the credenza after slipping the disk in her pocket.

Savvy snickered at me. "You think you might like to eat something?"

In nothing flat, she whipped up eggs, toast and sliced oranges. Curled up at either end of the sofa, we ate a lunch laced with more margaritas.

The ease with which she took over my care, coupled with tequila, drained the tension right out of me. As I tried to pick the salt out of my lap, I marveled to my friend. "You're the best, Savannah. You know that?"

"Yeah, I do. Come on, I'll tuck you in for a nap." She pulled me up by one arm since my bottom wanted to remain connected to the cushion. "I think Wayne sounds awesome, honey. You mind if I have his phone number?"

I turned back in a slow-motion kind of way and stared down my nose, trying not to cross my eyes. "Don't trust him. I'm not sure about him yet."

"I understand. I think I need to know his 4-1-1, though, in case we see either of your assholes again—Jesse or Alan."

I pointed toward the kitchen as she led me to the bedroom. "Look in my purse on the counter. It's in my wallet." She lowered me to the bed. I bunched the sheets and comforter up to my neck and floated away.

After what seemed seconds, Savvy shook my shoulder. "Hey, sleepyhead. This guy's at your door saying he's come to change the locks. Get some clothes on."

My eyes fought to see past the haze. "He wasn't supposed to be here until tomorrow," I said with a thick tongue, dry mouth.

"Yeah, well I asked him to come today," she said.

I stumbled into jeans and a sweatshirt and washed my face. Savvy handed me three aspirin and a Coke. An hour later, all my locks were new. I gave the guy a sandwich and a picture of Alan, promising him a reward if Alan showed up to get a key. Promised him a case of beer if he told his friends in the business. I showed him my bruises as proof of what could happen again.

Savvy glanced at her watch. "We gotta get your brats, don't we? Let's get going before the school sells your kids to the highest bidder."

"Mom has them," I said, thanking the heavens she did. Between now and tomorrow I had to learn how to hide the bruises. Savvy ordered pizza.

"I have to say, you're worth looking at again," Savvy said.

Empowerment and drink had replenished my depleted supply of spunk. "A gun's going to stay closer to my shooting hand. I'll be ready if it happens again."

She laughed. "There you go. Blow his balls off. They keep coming if you hit anything else."

I laughed heartily, the jocularity thrilling.

I handed her a glass of ice and Coke, and we sat down at the kitchen table, shoving pizza crust and paper plates to the side. A pain from my left hip reminded me to sit to the side. The ice cubes soothed my swollen lip. "When do you need to go home?"

"Don't worry about it. I'm playing bodyguard. You'll need my services as babysitter tomorrow anyway, unless the kids stay at your mom's again."

"Really?" I asked. "What makes you think that?"

She toyed with her bracelet. "A little voice told me from Atlanta. By the way, he said to call him sometime today."

I dropped a cube back into the glass and wiped my hand on my pants. "I should've known you'd meddle."

"Damn straight! I've got to meet the man who turned your world on its ear."

I scoffed. "Name me a man in my life who hasn't?"

"You need to meet with him, Slade. Go someplace and talk. I'll doll you up right. If I can't make something work out of your closet, we'll go shopping."

"He's not a boyfriend, Savvy." I thought those words over. "I'm not sure what he is."

She paused. "I grilled him for almost an hour."

"Watch it. He makes a great first impression."

"And I'm no fool. Step back for a moment. Some agent drags a derogatory statement out of you, but this one wants to help you out of this mess. I'm not telling you to jump in the sack with him, just accept the help. Meet somewhere, chat, and y'all get your act together, plan what needs doing."

"What's wrong with here?" I asked.

She did her girlfriend hand wave toward my kitchen, then the bedroom. "You hide in this house, Slade. Go where you aren't reminded of anything. Find someplace neutral. Enjoy yourself."

But I still knew so little about Wayne, unsure of what I thought I did know. And I had no idea what he was coming back here to do about Jesse, and if it would do any good. He seemed to feel responsible though. At least that suited me.

I chased away the dilemma, my brain still crammed with cotton. "Enough of that. What's wrong with my clothes?"

"Let's just say you're office by day and soccer mom by night."

The phone rang, the caller probably Wayne since I'd not called back. I wasn't going to get into a habit of reporting to him.

"Hello?"

"Where you been, Slade?" Jesse drawled. "I've been hunting all over for you."

Surprise stole my voice after hearing his slither across the phone line. I'd almost backtracked to normal till now. I rose and moved to the entry hall to pace.

"Slade? You avoiding me?"

"I've been busy," I said low. "You're not the only farmer in Charleston County, Jesse."

Savannah perked up at the name. She set down her glass and walked over.

Jesse coughed. "Some badges told me to mind my business. You could've at least told me they were coming."

"They surprised me, too. Backed me into a corner. Nothing I could do about it."

His voice thickened. "So what happened to my money?"

"They've got it. They're making me put it on your loan."

He yelled. "You double-crossing whore. You don't know who you're dealing with. You—"

Savvy snatched the phone from my hand. "Mr. Rawlings? This is Special Agent Hipp. I thought we told you to back off?"

She handed me the phone. Only a dial tone. "I think I scared him."

"Oh my gosh, Savannah. You gotta be careful with this guy."

She shook her head and returned to her seat. "He'll think twice before calling now, and he might not come over if he thinks you've got a watchdog. Now. All you've got to worry about is what to wear tomorrow night."

I grimaced at her simplistic remark. "I wish."

Manicured fingers straightened the front of my shirt. "Honey, please. Lighten up. No need looking like a bag lady. You can still feel good about yourself." She swayed her head, grinning, her earrings dangling, a suave come-on in her voice. "You'll feel like you're in the driver's seat."

I grinned. "I knew there was a reason I invited you over here, Special Agent Hipp."

"Of course. I'm the tempest in your storm, the eye in your hurricane, the—"

"The bodyguard who kicks ass."

She winked. "That, too."

CHAPTER 21

The doorbell rang. My hair crimped crooked on the left. This curling iron was a piece of crap. Sticking my fingers under the faucet, I eased out the mistake and reached for the blow dryer.

"I'll get it," Savvy yelled from the living room. "Take your time." In two days, she'd become a fixture in the place. We'd retrieved the kids from Mom's, and Savvy would stay with them while I met with Wayne. Ivy was thrilled with my friend, Zack enamored. They were both upstairs, taking baths.

Feeling female dredged up a self-worth I'd long forgotten, but my stomach fluttered, bordering on nausea. I brushed out a strand of hair and attempted the iron again, then gave up and headed for the front foyer, hands fidgety.

I drank in the broad shoulders and trimmed beard of the man standing in my entry hall, intently talking to Savannah. Even with her back toward me, Savvy's posture said she meant business. Looking over his interrogator's shoulder, Wayne's slow deep grin set my heart skipping, and his wink about did me in. I hated it.

This was business, for God's sake. A time to regroup and analyze where we stood, how to handle Jesse, mastermind how to keep our jobs. On one hand I had no business trying to give any impression of leading this guy on. On the other, I deserved to feel better.

Wayne wore creased new jeans, a beige dress shirt and a leather jacket that hung clean and sexy without the bulging holster. "Look at you," he said, abruptly interrupting his one-sided chat with my girlfriend.

Savvy had outdone herself with me. My cream cashmere sweater draped loosely over matching slacks. An amulet and chain hung around my neck, tasteful gold hoops on my ears, courtesy of her overnight bag. I looked more than good; I looked damn fine.

He stepped around Savvy and paused, his eyes obviously taking in my face, the bruises. Then he reached for me. I took a step back and threw a panicky glance toward Savvy, then stiffened as Wayne wrapped me in his arms without invitation.

Savvy raised her eyebrows, hand on a hip. Wayne completely enveloped me, forcing me to inhale a mild musty cologne and leather. Hesitant for a moment, I lightly hugged back. At my touch, he squeezed harder, and Alan flashed across my mind. The pressure on my chest, the inability to breathe. The same smothering hold to keep me from moving. Red-faced, I pressed my hands against Wayne's jacket. I couldn't do this. We didn't need to do this.

Terror flew over me. "I can't," I said, and ran back into the bedroom.

The necklace went back in my drawer, the earrings thrown on the bed. Nerves danced under my skin at the thought of a man holding me. The sweater landed in the sink, the pants on the floor. Where the hell were my jeans?

Someone rapped on the door. "Slade?" Savvy's voice spoke on the other side. "What's wrong, hon? Talk to me."

"I can't. I just can't," I shouted as I slid hangers across the pole. Thank God. My favorite jeans hung crooked behind my office slacks.

I shoved a dark brown turtleneck over my head, pulled my hair out from inside the neck, and grabbed my goose down vest. Socks and five-year-old boots completed the package. After a hard brushing, my hair fell like it was supposed to, only a tad puffier.

"Slade." This time it was Wayne. "Let me in. Savvy says we need to talk about what happened yesterday. What is it, CI?"

My hand rested on the doorknob for a moment as I inhaled deep two, three, four times. I was back in my own skin. No pretense of a date or anything resembling a date. No doubt I had to talk to Wayne, but no way would I send mixed signals. I needed the case closed, not a new relationship.

After counting to ten, I opened the door. Savvy stepped back, staring. Wayne eyed me, a worried mask on his face.

"Now we can go talk," I said.

They inadvertently stood in my way, obviously not understanding my behavior. Suddenly I could still smell Alan on me in that room, see the spot on the floor. "Back up, back up," I said. I pushed past them before I freaked out again.

Savvy reached me first as I poured a glass of water at the kitchen sink. "You're worrying me, hon." She didn't mention my destruction of her makeover.

I gestured toward Wayne, then Savvy. "Wayne, this is Savannah Conroy, my counterpart from Beaufort *and* my best friend. I believe you've spoken."

Wayne shook her hand, playing along. "My pleasure."

"Good," I said. "Now, let's go."

Savvy handed me my purse. She hugged Wayne tight and whispered something in his ear.

Wayne held the door handle, waiting for me. Savvy took my arm and put her back toward Wayne. I could still see the stain on my bedroom carpet through the open door. She saw me glance.

"Now you understand why you can't meet here," she said. "Go chill. Have a drink, or don't, I don't care. But the two of you have got to talk." She nodded toward the stairs. "I'm here with the kids. Take your time." She shuffled a step over and whispered, "Just give the guy a fair shake, okay?"

She hugged me and nudged us out, locked the door with animated purpose then waved through the glass. Wayne started to offer me his arm, and I pretended not to see it. Inside the Chevy Blazer, the upholstery held his scent. I tried to breathe shallow. He got in.

"This isn't a date, Wayne."

He tilted his head in acknowledgement. "It's whatever you make it."

Some of my apprehension settled at his reply. I set my purse on the seat between us, so relieved I'd dressed more casual, more me.

He started the engine. My hands lay in my lap, my wedding band gone after Alan's stunt. I'd spent two weeks with Wayne, but not unofficially, like this. His presence consumed me, my senses on razor edge. Even with my job and safety in jeopardy, my main concern at the moment was how to converse with the man. He'd helped and hurt me, burning bridges along the way, then gradually reconstructed them. I had no choice but to proceed forward, using him as a guide of sorts. I was leery of dealing with Jesse alone, and Wayne needed my knowledge of the farmer and the area. Our situation couldn't get more complicated.

"We have to eat, right?" he asked.

Dinner was safe, a public setting. "I could eat," I said.

We drove toward Charleston to Mount Pleasant's Shem Creek, far enough away from Ridgeville to avoid familiar faces. Wayne lightheartedly mentioned something about Savvy. I nodded and remained silent. He tried for a joke; I didn't laugh. My mind was burdened with a wheelbarrow load of concerns and unasked questions, but I didn't know how to start, like I'd step on my own tongue.

How much of Beck's information on Wayne was true? Was there more to his disciplinary troubles than I knew? Beck was an arrogant blockhead and had probably lied his ass off, but none of these agents told a clean truth. I smiled at something Wayne said, then watched a blood red Porsche pull up beside us and move on.

The biggest question was how to turn the tables on Jesse. How would we convince the authorities that a pig farmer was a legitimate menace? Until we crossed that hurdle, we remained in danger, both our lives changed for the worse.

"How's your sister?" I asked.

He stared ahead, not appearing distraught at my words. "Haven't found her yet." He seemed a lot calmer than I'd be missing a family member. Or was this a peaceful façade to keep me from going bonkers again?

"Is . . . is that normal?" I cracked one knuckle then rubbed it, scolding myself for the unladylike move. "Sorry, but I'm not sure how to talk about her."

"She's missing. She's done this before." He stretched his neck to the side, as if limbering up. "I have my feelers out. She was involved with Pamela and DEA. I'm not sure the disappearance is her doing or not. I've searched her old haunts, can't find a damn clue."

His voice mellowed there toward the end.

"I hope it all works out," I said.

He drove with just his right hand. "I have an ex-coke addict for a sister. Or at least I hope it's still ex. She disappears, and when she returns, I know she's not dead." He watched the road. "Not something I'm particularly proud of, but she's family."

"You're not your sister. Besides, you're a cop."

He laughed through his nose. "Tell that to other cops."

The worst my sister ever did was slip out of the house at one in the morning, smoke a joint and skinny-dip in the country club pool. "Is she why they placed you on leave?"

He shook his head. "They'd like to use that, but no. They have enough with Eddie and the rumor about you. In their opinion, I'm not the textbook agent, so they ride me any chance they can get. Trouble is new agents look up to me, and I land results. My prosecution numbers rank top three in the Southeast every quarter. I'm a festering boil on management's collective backside, but they need me."

To think that I'd fancied his job cooler than mine. Between the two of us, we carried enough baggage for the Titanic.

He took us toward the bridge. "You have enough problems without worrying about mine. Tonight it's about Jesse . . . or how we can work together against him."

I watched water pass under the Ravenel Bridge, with no clue on how I'd contribute to catch Jesse. There was no setting him up now. We'd failed miserably at that angle already.

We crossed Shem Creek Bridge and turned right into a parking lot. The hostess at R.B.'s Seafood placed us in a corner overlooking the pier, mistaking us for a couple. A collection of shrimp boats bobbed in slow motion not thirty feet away. She handed us menus and left. Wayne set his down, leaned his elbows on the table and stared at me.

I studied my menu like it was a final exam. Part of me wanted to pretend, even for one night, that a past with Wayne didn't exist. He was a stranger in so many ways, so protective of himself, but that morning he'd followed me to the beach wasn't in my imagination. He'd kissed me. Electricity had sparked between us. It shouldn't have. It confused matters. We'd be smart to go our separate ways, but with our Jesse dilemma, we remained hitched to the same buggy. I waved down a waitress two tables away and ordered a bourbon. Wayne held up two fingers.

He turned back to me. "Ames may have told Jesse that no charges were being brought. So Jesse made his call to you last night. As for what Beck said . . . just keep in mind that his job is to make a six-year-old look like an international gunrunner." He unfolded his silverware from its wrap and put his napkin in his lap. "I've dealt with him for two straight days. He's no Boy Scout."

There was a sense of the demoralized young boy in Wayne. As I watched him slowly spin his water glass and rub a finger across the moisture on the tablecloth, I realized he needed my help as much as I needed his. He'd sacrificed his job . . . maybe in defense of me, maybe not. He maintained a need to finish his task, make amends after promising me everything would be all right. I could tell Wayne that he didn't owe me anything, but in all honesty, I felt he did.

His finger reached over, hesitated, then touched my forearm. "It must be really tough on you, all this crap."

"Let's see. I've been groped, lied to, stalked, shot at, run off the road and almost raped. Other than that, I'm fine." I reached for my starched cotton napkin, placing it in my lap, surprised at how much anger I'd spilled in those few words. I scanned over heads for the waitress. Where was that drink?

"Raped?" he said a bit too loud. Horror contorted what had been a pleasant face with a soft beard. "My God, Slade. How in hell did that happen?"

The diners at the next table stopped eating at the sound of his voice.

"Hush," I whispered.

He shoved his chair away from the table as if preparing to fight someone then and there. "The hell I will. Who was it?" Frustrated, he scraped his seat back toward me. "Goddammit, please don't tell me it was Jesse," he whispered. "I never should've gone back to Atlanta."

I'd fingered a packet of crackers from the courtesy basket on the table then opened them, guilty about leaving them crunched to crumbs for the next eaters. "My ex," I said. "Let's not go into the details. Let's just say I let my guard down, and I'd prefer not to relive it again."

He frowned. Then his eyes narrowed. "Son-of-a-bitch," he said low. "I thought I recognized new bruises." He rose and walked to the end of the porch, leaned over and looked down at the water long enough for me to down my drink and ask for another.

Diners rose to leave, chair legs scraping the planked floor. Wayne returned and sat, somewhat tempered.

"Forget Alan," I said.

He gripped the menu. "He and I need to chat."

By now we were alone on the porch. I searched for some way to change the topic. I just wanted my life back, Jesse gone, and Wayne . . . categorized.

"I shouldn't have brought him up," I said.

He rested his hand on my wrist without hesitation this time. "I'm sorry. Just enjoy your dinner."

I retracted my arm to my lap. We sat silent for a minute that felt like hours.

"Wayne," I said, unable to stand the unsaid between us.

The waitress appeared and I withdrew my hand off the table. She set down our tiny complimentary crab dip appetizer with my second bourbon. When she glanced at Wayne, he shook his head that we weren't ready to order.

How should I say this? "You kept secret about Alan and Jean," I said, figuring blunt was best.

"I know, and it ate at me. But you'd filed the papers by the time I found out. You were knotted up enough about Jesse, so why upset you about Alan when you two were already history?" He sat back, analyzing me. "At the time, I thought I was doing the right thing. Frankly, I still do."

The simple explanation made sense. Or was I trying to make it sound logical? "Well, I'm not a china doll."

"Savvy raked me over the coals, you know," he said, trying to grin.

"One of her many talents."

"She vowed to hunt me down if I was . . . how'd she put it . . . adding another pony to my stable."

I allowed a smile. That so sounded like her.

"And she told me more about Alan. Don't know why she didn't mention the attack."

"Maybe because she felt it my news to tell," I said.

Another frown creased wrinkles around his eyes. "Slade, he's as dangerous as Jesse now."

I pushed the small spreading knife through the dip, unsure how to react to such a bold statement.

He recognized when to change the subject. "So Savvy got you drunk, huh?"

I stifled a laugh. "She loaded me up for sure. She also had the locks changed and handled Jesse's call."

The instant replay of Savvy's parley drew a snicker from him. But the mention of the hog farmer threw us back into the case. "What are we dealing with? How did Jesse sound?" he asked. "I suspect he's on the warpath."

We couldn't escape the oppressive weight of events. We'd be foolish to think of much else. I needed solutions on how to save my life. By the time we'd finished eating and the waitress had cleared the table and brought coffee, we were deep into investigation mode, the case the mortar that bound us. Twice, Wayne held my hand, acting as if he could never let go, until I pulled away, needing my hands to talk. The third time I let him hold on. It seemed to make him more at ease.

CHAPTER 22

Oyster shells crunched under the Blazer's tires as we left the restaurant. Mom wouldn't have approved of this evening, and that irritated my conscience, like an annoying tickle in the back of my throat. But Mom didn't know about all the attacks, the threats, or the plots to slice and dice my career. Still, I sensed another demerit on the character I'd strived to perfect.

In the big scheme of things, Wayne appeared unwavering in his support, at least to my knowledge. I, on the other hand, doubted him at every turn. But then, almost everyone in my world misled me these days. Who the hell was I supposed to trust? I'd performed by the book in all aspects of my existence, yet here I sat, up to my eyelashes in a quagmire.

The restaurant had closed, leaving us in mid-discussion. This late we opted to cruise the coastal area until we could hash out all the details of this crazy storm that had compromised both our lives, until we reached a consensus on what to do about Jesse.

Wayne steered toward the beach side of the peninsula, the landscape monochrome under a waxing moon. I loved the palmetto trees and marsh that bordered this span of roadway. Despite the chilly evening, I eased the window down to inhale the salt air.

"I have serious doubts about Mickey Wilder's disappearance," he said. The shift in conversation came over as abrasive since I'd settled into being one with the scenery.

But I had suspicions about Mickey's death, too. "Why do you say that?"

"Not sure," he said. "Talk to me about Mickey. Everything you can think of."

I was eager to discuss my old boss, as long as the talk didn't incriminate him. "He was a good man, Wayne. Don't try to pin something on him. Mickey was far too solid to do himself in."

I repeated the story about his wife's death, how we were shocked about his debt and antidepressants, and how he'd taken a few files and disappeared that icy February day. Wayne stopped at a light, and I quit talking, the memories painful. He let me pause. At the green light we both started again.

"He often worked late," I said, "especially when he visited the islands. He could've been delayed at a drawbridge or stuck arguing with some farmer." Everyone's surprise had been palpable when he didn't arrive at work the next day. Hillary had joked about a hangover, and I'd shut her up with a glare. "McRae notified the cops when I couldn't contact Mickey at home. State Director Edmonds called the IG." Wayne already knew they'd found Mickey's car in a marshy tributary that emptied into the briny Intracoastal Waterway.

Wayne drove just below the speed limit, no rush. The dashboard car clock showed eleven.

"It dumbfounded me when they labeled it a probable suicide," I said. "Mickey wasn't like that."

As second in command, I'd assumed Mickey's duties. I could still recite the names of the other agents, the local law, even the single FBI dude named Ricky, who'd briefly checked in one morning. I never saw Wayne.

We exited the contemporary town of Mount Pleasant. "How come I never ran into you during that investigation?" I asked.

Wayne shrugged. "I spent most of my time in the field combing every road and potholed path interviewing people. Mickey practically died in Jesse's backyard, you know."

"Yeah. It's creepy going out there." I said. "Where'd they find Mickey's car exactly?"

He held his tongue for a moment. "You know where they found his car."

Yeah, I did. But I wanted Wayne to tell me.

"Three miles from the Williams' farm," he said. "Jesse's place is between the two." He glanced over. "Feel better?"

He slowed and eased into the parking lot of a closed tourist shop, where boogie boards hung in the window next to seahorse decorated beach towels. Wayne put the gear in park and turned to face me. "Beck messed with your head," he said. "I'm trying my damnedest to be patient about it. Believe me, I know what he's like. Just don't second guess yourself. Or me. I'm on your side."

"Maybe I should go home," I said, uncomfortable.

Without one person in sight, I still wasn't afraid of Wayne. I was more afraid of me and my unpredictable reaction to him. Both our agencies assumed we were an item. Had people around us seen the chemistry? We hadn't done a thing, yet I felt like we had. The car idled as he leaned his right arm over the back of the seat, fingertips grazing my shoulder. If he kissed me, I'd kiss him back, hard.

"Hey," he said. "Did you know that McRae's name is all over Williams' farm file—in the notes, on inspection documents?"

"He's the district manager."

Wayne nodded. "But how many times does a director check behind a manager as seasoned as Mickey Wilder?"

Directors didn't do field visits. Heck, I didn't do them if an assistant could. "McRae documented all those visits?"

"No. But Mickey did—after the fact. At least those times he knew about."

God, I missed Mickey. Jesse wouldn't have tried to bribe him. "So McRae was interested in getting the farm himself?"

"Well, he was reprimanded two years ago for steering a sale to his cousin," he said. "He's walked the edge of legality before."

The sale Wayne was referring to had occurred in Dorchester County. I loved the thought of McRae caught and called on the carpet. "So McRae is Jesse's partner after all," I said.

"Most likely, CI."

I gazed out the window. I'd worn worse nicknames.

He put the car in drive, drove out and paused at a junction. He let an impatient driver speed past on the two-lane road. The tide was out from the volume of marsh mud, glistening wet under moonlight. We were headed away from home, toward my beach.

"Do you realize McRae handled the environmental evaluation on that farm?" he asked, driving onto the road.

I should've known that. My office, not his, handled that level of menial paperwork. "I didn't look at who signed the environmental. That's so routine." I thought a moment. "There is some low land on a back corner maybe passing for wetlands. Mr. Williams used to raise hell about his tractor bogging down. We lower the property value on land with wetlands so the government doesn't become the owner, but there isn't enough on the place to make a difference." I remembered McRae's directive about the appraisal. "Damn."

Wayne glanced at me. "What?"

"I started to tell you at the farm that McRae asked me to lower the price of that place. Eddie climbed out of the bushes and I forgot."

"Did you do it?"

I shook my head. "I don't have the authority. He said he'd get it approved without me, and I didn't ask how. I didn't want to know. I'm in enough hot water as it is."

"That it?"

I flipped both hands out and shrugged. "Sorry. I can't know everything."

He frowned. "I didn't say it was your fault, did I? Quit thinking you can fix everything. And quit doubting my motives. Shit happens, Slade. You just wade through it."

I sat quietly and thought about the load resting on his shoulders, and how sane he continued to act in spite of the authorities taking his job. Wayne was right. When bad things happened, I tried to correct them, put everything back to right—control the direction. This fiasco came at us from all directions, inconceivable to control.

"Practice what you preach," I mumbled.

"Excuse me?"

"Nothing."

I almost said take me home, again, but I preferred his company to being alone, waiting for Alan to break into the house again—or Jesse to call. Wayne was safe, and yes, he was smart. But most of all, he was the first person to make me want to stray from the rules in order to get something done. A high-caliber turn on.

I inhaled, searching for level-headedness. This outing was a mistake. I was sick of needing a man I only trusted part of the time. I'd trusted Alan and gotten nowhere. The girls who fell for the rough guys in school escaped my understanding. They always got hurt, or worse. Wayne bordered on that image, a man capable of a bullet straight through the heart.

I was smarter than this.

We crossed the islands. Still I said nothing. He turned into the sandy parking lot. He leaned across me and locked the glove compartment I assumed held a weapon he was no longer authorized to carry. With a warm waft of leather, he turned to face me, his shoulders blocking my view of the waves.

Warm lips pressed mine, firm and polite, easing my head against the headrest. My mind emptied as my heart hammered. I caught a hitch in his breathing as he eased back, shifted the weight on his arm and closed the space between us for another kiss. I started to reach around his neck, hesitated, then let my hand touch the side of his head, a gesture of pure restraint.

I'd begun to like the big jerk before Beck had messed with my head. Was I too smitten to think straight, or thinking too straight to allow some semblance of affection in my life? I couldn't enjoy the kiss for fear of what was, what had been and what could be.

As we parted, Wayne whispered, "Care to show me your beach again?"

My head fought with the tingling in my lower belly. This wasn't right. This wasn't us. We were top-notch employees, admired by our peers, above the fray of social missteps and stupid mistakes.

I stared, slowly saying the words. "You and I know better than to take this further."

"The past is past. We deserve each other," he said, a grip on my hand.

I coaxed my hand away. "Maybe, but not now. We need to get out of this chaos first."

With a sigh he started the SUV and took a hard left, away from the sand and surf, away from the temptation to do what the agency had already accused us of doing. What we'd wanted to do for weeks. What I still wanted to do so badly.

In the dark I clenched my hands, so frustrated at dancing this tightrope. I felt like the only person trying to be proper, but the harder I tried, the more I messed up.

The moon reappeared from behind a scattered cloud, painting the small tips of the inlet water white. Oleander bushes bordered the highway, the flowers dormant for the cool season, leaves oily-black in the silver light.

"So what now?" I asked, in attempt to steer us back to legitimate conversation. "About Jesse?"

"You let me handle him. I need you to dig up information on McRae," he said.

I admired his professionalism, but couldn't help wonder if I was letting go of something magical.

"But mostly," he continued, "I want you to stay out of the line of fire."

His tone was hard, but I understood. I was better at research than fighting crime, and I needed something proactive to do. "What are *you* going to do then? You're no longer official."

He turned the SUV left, back toward Charleston and the interstate. "I know a few local uniforms who'll help me keep an eye on Jesse," he said. "Sooner or later the boy's gonna slip up at some dive and talk about drugs, stolen hogs, or how he did somebody in. Or, if we're lucky, how he ran you off the road."

I wasn't comfortable with dragging in more cops. "I don't trust the police. If you can't help any more than that, then I need to—"

"You're trained to make loans, not chase down a sleazy lowlife." His words bounced loud in the confinement of the Blazer. My insides twisted with discomfort. He immediately reacted to my posture. "I'm sorry, Slade. I'm not doing this right."

I tried to twirl a wedding band that wasn't there. "Doing what?"

"Making up for Beck, trying to put you back on balance."

He wasn't any different than I was. "Shit just happens, lawman. Wade through it. Quit thinking you can fix everything. I've learned I sure as hell can't."

He snorted, hearing his own words thrown back. "With everything else going on around us, I don't want to have to worry about you. That's the bottom line. It's making me crazy."

"It's all driving me crazy. Every damn bit of it."

Our feelings were splashed all over our sleeves, that part was certain. Neither one of us knew where we were headed, professionally . . . personally.

"Tomorrow, I need your help at the courthouse, to find out what McRae is up to. Can you get the time off?" he asked, more confident now. I understood why. Being proactive set aside the brooding, the hopeless mood swings.

"One way or another I will," I said.

He drove the remaining miles with one hand on the wheel, his thoughts to himself. We said nothing as if everything had been said. Maybe it had. Maybe it hadn't. We were tired.

Wayne walked me to my front porch. He kissed me goodnight lightly on the cheek, his long gaze implying we could've had more.

"See you at nine," he said. "And make sure you lock up."

With Alan still a concern, I went inside. Savvy peered at me from the living room sofa, bleary-eyed. I covered her with a blanket and toured the house, checking every window and door. I needed a fresh direction, but not necessarily with a fresh romance . . . not so soon. The kids were confused enough as it was.

CHAPTER 23

While the kids devoured yellow moons, green clovers and purple stars in their cereal, Savvy and I leaned against the kitchen counter sipping Columbian blend. Three hours' sleep made my mind thick as oatmeal.

Savvy turned her back to the kids. "So?"

"The seafood was delicious." I held my expression in check, like we spoke about recipes or the price of rump roasts at the Piggly Wiggly. "I'm spending the day working with him."

"Ooh, you're bad. Here? Or the motel?"

I slapped her arm. "The courthouse, silly."

She raised her eyebrows. "Thought the badge was gone . . . you know, no authority."

"It is. But we have to figure out what to do with Jesse, or we're both sunk." I touched her hand. "I'm so torn about him, Savvy."

She stepped closer and bumped me with her hip. "Lighten up, hon. Why not just see where this goes?" She put her cup in front of her mouth, leaned in close and whispered, "Did you two do it?"

I smiled. "No, of course not. We kept it professional."

"I would've done it," she said with squinting eyes and a scrunched nose.

Her humor warmed my soul. "You did put the fear in him, though, witch woman. You scared him to death."

"Damn straight." She rinsed dishes in the sink and shut off the faucet. "I've gotta hit the road, hon. My office called. Some crappy misunderstanding with one of my own farmers." She dried her hands. "You going to be okay? I mean about the other *him*?" She hitched a shoulder toward the kids, referring to their father.

"Yeah. Craig will notify the area locksmiths. A reward for anyone who catches him making another key might settle his butt down."

"You go, girl!"

The kids twisted around at Savvy's exclamation. She threw up her arms. "Tell your momma how great she is. Say 'Go, Momma!'"

"Go Momma! Go Momma!" they chanted.

I laughed, went over and hugged them. "Get your stuff. Time for school. The bus will be here any second."

Then I whirled and grabbed my buddy. "You're a Godsend,

Savannah. Regardless of what everyone says about you."

After a friendly arm punch, she retrieved her suitcase. I hated to see her leave. She made my world spin on a normal rotation, something I hadn't felt in a month of Sundays.

I glanced at the clock on the oven. Fifteen minutes before Wayne arrived. Last night had reintroduced us to each other's needs, and I felt better about him. I didn't see our evening as a date, but more like a reprieve from responsibility, an opportunity for an unencumbered personal connection during a time when professional demands had drained us dry. Today, however, would take us back into knee-deep muck.

WAYNE'S BLAZER ROLLED into my drive at 8:55. I met him on the porch and pulled him inside the house away from neighborly attention.

"Let me get my purse," I said. "Did you get much sleep?"

"Not really. You eat breakfast?"

"What do you mean not really? I dropped into bed and died." Actually, I'd lain awake for an hour concerned about Jesse, my children, my job . . . Wayne.

"I met with Jesse."

I dropped my purse and made no move to stop my lipstick from rolling under the credenza. "You what?"

He stooped down to retrieve the lipstick while I scooped the remaining scattered items back into my bag. "Come on," he said. "I'll tell you on the way. I'd like to get to the courthouse early so we have time to tour the Toogoodoo area."

He escorted me outside, and I hopped in his front seat. "How did you find Jesse?" I asked. "What did you *say* to him?" Or do?

"I staked out his house. His truck wasn't in the yard, so I figured he was shacked up someplace else. When seven rolled around and no lights came on, I called the sheriff's office. They patched me through to one of their guys on the road who promised to call me if he spotted Jesse."

"You're letting people know what we're up to? Is that smart?"

He slowed the car as traffic bottlenecked on the on-ramp, then shot free on the four-lane interstate. "I'm on my own. I need the resources."

"What did you tell the deputy?" Did these guys take each other's word that unconditionally?

He drove with a measured calm, right at the speed limit. No weariness, no anxious fervor to nail the bastard who'd upended our worlds. Pressure suited him. No bags under his eyes. I'd doubled up on make-up to hide my shadows and thrown the bottle in my purse for backup.

"I told him a farmer tried to bribe a government official and needed to be convinced to leave the official alone. Wasn't twenty minutes before the deputy called back to say Jesse was gassing up at TJ's."

TJ's was the small mom-and-pop grocery on Toogoodoo Road. Wood floors and all. "What happened?"

"I met the deputy there. We chatted with Jesse."

His piece-meal release of information had me grinding my teeth. By the time we reached the outskirts of the Charleston peninsula, however, I learned Wayne had driven to TJ's and found Jesse with a friend. When the deputy stepped in plain view, the buddy bolted. I imagine Ren did, too.

The thought of Wayne confronting Jesse drew visions of fat lips and bloody noses. Maybe even a broken arm or two. But Wayne showed no sign of a tussle. Didn't want him hurt, but I was entitled to wish ill toward the maniac we were after who'd wreaked such havoc. "Did you do anything to him?" I whispered as we passed Dorchester Road where cars fought to enlist in the morning commute.

"Not really."

"And that means . . ."

"I told him if he ever came near you, he'd never live to brag about it to his dope-eating buddies." He waved a driver in ahead of him, his gaze on the highway. "And he probably has a nasty headache and splinters in his back, courtesy of TJ's wood siding."

A childish side of me thought "cool." "He won't listen," I said.

"A smart man would."

I tilted the vent away from my face. "I'd rather have a bullet in him."

"We'll do this legally. We can't mess it up."

"Like you and me performing an unofficial investigation is legal," I said. "Hey, learn how to take a joke."

He reached over and took my hand, his attention shifting back and forth between the road and me. "Sorry. This guy's not right, CI. He's just not right."

VENTURING INTO old Charleston was like dressing up on Sunday and visiting the preacher. I loved studying the old buildings restored under the watchful eye of the Historic Charleston Foundation. We parked near the Wallace County Office Building on Meeting Street and made our way to the Register of Mesne Conveyance office, RMC for obvious reason.

We found the right room after several wrong turns. Charleston deeds, plats and mortgages could be hard to find with the county's huge quantity of real estate transactions and the added complexity of so many islands. Heir property without clear chain of title was a common issue in a county so steeped in history. General Sherman's march through the state at the end of the Civil War had devastated hundreds of title records. Many longtime residents still wouldn't mention his name, or spat when they did. I wasn't too fond of the General myself. My great-great grandfather had fought in the Mississippi Cavalry, Company F, along with five of his brothers. One of them had deserted, something we didn't discuss.

For some reason, courthouses made people want to whisper—as if the books and records could hear you. "What are we looking for?" I said, brushing old tomes with my fingertips.

"Not sure," Wayne said. "Let's start with the obvious, checking real estate deals along the road near Jesse. That's why I need you. You know the addresses and names."

A blonde clerk in her mid-twenties stood behind a counter. I started in her direction to ask questions. Wayne grabbed my arm and dragged me behind a tall row of huge books. "Shhh."

"What are you doing?"

"Look back. Make it quick."

Holding a stack of papers, McRae stepped up to the counter and grabbed the blonde's attention. He counted out cash and handed it to her along with the documents. She gave him a receipt, then he left. We gave him enough time to exit the building before we approached the girl.

With all the naiveté I could muster, I waltzed up. "Excuse me, but can you tell me what documents that previous gentleman was having recorded? He was a tall man, brown hair, blue sport coat."

Her juvenile pout broadcast her hesitancy to divulge someone's personal business. I knew better. Recordings were public information.

I continued, stopping her chance to refuse. "I recognize him from a conference last month, and I think we might be interested in the same piece of land. If he's bought it, then I'm plum disgusted." I turned to Wayne. "I told you we should have offered more money. You went home to *think about it*. Now look. I'll bet you dinner at Magnolia's we've lost that place."

Wayne winked at the girl and shrugged. "Hey, how about proving to my fiancé she's wrong? She's too compulsive for her own good."

I glared at him, having had so much practice with Alan. The girl, however, didn't pretend. She couldn't take her fake-lashed baby blues off Wayne.

She eased toward him, leaning way over, and held out the papers as if I didn't exist. "Here, sir. See if this is what you need." I doubted she meant just papers. Her boobs rested on the counter, giving us a peek at black lace.

"I'm not sure," he said scanning the legal description on the deed. I peered over his arm trying to read the fine print.

"I'll bet it is," I nagged.

He smiled at the girl. "Sweetheart, do you think we could get a copy of this? I'm driving her out there to show her this isn't the same place. I'd be deeply indebted for your help."

"Sure. Be glad to. That'll be fifty cents a page for eight pages."

He whipped out his wallet. "Small price to pay to save me a two-hundred-dollar dinner."

"Glad to help, Sir. Come back anytime. I'm always here," she said, her eyes promising more than copies.

We strolled away from the counter, studying the legal description and signatures. The deed didn't mention Henry McRae. The forty-acre tract, only a half mile from the Williams' place, showed a four-week-old land transfer from Ashton Legare to Palmetto Enterprises for fifteen thousand dollars.

"That's the group Jesse told me to make his deed out to when I prepared the bogus papers. Whoever Palmetto Enterprises is, they flat stole that property from Legare. That old man sat on his place dodging real estate agents for a decade. He just died this month."

We searched records until we found four other pieces of land within a three-mile radius of the Williams' farm, all of them with frontage on either Toogoodoo Road or Highway 174. I knew those highways. They were the key roads to Edisto Island, but the serious resorts were elsewhere on Seabrook and Kiawah Islands. Yonges Island, poor as dirt, served primarily as a thoroughfare to Edisto. Saltwater and brackish creeks, inlets and rivers crisscrossed and subdivided the lands. Unless McRae knew something I didn't, the property held no exceptional attraction or value.

Of course, one had to define exceptional. People stepped back in time traveling outside of civilization where a historical past and the present blended together. Pockets of plantation slave descendants lived incognito between pieces of water, dirt roads and pine-oak thickets dripping with Spanish moss. Tiny white churches numbered one to every ten houses. One day all that would be gone to commercialism when folks with enough money discovered another beach route. Edisto Beach already flaunted streets of vacation homes and a small resort on the far end of the island.

"You know these people?" Wayne laid out the four new deeds on a table. The recording dates spanned eleven months.

"I know one well enough to speak to—or I did." I pointed to a name. "He used to borrow operating money from me. Two of the others have lived on their places as far back as I know. The last one I'm not sure of, but I think she's in a nursing home. All these others are deceased."

Elderly people who had deeded their places away before they died. So why hadn't they left their property to a relative? Residents on these islands clung to land, in hopes one day it'd be worth ten times more as commercial enterprises crept out from Charleston.

"So why would they sell?" he asked. "More importantly, why would someone want all four places?" Wayne flipped pages to the signatures. "You know any of these buyers, like Elwood and Hankins?"

I nodded. "The names, but not the people. Jesse told me to put these on his paperwork before he changed his mind that morning he sneaked into my office, remember? He said they were from New York and partners of Palmetto Enterprises. We need to check for mortgages. The deeds are dated, but aren't recorded in the RMC office until a few weeks later. That means these transactions were one-on-one. No attorneys, probably, and no loan closings. I'll bet these properties are debt free. The owners sure lived long enough to have paid them off."

I smelled a scam on seniors, and it had to be a good one to con farmers off their land. Even if they'd retired from the tractor, their roots ran deep in agriculture. Such land stewards relished every aspect of ownership, whether they grew a crop on it or not. They walked it every day if nothing else.

Cross-referencing the deeds and names with mortgages, we learned that out of the five tracts, three held no liens. The two others had debt paid off within a week after signing the deeds. The mortgages were miniscule. People in their 70s and 80s avoided debt, but sometimes made good targets for entrepreneurial scams.

I hated the way this looked. "Someone practically stole this land," I told Wayne, striking my finger hard enough on the table to make a legal assistant peer over his glasses. "These properties may not flank billion dollar resorts, but they're worth more than what they sold for. That's a damn shame."

He gathered the copied documents, tapping them on the counter to make them even. "I want to see death records. Are they in this building?"

"No. They're on Broad Street. Since they're recent, hopefully we shouldn't have a problem."

Leaving the building and finding the car took longer than driving to the courthouse with the old city's one-way streets and bottle-necked traffic. We parked in the garage on Cumberland Street, and within thirty minutes held copies of death certificates. Same pattern. Deed signed, farmer died, then deed recorded a few days later.

We returned to the car. Wayne rifled through the legal descriptions again. "Can you point out all these places?" He gave me that smile. "And you wouldn't happen to have a map?"

"I can point out everything with my eyes closed. We can pick up a good detailed map at the gas station on the way out of town, if you like. I'll mark the farms for you."

We left the city via Highway 17. Urban evolved to suburban with smaller ranch homes bordering the asphalt. The houses and Quickie Marts stretched further apart until development signs suggested growth potential—next to nine-hundred square foot trailers, concrete block and red brick box houses. Transient migrant workers occupied sparse labor housing projects during tomato, cuke or melon seasons, enterprises rapidly fading away.

Tourists usually traveled down Highway 17 and turned south on 174 to reach Edisto Beach, dodging the teeny communities that held no commercial intrigue. We exited early on 162, like we'd done before to meet Jesse. The first real estate tract lay three miles south of Hollywood and one mile south of the place where they dragged Mickey's car out of the water.

Wayne lost his smile as he appeared lost in thought. My stomach knotted with fear of what we were headed into. A country drive used to relax me, but the further we drove from the city the more my gut twisted for reasons I couldn't put my finger on—other than Jesse lived out here.

CHAPTER 24

Wayne and I drove down Toogoodoo Road to the first farm property on our courthouse list. He remembered the place, and the now deceased Mr. Legare, from last year's search for Mickey. The old gentleman had once given Wayne directions.

The Blazer bumped through a cattle gate onto the forty-acre tract. We stopped and stepped out of our warm vehicle into a nippy wind that hinted of winter and swayed the golden, brittle heads of dried Johnson grass. Wayne's phone rang and he walked off into the tall grass to take the call.

Beck's words rang in my ears about Wayne's mysterious calls and suspect activity. He worried about his sister, and hopefully this call came from her. Wayne still held a secret or two.

Wayne seemed intent on his conversation, so I wandered toward the empty residence. The small Masonite-sided house sagged from fifty years of age, with several of the siding planks cracked, chipped or fallen on the ground. A lean-to carport adjoined a kitchen entrance. I tip-toed and peered through the small window in the door. As my weight leaned forward, the door swung open. Inside, a square Formica aluminum table sat in the middle of the room on faded linoleum showing wear from years of supper ritual—predominantly under one worn, tired chair.

My grandfather had sat in a chair like that. My mind wandered to my grandparents' home in Mississippi. My two-week visit each childhood summer had coordinated with vacation Bible school at the Methodist church down the road from their cotton farm. I remembered Grandpa sitting at a yellow Formica table, cooling hot coffee on a saucer and paying my little sister a nickel to say damn in front of my mother.

"Hey." Wayne shook my arm, pulling me out of my reverie. "Note anything?"

I tossed the nostalgia and surveyed the place. "Only thing going for it is some minor road frontage. Where's the second tract?"

Farm number two was twice as big, with a home, a barn needing structural repairs and an old chicken house. Waist-high weeds and woody shrubs in the open area indicated fields that had lain fallow for at least five years. The breeze carried the faint scent of old hay, fertilizer and dried corn. Another example of an elderly farmer giving up hope on making a living from the land.

My job dealt in its share of highs and lows. Each fall, I prayed as my borrowers counted bushels to the acre, praying as hard as they did that their balance sheet tilted toward the black once they paid bills. But I'd seen many go down, the red ink having bled way too long.

Losing a farm broke people harder than shoe store owners or coffee shop baristas. Farmers rarely recovered. City folks didn't understand the deep connection. These elderly farmers on our list released their places for pennies, during the stage in their lives when they no longer needed to meet mortgages. Made no sense.

On the way to farm three, we passed by a stretch of migrant labor housing that Mickey financed twelve years ago. The thousand square-foot brick boxes looked three times their age due to hard use, but they were posh facilities to transients. They stood empty off-season as evidenced by the boarded windows.

"I interviewed a dozen people in those houses last year when I searched for Mickey," Wayne said, following my stare. "My Border Patrol Spanish came in handy, but they saw me as *la Migra*, immigration. Hard to get anything out of them. They live a damn hard life."

After covering all the farms on our list, none of the properties proved remarkable. Their locations placed them within a six-mile radius of each other, all transferred to Palmetto Enterprises by elderly people who'd died within a matter of days after signing. The elderly woman I thought resided in a nursing home didn't; her name appeared on a ten-day-old death certificate we'd located back in the courthouse.

The long shadows behind barns and fence posts indicated retiring daylight. "Can we head back now?" I asked. "By the time we make it to Ridgeville, it'll be time to get the kids. I'd call Alan, but . . ."

"No way. I'll get you there." He whipped around on a sandy driveway and headed north. "Let me get some gas, or we'll be walking."

We drove into TJ's graveled lot. The family that ran the wood-sided store lived in a doublewide a hundred yards out back. Scrubby native trees hid the trailer, but a rutted path running down the side of the business into a thicket showed the curious where to find Mr. Tyson and his kin. Assorted blonde and red hounds kept the inquisitive away.

Wayne parked alongside the pump and filled the Blazer's tank. We stepped inside to pay and pick up a soft drink. A couple of migrant laborers hung around in no apparent hurry. Mr. Tyson stood behind the counter keeping one eye on them and the other on a fishing show on the 32-inch flatscreen television mounted on the wall—a contrast to the yesteryear feel of the place.

He sported a camouflaged ball cap and a blue flannel shirt, the buttons straining the threads, a Southern Pride belt buckle digging into the overhang of a well-fed belly. His teeth spoke of tobacco and age, but the deep, tanned wrinkles in his face defined a man who laughed a lot and enjoyed the outdoors. As a rookie assigned to Charleston, I'd often stopped here for directions. Now, when I had the chance, I gassed up and asked him about grandchildren.

The door slammed behind me. "Hey, Mr. Tyson. How're the babies?"

The old man tipped his head toward me. "Hello, Slade. Getting' smarter than their grandpa every day."

"How ya' doin'?" Wayne asked retrieving his credit card.

Mr. Tyson turned to Wayne, waiting for payment. "Can't complain. How 'bout yourself?"

"Same. If I did complain, it wouldn't do me any good."

The old man chuckled with a gravel laugh. "You're right about that. Anything else I can get for you?"

"Just a sec." I threw a bag of spicy hot peanuts on the counter along with a Dr. Pepper in a bottle from the iced cooler within arm's reach. "We missed lunch, lawman. You want something?"

"Throw me a Snickers on the counter," he said. "And another Dr. Pepper."

Mr. Tyson grinned as the items added up. "Done?"

After we nodded, he ran the card. Wayne signed, then the storekeeper's chunky fingers punched buttons on an ancient NCR cash register that still *cha-chinged* and placed his copy of the credit card receipt in the drawer. The machine did little more than lock up cash and let people know where to pay.

Wayne laid a hand on the counter and stroked his short beard with his other. "Some information, if you don't mind. I was the federal agent assigned here a year ago when Mickey Wilder disappeared. I'm in the area checking out another situation."

Tyson's eyes squinted as he shoved the register drawer closed. "I recognize you. You and that deputy gave Jesse Rawlings a fine welcome around the corner there this morning." He winked. "Bet you thought I didn't see ya, huh? That one's trouble."

Mr. Tyson held up a finger. "Wait a second, son." He turned toward the drink coolers. "You boys come outta there. Either buy something or move on. This ain't a motel." He turned back to our conversation. "Sorry 'bout that. Damn transients steal me blind. Now what was we talking about . . . yeah, that Wilder fella. Nobody ever figured out what happened to him."

"Not even a rumor?" I asked, stepping aside as the workers paid for one Coke and a hot dog each.

Like a bobble-head doll, Tyson rocked as he made change and talked.

"'Fraid not. Only rumors that pop up 'round here is about McDonald's comin' in."

"Long way for people to come for a hamburger," Wayne said.

The store owner took a five from one of the migrants and made change. "Tourists stop here and complain all the time. Every once in a while I get some of 'em in here savoring our *authentic* culture," he said, pinching his finger and thumb together in a semblance of class. "I've heard 'em commenting more'n once about how they wished they had a modern place to stop at between the water and the city. Forty miles and an hour drive just inconveniences the hell out of 'em."

An absolutely breathtaking drive I adored. Blue herons flew overhead in slow motion like prehistoric birds. Palmettos grew wild amidst wax myrtles that stayed deep green year-round, accenting the marsh grass and wet, dark mud saturated only at peak tide. The scenery nourished me, but visitors flew down that stretch in their speed to reach sand and surf, oblivious to what God displayed. Springtime dizzied me when the azaleas, redbud and dogwood bloomed, turning rural homes into Americana landscapes, disguising the poverty.

Wayne laughed, pushing back his jacket and setting a hand on his hip. "You know how people with money can be."

"Wish I could experience it myself. I do believe I'd show a bit more manners," Mr. Tyson said, rocking back on his heels. "But all it takes is one of 'em to mention a fast-food place, and a local makes it hot news for Saturday night beer gossip. They think it's like winning the lottery, hoping the highway department or a hamburger joint will give 'em a million dollars for their patch of dirt."

I sidestepped around my partner to talk, but Wayne beat me to it. "You heard of any names in particular involved with the highway or some new development?"

A good question, but I felt the right to ask a few of my own. I didn't want to interrupt Mr. Tyson, so I waited.

Tyson waved, like he remembered what he wanted to say. As the man rattled on, I began to understand. Wayne could entice the man to gossip much easier than I could. I was too female and too closely affiliated with the mortgaged landowners in the area. Not a pleasant realization, but I could follow these rules.

The old gentleman folded his arms over the top of his belly. "Some say your boy Wilder got in the middle of somethin' real estate related. Some say he was dirty, others say he just got in the way. Doesn't matter, though, does it? Dead's dead, then people talk about you."

"Guess so," Wayne said.

I started to refute Tyson's words about Mickey. Wayne shifted his weight, lightly bumping me.

Tyson scratched his ear. "People come through here looking for land all the time. Before now it was only water frontage. Realtors ask me what families might sell, who's in financial trouble, stuff like that. I give 'em gas, take their money and don't tell 'em nothing. I know some mighty poor people that'd be fool enough to listen to these carpetbaggers, so I play the dumb ol' country boy." He grinned big with teeth too stained to flash. "They think I'm *quaint.*" His guffaw echoed around the store.

"Smart man," Wayne said, gathering up our purchases. I reached over and grabbed the drinks.

"Just been around a while," said the old man. "I recognize people for what they are."

Wayne shook the man's hand. "I appreciate your help, sir. You hang in there and don't let anyone take this place."

"No problem, son. No problem at all." He nodded to me. "See you, Ms. Slade."

Guess Mr. Tyson did know I was there. Hopefully my nickname wouldn't become *Sidekick.*

TWO-LANE ROADS led us from the islands. I directed Wayne to Savannah Highway to avoid the early side of interstate rush hour. Whether it was the car accident, or nervous exhaustion, I grew tired quicker than normal. A couple of times my hands tremored.

"You all right?" he asked when I stretched and studied my hands.

"I think so." Clenching my fingers, I didn't feel bad. I wasn't scared. What the heck was this? I'd handled stress and wasn't foreign to tension.

"Tell me if any of this gets to be too much," he said, and I detected a hint of the father-tone in him. The one that probably sent ex-Pamela packing.

As we drove, we analyzed and dissected facts, names and figures, struggling to make sense of the McRae connection to real estate fraud and an involvement with Jesse. Did McRae slug Eddie? Were Mickey or Lucas part of the scam, or were they murdered by chance? Did Ren tag along or serve a purpose?

I held my pen tightly to steady my hand, taking cryptic notes in the hope our scattered thoughts formed a pattern. "Did you come across Palmetto Enterprises in your investigations?" I asked, writing 'McRae' and an arrow to 'P.E.'

Wayne slowed with the traffic. "Nope," he replied. "While McRae wasn't supposed to be involved with those past inventory property sales, we never proved he made a buck or set up the deals. If the IG owned half a brain in its combined managerial heads, they'd let an agent watch these properties and see how they changed hands. With the appearance of

Palmetto Enterprises, I fear we have a more convoluted system in place. We've probably forced McRae underground."

"But we saw him file the papers," I said. "Guess that doesn't prove anything, huh?"

Wayne relaxed in his seat, as if he'd played this conversation before. "Without evidence of personal gain, nobody's going to do anything to him for delivering paper."

We were on the edge of something, though. We juggled too many clues, just too loosely connected. "Jesse knows Palmetto Enterprises," I said, "and Jesse tried to bribe me to get a farm in their name. That's plain illegal. After seeing McRae file the deed for Palmetto Enterprises, it's clear they're involved together in something."

"But what if Jesse knows these people, and McRae knows these people, but neither one knows the other knows these people?" Wayne said, grinning with mischief.

Just like one of those logic puzzles from high school: if green people are six feet tall and purple people are three feet wide, then how many eyes does a blue person have? I'd hated those damn things.

Frustrated at too many ragged ends, I reread my doodles and scribbled phrases. "Jesse did change his mind about using that company's name. What if Jesse and McRae, or whoever's involved, had a falling out? After all, what are the chances of both these idiots dealing with the same entity in Charleston County? Not Berkeley, Colleton or some other county. Just seems too coincidental."

"Not if there's a common factor in Charleston to capture everyone's interest," he said.

The pen clicked against my teeth. "Wait . . . McRae asked me something at the same time he told me to lower the price of that farm." Stress sure had shot holes in my memory. "I should've thought of this before."

"You going to get around to what it is you remember before you forget it again?"

I poked him in the thigh with the pen. "McRae asked me if I'd talked to the highway department about the Williams' farm."

Wayne stole a glance away from the car in front of him. "I don't recall the highway department being on your checklist of things to do when you foreclose, but you're the loan lady."

"You're right. It's not. I told him we didn't deal with the highway department."

"And . . . ?"

I shrugged. "That's it. He just asked me to check with them before selling the farm in case they found an issue with it. They don't have anything to do with Agriculture. A title search performed when we foreclosed would reveal any issues we needed to know."

Wayne shook his head, the pieces evidently not coming together for him either. "You know Mr. Tyson was just gossiping back there. Everyone likes to think his land's worth something," he said.

"Kinda what I thought. Edisto Beach is growing, but it's not Hilton Head. I'm sure big development will consume it someday, but this is Toogoodoo, miles away," I said. In a moment, something would click, and after I'd basically been recused from the discussion with Mr. Tyson, I wanted to be the one to solve this. "John's Island went through traffic chaos when resorts built before the infrastructure was ready."

"Good thought," he said. "Maybe we need to do more snooping in the annals of Charleston County government." He bobbed his head, confirming a plan. "Guess that'll be Monday's chore. The bureaucrats have abandoned ship for the weekend."

He shifted in his seat, his free leg propping a boot in a different position. The autumn afternoon sun flickered through branches and limbs of the immense live oaks that lined the highway. A hypnotizing effect, especially after a long day's work. Fender benders were as common on this route as the interstate.

Wayne tapped fingers on the steering wheel. "Dang these people move slow."

I laughed. "Guess you're used to Atlanta. Rush hour is a fact of life around here. We don't rush."

He grinned lopsided at me then turned back to his driving. A not-so-subtle message physically pinged inside me. Mom would have a cow if she knew her daughter looked twice at another man before her divorce was a respectable year old, much less final. Savvy would be proud.

He turned left on Dorchester Road, toward Ridgeville. "I'll leave you at your place and go back to the motel for a while. I've got phone messages to return, and I'd like a shower."

I'd forgotten he'd worked through the night. "Phone messages?" I asked. He answered to no boss. Pamela crossed my mind as did all the other women Beck had alluded to. The flash of jealousy surprised me, but common sense told me to get a grip.

"Duty calls," he said, pausing at the light.

What duty, I thought. *You're unemployed.*

We drove the last five miles in silence.

Wayne dropped me off at home with a hand squeeze, stirring my insides more than I wanted. As he left for his motel, my memory revisited Beck's accusations, and I wondered if an ex-wife was on that list of callers. He might need to run leads on his sister, though.

I chastised myself for trying to second guess the man. Who was I to ask about his messages anyway? One minute I question his loyalty, and the next I turn green over his calls. I threw my purse on the counter. None of my business. And from my track record, I wasn't the most astute judge of male character anyway.

A beer would file off my edges, but the kids beckoned. Without entering the house, I grabbed Daddy's Jeep and headed toward school. The parental car jam at Middleton Elementary School, home of the Blue Dolphins, always drove me berserk. Bus brakes squealed to a halt at the stop sign, then one by one roared in slow motion onto the highway. Parents lined down the road in the other direction. Not about to wait for a half hour while my kids walked around exposed to Jesse or Ren, I scooted around traffic and parked in the teachers' section. Let them give me a ticket.

Liberated students screamed and rough-housed as teachers and assistants waved hands and shouted in futility to calm the bedlam. I melted into a corner to surprise my urchins. Ivy's teacher pushed through the double doors, barking orders at her charges to simmer down.

I dodged kids, pushing past two lines of zealous tots to reach her. "Hey, Sally, did I miss my pair in all the pandemonium?"

Looping hair behind an ear, the freckled twenty-something faced me with a puzzled look. "They're not here, ma'am. Someone already picked them up."

CHAPTER 25

The teacher blushed through her freckles as I stood in the midst of everyone else's children but mine. "Their father picked them up, Ms. Bridges. Didn't he tell you?"

Too impatient and too embarrassed to correct her on my name, I apologized and marched to my car, stumbling off the curb in my irritability. In the car, speed dial went straight to Alan Bridge's voice mail.

"You son-of-a-bitch. How dare you pick up the kids without telling me?" I inhaled deep, twice. "Don't you start screwing with me . . . not with the kids. You don't want to start this fight."

Two blocks later, I realized he wouldn't call back, not after listening to that banshee rant. If I had it my way, the kids would remain with me for the weekend, maybe with Wayne sticking around. But I had no authority to confiscate Alan's visitation. Not without violating our separation agreement. He'd take me to court and drag in my work, the case, maybe even the close call with Smokey, convincing a judge I couldn't be a responsible parent.

Once home, after changing into tights, socks and a long sleeve turtleneck, I flopped on the sofa. I parked my beer on the end table, the hot chip bag against my hip, and phoned Wayne. Voice mail. Probably making his *important* calls. No way I could compete with his athletic, secret agent ex-wife when two flights of stairs left me winded. I upended the bottle and drained it, a loud sip at the end, resisting the urge to toss it on the floor and kick it, like it was Alan's head.

I turned up the chip bag to eat salty, extra hot remnants in the bottom and decided to try another beer. As I opened the refrigerator, I chuckled, knowing Alan would have two kids without a change of clothes. Zack wouldn't mind, but Ivy would give him fits. She'd march him straight to the mall. Wait a minute . . . oh, damn.

I slammed the refrigerator and ran to the kids' bedrooms. The school backpacks sat on their respective beds, dumped and exchanged for the new overnight bags I'd bought them just to visit their dad. Ivy's battery of toiletries was missing from the hall bath and Zack's room resembled a tornado from where he'd picked out his own clothes.

I beat my palm against the wall. The bastard sneaked into the house *again*. How the hell was he doing it? Ivy's key maybe? A new locksmith?

The phone rang.

"Hey, CI. Everything okay?" Wayne sounded jovial, much less secret agent punctuating his words.

"At least it's you, although I'd love for Alan to call right now."

Pause. "You want to try that on me again?"

I relayed the afternoon's calamity.

"He's messing with you, Slade. At least the kids are okay with their dad, right?"

"Yeah, but that's not the point," I argued.

He paused again. "Maybe that *should be* the point?"

"But . . ."

He was right. I was just plain mad.

"Why don't I come over?" he asked.

Then the alcohol in me asked the weighted question on my mind. "Make all your critical, important phone calls?"

"All three of them. I might have a deputy watching Jesse for us. And Eddie is much better."

"And the third?"

He sounded tired at my question. "Something about my sister."

"You found her?"

"No. You want to grab a pizza or something?" he asked, the subject tossed aside. The mention of his sister rubbed him wrong, and I hadn't graduated into his inner circle yet to know why.

"You want me to order delivery?" I asked, then rummaged through the junk drawer for coupons.

"Nope. I'll pick it up. The fewer people dropping in on you, the better. What kind do you like?"

"Meat lovers, extra cheese."

He laughed, the worry in his voice gone. "A carnivore, huh? No calorie counting in your house."

Ouch. "We could just do salads."

"Too late for a recovery. You made me hungry now. Meat lovers it is. Give me an hour."

It sure was a glorious feeling having someone worry, someone care, someone to share pepperoni and sausage with, who didn't resort to sarcasm or complete silence. His call had eased my concern. The man had once again made a crisis sound fixable.

In Zack's bedroom, my hands folded the jeans and tiny Spiderman underwear that draped the bed. I shoved the backpack aside and freed a wrinkled, size seven, Clemson tee shirt. A piece of paper floated onto the floor. I stepped aside.

With my toe, I turned the paper over, then feeling ridiculously stupid, picked it up. How many more Alan messages would I find? The thought of little fortune cookie notes hiding in the nooks and crannies of my home gave me the willies.

I unfolded the memo. A fine-tipped pen scrawled *I'm more than you bargained for.* The paper drifted out of my fingers back to the floor. I wiped my hands on my shirt.

I left Zack's bedroom as it was, note on the floor and clothes strewn on his bed, preserved for when Wayne arrived.

And I'd show him what? Alan's house, Alan's kids, Alan's adolescent messages? What the heck would six words on notebook paper prove?

My sock-covered feet padded to the kitchen. Retrieving the new bottle I'd meant to grab earlier, I settled back on the sofa and wallowed into the cushions. By habit, I hit Channel 17. Classic cartoons danced across the screen, but that was okay. Local news insulted my intelligence, and I didn't have time to watch a whole movie.

I checked the mantle clock. A half hour before Wayne would arrive. Shadows turned my Dover Yellow painted walls a medium tan, and I realized I was backlit in my house with the shades up. Jumping off the sofa, I made the same rounds as the other night, checking locks and closing blinds and curtains, rewarding myself with a swallow of Coors after securing each room. Back on the couch, I settled on the game channel, watching contestants vie for a million dollars.

The doorbell caused me to bolt upright, disoriented, wondering why I'd fallen asleep. Peeking through the side panel window, I eyed Wayne decked out in his brown leather jacket. He held a pizza box, a grocery sack and a plastic bag from the hardware store. I unlocked the door.

"Hi there, lawman," I said, leaning against the doorframe.

He laughed. "You doing something different with your hair?"

"What?" I reached up and ran my fingers through the tangled mess. My hair was my best asset, and here it was running berserk.

Wayne strode in, put a six-pack in the refrigerator, and opened the pizza box. "So what's up with Alan?" he asked, picking off a pepperoni.

His words lit a fuse. I ranted. Wayne leaned against the kitchen counter, his hands resting on the edge. He calmly listened, watching me pace the linoleum.

I stopped in front of him. "So what do I do?" He took his time answering as usual, so I returned to my pacing.

"You confirmed he picked them up at the school. They know what he looks like?"

"Yes."

"He has authority to pick them up at school."

"Yes."

"You left him a message on his phone to call."

"More like an ultimatum full of expletives, but yes."

He pushed away from the counter and held my arms, halting my movement. "Then you've done all you can do. Sit down and have dinner. We'll pay him a visit, if you like. Be thinking about something the kids forgot."

He popped open a beer for me, then one for himself. He took a swig. I set the pizza on plates. Our feet rested on the coffee table. Just a plain, lazy evening for a change.

I stood to get him another slice, and he slid deeper into the sofa, arms behind his head. The same man had sat in that very place and interviewed me a few weeks ago to see if I was party to a bribery scam. I scanned his body, amazed at the difference he meant in my life since that awkward introduction and caustic exchange of words.

"What you looking at, CI?" he said.

Okay, so the name had grown on me. "Nothing," I said. My hormones stirred like a blender on puree.

"You feeling better?"

I stood at the counter, knife poised over the pizza. "Yeah. I'm good." Life wasn't all that good, but my sanity remained intact. I had to admit Wayne had a hand in keeping it that way.

Wayne came up behind me, his hand resting on my shoulder. "Hey. How long does it take to grab another slice?"

I grinned, bringing my attention back to the present. "Sorry." I put pizza on his plate and handed it to him. He set it back on the counter, took the other plate from me and did the same. He turned me toward him.

My heart raced.

His fingertips drifted across my chin. "I'm worried about you."

I snickered softly. "Well, don't. Eat your dinner."

His eyes weren't meeting mine as I realized he traced my bruises, his gaze moving from my mouth to my ear, searching. I took a half-step back, reached up and covered that side of my face.

His hand rested against my neck, easing me back to him. "These aren't from the car accident, Slade."

I tried to look cute, eyes rolling. "How can you tell?"

"They're from Alan."

For a reason unknown to me, I blushed. Then his tenderness overcame my façade as a tear pricked my eyelid. I tried to pivot away, but he held fast, daring me to show my feelings, forcing me to be real to his face. "You're hurt."

"I'm okay," I murmured.

"He raped you, didn't he?" he asked gently.

Then I smiled, to let him off the hook. "No, Wayne. He tried, but he didn't get that far."

His arms drew me to his chest, hugging me firmly, but not hard, as if fearing I'd bruise even more. A sweet, long hug in my kitchen, lightly rocking with Wayne's cheek against the top of my head, my body wrapped with his for safekeeping. I reached around him and clung to his shirt.

Minutes later, he eased us apart. One hand reached behind my neck, the other in the small of my back, drawing me to him again, this time toward his lips.

The phone rang.

Zack and Ivy raced across my mind, startling me.

Wayne stepped back and shook his head with a grin. I thought I saw him catch his breath. "Answer it," he said, rubbing his neck. "It could be Alan returning your call."

I prayed for a telemarketer on the other end. "Hello?"

Words poured over the line, a bedlam of verbal nonsense. "Alan? Slow down, I can't understand you."

Wayne cocked his head, searching my expression for clues. "What?" he mouthed.

I shrugged. "Alan, are the kids okay?" If they were hurt, I'd draw and quarter him, then shoot the pieces. His whore could clean up the mess.

"What?" I yelled, as the words made sense. My hand shook and the receiver dropped out of my grasp. Wayne caught it, handed it back to me while resting his other hand on my shoulder. His eyes switched to investigator mode as they tried to assess the situation.

With the phone back in my hand, I shrieked. "What do you mean the kids are gone?"

Wayne took the phone. "Mr. Bridges, this is Wayne Largo. Slow down. Tell me what happened."

I grabbed for the receiver.

Wayne held onto it and put his arm firmly around my shoulders to contain me. "Call the police. Stay calm. Write everything down you can remember. We'll be right there."

"Where are Zack and Ivy?" I demanded, jerking loose.

"Someone attacked him and grabbed them in a parking lot. Throw on some clothes and get your purse. I'm driving."

I threw on a skirt over the leotards, grabbed my coat and we jumped into the car. Although Wayne sped like a race car driver, he wasn't fast enough to soothe my panic. My hands clinched my purse and the door handle, white-knuckled with a longing to crunch the bones and windpipe in Alan's throat.

I pointed out turns and street names, but otherwise remained quiet, unwilling to speak about the horrible atrocities spinning through my head. Verbalizing might make them true. Perverts killed children, often after performing ghastly actions . . . I tried to watch the road, but the headlines of other people's kids and their trauma kept floating back, getting in the way. I thought of words too often heard on the news: How did this happen to my family?

The apartment complex flashed blue and white from two blocks away. When we reached the parking lot, I jumped out before Wayne came to a complete stop. I tripped over my clogs and ripped the knee of my tights on the asphalt. He threw the car into park and leaped out, leaving the vehicle jutting into the lot.

He gripped my arm. "Wait a minute," he said.

I shoved him away and ran toward the apartment.

Three local cop cars parked outside the building, their LEDs lighting up the neighborhood, bathing us in a disco flicker. Pushing past an officer, I pounded on Alan's front door. "Let me in, you bastard!"

A uniform met me—Donald. I rushed past him, almost over him. Alan rested elbows on his kitchen table, his dress shirt splattered with blood drips. Dried red decorated his nose and lip.

The room tilted. White noise filled my ears and increased to a roar. Then just as suddenly, it died and disappeared.

"Slade, come back, honey." A clammy cold coated my face. My first stupid thought was whether Alan cared about someone else calling me honey.

Wayne helped me into a seated position against an armchair, on matted, cheap Berber carpet. Jean tended to Alan. She caught my glare and pivoted away, rewrapping the cloth around the ice bag. I wasn't in the mood for her either.

Alan's who I wanted.

"Where are my children?" I said through my teeth. "I'll see you rot in hell if they've been hurt."

Alan glanced down. Donald moved closer to him. Wayne gently held the back of my arm. I wasn't the bad guy here.

"Alan," Wayne said in a cooler voice than mine. "We need details."

My ex avoided eye contact with me, stupidly preferring to look at Wayne. "I picked them up at school. I can have my kids whenever I want," he said, then glanced at Donald. "Nobody tells me to stay away from my house, my family, my property."

I stood, straightening my shirt. "You moron. You raped me."

Alan's eyes narrowed. "In your dreams."

"Answer Agent Largo's questions," Donald ordered, his tone more impressive than his hundred-sixty pounds of uniform.

"Then what happened, Bridges?" Wayne asked.

"We went to McDonalds, did the playground thing. I took them to the river park. Zack fed the turtles fries."

Anguish cut into me at the vision. Tears welled in my eyes. Wayne tightened his grip on me, and I hadn't realized I'd taken steps toward my ex. "Where are my children, damn it?"

Alan held an ice bag to his temple. "It was getting late. I came back to the apartment. I was going to call Slade and tell her I'd picked up the kids, but she sounded mad on my voicemail. Served her right after she sicced the law on me." He stopped and drank from a glass of something I hoped proved lethal.

Silence filled the apartment. Wayne released my arm a bit.

"We . . . we got out of the car in the parking lot." Alan pointed toward the door, in the direction of the cop lights. "A man grabbed Ivy. He threw her in a car. Before I could run over, he grabbed Zack." Only then did he look at me. "I fought the guy, Slade. Honest."

Whether he fought the man or not didn't matter. In that moment I wished him dead, rotted and fed to buzzards.

Alan touched the bruising on his forehead. "The guy was so fast," he said. "He hit me over the head with something. Don't know if I blacked out, but by the time I collected my wits, the car was gone. I didn't even get the tag!"

I shook my head. "You really are a waste of humanity. I despise the damn day I met you."

Alan laid his ice bag on the table and shifted his pitiful gaze toward me, switching to a darker mode. "You were just easy ass all these years, you know it?"

"A real father would have died first rather than let anyone steal his children!"

"Slade," Wayne said low. "Don't go there."

What was the point? Alan didn't matter, not any more. All that mattered were Ivy and Zack.

"Alan," Wayne barked. "Pay attention before I lose my goddamn patience at your crap. Did you get a look at the guy?"

Alan's head snapped around, his words staccato. "White, late-thirties, a hundred eighty pounds or so, my height with dark hair, wearing jeans."

"Jesse," I said.

Wayne called Donald over, turned his back to us and spoke in a hushed tone to the man.

"This is that damn farmer in your bribery case?" Alan said. "You've jeopardized our children's lives over your bitchin' career?"

Guilt ripped through me in spite of logic telling me I didn't cause this disaster. Anger roiled in my stomach, dull thuds of pain fighting against digestion. The twitching in my arms wouldn't stop at will.

I'd kill Alan if he crossed my path again. If Ivy and Zack weren't returned, I'd kill him anyway. I turned for the door. "I'm going to find my children."

Wayne reached out and caught me at the threshold. "No. Leave this to the authorities."

"Jesse has my kids, and I'm not sitting around waiting for someone to fish them out of a creek." I exited the apartment, not realizing I lacked transportation.

Wayne caught up with me outside. "Listen, Slade. I know how you feel."

"Do you?"

"Jesse's shrewd. If you go blundering in, anything could happen. You can't put Ivy's and Zack's lives in any further danger. Jesse wants *you*, not them. You'll walk right into his trap." He opened the door to the car for me. "The authorities are well-trained for these sorts of situations. You're not."

He got in the driver's side. "Let's go back to your place."

I stared at flickering police lights, replaying what probably happened amidst the cars parked before me. Scanning the lot, I wondered precisely where they'd been snatched.

Wayne touched my chin and drew my face around. "Slade. We'll get them back. Stay strong."

"Shit, Wayne. That's all I've been is strong . . . while the whole damn world disintegrates around me."

He started the engine. "The police'll keep us posted. They have all our cell phone numbers including your parents. You need to be home when Jesse contacts you, and I have no doubt he will."

South Carolina's State Law Enforcement Division, SLED, would step in with a kidnapping involved. So might the FBI. I knew that much. But they were crazy, and so was Wayne, if they thought I'd sit still. "You can't expect me to hang around waiting for the phone."

Wayne turned the ignition back off.

I slapped my leg. "Let's go find him," I said, an eagerness surging through my belly. "You and me. We locate him and then call the police."

"Don't do this, honey." He reached to stroke my hair and I dodged him.

He sighed. "I'll hunt him, though. You can tell me all his favorite haunts and dubious friends."

Without a plan that made more sense, I put my hand over his in mock agreement. He kissed my hand, pleased he'd regained control. "Good," he whispered. "It'll be all right."

We drove in silence. I stifled my panic, a Herculean effort as pressure mounted inside me. The pressure grew into pain. My eyes closed, I rubbed my chest, suddenly realizing I rocked in my seat. Jesse got even while I'd eaten pizza and entertained a man. How did I get so irresponsible? What the hell was I thinking? Raising the children alone would take all of me. Shit. My hands fisted, I rubbed them on my thighs. Shit, shit, shit.

By the time Wayne stopped in my driveway, my search plan held a quasi-shape. Jesse wouldn't know how to handle an angry female with a .38.

Wayne opened my car door and tried to drape his arm around me as I stepped outside. I shirked away. All I wanted was my privacy and room to finish my plan.

My microwave clock read ten. I called my parents and sister on the cell, leaving the phone line open for law enforcement and Jesse. In spite of my request to be left alone, my family demanded to come over and spend the night. They wanted to be with me when Ivy and Zack were found. Other options went unsaid. Hell, this wasn't a birthday party or a celebration for someone's promotion. Having parents all teary-eyed, walking around on egg shells, would feel more like a wake.

Wayne met my parents at the door. Mom stared a hole through him, then at Daddy, the unspoken message being for him to take charge and get answers. Wayne spoke first.

"We meet again, sir. Wayne Largo. Wish we could have met under better circumstances." He held out his hand. Daddy shook it firmly as any southern gentleman would do to friend or foe, until the moment was right to deal appropriately with either.

Appeased for the moment, Daddy stepped aside to let Mom enter, never letting Wayne out of his sight. Wayne locked the door behind them after scanning outside. From the slight nod of his head, Daddy liked that.

Mom rushed to hug me, crying. "Oh, God, baby. Tell us what's going on."

How many times would I have to tell this? I stood and walked toward the kitchen, impatient at my mother for no good reason. Mom followed.

"Don't," I said, hand out. "Just don't. Y'all leave me alone, okay?"

Mom's face blanched, but she sat on the sofa, kneading a tissue, silently seeking Daddy's tacit advice with her searching eyes. My den opened to the kitchen, without much of a hiding place, but the distance kept me from choking on the emotion in the room. I knew I sounded rude, but tough. Everyone could get over it. My filter was gone.

Daddy arched his back and stretched tall, reaching under his coat. He pulled out his 9mm and a Colt .45. He clunked his temporary arsenal down on my coffee table.

"Whoa!" Wayne said, advancing toward him. "Not sure we need all that."

"Son," Daddy said, running a veined hand through his thick salt-and-pepper hair. "You're never sure when you might need firepower, but it's nice to know it's there. Don't you think?" He pointed to Wayne's gun on his belt. Only then did I realize he'd donned a weapon in the chaos. "I take it you know how to use that thing?" Daddy asked.

"Yes sir." Wayne pointed to Daddy's weapons. "Can I assume you know how to use yours?"

"Been hunting since I could walk. I served twenty years in the military, including a year in 'Nam. Slade knows how to use hers, too." He turned to me as I sat back down with a glass of water. "Honey, you still got the .38 I gave you?"

"My gun's in my purse."

Wayne started to say something about that, then caught himself. Instead he chatted with the arriving cops. He soon left to join the search. I'd given him all the possible places Jesse might be. Mom made copious amounts of coffee and sandwiches while Daddy polished his armory. I'd never seen him so resolute.

The hubbub of so many people kept me from folding within myself. I pretended the kids escaped and hid somewhere in the night instead of being in the hands of a vile redneck monster who wanted a piece of their mother. Just as I'd expected, however, an hour later everyone sat lifeless, gaping at television or the carpet. Mom stirred the air by offering seconds and thirds on coffee. God, I needed to get out of here.

Minutes ticked into hours, Jesse obviously intent on making me suffer. My thoughts turned sour as I questioned Alan's actions, motives, emotional instability. I already knew Jesse's.

"What about Alan?" I asked to no one in particular. My abrupt words caused heads to rise. Donald had volunteered to watch the house, serve as liaison to the others out scouting two counties. He sat across from Mom and raised his brow at my question.

"Forget he's my ex," I said to him. "He's horribly nasty when he wants to be."

Mom cast a pitying look. "But they're his kids, too, Carolina."

The use of my first name laced with motherly patronization grated on me like nails across a chalkboard. I turned away before I said something wrong.

"They'll question and check out everyone involved, Ms. Slade," said Donald. "Including Mr. Bridges."

CHAPTER 26

A sleepless nine hours later, still seated on my front porch swing, I wrapped a denim jacket across me to shield the bite of a blustery front. Dawn arrived as depressed as I felt, dark clouds hanging low and pumped with moisture, resting atop the pines. Zack and Ivy didn't have coats.

I knew the statistics. Few kidnapped victims survived past twenty-four hours.

Our house echoed without them, and I hated the morbid vigil inside. I craved a gun in my hand and Jesse in my sights. Daddy only taught me to shoot at targets; I didn't hunt. Maybe it was time to learn.

I hadn't wasted those hours, though. I tried to put myself in Jesse's mind, a well-known face in the rural community burdened with hiding two kids. I knew every creek bed and abandoned shed. Wayne didn't.

But he'd convinced me to wait for Jesse's call. History proved that the bad guys spoke to who they wanted to, or not at all. Key clues vanished, babies died when parents didn't follow procedures. Sometimes they died anyway.

But Jesse didn't call. Nothing added up. What did he want? Not my kids. And if he used them as bait for me, then why not call and draw me out?

Follow procedure, they'd said. Sure. Like I'd done when I called in the IG to arrest a farmer. Sometimes the goddamned rules didn't work.

The front porch creaked. Wayne had come back two hours ago – to update and catch a nap. He looked like hell.

"I don't want to talk," I said.

Wayne slumped down on the swing, his face drawn and bags under his eyes from being out all night with deputies. Four hours sleep in three days.

He reached over and brushed my hair back "You don't need to be out there hunting, Slade. Trained people are doing all they can for you."

I stared into the winter-bare crape myrtles, their skinny branches tremoring from the light rain. "I'm tired of people telling me what I shouldn't do."

His leg moved over and pressed against mine. "Waiting's the hardest part."

"So they say."

Wayne stood, hands in his pockets, observing the porch slats. "I have to tell you something."

"I already know," I said. "Jesse would've called by now if he was interested in demands." My words misted white on the air. "And now I wasted time I could have spent finding them."

He turned slowly and headed to go inside.

I bolted from the swing and circled around in front of him, stopping him with a jab to his chest. "He might have met with me if I'd called him. We could've cut him a deal. We met him before, why not again? The area isn't that damn big, Wayne. Where the hell is he?"

"I don't know. We'll work it through."

"Work it through? This isn't one of your damn missing livestock cases!"

"I'm sorry, Slade. What else you expect me to say?"

"What, sorry for bringing all this down on my family, or sorry you ever met me? Sorry for Eddie? How many types of sorry are there?"

His face darkened. He turned away and leaned on the railing. Fat rain drops now fell from the sky, plopping on the pine straw.

My shoulders shook from the surge of adrenaline and cold air. Silence hung heavier than the rain clouds. Alan wasn't here for me to lambast; Wayne was. But he mollycoddled me, making my bitterness fester.

He rested his forearms on the rail, his head almost in his hands.

Damn it, give me a fight, Wayne. "Talk to me!"

The big oaf just stood there. No answer. No body language.

I slapped the house siding, the sting jolting into my wrist.

He spun around, his fingers embedding into my upper arms. "Listen to me, and you listen good." His booming voice bounced around the porch, and his gray eyes stared hard. "You're the reason I'm here. You, Slade! I know you're on fire about this, but . . ." His hands released me with a shove, shifting me off balance. I caught myself in time to see him stomp into the house.

"Wait a minute. We're not done here," I shouted. That wasn't a fight. That wasn't even a discussion. "To hell with you and every-damn-body with a badge! You told me to wait here. Where's that gotten me?" Mockingbirds scattered from a loblolly pine, choosing the weather over my wrath.

I turned at the sound of hinges, expecting Wayne to resume where we left off. Instead, Daddy stood there with a cool, condescending gaze on his face. Realizing everyone inside probably heard my outbursts, I sensed he felt the need to check on me.

"I thought I brought you up right," he said.

I blew out hard, a grunt of disgust. "You did, Daddy. But you never taught me how to deal with this."

"I know you're under a lot of pressure, girl, but cut the guy some slack."

The door swung open again. Wayne marched past us down the steps.

"You aren't going without me this time," I said. "I'm coming."

"No, you're not," he shouted back.

"You don't know the area like I do," I argued.

He fixated on me, cell phone in his hand. I halted on the steps, Daddy behind me.

"I just got a call from Atlanta. Let me talk, please." The last word came out as a plea, and caught me off guard.

"You don't answer to Atlanta anymore," I said, each word dropping in volume as I sensed his despair.

He spoke a few moments longer, then came back to the steps, ignoring the rain wetting his shoulders. "Kay's vacated her apartment."

The name escaped me, and it must have shown on my face.

Frustration furrowed his brow, the lines around his mouth. "My sister, Slade. She's disappeared, remember?"

He ran a hand over his face. He stepped into the yard, alone in his frustration. Daddy touched my shoulder as if telling me to tread carefully.

Wayne turned and begged me to understand. "We're all each other's got, Slade. This is my little sister. She's involved with a DEA sting operation of Pamela's."

Although he'd told me little about the situation, I hadn't asked. Maybe I should have.

"She didn't check in. They can't find her. She's not answering her cell. I've got to make some calls." He jerked toward the car then back toward me, agonizing over his dilemma.

"So you need to go?" I asked weakly, reliving Wayne's disappearance to Atlanta before, leaving me to face Beck alone.

He stomped up the steps soaked, the cold rain dripping from his hair. I stepped back, bumping into Daddy who moved to the side. Wayne leaned over, his face inches from mine. "No. I'm not leaving you, Slade. I'm not who Beck said I was. I'm here, with you, for the duration of this shit. Please tell me you understand that now."

I quietly said, "I get it."

He went inside.

I wrapped my arms around myself, then Daddy lent me his.

"I'm going out, Baby Girl. I'm finding those children if it's the last act I do. Stick by the phone. I'll call you every hour."

I squeezed the suede of his coat in my fingers. "I can go with you now, Daddy. Jesse won't call."

"You're not exactly in the best frame of mind to chase around the countryside with a loaded gun." He released me. "Let me get my coat," he said, which meant his weapons.

Daddy's car soon drove out of the subdivision. Five minutes later, Wayne reappeared in dry clothes and combed damp hair. He strode past me with a vicious, hard intent. He drove away as well.

I still stood watching where their taillights had disappeared when Donald came out on the porch a few minutes later. "Ms. Slade?"

"What?"

"I couldn't stop your father from searching, but I can detain you. Both men said for you to wait here."

"You might have to try," I said, disgusted at the order.

He sat down on the swing, this boy-child cop younger than me, and started talking. He explained how law enforcement searched. By the time he got through, he'd shamed me into staying home, as if going out was for my sake only.

But by the time he'd stepped into the house, I'd changed my mind.

I pulled out my phone. "Daddy? I'm going out looking. You can come back and get me, or I'll do it alone."

I hung up and went back inside.

In my bedroom, I dumped my purse on the bed. Makeup, tissues and lotion remained behind. Wallet, gun from the nightstand and ammo from the closet went in.

When the deputy stepped in the hall bath, I walked through the kitchen to the garage, coat in hand.

My mother looked up from wiping the counter for the twentieth time. "Where do you think you're going, Carolina?"

"Can't stand waiting in here," I said, and left.

Daddy met me at the garage. He tried to send me back in the house, but I stood defiant, the keys for the borrowed Jeep ready in my hand. So he wrapped his fingers around my forearm, making me stare into his tired blue eyes.

"This is far too dangerous a game for you."

"I can go with or without you, Daddy."

"Then I guess you'll need company."

Ordinarily I'd have said no, but he wouldn't have listened to me anymore than I was listening to him. I'd spent many memorable times with Daddy when I was growing up, including target shooting at the firing range. He hit what he aimed at. He taught me to hit center, too.

"You go sit in the car, and I'll tell your mother we'll be back soon." He stopped on the step and looked back at me. "Where're your umbrellas?"

AFTER FIVE HOURS of scouting the properties Wayne and I had visited two days ago, Daddy and I found nothing. The Williams' farm held the same abandoned air as before. Entering the barn, I slung the door hard, screaming Ivy's name. Another time I'd have laughed when the top hinge fell off. Drops pummeled the tin roof as I climbed into the loft. We scoured the shed and overturned barrels and crates—kicking one or two around for the hell of it. The sky rumbled in the distance.

Wearing his hunting boonie hat, Daddy walked with me under my umbrella toward the irrigation pond, leading the way through waist high grass, intensely searching for . . . signs. Periodically he stopped and visually surveyed the landscape. Then he froze. I rested my hand on his back, afraid to ask what he'd seen.

"What's that?" he asked, raising his hand over his eyes.

I squinted ahead. Something scrunched, maroon and muddy lay at the fringes of the shallow water of an old irrigation pond. A buzzard waddled around the object pecking at its edges. It took a bite, stretched its neck inspecting for rivals, then tugged at its prey again, fighting for a piece that wouldn't let loose.

Zack had worn a red Henley under his flannel shirt when he'd disappeared.

I shoved Daddy aside and tossed the umbrella.

He bellowed at me as I shirked his grasp. "Wait, Slade . . . don't."

Panting and grunting through the soggy ground, I ran the thirty yards, mud sucking my shoes, dragging me down. "Get away," I yelled, waving my arms. "Get away!" The bird stared at me with stark yellow eyes, waiting to see how close I'd get. He squawked and took flight as I narrowed the distance, flying over close enough for me to hear the flap of his wings.

The small doe lay open, her intestines exposed. Rain diluted the blood, spilling it onto the ground where it mixed with the mud and was gone.

Each of my sobs brought a small moan with it. I stooped over, my hands on my knees.

Daddy caught up and turned me away from the carnage, holding the umbrella over me. "Shhh, hon. Come on." Holding my hand, he led me back toward the car while images of my children drowning in any of a hundred ponds, creeks and inlets in the area haunted each step. We circled the pond and left via the bent grass path we'd made coming in.

We hollered across acres of fallow fields and miles of woods and farm roads, our voices falling flat in the moist air. I fought the urge to scream uncontrollably as my babies' names hurled off my tongue over and over. Daddy's booming voice echoed off buildings, countering the shrill in my own.

My wet sneakers turned my feet to ice, and muck covered the floorboard of my car. Daddy turned on the radio, scanning for the weather. A man warned people to stay inside and to expect fifty mile-an-hour gusts and rain up to three inches. A day in Jesse's favor. Daddy tried to call and update Mom, but the signal deteriorated worse than the weather.

I spotted Harold Harwick bent over a tractor's churning engine under his pole shed. We turned in, honking as we drew up, and parked under the shed's lip.

The tractor choked down, and the middle-aged farmer, dressed in flannel, denim and a straw hat, walked over to the car as I rolled down the window. "Slade. What you doing out here on a Saturday? Don't you know there's a storm 'sposed to hit this afternoon? Thought I'd get something done before it did."

Only then I noticed the rain had stopped. "I'm hunting for Jesse Rawlings. You seen him?"

Harold tucked an oily rag in his pocket, a matter-of-fact look on his face. "No, can't say I have."

I inhaled a curse. "Did you see him yesterday? Maybe he drove by? You know his white truck, right?"

"I'd know if I saw him, young lady. Did see his brother, though. Driving that beat-up Fairlane. Went by here an hour ago, driving too fast for wet roads." He pointed up the highway toward Jesse's house.

My heart leaped at the confirmation. Ren and Jesse were never far apart. "Anyone else in the car? Maybe a couple of kids?"

"Not that I noticed. Can't see much from here."

Ren might be involved, but that was hard to predict. He showed half the cleverness of his brother, a fraction of the spunk, and mental faculties we weren't too sure of. He worked odd jobs on various farms when he wasn't tending his own hogs, and collected a small Social Security disability pension.

"Mr. Harwick, you sure it was Ren and not Jesse?" I swallowed the panic in my words. "They look a lot alike. It's important."

"Well, didn't see much of him as he sped by, but I know that car."

Disappointed, I slumped in my seat. "Thanks, Mr. Harwick."

He backed away as I put the car in reverse. "You better get out of this weather," he said. "Bad day to be conducting business. This is a day to stay warm and dry over a hot meal with your loved ones."

I nodded at the irony and backed out, threw the gear in drive and spun a second before reaching the highway. Daddy patted my knee. "Sorry, gal. He didn't know."

The three miles to the hog farmer's house took two minutes with my foot slammed on the gas pedal. Jesse would hide out, but Ren might be

Lowcountry Bribe

home. Doubt niggled at me as I recalled Ren's shortcomings. He only did what Jesse told him to do, but I'd be willing to scare him shitless in order to find Ivy and Zack.

"Want me to drive?" Daddy asked as we blew past an elderly couple in a car creeping along. I watched them swerve to the road's shoulder in my rearview mirror.

"Daddy, let me drive. Let me think."

"Then slow down," he scolded. "These roads are slick. We can't do squat mired up in a ditch."

I recognized the bold censure of a man keeping his fears in check.

We roared onto Jesse's driveway hidden on one side by wax myrtles and neglected ligustrum hedges ten feet tall. A police car sat in a thicket a hundred yards away, manned by a deputy. I braked. The car skidded to a stop on the hard scrabble.

The Rawlings house was a run-down, paint-thirsty shanty. Two-by-tens resting on concrete block served as steps. Old tee shirts and dishrags insulated iron pipes leading from the well to the house. Puddles stood inches deep in various parts of the yard.

Three windows vented the side facing us. I sat still watching for curtain movement. Chickens huddled beneath the rotted floor sills. Zack would've thought chickens living under a house very cool.

"Stay here," I told Daddy. "Jesse's momma might let a woman in, but the both of us will scare her off. If a man answers—"

"I come running," he said, patting the big Colt .45 in his lap.

The weather-rotted porch sagged and groaned under my weight. I jumped when the door flew open. The protective hand on my purse felt the outline of my gun.

A woman the size of a combine loomed before me. Her scowl deepened ruts in her forehead. Jesse didn't inherit her mean and lifeless eyes, but I could see Ren's mouth carved in her face.

"Ms. Rawlings, remember me? I'm Slade from the Department of Agriculture." The old greeting I used for work spilled out. "Hate to bother you on a weekend, but I need Jesse."

"Ain't here."

"How about Ren?"

She glared down her nose. "Ain't here neither."

The kids could be inside despite all the efforts of the police. Jesse might've slipped them back in at any time. A lone cop parked a quarter mile away wouldn't know. "Can I come in?" I reached for the screen door handle.

She stepped back inside and yanked the door shut. "They ain't here. No kids, either. No one's here but me."

I flinched at the word "kids." "I need to speak to Jesse, ma'am."

Thunder crackled, ripped, then boomed.

"Lord A'mighty," she screamed, jumping back.

I banged on the screen frame again. "Ms. Rawlings!"

"Go on," she said. "Cops done been here three times." She waved her hand as though swatting flies. "My boys wouldn't take nobody's kids."

Guess even a buzzard protected her babies.

"Those are my kids, ma'am."

"Don't care whose they are. Last thing I need is more kids. Aren't you the one with eyes for my boy? The loan woman? You're probably here to pester Jesse for money, like a farmer's supposed to make a decent livin' *and* pay you. Ain't he got enough troubles without the likes of you chasing him?"

My hand grasped the screen door handle and pulled it open a few inches. "Please let me come in."

Ol' Momma jerked it shut, this time catching the hook on the inside. "You ain't comin' in my house."

I yelled through the screen. "Zack? Ivy? You in there?" The handle wouldn't budge against the small iron hook, unless I put my whole weight into it. In a minute I would. "What are you hiding in there?"

"You're crazy. Go on before I call the cops on you."

Daddy eased out. "Everything okay up there?"

Anger drove my hand into my purse, fingers wrapping around the gun. If my babies were in that house, I was getting them out. "Open the door or—"

Gravel crunched and water splashed as a car sped up behind ours, the bushes and rain hiding the make and model. I whirled around, my .38 in hand. Daddy'd already stepped out and drawn his weapon.

CHAPTER 27

Wayne bailed out of his Blazer and froze, flashing his palms up. "Lower the weapons!"

Jesse's momma screamed, "Oh, Jesus—Jesus, save me!" before she slammed the wooden door.

I lowered my gun and stepped down off Jesse's porch. Daddy already held his weapon in check. Wayne marched up to me, boots sloshing through puddles. "The sheriff's office called. What the hell are you doing?" he yelled over a new rumble of thunder.

I tucked the .38 back in my purse and went to walk around him. "I still need to get in there."

He snared my arm. "What's wrong with you?"

"I know the area. I know Jesse. I know my kids. Who else is better suited to find them?"

He glanced at Daddy, who returned a grimace. After a deep sigh, Wayne moved forward. "We already scoured this place. The kids aren't here."

Daddy spoke up. "He's probably right, Baby Girl."

I glared at my father. Everything I said and did seemed to reflect a woman out of her mind to him, Mom, the police, even Wayne. Grief and anxiety gnawed my gut raw, but my intellect worked just fine. I thought sharper now than I ever had.

Wayne greeted Daddy with a nod. "I've got a lead," he said.

I gripped his jacket. "From who? What about?"

He peered at Jesse's house, then the low cloud leaden sky. "Let's talk someplace else."

"Daddy, you drive." I tossed him the keys. "Follow us to TJ's." Poor Daddy followed my orders, not knowing what or where TJ's was.

"What did you find out?" I asked as Wayne fired the engine and eased the car onto the highway.

"They received a hit on the Amber Alert for the kids. Didn't you bring your phone?"

"Screw the phone. Mine doesn't work out here anyway. Someone saw them? Where are they?"

Wayne's behavior already told me my children remained lost, but maybe they'd been spotted, and cops followed the car they were in. I wanted proof of life, confirmation they were alive.

"No one's seen them, Slade. Slow down. Let me pull in and park." I wondered what was so good about what he said other than the kids weren't dead.

He parked the Blazer onto TJ's lot. His eyes were weary. "They stopped Jesse's truck in Savannah."

Daddy parked, ran over and slid into the backseat. "What's happened?"

My heart still skipped triple time. "They found Jesse's truck, Daddy. It's a start."

Wayne looked at me long before answering. "They picked up Ren driving the truck. They're questioning him."

My grip dug into his forearm through his jacket. "So Jesse was driving Ren's car. Daddy! Mr. Harwick saw Jesse. That means the kids probably are still around here."

"Wait. What?" Wayne asked. "Who's Harwick?"

I twisted around on the seat with a bounce. "I questioned a farmer who said he saw Ren." I pointed up the highway, wagging my finger. "Said he saw him here, on this same road. Driving his beat-up car, just today."

"You sure?" Wayne asked, his head forward as if to hear me correctly.

"Are you sure your guys have Ren?" I asked. "If so, it was Jesse in Ren's car."

Wayne snatched his phone off the seat.

I rattled off instructions. "Tell them the brothers resemble each other. Tell them since they have Ren, Jesse must be here. Tell them it's easy to scare the piss out of Ren. And make sure—"

Wayne placed his phone flat over his coat. "I know what to tell them." He relayed the information and then his voice rose. "What do you mean his car was in the shop? Well, it's been spotted here on the road. Call me back at this number when you can confirm that." He snapped the phone shut. "They'll call us when they have more."

"More damn waiting," I said. "I'd have information out of Ren faster than this, and make him happy to provide it." Wayne said nothing, his patient expression stirring my ire. "He's not that smart. Good grief," I said. "This is crap. I can't deal with all this goddamn crap."

Wayne glanced at Daddy then back at me. "Thank heavens you didn't go out alone."

"Oh would you shut up about what I should or shouldn't be doing!" I opened the car door. "I'm questioning Mr. Tyson and anyone else in the store." My right foot hit the gravel about the time Wayne grabbed the tail of my coat.

I yanked back. "Stop it!"

"If you're going to act like a tornado, at least let me open the conversation. You'll scare everyone away with that hellfire approach of yours."

I stared into the rain clouds. I wanted to kick someone or something into the next county, and Wayne happened to be in my line of fire.

A slim, elderly man in a faded denim jacket stepped out of the store, hoisted a brown paper sack in the crook of his arm and climbed in his faded blue pickup. I jogged over and knocked on his window.

"Have you seen these two children?" I asked.

My creased photo of the kids snagged his attention as I wiped off water with my sleeve and splayed the picture from my wallet on the windshield. He shook his head, the window still up.

"Please. Think harder," I pleaded. "Do you know Jesse Rawlings? We suspect he has them. Or maybe his brother Ren?"

I slapped the picture on the glass again, mad he wouldn't roll down his window.

He locked his door. "No, ma'am," he yelled. He started his engine.

I leaned on the old truck, fearing he'd leave without weighing his answer fully. "They might look a bit older. This was ten months ago."

He shifted into drive.

"Zack is a bit heavier. Ivy grew like a weed, so she's about two or three inches taller." The man surely understood. He lived around here. I wanted him to open his eyes, analyze every car, every person, watch the landscape as he drove by, and call us.

He backed out and drove off, the movement snatching the picture from my hand. It fluttered to the ground. I picked it up, wiping the moisture off on my coat.

If I approached everyone I saw, sooner or later, someone would have seen the kids. Oh, damn it, I should've given the guy my card. I pressed knuckles into my eyes, willing myself to hold the pieces of my fragmented soul together.

"Carolina," Daddy called from the storefront. "Pull it together, girl. You can't help anyone like this."

The bell rang overhead as Daddy held the door for me. Displays of Zippos and scratch-off lottery tickets lined the long wooden counter. Next to the register sat a gallon jar marked: "Help Justin Fight Cancer." An eight-year-old boy in a green plaid, button-up shirt and a clip-on tie stared out at me from a school photograph.

Wayne shook hands with Tyson and introduced Daddy. "We need to ask you a few questions, if you don't mind," he started. I twisted a button on my coat. Mr. Tyson listened with no animation, no reaction, as if the words needed to take root before he understood.

The boy's picture drew my attention. His crooked, gapped-tooth grin made him appear happy in spite of the disease that ate him away.

Jesse might've stood right here in this spot anytime this weekend. On Saturday he could've picked up booze and forgotten my children needed supper. He wouldn't buy Frosted Flakes and a quart of milk for their Saturday breakfast. A Saturday without cartoons. My belly knotted. My imagination would consume me if Wayne didn't cut to the quick. The coat button wrenched off in my hand.

"Mr. Tyson," I said, stepping up and plopping an outstretched hand on the counter. "Have you or haven't you seen the two missing children? We don't have time to chat."

"Carolina," Daddy warned.

I stared into Tyson's eyes. I didn't care about manners.

Tyson shook his head, ignoring my misguided behavior. "Deputies been through here a couple of times asking questions. Haven't seen hide nor hair of any young 'uns that didn't belong around here."

"They're my children, sir." I thrust the picture of Zack and Ivy in front of his face. Tyson tilted his head up, pushed my hand farther away and examined the photo through the bottom of his bifocals.

"We think Jesse Rawlings may have them," Wayne said. "Have you seen him in the last twenty four hours?"

"Wish I could say I have. Jesse usually comes in on Friday for a few beers, but not this weekend." He lifted his glasses off his nose and peered at me with a softness in his eyes. "Sorry, gal."

Wayne rubbed his beard, no longer neat as a three-day-old stubble inched up his face and down his neck. "Maybe nothing, but what did Jesse buy last time he was in here?"

"Junk food, as always. It's never the same thing. He bought quite a bit, though, which probably explains why he hasn't been in here lately." He shook his head. "He wouldn't know a vegetable if he grew it himself."

We'd depleted Tyson of all he knew, which amounted to zilch. Wayne shook the man's hand. He left an IG business card with his cell phone number on the back. I grabbed the card and wrote mine on it as well. "Please call us about any hint of anything," I said.

Tyson tried to smile. "I will, gal. Good luck."

Daddy and I climbed back into the Jeep. Wayne leaned in my window. "It's time we went back, Slade. It'll be dark soon."

"It's cold, wet, and they don't have jackets. What if they haven't eaten? What if they're hurt? What if . . ." Not having an immediate plan undermined my efforts to stay strong and argue my case. The nights were black as licorice out here, thirty miles from city lights. "The rain is filling up the creeks." My voice hitched.

I reached in my pocket and tiny shreds of tissue fell out. Frantic, I opened my purse and reached for the packet of tissues I'd tossed on the bed at home. My nose needed wiping. I set the gun on the seat like it was Chapstick and ransacked the bag.

"Where's a tissue?" I said through my teeth, turning the purse upside down.

Wayne reached over me, picked up the .38 and put it in his left coat pocket. "Let's go home. We'll get up early."

"I can't stop," I protested. "What would they think if they knew I quit looking? How can I go home to a warm house and soft bed when they could be in a barn, a shack, the trunk of a car? Hell, the woods! If they're wet, they'll get sick." The words tumbled out faster than I could think, racing to the bottom of my despair where I was about to meet them and come unglued.

Wayne's phone rang. He stepped away from the car.

Daddy stroked my back, something not done since I was ten years old. "Wayne's right, honey, and I promised your mother we'd be home by dark. You can't search at night. It's too dangerous. You could miss them."

I snapped at the last person who deserved it. "Don't you understand, Daddy? If it's too dark and too dangerous for me, it's doubly so for them."

"And what good are you to the kids if you get hurt?"

Wayne glanced back at the tone of my voice, cell phone still at his ear.

"I can search a few more places," I said, eyes on Wayne, trying to watch for any sign of progress in that phone call. "Would Mom quit looking for me if I'd gone missing? Would you?" Wayne hung up with no emotion. I turned for my father's answer.

Daddy shook his head.

"I didn't think so."

Wayne returned. "Ren lied. When they asked where Jesse was, he said he didn't know. When they asked him why he was driving Jesse's truck, he said his car was in the shop. He drove the truck on an errand in Savannah, at Jesse's insistence. He has no clue about the kids. They're about to let him loose."

Studying the rain rivulets on the windshield, I tried to map a course of action. "They're nearby, you know."

Wayne's slow movements revealed his exhaustion. "If Jesse wanted to hurt them, he would have done so. He only wants you. If you go searching in the dark, tired as a plow horse, he might get you. I say we start again in the morning."

I turned the key in the ignition. "I'm searching down a few more roads. You can follow or not. Daddy, you can ride with me or go with him." Daddy buckled his seatbelt. Wayne walked to his Blazer without argument.

I drove south toward Edisto Island. Six abandoned barns and four dirt roads later, I switched on headlights, turned around and headed north toward home. Wayne's headlights stayed a steady four car lengths behind. I jerked impatiently off the road to search one last time, my tires skidding six feet before catching. High-stepping through dark vegetation soaking my jeans, I fell over a rusted, weed-covered disc harrow, blades dangerous enough to slice me in two. Raising up off my knees after groping for the flashlight in something I assumed to be mud, I caved to the futility of rambling blind.

I screamed, the noise scraping my throat raw. My flashlight shattered against a fence post sending batteries, plastic and glass in all directions. Daddy and Wayne ran toward me.

"Leave me alone!" I sobbed. "Stay away, goddamn it. I don't need your sympathy. I need my kids! Somebody find my children." My body stooped, head touching the ground as I cried fierce, savage wails of agony.

The two men halted in the high grass. After I'd released the brunt of my frustration, Daddy took the reins. "Carolina, stand up and get in the car." His tone and the use of my first name brought back memories of a twelve-year-old's piano recital disaster. He'd held me as I cried, embarrassed I'd let the world down over a forgotten chord.

Drained, I rode back without words, Daddy driving. Words felt sacrilegious. I let a few tears fall in the dark, not caring that I couldn't feel my feet. My father threw the heat on high and used a barbecue napkin from my glove box to wipe the fog off the window. Then he handed me a few dry ones.

"Baby Girl, you've got to collect yourself. Coming apart don't help Ivy and Zack a damn bit."

I sighed ragged. "I know, Daddy. I'm sorry."

"I'm not the one you owe an apology to. That man is killing himself for you. His sister's disappeared and they ain't found a sign of her. Yet here he is helping you. He hasn't slept a wink since he left the house yesterday morning."

I hung my head, disgusted at myself. I fingered the napkin, furious enough to blow a bullet hole through Jesse's sarcastic, good-old-boy face, no matter how many years it landed me in jail. He'd turned me into someone I wouldn't care to meet.

CHAPTER 28

Sunday came and went as the three of us scoured every cow path and asphalt road on three islands. Once we were home, Donald gave up his vigil with a vow that he would remain in close touch and keep searching, his unspoken message being no point in guarding an empty house. He was too kind to be that blunt. He left. Mom fixed country fried steak, her contribution to the cause and personal attempt to stay occupied. We ate in silence, eating little, no one wanting to discuss the day's failure. I fell into bed, dropping asleep before I could cry.

Monday morning, I bolted awake with an urgency coursing through my arms and legs to move. I scrambled upright in bed, my heart hammering. Wayne lifted his hand from stroking my forehead. "Shhh. Just me."

My panting slowed as my thoughts collected. "What time is it?"

"Eight. I already checked in with SLED. Nothing new."

Feet hitting the carpet, I ran to the bathroom, then to the closet, still wearing yesterday's clothes. "Why'd you let me sleep so long?"

"You were exhausted."

I vaguely remembered the night before. "Where'd you sleep?"

"On top of the bedspread, next to you. Every place else was taken."

He didn't seem to care who knew he'd shared my bed. He mumbled something.

I stumbled outside the closet, one leg in my jeans. "What?"

"You sure you're up to going out again?" he asked, scratching his beard. "I still think you ought to be here."

I fumbled with the buttons of a flannel shirt. "It's not open for discussion." I grabbed my purse from the dresser top. "I need the gun."

He rose to exit the bedroom. "You'd plug six rounds into Jesse before we asked him questions. I'd only see you on visiting days at the penitentiary."

"Whatever." Head clear now, I recognized the common sense, but I still wanted the comfort of a weapon.

I ran upstairs and grabbed a shopping bag from Ivy's closet, cramming it with a blanket, several pairs of socks and two of her oversized sweatshirts. One would fit Zack.

Downstairs, Mom slept in my spare bedroom. Daddy snored on the sofa, his way of standing guard. I avoided the temptation to kiss his sagging cheek. He needed his rest.

We left through the garage. As we stepped outside, I paused. A television truck was parked next to the driveway, and a host of reporters jogged over. We hurried into the Blazer and slammed the doors. Matt Claussen, the square-jawed, handsome blond guy from Channel 4 News, maneuvered in front of the car.

They already knew my kids were missing. All they wanted was a sympathy piece, preying on the crumbling mother. "Run the idiot over," I said, angered at the gross lack of empathy.

Wayne laid on the horn, and the local celebrity almost did the splits leaping clear to the sidewalk. Cameras, hands and bodies demanded our attention like a street gang. I shook a fist at them. "They're trespassing. They're rude. They're—"

Wayne clipped a tire over the curb and accelerated away. We headed toward the interstate.

A few miles later, I pointed as the intersection whizzed past. "That's where we turn."

"We're going to your office first."

"Damn it, why?" I had worked a mental list of new roads and isolated places to search.

"To grill some people," he said. "It could lead to other things."

"Every minute is less daylight." An anxious urge to find the kids climbed back up from whatever abyss it had slept in. "Don't hold me back again. I won't stand for it."

"Just trust me."

I caved to his judgment, if only to speed things up.

We parked outside the Charleston agriculture building. Wayne barreled into the office like a Marine. I followed, curious to view their faces, anxious to hear their excuses, eager to be done and gone.

Jean gasped. Ann Marie stared wide-eyed, as usual.

"Everyone here?" Wayne commanded from the middle of the room. The two women shrank back in their chairs. "Where's Hillary?" he asked.

"In here." Hillary appeared from her office with one hand on her hip and the other holding papers. For a change she looked sharp in a plaid skirt and red knit sweater. As if she planned to meet McRae at the Motel 6. "What's your problem?"

Wayne's tone gave him a bigger-than-life appearance with his announcement to all. "We believe Jesse Rawlings kidnapped Slade's kids. Somebody in this office knows more than she's saying. You can talk to me, or you can talk to SLED, the IG or the cops. I can have them all here with a call." He stopped in front of Hillary. "Let's start with you."

She retreated to her office. "You've got no authority here," she said over her shoulder. "You've got no authority *anywhere*."

"Oh, but I make for a fine witness," he said. "And from what I've seen and heard about you, I could make a difference in your future. Trust me."

"Whatever," she said, but didn't try to stop us.

I followed Wayne into her retreat, smelling Hillary's knock-off Gucci cologne the minute I crossed through. She barely sat in her chair before Wayne leaned on her desk with fisted hands. She pretended to work, her jerky movements shifting paper. Wayne moved the papers out of her reach. She stared up at him, menacing yet scared.

Her veiled arrogance was no match for my impatience as I strode behind her desk and got in her face. "What do you know?"

Her gaze shifted from Wayne to me. "You two are insane. Get out."

I reached out, as if to grab her sweater. She snapped backward, her chair rolling against to the wall. "Don't you dare try to assault me," she said.

"I might be insane," I said, "but if I find out you kept information from us, I'll skin you with a dull knife and nail your hide to a fence post."

"I don't have to talk to anyone." Her fingers trembled as they reached for a folder. She spoke down to her file. "The law would already be here if you had anything."

"Oh, like *that* sounds innocent," I said.

Wayne reached over and closed her folder. His words softened, but they weren't nice. "I think someone used you for sex. Might add a whole new dimension to this story."

I snatched the file from her hands.

Wayne squeezed my forearm, not taking his eyes off Hillary. "Maybe you worked a deal with Jesse?" he said. "You fed information to him to harass Slade, kill her dog, steal her children."

Color drained from her face. Frankly, I couldn't see Hillary going that far, but any con, lie or method that garnered clues was fair play as far as I was concerned.

"I haven't done a thing," Hillary said, staring at us a moment before her attention returned to her desk.

"That's bullshit and you know it," he said, voice controlled and chilling. "Your pillow talk and calls tipping McRae regarding our activities in the office are enough to nail you. McRae is a pipeline to Jesse. Whether you know McRae passed information to Jesse or not, you're still responsible for whatever Jesse does as a result."

Her eyes widened.

Wayne paused. "The only way to help yourself is to help us."

She remained frozen. Her stare moved off us and fixated on the wall.

"Well," he said, reaching over and rotating the chair so it faced him.

"You go ahead and tough it out. But if something happens to those children, all bets are off and you're going to prison."

Her arms crossed in front of her. Even trembling, the posture still spoke defensively.

"Seriously, Hillary?" I said, irritated.

"Okay," Wayne said. "Shall I let Slade ask her questions . . . behind a closed door?" Wayne stood straight. "She's been itching to deal with you."

I winced, uncomfortable with his depiction of me, but not sure how far he was from the truth. Agents apparently picked a course of action and tackled it, true or false, seeking a rise out of their targets. Hillary's complexion color scared me. What if she knew nothing, just like she said? Lately, people took shots at me using fictitious ammunition. They inflicted enough damage to make others assume me guilty. Using their tactics on Hillary felt dirty . . . but necessary.

Hillary couldn't have children. Maybe she didn't understand what all this meant to me. She loved acting out, and I wondered if she behaved badly because she suffered such a shallow personal life, like Lucas.

Her eyes blinked and widened again. "Why harass me?" she said. "Slade has obviously pissed someone off. Maybe she ought to watch whose toes she steps on next time."

Scratch the sympathy vote. I gripped her wooden nameplate as if it were her carotid. No longer pitying her rough upbringing and abusive home life, I wished she would choke and die.

Wayne stepped back to let me play bad cop. I wasn't pretending.

Moving around her desk, my face moved close enough to count her eyelashes. "The police will talk to your husband. He'll learn about your affair with McRae. How long has it been since your truck driver smacked that pretty face of yours? I've seen your bruises. Let's spread the details of your pitiful life all over this state. How does that feel?"

Her unblinking eyes almost popped out of her head.

"You're an open book, lady," Wayne said. "So are McRae's other two women. Are you doctoring files, hiding paperwork, hoping he'll leave his wife or promote you in exchange for services rendered? Surely you didn't think you were his only lay?"

Internal Affairs Agent Beck broke me using practically the same wicked line about Wayne. Hillary's chin dropped to her chest. "I just fed him information and hid the file."

"What about Jesse?" Wayne asked.

"I'm not involved with him, or any kidnapping."

So she's only part guilty. "What *are* you involved in?" I asked.

She opened a drawer and lifted a file I'd never seen—labeled Larry Smith. "Henry told me to keep this for him." She dabbed at moist eyes.

"Larry Smith is sort of Jesse."

Wayne grabbed the file and flipped through the papers.

My office, the center of illegal activity. Now I was really pissed. "What else?" I demanded.

"Henry and Lucas created the file. Henry said Larry Smith was a landowner who no longer had a loan with us. I think he might be dead. I don't know. Jesse sold equipment and hogs through this name to avoid taxes and loan payments. Henry and Lucas got a cut." Tears now diluted her cheap mascara. "He hates you, Slade," she cried. "He spends more time talking about you than me."

Big hoo-ha. I already knew Henry hated me.

Wayne dropped the file on the desk, and Hillary jumped. "Call McRae's office and see where he is." He pointed at her. "Don't even think about telling him we're here."

She shook her head in understanding and dialed the district office. She hung up quickly. "He's not there. They don't know where he went."

Wayne scowled and dialed his cell phone.

"I did what you asked!" she pleaded. "Don't call my husband."

Wayne spoke to someone, then flipped the phone closed. "SLED is on their way over here with an FBI agent." He waved the file. "They'll appreciate this." Wayne motioned for me to follow him out of her office. "When they get here, we're leaving."

His instincts to come here had been dead-on. "Drop me at home," I said. "I'll take my car to the field. You can chase McRae."

"Slade, you went nuts yesterday. Don't go out."

I heard a tiny pneumatic whoosh. McRae strolled in.

My throat constricted at the sight of him. Here was a man who'd exhibited no redeeming qualities the entire time I'd known him. My mental faculties skipped from one scenario to another, seeking words to put this man in his place instead of my hands gouging out his eyes. I'd verbally jousted with him far too many times and won. With the stakes so high, this time should be no exception.

But he had a lot to lose and he couldn't stay away. He had to know what we knew.

But he turned to Wayne. Of course he would.

"Mr. Largo, I presume," McRae said. His gaze fell on me. "With my favorite manager." Pale lips grinned wide, thin and confident. "So sorry about the children. Any news?"

My nails dug into my palms. "You tell me."

Wayne stepped between us, a defensive posture to stop whichever one of us decided to make a move. "We need to talk, McRae."

My boss laughed. "I bet the IG would love to hear about this unofficial visit. What's your boss' name? Ledbetter, was it?"

As the old taste of hate for McRae raced through me, I wondered who told the man we were here. I scanned the room. We'd occupied Hillary. I pointed at Jean's empty chair and Ann Marie gave a shaky shrug. Of course it was Jean.

A fretful Hillary hugged the doorjamb of her office, McRae watching. "I see the staff has been cooperative."

Hillary closed her eyes and rested her forehead on the frame.

"Quite," Wayne said, his glare hard, his voice harder. His rustic, unkempt appearance gave him a brawler image compared to McRae's sleek and seamless polish.

McRae's jaw tightened as he sat on the edge of Jean's desk and unbuttoned his suit coat. He flapped his tie. "My only crime is adultery, if you call that a crime. If Ms. Traywick took it upon herself to get illegally involved with something, that's her problem. Makes me wonder where Slade was while her employee strayed." He scoffed with a tilt of his head back. "Once again, the Charleston manager falls short of expectations."

I stepped around Wayne and slapped McRae off the desk corner. He clumsily regained his balance with some sidesteps, reaching up to hold his cheek. The sting on my hand recharged me, enticing me to do it again in spite of the creepiness of touching him.

Wayne moved in the way. "We'll sort this out in Hillary's office."

Hillary scurried away from her office, not wanting to get involved. McRae strolled in and propped up against the wall, arms folded with a demeanor of calm control. His cheek flashed red with my hand's imprint.

Wayne entered, stoked and primed. I closed the door. "Sit down," he said to McRae.

"I'll stand."

Wayne gripped the back of a chair. "So your arrangement with Lucas Sherwood disguised the sale of collateral through Jesse Rawlings and his alias of Larry Smith. Did Mickey Wilder refuse to go along? Is that why he disappeared?"

McRae's eyes narrowed. "You're trespassing on government property, Largo."

Wayne rubbed the portfolio. "We have the file that I believe you ran over here to collect from Hillary."

McRae stared down his nose at each of us. With the tension thick in the tiny ten by ten office, I wondered when he'd bolt, almost welcoming the interruption to physically tackle him. Someone smelled nervous, almost sweaty. I wondered if it was me.

Wayne gestured toward me. "You used your affair with Hillary to keep an eye on Slade. And since you're so connected with Jesse, I suspect we can tie the children's kidnapping to you as well."

McRae unfolded his arms. "You have nothing on me."

Wayne's brow raised. "Really? We're up to murder, kidnapping, kickbacks ... how about the attack on my partner? Then we've got bribery, embezzlement, and of course, conspiracy and falsification of government documents."

Wayne stoically tested McRae, inert in this blinking game of words. At the moment, Wayne and Beck held a lot in common, and it didn't bother me at all.

"I don't kidnap kids or murder people." McRae faced me, his voice oozing sarcasm. "You making stuff up now, Ms. Slade? Kidnapping and murder? What a crock."

My hands balled on my hips. "You're pathetic, Henry."

McRae gave a faux grin, fooling no one. The allegations gave him pause. "Sounds like a lot of empty allegations to me. No proof."

I laughed. "I've got plenty of proof that you're pathetic, Henry."

Wayne moved into McRae's space, six inches separating the toes of their shoes. "You better pray we find those children. Jesse won't take kindly to shouldering the whole mess himself."

McRae shrugged. "If Jesse snatched them, he did it on his own. I didn't know anything about it until Hillary called last night." The man's eyes squinted with anger. "That farmer is uncontrollable. Hell, my money's on Jesse for Wilder's disappearance."

I yearned for the chance to sink my fingernails in his face, break his crooked nose, bust his lip. Wayne caught my attention with a glance, an attempt to diffuse my anger. My temper festered behind the crumbling retaining wall of my good sense.

"What about the crooked paper with the landowners?" Wayne asked.

"Sorry, not sure what you're talking about." McRae said.

"Slade's research, the courthouse records, and the locals spilling their guts," Wayne said. "You forget I learned a lot about this area working the Wilder disappearance." He paused. "And don't forget your long-distance partner."

We weren't sure about the partners and didn't have squat to confirm McRae's transgressions, but Wayne sounded convincing enough to make even me second guess the facts. He named three of the properties we'd researched, including the one we saw McRae file papers on in the courthouse.

McRae sniffed once. "We bought land along those highways in case the government decided to widen them. All on record. Businesses fight for road frontage leading to water. Nothing illegal about that."

More farmland could be involved than we knew. I couldn't see Mickey tolerating farmers getting taken advantage of. "Mickey would've said something to you," I said.

"Mickey didn't know," McRae replied, hands digging deep in his pockets, too relaxed for my taste.

"Where'd you get the money to buy the land?" Wayne asked. "Uncle Sam doesn't pay you that much."

McRae's gaze flitted about the room. "My business."

"I've locked up more people over a simple paper and dollar trail than anything else," Wayne said. "I'll put the pieces together."

Hillary knew little and McRae was stonewalling. Time to hand them over to the authorities and let them sort it out. I moved to the door, taking the knob in my hand. "I'm sick of this. Let's go."

Wayne held up a finger, begging for another minute. I grabbed a chair over and sat down, dropping my head in my hands. In exactly one minute, I was calling Daddy to come get me and search Toogoodoo again.

I raised my head. "Who is Palmetto Enterprises?"

McRae snorted. "Business acquaintances. Jesse wasn't trustworthy. I dropped him once I found them, though I have to admit Jesse was a good talker. Some of those codgers sold their places at a premium."

"Why'd so many of them die before the deeds were filed?" Wayne asked.

McRae's mouth hung open. "What the fuck are you talking about?"

I jumped up. "Those poor old people died before the deeds were recorded, you moron. Like you didn't know."

"You're lying," he said, with less wrath and more smug.

"Once a conspiratorial relationship is forged and the first overt act occurs, all parties are equally liable for the acts of each other," Wayne quoted. This sounded real, or a damn good bluff. "You're screwed, McRae. That bogus file ties you to murder and kidnapping. Federal statute. Sentence without parole."

Wayne moved into McRae's space. "But Mickey found out, and you had your partner get rid of him."

McRae frowned. "Absolutely not."

"He had to suspect Jesse sold equipment and hogs for personal use," I said. "He had to wonder why small land changed hands so easily. Oh, my God, you helped dispose of Mickey."

"No," McRae said. "I know nothing about that."

"Hope you have proof of that, hoss," Wayne said.

"So why'd you suck me into all of this?" I asked.

"We couldn't afford for the Williams' place to go to public bid. Jesse thought he'd get you to work a deal. I warned him you didn't know how to cooperate on anything."

My watch showed two hours since we'd arrived. A new wave of fear for the kids rushed over me. "That's it, Wayne," I said as I stood.

Wayne moved in on the seated McRae, making the man stand and back up. "I'd enjoy beating the hell out of you, but I don't have the time."

Wayne pushed him down the wall, along the sheetrock until he reached a metal conduit of computer wires running down from the ceiling. He then slammed my boss against the wall, the pole hitting him square in the back. "Where are those children?"

"I don't know," McRae hollered. "I don't give a damn about her fucking brats."

If McRae was telling the truth, Jesse was probably flying solo with a plan of his own steeped in simple vengeance for me. We had no clue what he was up to, and we'd wasted gobs of time coming to that conclusion.

McRae shook like the nervous dog he was. Wayne gathered McRae's shirt in his fist, and without a punch, McRae's knees gave out. Wayne let go.

A middle-aged SLED agent peered in. "Everything all right?"

"Fine," Wayne said through his teeth. He shoved the file into the agent's hand, pointing to McRae then to Hillary. "This idiot and that woman are up to their necks in a conspiracy to include murder, maybe snatching the Bridges children. Give this file to the FBI agent en route." Wayne reached into his pocket. He tossed the man a small tape recorder. "Their confessions are on here, proof of several felonies. Give that to him, too."

"Whoa," said the agent, holding an item in each hand. "How about you sticking around and helping us answer some questions?"

"That one," he said, pointing to McRae, "told me enough to know my butt needs to be in the field looking for those kids. I'll come in later."

"No, I think you'll stay—"

"Hold that thought," Wayne said as we ran out to the SUV, giving no one the chance to stop our departure. Storm clouds, angry and dark, warned of more rain.

"I'm taking you home," Wayne said, turning off the radio announcer reporting high winds by three this afternoon. "No argument." He accelerated out of the lot, tires spitting gravel.

I grabbed the dash as he turned the corner. "I don't think so."

He slowed down at a red light, then gunned the gas as it popped green. "Damn it, Slade. I move faster alone."

I do, too. "Fine. Take me home."

We drove in silence. Wayne couldn't acknowledge my personal need to protect all I had left. I wasn't the one needing a bodyguard. Ivy and Zack were. Why couldn't anyone understand that?

Daddy stood beside his car in my driveway. As I tried to get out, Wayne dragged me back by my coat and tried to remind me why I couldn't go. I pulled free, tired of being literally jerked around.

"I'll call," he said. He drove off, leaving me under Daddy's guard.

In the house, I threw on a sweatshirt and grabbed my raincoat, running back to my dresser for extra socks. The kids' bag sat in the kitchen, unloaded when Wayne had dumped me off.

Daddy appeared in my bedroom. "What are you doing?"

"What I've got to do." I brushed past him to the living room. His pistols lay on my oak coffee table. "No, you don't," he said.

"I'm going, Daddy," I said snatching up the .45. "You said you'd do the same for me." I ran to the door, clutching my purse off the kitchen counter on the way.

"Then I'm coming—"

"No, you're not. I love you."

"Carolina!" Daddy bellowed as I opened the garage door. That bellow used to stop me in my tracks when I was ten, but not this time.

I started the car and left. Of course, a torrential bottom dropped out of the stormy sky. I couldn't see twenty feet past the front of my car, but I'd chase those twenty-feet views for however many miles were needed to find Ivy and Zack.

CHAPTER 29

I shot down Savannah Highway, driving like a bootlegger with badge heat on his bumper. First on the agenda were five dead-end roads we'd missed the day before, then Jesse's house to talk to his mother again. I'd scan every creek, marsh and shanty in between.

Two hours and one wind-bent umbrella later, I'd covered eight stops, each time fearful of discovering the worst, sick at not finding Ivy and Zack. My hair clung to my face and neck, and I couldn't chase away the damp chill, in spite of the heater. The wet air kept the inside of my windows spotty and fogged.

Crossing the rushing, rain-bloated creek brought back thoughts of Mickey. Would Jesse kill children like he did Mickey . . . and the elderly people who'd mysteriously dropped dead before the deeds to their farms were recorded? So many dead people. And this weather gave him his best chance to dispose of bodies, especially little ones.

In the damp, cold air, a shudder raced across my back. My arms ached from gripping the wheel, and from the metal taste in my mouth, my lip was chewed raw.

As I crossed the Toogoodoo Bridge, I tried to think like Jesse. This far from home, the kids would be scared out of their minds. He could tell them to stay put and they would. He wouldn't babysit. Hogs needed feeding since Ren was in Savannah. Jesse would dodge the cops. God knows what other business he was conducting . . . what other people he'd kill. Wet and scared, I shivered again.

Thunder cracked the air, the subsequent rumbles echoing into the distance. I stared at the road through flip-flop wipers as the deep bass convulsion faded away. Sheets of water coated my windshield. I twisted the knob, raising the speed of the wipers. I could barely see the center line.

Two-hundred-year-old oaks dripped with ten-foot tendrils of sopping wet moss, and I remembered taking the kids to Angel Oak, letting them climb on limbs wider than they were tall. They'd laughed about the old tree being the Keebler cookie house for elves.

I'd been a good mother. *I was a good mother.* After all the hugs and kisses, their material needs were more than met, unlike the poor children who seasonally lived in the labor houses now passing my window.

The labor houses!

I slammed on the brakes with both feet. The car spun, gliding across slick asphalt, one wheel dropping into a shallow ditch with a lurch. It stopped half off the road. Rain hammered the roof. Damn!

Remembering Daddy's instructions, I teased the gas, seeking a break. When the tires whirred and I didn't move, I lifted my foot, sickened at my stupid dilemma.

Why hadn't I remembered the labor houses without stomping the brake? They sat close enough to Jesse's place to be convenient. Plus, they remained vacant this time of year. The shacks lined in a row leading away from the marsh, a stone's throw from the bridge.

The perfect hiding place.

The vehicle's front end jutted into the road, the headlights shining halfway up a copse of white oaks across the way. Thank goodness for no traffic. I barely tested the gas again. Still spinning.

Then I saw the high headlights of a big truck barreling toward me.

I threw the transmission into reverse, pumped the gas once, then jerked the gearshift into drive and floored it. Daddy's Jeep bit into the wet ground and lunged back into the opposite lane, narrowly avoiding a deep ditch channeling a roaring flood of water toward the creek.

The truck shot past me, horn blaring.

Trembling, I repositioned the car and drove back toward the creek to inspect the unoccupied labor houses.

Weather and neglect had hardened the driveway of the first house and turned it into part of the threadbare yard. Heavy shaded trees encouraged black mildew to creep across shingles and eaves.

I stopped, the sudden shift to park giving the car a lurch. I scanned the situation. No curtains. No sign of life in the house. The rain abruptly ceased, almost making me jump. Random hits of water from the oaks peppered the hood and roof as if telling me time was ticking.

Trepidation shot through my body. Adrenaline had fed me to this point. Now that I stood on a precipice, was I prepared for what I'd find?

Angry at my dark doubts, I shot out and slammed the door with a force that had been waiting days for release. Slipping on dead leaves and moss, I ran to the first front door, expecting to kick it open. It wasn't locked. I stepped in, shaking myself off on vinyl flooring worn through to concrete slab.

Prefab open cabinets hung in the kitchen, the tile cracked, bent up and split. Receptacles dangled from the wall. Water dripped through the range hood into a spot where the stove used to be. Down the hall, toilets missing their inner mechanics sat coated in a grunge of unidentifiable substances, floors spongy from their overflow.

Poor wasn't pretty.

The thought of my children in such an environment infuriated me. "Zack? Ivy?" I slung doors open, waving the .45 in outstretched arms. Ready to shoot cockroaches.

I went from house to house, all of them cookie-cutter copies of each other. Some I had to force my way into, while others welcomed me with wide open doorways. One by one I searched for my children. The seventh house had locks intact. I circled it, banging on cracked windows or plywood substitutes, making all the racket I could, listening intently for cries of "Momma." My throat turned to sandpaper as I repeatedly yelled their names, while rain now pelted sideways with the rush of a cold wind, soaking me to my underwear.

Around back something bumped—a limb on the roof? A current zipped through me. Wild dogs, squirrels, even bobcats inhabited the area. Then I heard what every desperate mother longs to hear.

A child's cry.

"Zack?" I tucked the gun in my waistband and grabbed the edge of a plywood sheet over a window, fingers gripping, yanking. The slick wood refused to give. I bolted around to the front door. The padlock held fast. I tried to muscle it open with my shoulder. Then I kicked it, over and over. Instinctively I reached for my weapon, but hesitated. An accidental bullet through my own child would destroy me. "Zack? Ivy?"

No response.

I backed up and scanned the front of the house. Older boards covered the windows, some gapped as if haphazardly put up in a lazy effort to keep out the weather. The board on the back, however, had been anchored fast, with purpose. I ran to the back again. "Ivy? Zack?"

Muffled cries of "Momma" sounded again, then beats against the other side of the plywood.

"Stay right there," I shouted. "Stay at this window."

Methodically I made a sweep, gripping each sheet of wood on each window. Some shifted an inch or two, but none gave. I reached the back door, splintered, peeled and rotted at the base. I kicked it. It cracked. With fanatic fervor and the first scent of advantage, I laid one kick after another on the weak point until my foot broke through. With my shoulder, I rammed it again and fell into the house.

I rose, pulling a long splinter out of the underside of my forearm, and then stood poised, listening. Gun in front of me, I slowly crossed the dark, damp kitchen.

Cries rose loud, pleading.

I ran down the short hall of the tiny house. The bedroom door held another padlock, latched in a newly installed hasp. I stepped back and leveled the gun. "Zack? Ivy? Get away from the door," I called. "Way back."

"Momma!"

"Are you away from the door?"

"We're in the corner, Momma."

Their voices told me they were to my right.

I aimed left. The shot deafened me as the weapon recoiled. Ivy screamed. I kicked the shredded door open, the cheap wall construction caving to the pressure, and threw myself into the arms of my two dirty, scared babies.

Wrappers of cookies and crackers scattered the floor, along with several empty soda cans. The place smelled like a garbage truck. The kids had used the closet as a bathroom, bless their hearts. Plywood over the window left them in darkness except for cracks of daylight sneaking around the edges. By the looks of things, Jesse had dumped them off with a small stash of snack food and hadn't come back.

My hands traveled up and down them feeling for welts or cuts. I saw no blood, and they still wore the clothes they'd gone to school in on Friday. "Are you hurt?" I asked, hugging them madly.

Ivy showed me a scratch on her leg and a bruise on her elbow, probably from being thrown in the car. *Good sign.* Scratches were easy.

"Is that all that's wrong, baby?"

She started to whimper. I held her at arms' length, scared of how she'd answer my question. "Did he hurt you in any other way, darling?"

"He knocked me down." She showed me a torn knee in her jeans. I squeezed the breath out of her. Thank heaven.

Zack, ever the little man, fought his tears. I hugged him hard enough to make him groan. "How about you, guy? You okay?"

He gave a courageous nod. "I didn't hurt *my* knee, Momma."

I laughed, my eyes wet. "Wonderful. Let's get in the car. Lots of people are looking for you two." Jesse could show up at any time. Two gunshots had to alert somebody.

As we stepped to the door, a red Toyota turned into a driveway two houses down. I yanked the kids inside by their shirts and shoved my hand into my coat pocket for the gun. Jesse could have other cars, friends or partners.

The driver stopped, backed up onto the highway, then headed in the direction he'd come from. I loosened my grip on Zack's collar and ushered both kids toward the Jeep. We ran, splattering our legs with mud, to where I'd parked at the first house.

Ivy jumped into the front seat.

"Quick," I said from habit. "Buckle up." I cranked the car and turned on the heater, craning my neck from one direction to another.

"Grab those sweatshirts out of that bag," I told Ivy. She threw the oldest one back to Zack. When he put on the lavender top without whining, I knew he was cold.

She then tossed the shopping bag in the back, out of her way. Tears and rain cut tracks through the smudges on her cheeks. "How'd you find us?"

"I know these parts well, honey. But I'd find you anywhere." She undid her belt and slid next to me in the car. I wrapped an arm around her and kissed her forehead. *I'd kill for you, baby.*

I raced north toward home, fingers dancing across my cell phone. No answer at Mom's. I tried my house and heard nothing. The phone's screen read "call failed." No bars. No service. Charleston was well over thirty miles away. With this weather, people were harbored inside, oblivious to those on the roads, ignorant to who chased who and who tried to kill each other. If I tried driving home without letting anyone know I had the kids, I ran the risk of being spotted and followed by Jesse. He could run us off the road and we'd be at his mercy. I had a gun, but so would he, and I didn't want to risk some showdown. He could kill us all and design it so no one would know what happened.

I had to make at least one call. But where? I had no idea where to find a county sheriff's satellite office out here.

But cops were searching the island. One of them could probably reach TJ's faster than I could drive home. Plus, I wanted authorities to grab Jesse ASAP.

I drove the short distance to the country store, the only place I trusted anyone at the moment. Sloshing through puddles in the parking lot, I parked behind the store, hiding my car from the road. Mr. Tyson's eyes widened when we scurried out of the weather into his store.

"Look what I found, Mr. Tyson. They were hidden away at the labor housing camp right down the road." My voice shook. I wanted to laugh, dance, turn a cartwheel, hug and kiss everybody in my path. My kids were safe. I rubbed each of their heads again.

His big arm waved us over to him as he waddled out from behind the counter. "Good gracious almighty, let me help you with those youngins." He reached out to hug me. "Come to the back and we'll get 'em cleaned up. Bet I can find something to fill those tummies, too." He turned to his chubby, slightly challenged daughter, about my age, one long braid down her back. "Margaret? How about catching the register for me? Can you do that?"

"Yes, Papa." Margaret grinned at us as she stepped away from stocking baked beans to take her father's place up front. The kids stared untrusting at the simple woman as we walked through to a room in the rear, behind the coolers.

A vinyl sofa sat against the long wall and a brown plaid recliner older than me rested under the window, both facing a retro color television with rabbit ears trimmed in tin foil. A wooden door opened to the back stoop. I checked the bolt. Mr. Tyson took each child by the hand and placed them on the sofa, patting each one on the knee as they shuffled their fannies against its back. "Sit there, and I'll be right back."

They peered around at the old wooden walls, dated furniture and stacks of tackle and boxed dry goods in the corner. I smiled and squeezed them again, unable to take my eyes and hands off them.

Tyson came in with goodies. Of course the kids wanted the cocoa first. Their fingers felt like ice. I placed my gun on top of a cabinet, slipped off my raincoat and stooped in front of Ivy and Zack. Damn, I'd forgotten the blanket in the back seat where Ivy had thrown it, still in the shopping bag.

"Mr. Tyson, may I use your phone? My cell isn't working out here."

Ivy stopped in mid-bite of a chip, her eyes alarmed.

"Shhh," I cooed. "I'm just going to the front of the store to call your daddy. Okay? Mr. Tyson'll guard you."

The old man nodded. "Sure, Ms. Slade. Make your calls. Let's see if I can find some cartoons on this ol' TV." He snapped his suspenders, and Ivy discovered she could still grin.

Back in the front of the store, Margaret stooped over, organizing something under the counter. I found the store phone and moved to the front window out of her earshot. Reluctantly, my first call went to Alan.

"I found them," I said, delighted at the relief of saying the words.

"Where?" he asked. "I'll come meet you."

A reply escaped me for a moment. "Don't you care how they are?"

"If they weren't fine you'd be upset. Of course I'm thrilled you found them. Tell them their daddy loves them. So where are you?"

"I'm at a place called TJ's in the Toogoodoo community. You don't have a clue where it's at. I'll be leaving to come home before you could get here."

"So, you're leaving now?" He asked the question as if I were getting off work and hitting rush hour. The average person would have been thanking God, Allah, Mohammed and Mother Nature, ecstatic beyond measure. "I'll meet you at the house then," he concluded.

"Fine. I'll call you when I'm almost there." He hadn't even asked to speak to them, but his shortcomings weren't my problem anymore.

The best call came next. "Wayne, it's me."

"Where the hell have you been?" he demanded. "Your daddy called me in a fit, and I've got deputies looking for you."

"I'm at TJ's."

"You're a walking lightning rod for Jesse. Get out of there."

"I've got the kids."

He paused. "I'll be damned. I take it they're safe?"

"They're scared and dirty, but in good shape. I found them in that labor camp near the creek."

"Damn," he said. "We should've looked——."

"I've already kicked myself." The image of them sleeping in that damp, cold shack drew a lump in my throat. "I've called Alan. Can you call the authorities? I'm not sure who . . ." I coughed, then swallowed tears. Coming down off all this adrenaline drew thoughts of what might have been. "Wait. I can't . . ."

"Don't talk about it. You just stay put. I'm ten miles away. I'll see if a deputy can get there sooner. Where's Alan?"

Someone tried to beep in on the line. I looked at caller ID, the number unfamiliar. Remembering this was Tyson's phone and not mine, I put it back to my ear and let the call go to voice mail. "He's back home. I told him to stay there."

"Good. Listen," Wayne said. "Don't go anywhere. I mean it! No more disappearing acts. Y'all lock up the place and let nobody in. Hear me?"

I laughed, a foreign experience. "I promise," I choked through sniffs and snivels. "This time I've got no place else to go."

Life was suddenly worth living again. Sniffling, I realized how tense I'd been. I'd sleep like a wore-out coonhound once we got home, with both the kids in my bed.

Wayne lightly laughed on the other end. "You okay?"

"Fantastic." I sniffed again. "Please hurry."

"Will do."

Wiping my cheeks with my sleeve, I turned toward the back to sit with Ivy and Zack, possibly beg Mr. Tyson for my own cup of hot chocolate. Then I remembered the blanket.

"Margaret, I'm going outside to my car to get the kids' clothes and blanket."

"We got blankets, Ms. Slade. Don't go out in that rain. Let me look in the back."

I remembered Wayne's orders to remain inside. "I already checked the back door. Do you think your daddy would fasten the front? Not let anyone in until the police arrive?"

She nodded as I watched her backside sway toward the rear. "I'll go get him, Ms. Slade. Daddy sure worried 'bout you last night."

"That's sweet of him."

Margaret disappeared and I glanced up at the television on the wall, the weatherman warning folks to stay off the low streets of downtown Charleston. They were flooded two and three feet deep in spots.

I wiped my chin with the back of my hand, still drenched. Spotting napkins on the coffee-hot chocolate counter, I pulled out a couple to wipe off, but they shredded. A roll of paper towels stood to the left of the cash register. I leaned over, reached it with the tips of my fingers, and pulled it toward me. After unrolling four sheets, I buried my face in them, rubbing up into my hair then down into my collar.

I turned. Jesse stood four feet away, inside the door, grinning a toothy smile.

A heavy fist rammed upside my head, sending a yellow streak of lightning across my sight. My legs crumpled, and my last thought was of Jesse stealing my children again.

CHAPTER 30

I woke up sprawled across the cracked vinyl backseat of Jesse's car, or rather his brother's car from the looks of it. The tires hummed over blacktop. He'd bound my hands and legs with duct tape. The vehicle's interior reeked of rancid chewing tobacco, motor oil . . . and hogs. We traveled fast.

My head ached as I struggled to sit. My feet hit empty beer cans in the floor, announcing my consciousness.

"Lay down," Jesse shouted, "or I'll put you to sleep for good."

I fell back down on the seat and closed my eyes. Oh God.

"Have a good nap?" he asked.

He was going to kill me. What other option was there? I couldn't remember if I said how much I loved the kids back at the store. I'd touched them, hugged them, but had I said the words? I clenched my fists, nauseous at the twist of events, angry at fate's nose-thumbing at my efforts to do right. That's when it hit me. He'd settled for just me.

I zeroed in on the back of Jesse's head, trying to will an aneurysm. Instant death. Instant reprieve. He'd run off the road, maybe roll the car. I'd rather take my chances on surviving a wreck over facing Jesse. After what I'd tried to do to him, he had to be pissed.

With Ivy and Zack safe elsewhere, I could refuse to play victim. "You're in a load of trouble already, Jesse. Why make it worse?"

As if he'd read my mind, he said, "Hope you said good-bye to your brats back there."

Magnificent. Confirmation they were still at TJ's. I strained my wrists against the tape. "This thing has gone way too far. If you give up now, the lawyers might do something for you."

His head shook. "Can't do that, sugar. Still got business to finish with my partner." He snickered. "Can't wait for you to meet him."

"You moron, they arrested McRae. He's not coming."

"He ain't no part of this."

How stupid did he think I was?

The vehicle moved too fast for the wet road. A hovering sensation sent flutters through me as we half drove, half hydroplaned wherever we were going. "I might move on, though," Jesse said. "Ha! So much for the loans I owe ya', huh?"

A horn beeped three times behind us, and Jesse slowed. "There's the son-of-a-bitch now." Our car accelerated again. "He'll just have to follow."

The muscles in my neck cramped from trying to twist and see. Where were the cops Wayne had called? I was lying in the car everyone was looking for, for God's sake. This appeared to be the infamous missing Fairlane.

We veered left, off the highway, and drove over a potholed road, each bump jabbing the seatbelt buckle into my ribs. Rain traveled in horizontal streams across the side windows, and my head bounced on the seat.

We stopped at last, wet brakes squealing. Jesse got out, and I heard a gate or door groan on rusty hinges. He hopped back in and drove into the darkness of a building. I recognized the crooked trusses of the Williams' barn: the place where I'd rendezvoused with Jesse, when Eddie had gotten hurt, when the tape of the confession had disappeared and my life had fallen out of orbit.

The Ford's engine coughed twice, then died.

Rain pounded the tin roof, then let up, then cut loose heavy again. The noise of such a storm served to Jesse's advantage, able to shroud gun shots as if they were thunder. The closest neighbor was a mile away. I tried to sit again, but Jesse's cold glare over the back of the seat convinced me to stay put.

"Let me go and I won't say a thing," I said. "You can hightail it to Mexico for all I care."

He opened his door, lit a cigarette and propped a boot caked with mud on the open window ledge. Dank odors of dirt, fertilizer and old machinery crept in. He puckered and blew a long, slow puff of smoke. "Mexico. Who moves to Mexico? They all run here, so must not be anything down there."

I thought I heard a car door slam and tilted my head, listening. The familiar squeal of the barn's wet hinges indicated we had a visitor. Sloshing footsteps set my pulse racing and fear set in deeper when Jesse wasn't disturbed at the guest.

Alan peeked in the window. "Hey, honey bunch. How's your day? Catch any bad guys? Screw any more agents?"

A wave of hysteria washed over me. I blinked rapidly, trying to switch to a scene that made more sense. I clenched all my muscles, seeking a grip on reality as it struggled to slip away.

Alan moved away from the window and made his way to the passenger door.

Jesse frowned. "Where the hell you been?"

"Got here as fast as I could. Never been in Hicksville before," Alan said. "I called you as soon as she called me, so quit complaining." He sat down on the front seat. "Now what?"

A kick in the gut would have bruised me less. Men from opposite ends of my world knew each other—knew each other well. Moreover, I'd never caught an inkling of a hint.

Jesse nodded toward me. "That high-and-mighty lady of yours doesn't have a clue. You did good."

"Wonder Woman. She thinks she's Wonder Woman," Alan said.

Jesse belly-laughed. "You're shittin' me. She wear a costume when you screw her? Damn. Makes me hard just thinkin' about it."

Alan chuckled. "She don't give it up that easy, man. I took what's mine." He propped his sneaker on the door, miming Jesse, minus the cigarette. "You were supposed to deal with her by now."

"To think I lost sleep about divorcing you," I snapped.

"You should've taped her mouth," Alan said.

Jesse shook his head. "Hmm, hmm. You married a worm, Slade. Hell, even I can see that."

"Keep pissing me off, and your cut drops to ten," Alan said.

Jesse peered over the front seat. The creep's detached coolness gave him an arrogance I'd never seen. "Your husband wants you dead. Not only does he get the kids and the house, but life insurance to boot. Not a bad idea from such a white-bread guy."

"Why didn't you kidnap me instead of the kids?" I thrashed, kicking cans across the back floorboard. "Why'd you have to scare them out of their minds, *Dad*? You sick piece of shit, they're your flesh and blood. They're babies!"

He shrugged. "They were bait, sweetheart. They weren't hurt, and they'd always think this guy did it." He nodded toward Jesse. "The plan was supposed to be so simple. Jesse takes the kids and you come looking for them. But you called in the feds." He scowled at Jesse. "Of course, dumb ass over here had to offer the bribe for this place."

Jesse lit another cigarette. "That part's not your business, Bridges."

"It was a simple plan, dude. Damn!" Alan shifted to his left, looking back at me. "And what beats me is the fact you took three days to find the kids, Slade. And this dirt farmer had to go deal crank, crack, or whatever, or we'd have nabbed you sooner." He rolled his eyes. "We put them right under your nose. What happened? Rambo cramp your style?"

I stared at the heartless beast I'd inaccurately described to my attorney as a wimp.

He pivoted back around, relaxing against the seat. "It's a damn good plan. I'm the distraught husband waiting for his wife to call about his kidnapped children. You're found dead, and Jesse does a disappearing trick. He's done it before, eh, hog farmer?" Alan's whiny voice mocked the script. Then he raised a thumb's up. "Oh, that's right. I'm waiting for you and the kids back at home."

I writhed against the tape.

Jesse reached both hands over the seat and grabbed me by the shirt. I screamed and shut my eyes, expecting another fist. "*Shut up*, woman. I'm just sitting you up."

Nausea rose and fell in my gut. Jesse actually seemed the better of the two men.

Being vertical made me feel less vulnerable, but my heart continued clamoring. Thank God the kids were safe, but thinking about them raised a new fear. Alan would be the one to raise Zack and Ivy.

I leaned forward. "Please. Don't do this, Alan." Surely the man retained some residual affection for me after twelve years. As ridiculous as the situation had become, he was my chance to stay alive.

His quick twist around caught me by surprise as the slap stung my cheek. "Shut up, *Carolina*."

So much for hoping.

Where was Wayne? Where were the police? Wayne had maps to each place. He'd backtrack and scout this area again. He'd do it fast, too. Damn. I'd said such horrible things to him. His sister was missing, yet he'd chosen me and mine. The kids must've freaked when I disappeared from TJ's. What will they think if I never come back?

Stop it. Focus. You're not dead yet.

I couldn't run, scream or hope to be heard. Could I turn one man against the other? They weren't exactly blood brothers.

My gaze met Jesse's. He'd been watching me fret. "You could've done worse, Bridges," Jesse said. "Look at her. Nice body, makes good money. Nobody this good looks twice at me." His gaze continued to undress me. "You don't prefer this ass to the bitch you're porkin'?" He sucked his cigarette and blew the smoke at Alan's face. "You got shitty taste."

Alan waved the smoke away. "You didn't have to live with her. She had to do everything right. The whole world was black and white." He ran his fingernail along the seam on the seat's faded caramel upholstery.

Jesse cackled. "I'd have divorced you, too."

"Asshole."

"Who kept you in dope for six years?"

Jesse peered over his shoulder. "You didn't have any idea, did you, sweetheart? I've known your ol' man from when he sold tractors with his daddy. We met at an auction. You apparently told him some bizarre drug rumors about me and my momma, and old Alan here looked me up. Lucas knew. A real good guy. Helped us dispose of a few plows and a whole slew of pigs." He took a long deep draw on his cigarette; his chest expanded, held a moment. "His nerves melted so bad there at the end." He released the smoke. "Glad he took himself out. Saved me the trouble."

He grinned. "I was there, you know. Watched the son-of-bitch blow his brains out." I cringed as his earsplitting laugh bounced around the car. "My prints all over the room, and nothing anyone could do about it because I'm one of your customers."

Lucas' note made sense now. He'd been tired of condoning the criminal behavior of these two and probably feared jail. Guilt made him eat the bullet. In his own benign way, he'd taken a jab at Jesse by killing himself in front of the farmer.

Jesse slapped Alan's shoulder hard. "I started to dump your dear sweet hubby a year or so ago back when I moved up to real estate. Couldn't pass up that insurance money, though. Imagine me using your life insurance to pay off the farm *you* helped me get. But you got all noble." He cocked his head toward me, speaking to Alan. "Your wife took me for a ride, too. Impressive. If not for McRae, I'd a been caught."

Alan thumped Jesse's headrest. "Get this over with. The police'll be all over this place like fire ants in no time."

"So kidnapping the kids and me had nothing to do with the bribe?" I asked, fighting to make sense of this nightmare while stalling for time. "What did I do to merit this, Alan?"

"You *are* dense," he said. "We're killing you, sweetheart. No deep thinking necessary."

The farmer tossed a butt onto the ground and stepped out from behind the wheel. Alan watched Jesse stroll to the back of the car. "Where you going?"

"Getting my stuff out of the trunk, bonehead." Jesse jiggled keys, then opened the trunk. I heard bumping, then a whump. The lid shut.

I trembled. I wanted the suspense to end, yet I didn't. I yanked my arms against the tape, feeling the strain against the sticky cloth. "Alan, cut me loose."

Jesse reappeared, shotgun in hand. Ren stood beside him with another.

Alan stared at the unexpected partner. "What the hell's he doing here? Wait. You stashed him in the goddamn trunk?"

Under normal circumstances, I'd have laughed at Alan's surprise. Everyone knew Ren rarely left Jesse's shadow.

Alan seemed skeptical, Jesse calm, thinking. Ren waited for direction.

Time stopped, as if God gave me a chance to rethink my life as the partners analyzed their deal. I pictured the faces of my children. If I lived, how could I explain about their father turning criminal? If I died, they'd live a lie with a murderous bastard. They'd never been to a funeral. How would they deal with going to mine? Would I be too messed up for an open casket?

"I gotta make sure the area's clear." Jesse stepped away from the car. "Be back in a second." He thrust his gun toward me. "Watch her," he told his brother. "And keep an eye on him, too."

Jesse left. I sat quietly until he was gone out of earshot.

Without the testosterone clash, I seized the chance for one final plea. "Alan?" I whispered.

"What?" he snapped.

I waited a second to see if Ren had heard. He stood with gun pointed down, scanning the area around the barn, with the occasional back glance at us. The rain slowed then roared, drips coming through the tin roof in places.

I scooted closer to the front seat and whispered. "You think you're the only one I called when I found the kids? The cops will be looking for me. Everywhere—including here. This is the farm Jesse wants. You can take out Ren." Maybe somewhere in that seditious brain was the college sweetheart who couldn't wait to see me after class. "Let's leave."

"Like I'd trust you."

"Yet you trust *him*?" I whispered. "Jesse's car is in here. Your car's outside for everyone to see. Are you that stupid?" Damn. "He'll kill me, then double-cross you."

"Thanks for the heads up, babe, but I got everything covered. You called me about the kids. I intercepted Jesse's car." He tapped a finger on the seat back. "It'll look like I tried to rescue you." Then he spoke under his breath. "And I took care of our guy in the process. Make that two. This one don't seem to have half a brain."

I wasn't feeling the love at all. "What about me?"

His lip slid wide and mean. "I've gotten used to the idea of living without you. Thanks for filing the papers first."

"It will crush the kids if you . . . hurt me."

"They'll be fine. Time heals. I'll raise 'em right."

The hell he would. "Don't be an idiot, Alan. Get us out of here before it's too late."

"First I'm stupid, then I'm an idiot. Not too bright for someone trying to save herself." He shrugged like killing was a Sunday afternoon pastime. "Jesse's just a thick-headed ox. He doesn't have enough smarts to cram in a thimble." He whipped out Jesse's roll of tape. "Enough of this talk. I've had enough mouth from you to last a lifetime."

Grunting in anger, I dodged until he grabbed a fistful of my hair, shooting pain into my scalp, and held me still enough to wrap utility tape across my mouth, overlapping it behind my head, partially covering my nose. Ren watched as if taking in television. I kicked the seat, screaming.

"You," Alan said, pointing at me, "are a pain in the ass to the very end. I should have—"

"You should have what?" Jesse asked.

He stood three feet away. The shotgun rested in both hands, his feet spread wide for balance.

"Hurt us, brother," stammered Ren.

"Yeah, I know, bro. I heard him."

Alan blanched white as my best silk slip.

Jesse leaned toward me. "Thanks, Ms. Slade. He ain't worth shit. No wonder you kicked him out."

I sat immobile at the uncertainty of the next few moments I'd mistakenly had a hand in creating. Jesse leveled the shotgun. "Get out of the car, Bridges."

"Hold on. I was messing with her."

"Sure you were," he said. "Get out. And toss the pistol on the ground."

Alan stepped out and moved toward the barn door. I shifted sideways to see out my window, my breath quickening. Jesse followed him, the gun muzzle pointed at his gut. "I said lose the piece."

Alan dug the .22 out of his jacket pocket. It hit the damp dirt floor with a muted thump.

Alan's face flushed. Jesse's murderous eyes widened along with a sneer that turned my blood cold.

"Getting greedy, huh?" he said. "You got balls enough to take me? Not like you were exactly armed with that pea shooter."

"I never intended to take you, Jesse. I swear." He pointed toward the .22. "That was just protection . . . for coming out in the boondocks. Don't forget the money."

"Well," Jesse drawled. "Since you're not happy with the old arrangements, here are the new terms. I'll keep you alive for seventy percent of the insurance money."

Alan frowned. "You're outta your mind."

Jesse racked the shotgun.

"Whoa," Alan shouted, arms out in front. "Fine."

Jesse laughed. "Like I could trust you."

The shotgun blasted Alan backwards. He fell to the ground, his left knee and thigh shattered.

"I changed my mind days ago, Bridges."

Alan's cries fell to a whimper, head bobbing up and down as he squeezed his leg to stop the blood. "Kill me and you won't get anything." He gulped air, his face tight with agony.

"You never meant to give me the money, and would've turned me in before it was all over and done with. And I like your wife better than I like you."

"You don't know that," Alan panted. "You would kill me if I didn't pay you. You'd harm my kids."

Jesse laughed long and loud, into his belly. "You don't give a flying fuck about your kids. Killing you would still mean I get no money. Besides, thanks to your wife, the feds are after me. When she dies, they'll come at me hard and fast. I don't exactly have the time to hang around and wait for you to bury her and file paperwork." Jokingly he raised a brow. "Do you realize you still owe me five hundred dollars?"

Alan's arms raised in front of him, shaking. "I'll pay you. I'll pay you."

"I have the money from the farm deals, dude. More than you ever planned to give me. Hell, anything is more than you planned to give me." He racked a fresh round into the chamber. "You're a damn liability, *partner.*"

Alan whined, "I'm sorry. Please! Let's renegotiate."

Jesse pivoted and stared at me, his eyes crazed and eager. I anticipated the long dark gun barrel being my last perspective on life.

"You understand, don't you, Ms. Slade?" he said with a hard voice that pile-drove a chill through my gut.

The second shot splattered Alan's brains against the wall and across the stacked, rusted irrigation pipe.

My eyes squeezed tight, but not tight enough, trying to hide the slaughter—and avoid seeing the next shot come at me. All I could think about was Wayne saying I should stay by the phone back at home and let him deal with Jesse.

CHAPTER 31

Rain renewed its roar, pounding overhead. Jesse hopped into the front seat of the rusty Ford sedan, and I heard the clank of metal against metal as the shotgun hit the seatbelt buckle. "Get in, Ren. We gotta go." Jesse jerked his door shut. "I'll drop you off at the house. You got hogs to feed. I got plans."

"Wanna go with you," stuttered the brother, still standing outside the car, obviously unable to think and get in the car at the same time. "I got plans, too."

Jesse snickered. "Not this kind of plan, bro. Ms. Slade ain't no hog. She's for me."

I looked away. Death seemed preferable to what I guessed Jesse had in mind.

Ren pleaded with slurred words. "Give her to me. Then I go home."

I struggled to withdraw inside myself, wondering how women mentally escaped their bodies while being violated.

Jesse cranked the engine. "I'll handle her. She was gonna sell off all your hogs and kick us out of our house."

"No," Ren whined.

I kicked the seat, vehemently shaking my head with grunts. Ren had to know Jesse was playing him. Ren's slow gaze met mine.

The car died.

"Shit." Jesse cranked it again, and when it turned over, he threw the car into reverse, backing the heap up a few feet, then stopped. "Get in, or I'm leaving you here."

Ren jumped in the front seat. "She ain't takin' my pigs."

"Fine," said Jesse, "but do what I tell you, okay?"

"Okay. But I'm coming with you." Ren set down his shotgun, butt on the front floorboard, the muzzle aimed at the ceiling. Jesse shoved it down out of sight.

"Then stay out of my way, bro. You hear?" Jesse said. "Lie down," he yelled at me, and then backed out of the barn. "You owe me," he said over his shoulder, arm resting over the seat back. "I did you a goddamn favor though you won't enjoy being a widow that long. Stupid son-of-a-bitch would've backstabbed me faster than you." He hit the steering wheel. "Everybody fucks me over. How you supposed to trust anyone?

Farmers work hard for a living. We deserve respect."

Head buried in the seat, my limbs still trussed to the point my feet lay numb, I prayed every prayer I'd learned since third-grade Bible school.

We turned right. Jesse drove about fifteen minutes, best I could calculate. Several miles ahead, the road would end at a touristy area on the Atlantic shore, deserted this time of year. An assortment of dirt roads, creeks and wetlands veered off the asphalt as potential seclusion.

"The Lord is my Shepherd, I shall not want . . ." The rest of the psalm escaped me so I repeated the same line in my head, until it sounded bizarre. Of course I wanted. I wanted to live.

Jesse turned off the highway, on to a fine silt road peppered with shells. The Ford bounced hard once, then several times in succession. Shocks squeaked as the wheels struck holes and the exhaust pipe scraped the ground. Jesse jerked the wheel left. The car's interior darkened as we came to a stop. I could barely see the edge of a tin roof through the rear window, but we weren't under a carport. The roof was at least twenty-five feet high. Storm clouds, trees and building gave the place a midnight feel.

The engine shut down with a shudder, grunting with each shake. Why hadn't this piece of shit died on the road, where someone might spot us?

"Tucked in nice and cozy," Jesse said. He got out and opened my door, the dome bulb brightening the interior like a flashlight. Jesse reached to flick it off.

Ren stumbled out, shotgun in hand.

"Good, it stopped raining." Jesse dragged me out, and leaned me against the wet car. He waved a switchblade.

I tried to back up, doing no more than drying water off the vehicle.

"Be still." His knife sliced through the ankle tape. My toes tingled with the rush of circulation, and I nearly stumbled on quivering legs. Jesse caught me and propped me back up.

Ren stood watch.

The moist air clung thick and stagnant, chilling me quickly in damp clothes, especially with the temperature dropping. I recognized Drue Limehouse's open-air packing shed from my summer visits, inspecting the season's tomato crop as it passed on conveyor belts past migrant sorters who culled and graded. This time of year it sat idle. The enterprise hid behind clumps of oaks, wild palmettos and random crape myrtle someone planted eons ago, a hundred fifty yards off the highway. I never would think to search this place. How the hell would Wayne?

I grunted against my sticky muzzle to get Jesse's attention. I figured the more we conversed, the longer I lived.

The knife danced before my eyes again. "Imagine if I slipped with this thing. I could slice that perky little nose clean off." He chuckled and pressed the cool blade against my cheek, then ran it down toward my neck.

I stiffened, fearing he'd see the rapid pulse in my neck and go for it.

He pulled back, his grin maniac, and ripped the tape from my mouth, the dangling ends still stuck to my hair. "There. Is that better?"

I gulped air.

"Scream and you eat this blade," he said with a snarl. "I've had my goddamn fill of you." The blade rose up and down in his hand, accenting each word with swooshes. "You know how many times I could've had you? For years you talked down to me like my mother. Do this, Jesse. Don't do that, Jesse. Then Bridges came up with his stupid insurance deal, but it didn't take me long to realize he just wanted to off you. Damn pissant didn't have the guts to do it himself." He waved his arms. "All I'm doing here is tying up loose ends. One down."

I inhaled deeply to collect myself and caught an overwhelming whiff of the peppermints he carried, mixed with the scent of tobacco. Jesse lobbed Ren one of his candies. The brother grabbed it in midair. Throwing the gun on the ground like a child's stick horse, he wrestled with the mint's wrapper.

"Ain't decided 'bout you yet, though," said Jesse. He removed his cap, ran his fingers through what I used to consider gorgeous thick dark hair, then replaced the hat like I'd seen him do a hundred times. He bit off a wedge of chewing tobacco he'd retrieved from deep in a pocket. I'd never seen him take a chew before. There was a lot about Jesse I didn't know.

I gushed out words, any words. "The Williams' farm thing wasn't my fault." What was I supposed to say? I called in the feds? Tried to get you busted? Fact was, I *had* crossed him.

He laughed. "I wish you could've seen your face when you found out your husband knew me. Funny, huh, Ren?"

Ren moaned enjoyment, smacking on his candy. "Funny."

Jesse smiled adoringly at his brother.

"But I was getting you the land," I blurted, grasping every angle I could.

"You were trying to lock me up." He whipped his blade under my chin, pushing it into the soft skin of my neck, then his finger wiped the spot. The digit went into his mouth, and he licked his lips like his brother with a piece of candy.

At the sight of my own blood, even so little of it, my head swam. "I gotta sit." I moved over and rested my butt back down on the car seat and leaned my head over as my senses tried to wander out of my grasp. I struggled to stay clear . . . keep him talking. "What about McRae?" I mumbled.

"What? Can't hear ya'."

"What about McRae?" I said again, raising my voice.

"What about him?"

"He said you handled the landowners. What does that mean?"

Jesse propped a muddied boot on the back tire next to me. "I talked to the old farts with the land, then I made sure they met their Maker. Three of 'em was at death's door anyway."

I scrunched my face, eyes shut.

He stooped down and rested his hands on my thighs. I jerked alert and saw the chaw juice in his teeth. "I signed the deeds. I know about selling land. You taught me with my loans and all."

Great. I was Jesse's mentor. I was a paragon of a woman, teaching him the means to crime, murder and mayhem. And to think, less than a month ago I'd felt sorry for this uneducated man who dressed up to come see me in the office.

"Get up and walk to the shed," he said. As if on cue, Ren picked up his shotgun.

My blood went frigid. "Why?" Like a kid being told to go to his room, I wanted to know my fate before it happened.

He yanked me up and pointed to the concrete steps leading to the platform. "Get going or we can end it here."

Since sorting and shipping vegetables was a hot job in the most sweltering part of the summer, the platform had no walls, just a huge raised slab floor littered with tables, broken crates and conveyor lines, built like a huge pole barn with a tin roof. One end, however, was enclosed, and wooden stairs led up to the office where an overseer could watch the work below without all the disruption, smells and oppression of June and July temperatures. Even if someone glanced around the shed, they wouldn't see us upstairs in the dark. I could be killed, left to rot, my bony remains found when they cranked up the conveyor in the spring.

He lifted me up and shoved. "Move."

I lost my balance and fell into a pile of wood crates. Hauling me up, Jessie slung me forward. "This ain't your office and there ain't no more rules. Get up those stairs!"

Ren watched.

Jesse wheeled around to him. "You stay here as guard. That's real important. Me and Ms. Slade gotta talk about keeping your hogs, bro."

Ren gripped his gun tighter and nodded. "Okay."

My shins throbbing from stumbling into the crates, I stopped halfway up the stairs. "Ren. I want you to keep the hogs. It's all okay. Jesse and I don't need to talk. When do you and I get to have our meeting?"

His arms drooped, lowering the gun, a wide grin on his face. I shivered at what he hoped. "Meeting," he yelled.

A fist to my back caught me off balance. I tripped, up one step then back down two. As I tried to stand, I fell, unable to balance with taped hands. Stairs jabbed into my ribs as I hit.

"Get up," Jesse said.

I rolled to my side. "I can't."

"The hell you can't. Get up." He gripped my taped hands. The angle wrenched my shoulders. I twisted, trying to remove the pressure, and lost my balance again. I slipped from his grasp and fell. The momentum carried me back into him, over on my side, bouncing three more steps down. The two-by-six railing kept me from sliding through the gap to the floor twelve feet beneath.

"I can't walk like this," I said, wedged and contorted to the point I wasn't sure how to stand. "Please, just cut me loose. Where am I going to go?" I whimpered.

"Shut up," Jesse murmured through his teeth. He pulled out his knife again and cut the tape, only to quickly slide the blade under my chin. I stood slowly, the knife following. Jesse inched his face closer. "You are mine," he growled. "I fucking own you. Nothing is your call any more. It's all me now, get it?"

I nodded, afraid to rub my aching wrists, fingers numb from no circulation.

"Say it," he said. "I own you."

The gravelly, guttural command spread fear through my core, paralyzing me. I was afraid to cover my face, block him out of my vision, for fear he'd gut stab me. Any misbehavior on my part could end my life on the spot.

"Say it!" he yelled.

I jerked at the shout. "You own me."

He kept a watch on me and pointed behind him to his brother. "Ren, stay down there. She's lying to you about a meeting."

Ren craned his neck from about thirty feet away. The smile washed off his face, like a kid promised a cookie then told they're all gone.

I wanted to tell Ren he could keep his hogs, even buy more head. Anything to win him over, but the words stuck in my throat, knowing Jesse's blade hovered a foot or two behind me. He shoved me onto the landing, kicked open the door and pushed me inside. Then he returned outside, obviously to calm Ren.

Body shaking, my first instinct was to find a corner and crawl to it and hide, but I couldn't see. My eyes took a while to adapt. Finally, I made out the twelve-by-fifteen room. It contained one military surplus metal desk butting against a dented file cabinet missing its lock. A dark naugahyde couch bore cushions worn flat from fat-bottomed truck drivers and produce brokers. I found a switch and turned on the overhead light. A pressboard lacquered end table held magazines about farm equipment and NASCAR, while a calendar hung on the wall, a buxom woman straddling a motorcycle.

Jesse blew into the room. "What the fuck?" He shut off the light with a swat. "What do you think you're doing?" He shoved me down onto the sofa. "Done got Ren all riled up now, you dumbass bitch."

This dingy room was going to be my last place on earth unless I collected my wits. Then anger rushed in, laced with sarcasm. "What, no candles?"

"Beats both of us on top of you in the back seat of the Ford."

My flash of ferocity vanished as my body shrank against the thought painted by those words. Searchers had to be within a mile of here. Noise or light might signal someone, but there was no light now. I could barely see Jesse. A gun blast might do it, but the wrong people held the guns. Again, I ran my mouth to buy time. "Did you kill Mickey?"

"Maybe."

"What the hell happened to make you like this, Jesse? I've been good to you." Surprisingly, it continued to grieve me to see who he wasn't.

He shrugged. "Maybe I was dropped on my head as a baby. We deviants have all kinds of reasons." He spat. "You can't tell me your husband was worth a tinker's damn. What happened to him?" His jaw muscles worked the wad in his mouth. "Hell, what happened to make you marry the likes of him?"

"Guess I screwed up," I said, scraping the barrel for delaying tactics, amazingly using the truth.

He picked something from his teeth and flicked it away, then spit. "In more ways than one."

"I've helped you for years," I said. "I'm sure we can work something out."

"You messed us up, Slade. I was gonna blackmail McRae." He kicked the desk. "Now I gotta start over somewhere else."

Even scared, I yearned to understand the crap I'd fallen into. "McRae dumped you."

"Really?" he said with rancor. "Tell me something I don't already know."

"I hated his guts, too," I said, shaking, fighting not to.

"If I'd gotten Williams' land, McRae would've been forced to deal with me. He wanted it." Jesse raised his arms, animating his frustration. "But you kept doing the wrong things. McRae tucked that guy from the highway department into his pocket, and the two had enough money to pay me if I'd gotten it from you in time. I could have done so fine with that deal."

Mike Hatchwood. The Georgia guy who loved coming to Charleston. McRae had told me to expedite a sale to him for the Williams farm at a lower price. I'd thought McRae had just wanted the place prudently sold. I'd been awfully dumb for a smart lady.

Jesse eased beside me on the sofa and touched my hair.

Rain and body heat mixed a nasty blend of smells on the man. Ren usually delivered the odors to the office, but Jesse's evasion from the law left him stinking of sweat and sour mud. I could hear the wet, sticky tobacco working against his teeth.

I wracked my brain for more dialogue. "You tried to kill the other agent," I said, my voice wavering.

"Ren," he said. "He does whatever I tell him."

Jesus, Ren had a violent streak, too. I tried to forget the rumor of Ren's daddy being his grandfather.

"So Ren killed Mickey," I whispered, a statement to myself.

Jesse leaned in. "No. Shut up."

Instead, every joint, muscle and tendon clenched in me. He lifted his hand off my face, then smoothed his knuckle down my neck.

I shifted out of reach. "Ren wouldn't kill my dog. That was your truck."

Jesse moved in and licked my ear. "No wonder Alan got tired of your mouth. Let's see if I can find a better use for it." His hand cupped my chin, then gripped tight, and forced my face toward him.

My stomach roiled. I swallowed bile. "Don't hurt me," I said, unable to say the word kill. "I could grow fond of you. I mean, you're not a bad looking man."

"You hate my guts."

"Cops are searching for me all over the place, Jesse."

He grinned. "They ain't lookin' here."

"Let me go, and they won't be as hard on you. You can take me in and tell them you saved me from Alan."

He stood and leaned one knee on the couch, his belt buckle within a foot of my face. "You don't have a say-so, Ms. Slade. Not anymore. For three thousand dollars, I believe this evening is mine, bought and paid for."

CHAPTER 32

Jesse hovered over me, his eyes burning with lust. The cold fake-leather sofa creaked as my body tensed and his weight shifted closer.

"Don't, Jesse."

The stench of stale sweat mingled with peppermint and tobacco. Repulsed at the idea of being a rape victim, I reared back, across to another cushion, and kicked out, my foot glancing off his upper groin.

"Oh, you little bitch." His scowl was comical. "Thought you'd damage the package, huh?" He rocked back and forth, his hands pointing toward his crotch. "Can't touch this, babe." Then he leaned toward me. "But it'll touch you."

With his temperament change came my own. The image of rape reminded me of Alan's attack in my bedroom. The knife had scared me witless, but Jesse'd unclipped the sheath, slid in the knife and laid it on the desk. I fought a whimper at the forecast of his intentions. Rape—that was something I could possibly overcome given half a chance. I'd done it before. Somewhere in the process, the man was vulnerable. At what stage was yet to be seen. "Wouldn't want to touch it," I said. "I imagine the hogs would get jealous."

He smacked my jaw, knocking me off balance. I hollered, "Ren! He's hurting me."

"Shut up, or I swear . . ." His whispered chuckle ran shivers up my back. "Was it true what your husband said?" He reared upright.

"I doubt it," I said, clueless to what he meant.

"You know. Come on. I want to see you play Wonder Woman." He unzipped his jeans.

A bolt of horror took my breath. My attempts to inhale caught until I could reach deep enough to scream. "He's killing me, Ren. You're going to lose all your hogs."

Clamping a hand around my neck, Jesse cut my scream short. His other hand snatched open my flannel shirt, yanked my tee shirt out and popped loose the snap on my khakis. I strained against his grasp, feeling hot blood rush into my face as I grunted and twisted, my hands trying to push him away.

"Shake it, Slade," he sneered. "Give me a belly dance."

His grip was strong. He shoved me flat.

I dug my butt into the cushions and tried to kick him off. He saw me coming. The back of his hand knocked me into another star-laced dimension. When my head cleared, I lay exposed with my pants and underwear around my knees. One of Jesse's huge hands pinned my arms over my head, his eyes studying my nakedness like an adolescent boy seeing porn for the first time.

I couldn't kick back now. I resisted temptation to give in and let him have his way, just so all this would pass.

"You're breaking my arms."

"Tough shit," he said.

"I'll keep talking, screaming."

"I'll cut out your tongue."

"I mean . . . don't you want it served up soft and easy?"

He ran his hand down my stomach. "No matter to me."

His gaze traveled the length of me, and with any kind of light he'd have seen my goose bumps of alarm. But with his moment of lust and mental preparation, he eased his grip. I arched, yanked a hand loose and swung a fist at his face, exhaling with the effort. I missed. He didn't. Blood spurted from my nose, sting in my eyes.

He slapped my hands away from my face and pinned my wrists over my head with one hand again, his other groping to get my pants completely off. "I'll cut your fucking throat and take you dead," he whispered. "Ren'll take you either way."

Blood choked my airway. I coughed, spraying red droplets across Jesse's face, exactly where I'd aimed.

Ren burst into the room. "Ms. Slade."

"Oh, Jesus fuckin' Christ," Jesse shouted. He pushed back off me. One fist on his waist, he stood with a hip cocked, his belt dangling, dragging his open jeans low on his behind. He pointed with the other hand. "Get out, bro. I didn't call you yet."

"Don't kill her. I need my hogs."

It was the first complete sentences I'd ever heard from Ren. His lucidity contrasted with the greasy, second-hand appearance. Maybe he could be reasoned with.

I scrunched back into a semi-raised position, blinking hard from the nose slam. "Ren, your brother is planning to go away. He won't be here to save your hogs or take care of you. He won't be paying for the farm anymore. And if he hurts me, you lose everything."

"No, no, no." Ren gripped his shotgun in one hand, his other opening and shutting as he flexed his heavy arms out and in with each wail.

Jesse's glare turned poisonous. He hiked up his pants and buttoned them, ignoring the zipper. "Shut up, bro. Damn it all. Your hogs are fine."

Ren pointed at me. "She said—"

"She's lying. Aren't you listening, you dumb fuck?"

"I don't lie, Ren," I said curling my legs up under me to avoid giving Ren any sexual ideas. "I have never lied to you."

Jesse's punch to my shoulder whiplashed me to the couch. "Shut up."

But as soon as Jesse's attention reverted back to Ren, I reached for my pants, slipped them up, and re-clothed, my feet now on the floor as I eased to the edge of the sofa. "Why do you think he didn't want you here, Ren? Our meeting was private. He said so himself. He didn't want you to know that he's leaving. Tomorrow . . . he's taking his truck and going to another state. You know how he sent you to Savannah yesterday? Well, that was practice. This time will be for good—without you."

Ren gaped at me, hanging on every word like they held a secret prize. "Shut up," Jesse yelled.

Through the high-pitched tone in my head, I struggled to reclaim ground I'd gained with the simple brother. I managed to croak, "Have I ever taken your pigs away?"

Ren raised his gun loosely, uncertainty on his face.

Jesse made a casual move for it, like an instructor taking a weapon from a novice. "Put the gun down, buddy."

But Ren was leery, and his brother's attempt to take his shotgun evidently rubbed him wrong. He squeezed it harder.

Jesse frowned. "I said let go. Don't be an idiot."

Four hands gripped the weapon, wedged between the men one moment, separating them by a foot the next.

I jumped up and backed against the desk, refastening my clothes.

Then the slight disagreement turned into a tug-of-war, Ren with his two-fisted grip and Jesse one-handedly shoving the gun's muzzle away from himself while gripping it in a tugging match.

Under Ren's power, Jesse backed into me, twisting, trying to leverage his feet, finally butting one foot against the desk's base. Ren yanked harder. Jesse fell against me and I leaped aside, envisioning a random blast accidentally cutting me in two.

My hand brushed the discarded knife on the desktop, still in its sheath. I clutched the hilt.

The men now tussled. The knife felt heavy in my hand.

Ren released one hand and punched Jesse in the face. Jesse threw one of his own.

I stepped forward in a slow motion effort, envisioning the entire blade in Jesse's back. This was my chance. Jesse's eyes widened as he caught a glimpse of me. His moves escalated. He writhed harder, at the same time trying to put Ren between us.

I imagined the feel of skin, muscle, then bone against the blade in my hand, and froze.

Ren raised the gun and kneed his brother's gut. Jesse lost hold of the shotgun, doubled over long enough for the simpleton brother to drop the weapon on the floor and follow through with a two-fisted one-two blow to Jesse's cheekbones.

I released the knife and snared the gun by the muzzle. Hand over hand, I reeled it in, flipped it around, and pointed it at the entangled men.

"Stop or I'll kill you!"

Jesse reacted first, Ren a split-second behind him. Even as he panted, Jesse's eyes clearly showed an analysis of his options, sorting out how he'd react next. Ren did what he was told, but maintained a wary attention on his brother.

Jesse grinned.

An "oh shit" rolled through me. I gripped the gun tighter.

He winked. "Did you think to check the safety?"

I held my breath. If the safety was off or I even looked to check, I was finished. Suddenly, I realized the futility of my winning the day against two grown, muscular men. I should have just pulled the trigger. "Listen," I started, "both of you—"

In one motion, Jesse reached for the knife on the floor with his left, the gun's muzzle with his right.

Flash filled the ten-by-ten room, and a monstrous explosive clap ripped through my ears as I fell back against the desk. When I opened my eyes, Jesse no longer stood before me. He leaned against the wall, his back pressed into cracks made in the cheap paneling. Dead center of his torso, a dark hole the size of a big man's fist became home for all nine of the double-ought pellets from the twelve-gauge shotgun. I became intensely aware of the burnt aroma of gunpowder.

Silence hung thick and overwhelming. Didn't know whether I'd lost my hearing or there just wasn't anything to hear.

Jesse's knees gave way, and he slumped to the floor, his facial expression holding an uncanny resemblance to his brother's. His body made no sound as it hit.

Ren wrenched the gun out of my hand. I banged into the desk, trying to scamper back in the small space. I expected a secondary attack, any instant another blast.

Then my heart leaped at the miniscule chance Ren's scattered brain cells had found a common bond with me. Feigning ignorance of the dead body five feet away, I eased three steps toward the door. Ren grabbed my upper arm. I heard my own clipped cry through the tinnitic whine in my head.

"Wait," he mouthed. It was only then I realized I couldn't hear.

What now? Still no one knew where I was, and Ren's thoughts ran squirrelly.

Strolling to his brother's body, Ren lifted Jesse wound-side down on his shoulder, jolting the limp man once for better placement.

I ran out the door. My sock feet skipped steps and leaped over the final four to the tomato shed floor. Swinging myself around the rail, I bolted toward the back of the facility. Items in my way got kicked, my toes cut for sure. Jesse'd taken off my sneakers, and I'd left them behind.

Slinging the driver's door open on the rusty Fairlane, I flung myself behind the wheel. My hands groped the steering column, the visor, the floor. Of course, no damn keys. I scrambled out and tried to see in the moonless night where to run next.

Ren appeared on the shed's landing, whistling a tune I couldn't hear. I sprinted on what I could make of the packed silted road we'd come in on, the coloring slightly contrasted with the grass in the night pitch. The path would lead to the two-lane.

I tripped and fell. I cursed my inept ability to save my own behind and dug my feet into the silt. Wet like my beach, the packed ground let me get back up. My right arm collapsed under my weight. That's when my nervous system registered serious pain in my bicep. I couldn't see a wound in the dark, but the knowledge of one was there. I rolled to my left to remove the weight on the injured limb.

Ren ran up, gripped my crippled arm and lifted me, the roughness shooting fireworks of raw agony into my chest. Blood had soaked his clothes where he'd hoisted Jesse. He mistook my backing away in disgust as an attempt to escape and yanked me closer before shoving me back toward the car. Now I wore the same blood, the stickiness evident on my hand and wrist, probably my neck.

I let him show the way, moving any direction I had to in order to take his pressure off my arm. Alan's .22 in his hand confirmed I'd been shot.

"Can't hear," he said, the gun tapping the side of his head. "You either. Got your attention this way." He waved the hand piece. "Come on." He turned around, expecting me to follow him to the car, the shed, whatever.

He wasn't even mad.

I had no choice. Running would put a bullet in my back.

Jesse lay in the back seat I'd become intimate with earlier. Ren pushed me into the open driver's side, using the pistol to nudge me over so he could get behind the wheel. He threw the shotgun in the back on top of his brother.

"Come see my hogs," he said, and drove up the path. At the highway I searched for headlights, but the road disappeared into an onyx gloom, bordered on both sides by greenery turned black in the moonless night.

I dug fingernails into the dashboard, cradling the throbbing right arm in my lap. Ren's foot mashed the gas then let up, flying us at eighty then sliding down to fifty only to stomp the pedal again as if he'd forgotten he needed to get somewhere. Jesse's mixture of aromas thickened the air as the heater reached temperature, curdling my stomach. My breaths turned shallow. I covered my nose and mouth with my good hand.

The fifteen minutes crawled as I expected each swerve to send us into a creek or against a tree. He turned the car onto an unkempt path I'd forgotten existed. We headed to the back of the Rawlings hog farm, about a hundred yards behind his mother's house. The car bounced on ruts and in and out of mud holes, shocks groaning with effort. When we rolled up to the fence, Ren wrenched the gearshift into park. The car coughed and heaved.

By now, Wayne would be hunting me, cursing me, himself, and anyone in his way for events beyond his control. Recovering old tracks, authorities should have found Alan. But like Wayne had said when the Rawlings' mama slammed her screen door in my face, Jesse wouldn't come back here. Too obvious. Nobody would look for me at this location, not until they'd looked everywhere else.

Headlights appeared on the highway back up near the house. I listened for the sounds of sirens, slamming doors and human voices, any sign of help. I inhaled, sniveling and sucking in salty tears and blood from my nose, causing a cough.

Ren put a finger on his lips. "Shhh."

The unknown car passed by the dirt road, two hundred feet away.

I released a moan.

Ren shook my arm, motioning me to get out of the car. He held onto the handgun, leaving the shotgun on the back seat floor. He heaved Jesse onto his shoulder and swung the handgun like a highway worker moving backed up traffic. I remained standing by my door. Ren waved me to catch up. I turned to close the door, and he headed toward the hog pen, so I left the door ajar, the dome light on.

I'd seen the place several times, but not lately. Lucas had overseen livestock inspections. The ground rose and fell, uneven under my unshod feet. Ren stepped around a mud puddle I couldn't see, him knowing how to walk the route blindfolded. I mimicked his step but misjudged another, coating my left foot and cotton sock in water and muck. Wind whipped past us, dipping the temperature as it went. I guestimated the cold in the forties and drew my buttonless flannel shirt around me. My coat still hung at TJ's.

I'd left Ivy and Zack seated on the old vinyl sofa, waiting for me to return after calling their daddy. Now they'd be orphans. I rubbed my eyes, wiped my face. Tears felt like frostbite on my chapped cheeks. I couldn't feel my toes.

Ren reached the hog parlor's main door. We'd financed its construction when I first reported to this office, one of the first capital improvement loans I ever made. The cement floors slanted liquid out of the pens to the outside, draining into a lagoon fifty yards back, if I recalled. Crates lined up inside for climate control, and pens opened outside so the hogs would enjoy fresh air. Nothing spectacular, just practical.

Once upon a time the brothers had managed brood sows, taking the offspring from babies to 250-pound market size, but at my suggestion they'd moved to purchasing feeder pigs and fattening them up instead. Jesse's baby pigs fell prey to every calamity under the sun, and he always found an excuse for his boar's lack of performance. At peak capacity, the men could've managed twenty sows or five times as many feeders, but I never saw that happen. Thus the reason to alter the operation.

We walked inside the two thousand square foot building, and I waited for Ren to turn on the light. He kept going, never seeking a switch. Of course not. A light would tell Mama he was home, and I imagined Mama not being too keen on seeing a dead son.

Ren trudged past the rows of hog pens. "Come on," he said, glancing back to make sure I followed. Animals in crates on either side of us squealed, bumping against the walls in recognition of their owner. Their gleeful grunts told me I could hear again. Their odor told me nothing had impacted my sense of smell.

Ren led us through a caged gate into the open area behind the building. I'd thought my feet couldn't get any filthier until we stepped into the gunk of part mud, part pig crap, saturated by the storm and urine. My feet were so cold they moved like wooden blocks on the end of my legs. I welcomed the crap. It was warmer than the shallow puddles and frigid night air.

Jesse's body hit the ground with a smack, face up. Ren stood and stretched the kinks out of his shoulders, standing taller than I'd ever remembered him. Hogs thumped harder against their crates.

"Jesseeee?" A light came on in the back yard. Old Momma hollered from the back porch, her voice rising up at the end. The name came out way too similar to a hog call. I marveled she yelled her son's name with every cop for fifty miles hunting him.

"Mumma, here," Ren shouted, a heavy masculinity to his words.

"Get in here, Ren," she yelled. "Jesse with you?"

Ren's head ducked as if she could see him. "Yes'm. Feedin' pigs, Mumma." He prodded me with a finger. "Dig."

With that lone word, he dropped to his knees and scooped the mess, starting a hole. He lumbered up and found a shovel, then returned to the task. He knocked my leg with the handle, waving for me to follow suit in the squalor, using my hands.

Anything for a distraction from the bullet wound in my right arm. Anything to avoid a date with Ren.

Gunk wedged under my fingernails and splattered my face. Twice Ren almost hit my one working hand with the shovel blade as he chopped the dark wet ground. When I jerked away, he scowled and bumped me with the tool to resume work. We dug two-feet down when he shoved me with the back of the blade to stop. I dared to catch a glimpse of Jesse, his eyes still open, still stunned at the ridiculous nature of his demise. Our task had dappled him with sludge from head to toe.

Shivers rocked me. Wet, caked pants and shirtsleeves insured I stayed frozen. My buttonless flannel shirt flapped and I wrapped it around me for the umpteenth time, even knowing it did no good. The physical labor released a new level of pain in my arm. Teeth chattering, I clenched them to avoid biting my tongue. Coordination floundered, my limbs like sticks.

Rolling him like a barrel, Ren moved Jesse to the hole. The body landed with one arm under, one sprawled across the ground. In a moment of tenderness, Ren gently lifted the arm and laid it alongside his brother. Then he shoveled in the muck.

I rocked in place. Ren's coat looked so warm.

Jesse's body barely covered, Ren admired his work. Another shiver seized me, forcing a groan I couldn't stop, which obviously caught Ren's attention.

"Thanks, Ms. Slade. You help me good," he said. "You always do."

He wasn't right, unfortunately disconnected mentally and socially. He concluded I'd helped him with Jesse like I'd helped him with his farm. DNA and environment had molded him into a pitiful soul. Hurting, scared and frozen, I still pitied Ren.

I faltered as I stood to back against the gate leading inside the parlor. But instead of grabbing me, he reached beside me and let out the hogs from one of the crates.

"See? Pretty pigs." He clucked and whistled, conversing with the swine. Two hundred-pound animals snorted and grunted, banging off each other, vying for the exit. I held onto the slatted pen until all but one had run to Ren. Passing through the gate and latching it behind me, I rushed for the aisle we'd come in through.

His snorting pets surrounded him, snouts curious about their disturbed pen, and Ren struggled to wade around porcine obstacles. A large hog leveraged him against the door such that he couldn't open it, and he kicked at the animal to buy some room.

I ran on what felt like stilts. My numb feet couldn't maneuver the floor, and I staggered, catching myself against a wall. The jolt of agony through my bullet wound sprayed spots across my vision. As I steadied, headlights appeared from the direction of Ren's car. My heart hit my ribs as hard as the hogs banged their cage. Blinded by car lights and pain, I had no damn clue where to turn and spun left, then right, trying to remember where it was safe for me to run.

"Mumma," yelled Ren, fright in his voice.

I made my decision, running right, away from the house. Arms grabbed me, rough fingers gripping the raw meat of the arm wound, sending me to my knees. His thick leather belt squeaking and protesting the cold, a deputy dragged me into the grass. Donald. I screamed into his hand covering my mouth as he used my hurt arm to set me upright.

"Come on out, Mr. Rawlings," said a man in the dark. Another vehicle, flashing red and blue strobes pulled in behind the pair of lights already parked. I heard Ren's wails and whimpers. Hogs squealed and rammed their fencing. More cars pulled in.

"He's got a gun!"

My head snapped up. Ren wouldn't understand. He was a child inside, despite the perversions instilled in him by a crazy mother and sick brother. Safely away from him, pity welled anew. I realized he hadn't tried to rape or kill me like his good-old-boy brother. Jesse'd said Ren wanted a piece of me. I'd believed him.

I screamed for someone to listen. Ren was dense. He might not react as they expected.

Donald moved away and another man grabbed me as I tried to rise.

"Stop them, Donald," I said, crying. "He's slow!"

"Shhh, Slade," said Wayne, rocking me as we remained bent low.

A shot rang out. Hogs stampeded within their confinement, and wood creaked as the weight tested the nails. Squeals filled the air.

"No, no, no. Not my hogs," Ren wailed.

"Don't hurt his hogs," I croaked through a raw throat.

"It's all right," said Wayne. He sat on the wet ground and threw a coat over me. I couldn't stop crying.

I screamed. "Make them stop."

He wrapped his arms around me, distributing his body heat.

I heard a .22. My blood chilled.

"That's it," said Donald.

Gunfire peppered the thick night air.

"He's protecting his pigs," I yelled, unheard over the blasts.

The gunfire faded. Pig noises reduced to a lower pitch. More boots rushed toward the pen.

"No, no, no," yelled Ren's mother.

Wayne drew me sobbing to his chest. He crunched me in a hug, and I passed out from the pain.

CHAPTER 33

Four days later at the graveside service in Ridgeville, Savannah squished me with a hug, careful not to touch my sling. She rested her hand on Ivy's shoulder and then brushed her hand along Zack's cheek. "You okay?" she asked them, meaning me. They nodded.

"Yeah. Thanks for coming," I said through lips still thick where Jesse had struck me. Daddy walked up and took the children, ushering them to his car. I watched them go and sighed. "Those two are my main concern."

She smiled. "Of course they are, but who went to hell and back for them? Cut yourself some slack." Savvy nodded to my right, over her shoulder. "Don't forget about the rest of us, hon. We're here for you."

Wayne had come to the funeral, bless his heart. Eddie stood beside him, finally released for duty. Wayne gave me the respectable space required by social protocol in order to bury my husband, but his smile found me at key moments when people grated on my nerves, praising Alan as the church deacon, the good father, the wonderful husband. Simple eye contact with Wayne empowered me, giving me assurance that this chapter was over.

"You need anything, Ms. Slade?"

I turned and smiled at Deputy Donald James. "I'm okay, thanks." Here was a man who didn't shoot the bad guy or save the day, but served his purpose. There when Wayne wasn't, concerned when others weren't, he had dutifully filled assorted gaps when I'd needed someone to be there.

I patted his arm. "Scarecrow doesn't suit you, Donald."

He glanced to the side, fighting the mild blush creeping up from his collar.

"I think you're more of a Tin Man," I said. "More heart that you get credit for."

He smiled, hugged me gently, and moved aside as others approached to give condolences.

The kids had been told that their father died searching for them, a victim of Jesse and Ren. Small chance Ivy and Zack would learn the truth. I sat at the graveside, anxious to move away from my past, but devoted to giving my children the time they needed to remember theirs in whatever flavor they chose.

Ann Marie was the only agency employee in attendance, the only person honest enough to show her face and care. State Director Edmonds could not come because he was indisposed with federal officials. An unexpected twist had surfaced. Edmonds had been involved with McRae, spreading their acquisitions throughout the state of South Carolina. The shell corporation Wayne and I snooped around had represented Edmonds, McRae, a real estate agent in Kershaw County, and the highway department employee who'd pretended to be from Brunswick. Unknowingly, I'd taken down a politician, a director, a civil servant and a businessman who'd collected small parcels of land via unscrupulous methods to turn over for a premium when urban sprawl raised their value.

My stubborn decision to call in the IG proved the monkey wrench in the whole deal. Edmonds didn't know McRae had been working with Jesse to consummate deals on his own. So Edmonds had, in essence, called the authorities in on himself. Lucas became a simple casualty in a situation well over his head, but he'd helped in his own way. His death had been the catalyst to make Wayne ask for the case.

My gut had sunk into my shoes when a deputy told me they'd found Mickey's body beneath the very crates Wayne and I had sat on at the Williams' place.

The affair moved to my home around two PM where casseroles and bottles of wine and iced tea filled my kitchen. Three hours later the last of the guests left, and my parents whisked away Ivy and Zack while I met with Wayne. I planned to tell him I needed distance from everything surrounding the incident with Jesse Rawlings, including him.

We sat on my lamp-lit front porch in my mountain rockers, liquored coffee in hand. "I don't know what I would've done without you, Wayne."

He winked. "Not sure you even needed me."

"Believe me, you came in handy." I couldn't count the times he'd assured me I was smart, could hold on and make the right decisions, when all I saw were brick walls. During the many moments my "rules" didn't apply, he taught me to dig in and create my own. He'd dealt with my attitude, an attitude I'd never known existed until threatened and challenged. "I see you as Sam Spade now," I said, recalling an early conversation between us.

He lightly scoffed into his cup, steam rising off the coffee in the cool air. He moved his cup to the arm of his cane chair, as mine rested on my slung arm. The finality of the day, the case and Alan weighed heavy on my shoulders, leaving me too tired to rock, drained.

A dog barked a block away. "I'll miss you," he said.

I stared up through the pines at a night full of stars. "Beck still bothers me a little," I said. "Have you really met of a lot of women like me through your work?"

"No," he said shaking his head. "No string of women. Definitely no one like you."

"Glad to hear it."

He sipped his coffee once, twice, then set it on the porch, elbows on his knees. "I dated three women before Pamela, who was the only one I married. Now we're divorced. That's the long and short of it. No mystery, no secrets, no one-case-flings. I'm not the Casanova he described."

Wayne looked down at his boots. "I'm taking some leave, Slade. Probably be out of touch a while. Might be healthy for both of us that way."

He'd beat me to it. I hadn't expected it to sting.

"My sister hasn't shown up yet," he said, his voice monotone and firm. "She's done this before, only this time she didn't have people mad at her for cooperating with the feds." His chest heaved with a sigh. "I owe her my time now."

"I hope you find her," I said, standing.

He rose from his chair. His boot step toward me echoed on the wood plank. After a soft caress of my cheek, he slipped a hand behind my head, drawing me close for a long deep kiss. He rested his forehead on mine. "Stay away from hogs, CI."

"Take care of yourself, too, lawman," I said.

My eyes dry, I watched him back out of my driveway. I sat on the porch rail sipping the rest of my coffee, staring in his direction long after he'd turned the corner.

COFFEE CUP EMPTY, washed and put in the dishwater, I fed Madge and returned to Mom and Daddy's place. Savvy's car sat on the curb. I chuckled. Mom had out-charmed her, making her stay the night.

"Our heroine is home," said Daddy as I walked in through the garage. "You can put dinner on the table."

Savvy waved from the kitchen where she sat on a stool chatting with Mom. I laid down my purse. "Where are Zack and Ivy?"

"They crashed early, honey," Daddy said. "We fed them and they fell in the guestroom bed over an hour ago."

"Y'all go ahead and fix your plates," I said. "Let me check on them a minute."

My dark-haired beauty and her strawberry-headed brother slept hard, their little bodies hardly moving. I fought the urge to crawl into bed with my daughter, gather up my son in my arms. Zack's pillow was damp. He'd miss his father more than any of us.

I smoothed their covers, and turned to leave. Savvy leaned in the doorway.

"They're fine," she said.

"Yeah. They're good kids, aren't they?" I said, closing the door.

She stopped me at the top of the stairs. "You're better off without him."

I didn't know which *him* she meant. "Alan or Wayne?"

She squinted, mulling over the question. "From where I stand, I don't think you *need* either one. I label this the Slade-is-queen phase of your life. Do something with it. If nothing else, enjoy the kids."

Downstairs, Mom served something from paper bags onto her heavy white Spode dishes. Not the china, but not the everyday, eat-leftovers-on plates. Her way of dressing up take out. Of course her stainless and nice glasses adorned the table, tea in a glass monogrammed pitcher. We sat as Mom brought the first loaded plates, setting one in front of me like it was my birthday.

I lifted the bun. "What's this?"

"Why it's barbecue, Carolina." Mom hurried back for two more plates, Daddy on her heels to help. "With that golden mustard sauce you like so much. Just didn't have time to fix much else, you know, with today and all."

My stomach rattled empty, but my taste buds revolted. "This is fine, Mom."

Savvy stretched over toward my ear. "What's wrong?" she whispered. "You feel all right?"

I picked at the meat.

"Listen," I whispered back. "Next time I come over for dinner at your place, let's do chicken or seafood. Pork just doesn't seem appetizing to me anymore."

ABOUT THE AUTHOR

C. Hope Clark was born and reared in the South, from Mississippi to South Carolina with a few stints in Alabama and Georgia. The granddaughter of a Mississippi cotton farmer, Hope holds a B.S. in Agriculture with honors from Clemson University and 25 years' experience with the U. S. Department of Agriculture to include awards for her management, all of which enable her to talk the talk of Carolina Slade, the protagonist in most of her novels. Her love of writing, however, carried her up the ranks to the ability to retire young, and she left USDA to pen her stories and magazine features.

LOWCOUNTRY BRIBE's opening chapter took first place in the Phillip Mangelsdorf Award, third place in Alabama Writer's Conclave Competition and honorable mention in The Writing Show Chapter Competition as judged by bestselling mystery author C. J. Box. The novel enjoyed semi-finalist status (top 100 out of 10,000) in the 2009 Amazon Breakthrough Novel Contest, and ranked as a finalist in the Daphne du Maurier Award for mystery/suspense award sponsored by the Romance Writers of America.

Hope is married to a 30-year veteran of federal law enforcement, a Resident Agent-In-Charge, now a contract investigator. They met on a bribery investigation within the U.S. Department of Agriculture, the basis for the opening scene to *LOWCOUNTRY BRIBE*. Hope and her special agent live on the rural banks of Lake Murray outside of Chapin, South Carolina, forever spinning tales on their back porch, bourbon and coke in hand, when not tending a loveable flock of Orpington and Dominiquer hens.

She also currently manages FundsforWriters.com, a weekly newsletter service she founded that reaches almost 50,000 writers to include university professors, professional journalists and published mystery authors. *Writer's Digest* has recognized the site in its annual 101 Best Web Sites for Writers for a dozen years.

She's published in *The Writer Magazine, Writer's Digest, Chicken Soup, Next Step Magazine, College Bound Teen, Voices of Youth Advocates (VOYA), TURF Magazine, Landscape Management* and other trade and online publications. She speaks at several writers' conferences a year. Hope is a long-term member of SC Writers Workshop Association, Sisters in Crime and MENSA.

C. Hope Clark
Website – www.chopeclark.com
Twitter - www.twitter.com/hopeclark
Facebook - www.facebook.com/chopeclark
About.me - http://about.me/hopeclark
Editor, FundsforWriters, www.fundsforwriters.com

CPSIA information can be obtained at www.ICGtesting.com
Printed in the USA
BVOW072310120912

300244BV00001B/56/P